"Argylle condemns those who currently rule her," the princess continued. "Violence. Lawlessness. Her own people, here, among you, ready to make things right."

Her golden eyes swept the crowd, and Faron's insides tightened and his pulse quickened. How long had it been since he'd seen a woman so beautiful? Not since...since...

A face, a name, both threatening to return, but he fought them down, remembered the flames of the pyre Sariel had burned him upon. With his vision overwhelmed with fire, he watched Princess Isabelle draw her sword to end her speech.

"We are freedom, my friends. Freedom from the tyranny of the Casthes. Freedom from the vile faith of the east. Will you fight with me? Will you return to the homes you left, broken no longer, servants no longer, but instead free and radiant with the goddess's blessing?"

No hesitation. Every man and woman raised their arms and voices, crying out their acceptance. The hundreds of soldiers behind Isabelle joined in the chant, overwhelming it with a single name that the rest quickly took up.

Isabelle! Isabelle! Isabelle!

The Bastard Princess slashed the air with her sword. Her decree felt like it traveled for miles.

"Then, stand tall, warriors of Doremy, for this day, we go to war!"

Praise for
David Dalglish's Vagrant Gods series

"An action-packed tale of the cost of empire and those who refuse to bend. Full of characters you'll love, *The Bladed Faith* is a delightfully stabby and oftentimes beautiful exploration of what it means to hold out hope against impossible odds."

—Megan E. O'Keefe, author of *The Blighted Stars*

"Filled with intense action and complex characters who are easy to fall into, *The Bladed Faith* is what might happen if Final Fantasy crossed with *The Way of Shadows*! I loved it!"

—Rob J. Hayes, author of *Never Die*

"Dalglish's plotting and pacing are top-notch....This book is Arkane Studios' *Dishonored* meets D&D's divine magic."

—*Grimdark Magazine* on *The Bladed Faith*

"This dark adventure...will hook genre fans with its detailed world building, strong characters, and bloody, action-packed scenes. Readers who enjoy Mark Lawrence and Erika Johansen will root for Thanet's rebel team of misfits and...will eagerly anticipate the next book in the series."

—*Booklist* on *The Sapphire Altar*

THE
RADIANT
KING

By David Dalglish

ASTRAL KINGDOMS

The Radiant King

LEVEL: UNKNOWN

Level: Unknown

VAGRANT GODS

The Bladed Faith
The Sapphire Altar
The Slain Divine

THE KEEPERS

Soulkeeper
Ravencaller
Voidbreaker

SERAPHIM

Skyborn
Fireborn
Shadowborn

SHADOWDANCE

A Dance of Cloaks
A Dance of Blades
A Dance of Mirrors
A Dance of Shadows
A Dance of Ghosts
A Dance of Chaos
Cloak and Spider (novella)

THE
RADIANT
KING

Astral Kingdoms: Book 1

DAVID
DALGLISH

orbitbooks.net

Orbit
Hachette Book Group
1290 Avenue of the Americas
New York, NY 10104
orbitbooks.net

First Edition: March 2025

Orbit is an imprint of Hachette Book Group.
The Orbit name and logo are registered trademarks of Little, Brown Book Group Limited.

The publisher is not responsible for websites (or their content) that are not owned by the publisher.

The Hachette Speakers Bureau provides a wide range of authors for speaking events. To find out more, go to hachettespeakersbureau.com or email HachetteSpeakers@hbgusa.com.

Orbit books may be purchased in bulk for business, educational, or promotional use. For information, please contact your local bookseller or the Hachette Book Group Special Markets Department at special.markets@hbgusa.com.

Library of Congress Cataloging-in-Publication Data
Names: Dalglish, David, author.
Title: The radiant king / David Dalglish.
Description: First edition. | New York, NY : Orbit, 2025. | Series: Astral Kingdoms ; book 1
Identifiers: LCCN 2024017345 | ISBN 9780316576673 (trade paperback) |
    ISBN 9780316576680 (ebook)
Subjects: LCGFT: Fantasy fiction. | Novels.
Classification: LCC PS3604.A376 R34 2025 | DDC 813/.6—dc23/eng/20240415
LC record available at https://lccn.loc.gov/2024017345

ISBNs: 9780316576673 (trade paperback), 9780316576680 (ebook)

Printed in the United States of America

LSC-C

Printing 1, 2024

To Brit, Stephanie, and everyone else at Orbit who still believes I have worthwhile stories to tell.

The ISLAND of KAUS

Warmwind Mountains

Leyval

Vendom

Wendway Fort

Greenberg

Arbertown

Luelle

Clovelly

ARGYLLE

DOREMY

ARMANE

RUDOU

Faron's Cave

Barkbent Town

ETNE

THE LAND OF DRAGONS

Kaleed Swamp

ARGYLLE

Arbertown

Luelle

Clovelly

FAERIE HILLS

Faron's Cave

Barkbent Town

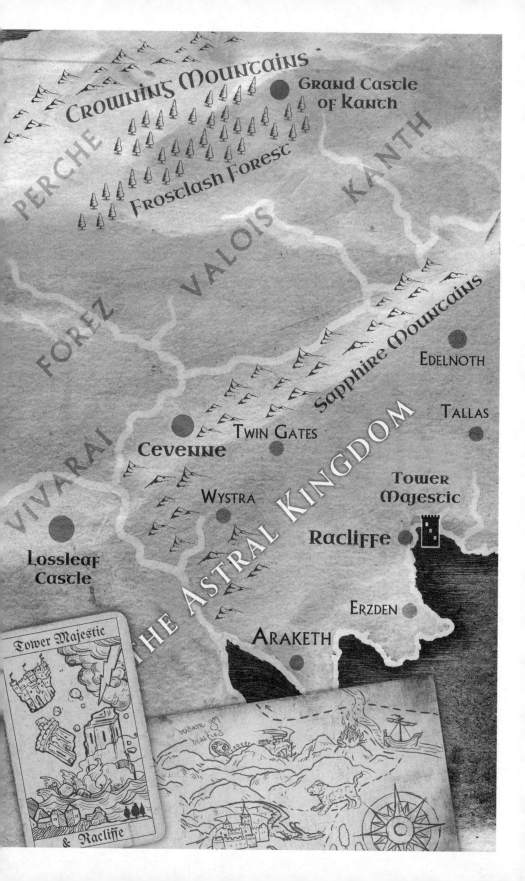

Prologue

SARIEL

D eep within a forgotten cave, Sariel's brother knelt in the heart of an unlit pyre. Sariel stood before him, an oil-skin in hand.

"Are you certain of this?" he asked.

"I am," Faron said. Though he was a kind soul, his voice was firm, and it reverberated throughout the cave.

So pure, thought Sariel. *So foolish. So broken.*

Sariel poured the oil across Faron's brow. It flowed through his brother's short black hair. Rivulets continued along the sides of Faron's handsome face and then splashed across his muscled chest and back. The drops continued down to the eulmore logs, stacked in preparation for the coming fire.

"You'll forget things," said their sister Calluna. She sat some distance away, her back pressed to the cave wall. She wrapped her pale arms around her legs and pressed her knees to her chest. Her long black hair formed a blanket around her. Protecting her. Hiding her. "It's been getting worse."

"It's what Faron wants," Sariel said, his voice soft and nothing like his brother's. He dropped the empty oil-skin on the logs. "To forget."

"Will you judge me for it?" Faron asked.

"No judgments, not for my kin." Sariel lifted his hand, summoning the innate power of radiance he and his five siblings all possessed. A blue flame burst to life in his open palm.

"Eder will be angry," Calluna said, referring to their absent brother. The flame's blue light flickered off the faint tears in her eyes, adding depth to the cold starlight that forever shone within her irises. Eyes they all shared. The mark of radiance.

"Let him be angry," Faron said.

"I'll miss you," she insisted.

Faron smiled, so warmly, so miserably.

"I know. Be well, Calluna. I'll see you soon."

Sariel almost extinguished the fire in his hand. He didn't have to do this. He need not participate in his brother's attempts to forget those he'd loved and lost. The idea faded as instantly as it had come. No, he would be here for his family, whatever the cost. He looked down at Faron and saw his brother's head tilted away from Calluna so she could not see his own tears.

"You're too soft for this world," Sariel said as the fire grew stronger in his palm.

"Then do it," Faron commanded with a tone that had rallied armies and frightened kings.

Not yet. Not until he checked with Calluna, who looked ready to shrivel into herself. His sister sensed his unspoken question.

"I'm here to the end," she said, her will strong despite the timidity of her voice.

Then let the damned deed be done, thought Sariel.

He tilted his hand. The fire flowed like liquid from his palm and fell to the stacked logs below. The oil caught. The fire spread. Smoke filled the cave as flesh began to blacken and peel.

"Until we meet again," Sariel said as, for the third time in his agonizingly long life, he burned his brother alive.

Part One

AWAKENED

Chapter 1

FARON

When Faron awoke, he was blind, and he could feel worms crawling through his flesh and organs. An overwhelming sense of loss and sorrow pierced his mind like a spear, receding as his senses returned. Whatever the cause, he could not remember it. Let memory fade as he focused on the now. Where was he? What had happened?

The pyre.

Yes, the pyre. Its ashes were beneath him as he lay on his back. The worms, the carrion bugs, they shouldn't...

The cave. Sariel and Calluna must not have properly sealed the cave. That, or humans had broken their way in...but no, they would not. They feared the qiyan too much for such a risk.

I do not know how long you have feasted, but it comes to an end. Leave me.

The thought echoed through him, projected by his radiance. He instantly felt the change. The carrion insects cut, bored, and ate their way to the surface of his skin. Faron clenched his jaw against the pain. Worms slithered like snakes from his wrist and belly. A beetle retreated out his nostril. He breathed softly and shallowly, not wanting to disturb whatever creatures occupied his lungs.

Blood, his blood, mixed with the ancient ash. The pain receded, and he slept again.

·

The next time Faron awoke and opened his eyes, he saw the barest hints of light. It seemed his sight had recovered. The stone was cold, and it felt pleasant against his bare skin. He pushed himself to a sitting position, crossed his legs, and bowed his head.

Warning was given, he told the smallest and simplest of creatures occupying his body. Maggots, squirming in his stomach. Unhatched eggs, laid upon his skin. He clenched his fists and let radiance shine through his body. It burned the invading creatures like fire, shriveling their bodies and popping their eggs.

He gasped when the effort was finished. The pain of it slowly ebbed away. Faron stood, stretched, and then tested his limbs. His balance was wobbly at first, but improved as he shifted his weight from foot to foot. Next he ran a hand through his hair, found it slimy with moisture and dirt. He desperately needed a river or lake to cleanse himself.

The cave was pitch-black, but that did not bother the eyes of those touched with radiance. Faron looked about and found a tightly wrapped leather bundle, poorly hidden underneath a pile of stones. Beside it was a plain but finely sharpened sword. Faron smiled. Little Calluna, always watching out for him.

Within the bundle, he found a fresh set of clothes, remarkably clean after an unknown amount of time spent waiting. He dressed himself in the dark, the measurements correct as expected, and then took in the new style.

A white shirt, lacking the ruffles along the neck and top buttons that had been popular when last he visited the markets of Araketh. Long stockings, and atop them, a pair of leather trousers dyed black with the bark of eulmore trees. Most impressive was the brown leather coat. It had a high collar, thick copper buttons, and six pockets, three to either side. A belt was sewn directly into the sides of the waist, allowing him to buckle it shut should he be marching or riding.

A jingle alerted him to a heavy coin purse in a pocket. Faron pulled it out and undid the drawstring. Within were dozens of silver coins, and he examined one of them. There was a tower on one side and five stars on the other, the designs unfamiliar to him. A new currency, then, minted during his recovery. He put it back, pocketed the purse, and then continued dressing.

The boots Calluna had chosen for him were plain enough, brown leather with adequate padding, the color matching his coat. He slipped them on and adjusted the laces across the back to tighten them. That done, he grabbed the sword and headed for the cave's entrance.

It seemed he was wrong to doubt his siblings' diligence. The cave was sealed with a heavy stone, and what cracks remained must have been filled with mud. Time, though, was merciless, and wind and rain had worked away the mud until it was mostly gone. Little streaks of daylight peeked through, as did a hint of wind.

Faron placed his shoulder against the stone, braced his legs, and pushed. Leaves crunched and twigs snapped as the boulder rolled several feet before stopping against a thin eulmore tree. Its branches shook from the impact, its many violet leaves shivering in protest. Faron breathed in the clean air and felt his lungs heal away the last of the damage.

"How many years has it been?" he wondered aloud. His brother Eder could calculate that with a glance at the night sky. Tracking the movements of the moon and stars had always come easy to him. For Faron, there would be no answering that question until he reached civilization. The idea excited him as it always did when he reawakened. With the passage of time, language would be shifted, clothing would be changed, and homes would have adopted new styles or improvements. Even the meals might be different, should new spices become favored or the wandering feet of merchants build new paths between various portions of the grand island.

The reminder of food set his already ravenous stomach to grumbling. Of the several reasons he'd chosen this cave, one had been a field of raspberries to the north. He started that way, the violet canopy above him thinning, then stopping entirely as he exited the forest.

What fruit grew on the bushes was not ripe enough to eat. Not summer. Early spring, then, he guessed, as he skirted the outer edge of the bushes. If it were close to fall, the leaves of the eulmore trees would have been drained of their lovely color, shifting from violet to an ashen white. It seemed he'd have to make do with a bloodier meal.

Faron returned to the forest and gathered the occasional fallen branch or twig. Once they were piled together, he placed his hand in their center, summoned his radiance, and set them alight. For such simple tricks, he felt nothing, but this next one would put a strain on him and leave him winded. Still, it would be better than spending hours hunting.

Faron sat beside the fire, closed his eyes, and let his mind drift. His consciousness slipped through his boots into the dirt below and then spiraled outward. The world around him grew more vivid, more real. He heard the faintest clatter of red squirrel claws clutching black bark and birds whistling their songs as they flitted about the canopy. Blue-breasted robins, building fresh nests to impress mates now the winter was over. Purple-and-gold woodpeckers, thudding their beaks in search of grubs and worms.

Should have checked my body first. You'd have found a much easier meal.

No bird or squirrel would be enough, not for his hunger of untold years. Farther and farther he searched, until he sensed it: a wild hog, foraging among the underbrush.

Come to me, he said, pushing his will into the beast. He saw it in his mind's eye like little silver threads arcing between his body and the hog's. *Like a spider,* Calluna had described them once, and as much as Faron disliked the comparison, he could not deny the similarity.

Minutes later, the hog arrived, docile and quiet. Dirt caked its hooves. Two flies zipped about its deep red hide. Faron lifted his sword, turned its edge, and pressed it to the hog's throat.

"A victim of circumstance," he told the beast. "Know that I appreciate you for it, nonetheless."

A single cut, and the blood flowed.

•

Come nightfall, and with a full belly, Faron cast his will once more into the forest. This time he meditated for an hour, the focus of his mind spiraling beyond his immediate surroundings. As he took stock of the wildlife, he debated. In his last lifetime, he had befriended a hawk, and before that, a raven. Birds tended to be his favorite companions, but when his mind skirted across a nearby coyote, her loneliness struck him.

Come to me, he told her, and minutes later, she arrived, having crossed half a mile of forest to do so. Her fur was a tawny brown intermixed with white. The gangly state of her limbs and chest provoked a frown. She was not eating well, but why? He beckoned her closer so he could put his hands upon her. Contact allowed him a better understanding. Radiance flowed, silver threads connecting, and he peered into the coyote's mind.

A mother. Six pups. Four pups. Then three. Then none. Poor food. A poor hunter, abandoned by her pack. She was a failure. A failure. A failure.

Faron withdrew his mind, but his hands remained, and he looked deep into her yellow eyes.

"You do not understand me yet, but you will," he said, bracing for the strain. This would be harder than lighting a fire or sensing for nearby hogs and squirrels. Little wisps of silvery light floated like smoke from his hands and into her body, shaping her, changing her. What mind she possessed sharpened. The speech of humans would no longer be gibberish. Her eyes widened, and he sensed fear and excitement overwhelm her in equal measure.

"You will not remain this way," he told her. "It is a change too drastic, and a strain too great, but I would receive your answer amid true understanding. You will visit lands beyond this meager forest. You will walk the cities of man and see their nations and people. Sometimes I will feed you, and sometimes you will hunt for me. The way will be dangerous, and mankind's trust of you fickle and wary."

Those round eyes of hers stared into his. Her entire body locked stiff. The concepts he spoke of were grand and foreign to her, and yet she understood them now. It was cruel, in a way, but Faron was no stranger to cruelty.

"Will you join me, and see the wonders beyond this forest?" Faron asked, releasing her. "Stay, if you accept. Run and be free, if you refuse.

I will harbor you no ill will should you reject me. The choice is yours, little coyote."

The connection between them faded, but he sensed faint echoes of her emotions. Her loneliness warring against her pride. The loss of her pups. Her vicious anger at a pack willing to leave her and her offspring to starve.

She turned away, just once, and then sat beside his fire. Her head tilted slightly. He could almost hear her voice in his mind.

What now?

"The intelligence I granted you will ease away," he told her. "But rest assured, you'll still be wiser than all other dogs, coyotes, and wolves. I suppose I should have your name. I would not demean you by calling you 'little coyote' forever."

His new companion glanced at the fire and the butchered hog beside it. Faron grinned.

"Go ahead," he said. "I've eaten my fill."

She tore into it with glee. Faron sat down, crossed his legs, and rested his chin on his hand. All animals had names, or concepts close enough to be usable as names. He closed his eyes and focused upon her.

What are you called? he asked.

She did not answer, not knowingly. Instead, a scent came to him, for that was how all coyotes knew themselves, and others.

Leaves, half covered in mud, wet with rain, bitter with a splash of blood, and yet, hovering about it, the final note of a wild iris bloom.

Faron chuckled at her.

"Quite a mouthful," he said. "Might I call you Iris, if only to save us time?"

The coyote cracked a rib free, chewed it twice, and then nodded.

"All right, then," he said. "Iris it is."

Chapter 2

FARON

Faron traveled east, deeper into the forest, aiming to visit the village of Clovelly on the other side. Once there, he could learn how much time had passed, use the coin Calluna left him to buy a room for a month or two, and then feel out what new life he wished to create for himself. Perhaps he might search for his siblings, perhaps not. It was much too early to make such decisions. The day passed uneventfully, which was fine with him. It gave him a chance to assess his new traveling companion.

She was a guarded sort, rarely keeping to his side. After several hours of traversing the brush-strewn forest grounds, she started limping. Upon noticing, he sat down and called her over. Once she agreed, he took her paw in his hand. A moment's thought, and he sensed the swollen tendons within, and a shape of bone not quite right.

"This will hurt," he told her before he squeezed, hard. To reshape, things must first be broken. She yelped and bared her teeth, but to her credit, she did not bite. Afterward, he massaged the paw and let a bit of radiance seep into her to soothe the tendons and reduce the swelling. After a few minutes of that, she laid her head on his lap, closed her eyes, and went to sleep.

He finished the mending not long after, but kept on massaging her paw.

An hour later, they resumed their travel, and this time, she did not stray quite so far. There was also more of a bounce to her step. She seemed old for a coyote, possibly in her sixth or seventh year, but there was no way to ask. Coyotes did not track the number of revolutions of the moon, only the shape of it, and how it affected the hunt.

"Eat up," he said when they stopped at a stream crossing. He'd packed what meat he could, wrapping it in the leather Calluna had used to store his new clothes. Two packages, one full of meat he'd cooked, the other, raw bits specifically for Iris. They ate and drank their fill from the stream, Faron using his hand to sloppily bring the water to his mouth.

"Next time, if there *is* a next time, remind Calluna to pack you a canteen," he muttered to himself as they continued their journey. After a few more miles, Iris's energy waned, her head sagging and her tongue hanging out one side of her mouth. He stopped again, and while she rested, he scanned his surroundings.

Near his cave, the forest had been nothing but eulmore trees, but here was not quite so uniform. Intermixed about half and half among the violet-leafed eulmores were shorter red oaks, their bark dripping with a sticky brown sap. It kept insects at bay, though some bears had developed tongues thick and dull enough to endure its foul taste to eat the vermin that got stuck. Their leaves were a fiery red, hence their name, and they mixed with the violets of the eulmores so that the sunlight painted the forest below in their wondrous color.

Against such a backdrop, mixed with the golden light of the setting sun, the smoke of a human campfire was all too easy to spot.

"Do you see it?" he asked Iris, and pointed. She looked up, sniffing as she did. A soft growl rumbled from her throat, and she bared her teeth.

"I doubt you've had many pleasant encounters with humans," he told her. "But you'll be around them during your travels with me. A few might even give you a comfortable scratch behind the ears, if you're polite enough."

Iris gave him a most impressive glare.

"Fine, then, don't be polite. Just don't bite anyone, either, since I will be the one they blame." Her ears flattened. "And yes, you should care about that, too. At least, you will, once you learn the comforts of a well-provisioned inn."

Faron led the way, surprised by how closely Iris trod at his hip. Perhaps she'd had a particularly bad encounter with hunters sometime in her life. It might even explain the lingering issue with her paw, though that was only a guess. Life was not easy as a coyote. Faron adjusted the sword sheathed at his hip, gave Iris a gentle pat atop her back, and then entered the stranger's camp.

"Greetings," he said to the lone man at the fire, who startled to his feet. One hand dropped to the knife at his buckle, the other reaching for a wooden staff resting beside him. His meal fell to the dirt.

"I have nothing to interest thieves," the man said, pointing the knife. His face was round, and his neck covered in a faint gray beard. He had a broad forehead and sharp cheeks; combined, they made his blue eyes seem beady.

"And I come not as a thief, but as a friend," Faron said. He gestured to Iris. "Might my companion and I enjoy your fire?"

The stranger lowered his knife after a moment's hesitation.

"Friendly company is always welcome," he said. "Join me."

Faron sat beside the stranger atop an overturned eulmore tree. Iris kept on the opposite side of the fire, and there was no disguising her distrust.

"Have you a name?" the stranger asked, settling down.

"Faron. You?"

The stranger's cheek twitched.

"Preacher Russell, at your service."

Preacher? Faron wondered. *Of what faith?*

Worship of the goddess, Leliel, was the dominant faith across the great island of Kaus, yet Faron saw no idols or amulets carved in her likeness. Russell appeared on the heavier side, and Faron suspected much of it was muscle. His hands were callused, as were his bare feet. Nearby were his boots, well-worn and most certainly not cheap. His outfit was peculiar. Though his trousers were plain, his shirt was a mixture of yellow and black, the differently colored threads neatly formed into rows.

Even more peculiar was his staff. Hooked to the top by thick wire thread was a closed glass jar. A collection of insects swarmed inside it, all kinds of beetles, centipedes, mosquitoes, and dragonflies. Most numerous of all were some dozen black horseflies.

"Strange to find a preacher out so far in the wilds," Faron said.

"Clovelly isn't too far away," Russell insisted. His voice rumbled. Given his size, he could be intimidating if he wished to be. The big man ate strips of salted pork, and he tore a little segment free and held it between his thick fingers. A flick of his thumb opened the lid of the jar tied to his staff, just enough to press the piece of meat inside. It hit the bottom of the jar, and the insects immediately swarmed over it.

"Even we holy men need time alone from the people we tend. Besides, if Father orders me out here, then out I go, without complaint or question."

Faron watched the meat disappear in moments. Not a single bug attacked another. Iris growled from the opposite side of the fire and then lay still.

"Might you answer me a question?" Faron asked, careful to keep his voice light.

"I am a preacher," said Russell. "I aim to give answers, so please, ask."

"What year is it?"

The preacher lifted an eyebrow. His cheek twitched yet again.

"My, you must truly love your solitude. We are in the eighty-sixth year of Father."

A new measurement of tracking time? That complicated things.

"I am not familiar with such years," he said.

Russell grunted and bit a piece of pork.

"A few of these far western kingdoms stubbornly refuse to adopt the proper calendar, so I suppose I should not be surprised. I believe it's somewhere around 380, or maybe 381 Years After. I could not tell you for certain."

Years After marked the time since the Anaon Kingdom united the entirety of the island. Its shattering had led to the rise of what were known as the little kingdoms, dozens of petty human realms eagerly dividing up the island and slaughtering one another in never-ending squabbles.

Faron kept his face calm as stone upon hearing the date. Almost seventy years had passed between his burning on the pyre and his eventual return.

"It seems I must spend our evening confessing my ignorance," Faron said. "Who is the Father, that kingdoms would change their years to honor him?"

Russell set his plate on the log beside him and wiped grease onto his trousers. There was no hiding his suspicion.

"Do you tease me, traveler, or have you spent so long in these woods you know nothing of the outside world?"

Faron flashed him a smile. "Think what you wish, my friend. I seek only to learn."

Russell grabbed his staff and shook it, agitating the bugs.

"Father is the mender of our sins. Father is the forgiveness that can soothe, and it is by his power that my prayers heal the sick and wounded. Here, let me show you. Look into my jar, traveler. Gaze upon the creatures trapped within. Do you see them?"

Faron did. They were angry and scurrying.

"Keep looking upon them," Russell continued. He held the staff closer, the jar swinging from the wire. "But this time, focus not on the creatures, but the empty center. Concentrate on that space. Do you see the light there? Do you see it, growing? Do you feel it, warming?"

His words were true. A light did shine within the glass, and Faron felt warmth in his breast. That warmth, though, was not the result of the spell the preacher attempted to weave. It was rage seething to be unleashed. Closer, closer, the jar. Closer, the preacher's hand and staff.

"Gaze into the light," Russell said. "Let it comfort you. Wash away your thoughts. Feel the life leave your limbs. You are silent. You are still."

The light emanated from the jarred creatures, an unseen force sucking golden, sickly swirls from their bodies. The flying bugs hovered in steady revolutions. Those who crawled ran in circles beneath it. Faron felt it trying to ease away his thoughts and relax his muscles.

This was radiance, the power controlled solely by Faron and his siblings. Somehow, a human, a *preacher*, was manipulating radiance for his own use.

"That's right," Russell said, drawing the knife from his belt. "It will all be over soon. Feel nothing. Await the dark."

Iris leaped over the fire, her teeth latching on to the preacher's wrist. Blood flowed across her tongue. Russell cursed and tried to kick her, but Faron had seen enough of the man's ill nature. He batted the jar and staff aside, and as it fell, he positioned himself so his leg absorbed the kick meant for Iris.

Faron's hand closed around Russell's throat and he lifted him off the ground. Russell thrashed wildly, his face turning red. The knife fell from his bleeding hand. Only then did Iris release her grip.

"It is a foul man who would murder visitors to his campfire," Faron said, slamming the man to the ground and pinning him to the earth. Silver radiance flared in the starlight of his eyes as vines erupted from the dirt to trap Russell's wrists and ankles.

"But do not worry, Preacher. I shall still have my answers."

Faron let go of the man's neck to grab the hastily discarded staff. The bugs within swarmed angrily, as if incensed by their new master. Russell's eyes followed him, wide and terrified. He said nothing, silent in his fear.

"Listen to me, and listen well," Faron said, halting in front of his captive. He lowered the jar so it hovered directly above the preacher's head. "You will not lie. Your tongue will not form the words. My ears will not believe them. The truth, as you view it. Do you understand, Preacher Russell?"

"My soul is steeled against the coming dawn," Russell said, shutting his eyes. "My heart is made pure from the past that enslaves."

A single pull, and Faron tore the jar free from the wires connecting it to the staff. He settled to his knees and held the jar closer, its glass bottom almost touching the tip of Russell's nose. The flies and beetles squirmed, clicking and biting to be free. Above them, in the center of the jar, the first bit of light began to glow.

"It is strange, to use such a thing as a focus," Faron said. "Why the insects? Need you their life, as a human, to concentrate the radiance?"

"Forgive my sins of the past, for they are many," Russell continued, ignoring him. "Guide my feet, Father, so I may not add to them as I walk."

Iris lay beside the fire, watching the pair. She bared her teeth every time Faron moved the jar. Though he was not privy to her thoughts, he could almost feel them drifting off her. She did not understand why he spoke with this man, nor let him live after his betrayal. The business with the jar, in particular, upset her greatly.

Faron used his free hand to pull the preacher's eyelids open. He disliked the jar, too, but he would grant Russell the mesmerization of that stolen radiance, and all its power. It was only fair.

The man's prayer sputtered silent as the gold shone upon him.

"You will not lie," Faron repeated, and this time the words sank into the preacher. Faron watched his eyes glaze over. "Your tongue will not form the words. My ears will not believe them. The truth, as you view it. Do you understand, Preacher Russell?"

"I do."

Faron let go of his eyelids and shifted the jar from one hand to the other. Nearby, Iris whimpered unhappily.

"Why did you wish harm upon me?" Faron asked.

"Because I was ordered to do so."

Orders? Faron's eyes narrowed.

"Explain these orders."

Tears ran down the sides of Russell's face. All the bugs gathered at the bottom of the jar, carefully circling to leave a little gap in the center so the golden light, so yellow it almost resembled pus, still shone through. Wings and carapaces fluttered. A lone praying mantis flicked its front legs along the glass in a steady rhythm.

"I was to travel the farms alongside this forest and watch for a man, pale of skin, dark of hair, and with eyes like...eyes like..."

"Like what?" Faron asked, leaning closer.

"Eyes like starlight."

Faron shook the jar, stirring the insects. The gold light within flared brighter.

"Hold nothing back, Preacher. Speak your truth."

Russell pulled against the vines holding him, but the attempt was weak and half-hearted. His eyes never left the jar.

"He would have many names, but Faron would be his favorite. He would be confused about the passage of days. Most of all, he would be dangerous. You, *you* would be dangerous."

The spell was already starting to break. Faron could manipulate truth and memory, but it was infinitely easier to do so upon a willing soul. Russell, however, quaked with religious zeal.

Faron hesitated. He didn't have to ask the overwhelming question in his mind. He could continue in ignorance. This might be a misunderstanding. Much could have changed these past seventy years.

"Who gave you these orders?" he asked, refuting that cowardice. He would not walk these lands afraid of the truth. That way would never be his.

"I was told they came directly from the Luminary."

Another name that meant nothing to Faron.

"Who is the Luminary?" he asked, again shaking the jar. Iris stood and growled. The insects within writhed like mad. The light pulsed, turning from gold to silver as Faron's own radiance poured into it, overwhelming the wretched stolen gold.

"He speaks for our Father, guiding us through the wilderness," Russell said. He bit his tongue, hard, but that did not stop the words. He continued, blood dribbling down his lips. "He is Mitra Gracegiver, the one who united the eastern kingdoms, founded the Church of Stars, and granted us our holy light."

The name "Mitra" meant nothing. Names could be changed. Holy light? The human's name for radiance. That they possessed the ability to control the magic filled Faron's stomach with fire. Just how many wielded a gift never meant to be tainted by their hands and lips?

"What does the Luminary look like?" he asked. When Russell did not answer, Faron leaned closer, his voice hardening. He grabbed the preacher's throat with his free hand. "What does Mitra look like?"

"Beautiful and wise, his hair, it's...He looks like..." The glazed look in Russell's eyes faded. He shook, his fear returning tenfold.

"You," he said. "He looks like you."

Faron cast the jar to the dirt and waved his hands. The vines receded. Though he was free, the preacher lay still, afraid to move.

"Begone," Faron said. "And remember that, though your life was forfeit, you were shown mercy."

The spell over, the preacher broke completely. He grabbed his staff and jar, scrambled to his feet, and fled into the forest.

Good riddance, thought Faron.

He sat by the fire, his chest constricting and his throat tight. When he looked down, he saw his hands were shaking. It seemed Iris noticed, too, for she trotted over and licked his fingers. She whined, and he sensed the question within.

"I'll be fine," he told her, and gave the coyote his best smile.

In return, she snarled, but not at him. Faron spun, his hand reaching for his sword, but he never drew it from its sheath.

His brother Sariel sat on the log by the fire. He looked sharp in a coat matching Faron's, only black instead of brown. His dark hair was long and loose, hanging halfway down his back. Across his shoulders rested his enormous sword, Redemption, untouched by time. It was crafted entirely from a piece of a dragon's jawbone. With the aid of radiance, unbreakable dragon bone had been sanded and smoothed so its hilt was soft to the touch, whereas the blade, its length half his height, was sharpened into a deadly weapon.

"Welcome back," Sariel said. He gave a smile that had seduced many a man and woman, for they did not see the truth behind it, nor the unbearable guilt and sadness that lurked in the stars of his eyes.

"We need to talk about Eder."

Chapter 3

EDER

*A*re you watching, Father? thought Eder as he gazed up at the clear night sky. *Are you ready for the souls to come?*

Eder descended on one of the Tower Majestic's seventy-five lifts, a square platform hanging from thick ropes tied to metal rungs bolted to all four corners and then given a wooden guardrail. Before him stretched the emptiness at the heart of the tower. Lanterns swayed along the other side of that enormous black abyss, hundreds of them, yellow stars a quarter mile away. A chill wind teased the thin fabric of his black robe and fluttered its silver tassels. A wind always blew through that vacuous center, as if nature itself decried its emptiness. The lift traveled smoothly, the boards beneath him groaning and swaying only a little, inevitable given the great distance they covered.

"There are nine devouts prepared for tonight," said Madeleine, the only other passenger on the lift. She was a brilliant young woman, her blond hair tied back in a bun to lend a severe look to an otherwise beautiful face. Like all officials of the Mind of the Father, she wore a black vest and trousers. Pinned at her breast was a silver pendant, a mimicry of the tower, with three stars beneath to signify her as a Celebrant, her order's highest achievable rank. Buckled to her waist was Eder's knife, sleek and silver.

"I have not the heart for nine," Eder confessed.

Madeleine crossed her hands behind her back. She stood beside him, the top of her head barely reaching his shoulder. He wondered if she saw the same beauty he did when gazing out across the expanse. The emptiness frightened most people, a quarter mile of nothing between the Tower Majestic's interior walls of hardstone. Far, far below swirled the ocean, sparkling faintly from the unobstructed starlight.

It was said, if one fell, one's heart would burst from fear long before one hit the water, and only a corpse would greet the hungry creatures of the sea. Eder suspected the people of the tower preferred that story to the truth, that the churning water would crush a body like a man's heel upon a cherry.

"If you have not the heart, then let others bear the burden," Madeleine suggested.

Floor after floor passed to Eder's right, hardstone jutting out from the tower's side to allow dozens of buildings to be constructed of wood and sandstone atop them. People moved through their tightly curled streets, human shadows lit by torches and starlight. More lifts moved up and down between the juts, crossing far shorter distances, many of them at an angle to connect the different floors. Those were pulled by liftmasters, strong men who twisted and turned gears connected to pulleys to safely and smoothly wind and unwind the heavy ropes.

Though stairs circled the tower's sides, it took most people more than an hour to climb them from top to bottom. Much faster, and easier, to take lifts to the many floors built into the hardstone. Most lifts would have multiple stops, but not the one Eder and Madeleine rode. It served a special purpose. Its only entrance was near the top of the Tower Majestic, and permanently guarded. Its only exit, the cold cells far below.

"This burden is mine," Eder said. "I will not force upon anyone that which I alone must bear."

He looked to the sky for strength. The Tower Majestic, two thousand vertical feet of hardstone, was built in an era long before humans, by a people forgotten to time known only as the Etemen. No matter how grand it was now, it had once been grander, for the tower rising out of the ocean had cracked in half and then collapsed onto the cliffside. This meant the upper portions ended abruptly at open sky.

A blessing, so far as Eder was concerned, for it granted those living within the sight of the stars glittering above.

Madeleine stepped closer to the lift's edge and touched the guardrail.

"Then rest for tonight," she said. "The cells can accommodate the devouts for a bit longer."

"The moon is full, and the devouts' souls are ready," Eder said. "They deserve their freedom, not another month trapped and waiting." He smiled at her. "Do not worry. I am long accustomed to these burdens. They will not break me."

"All things may break," Madeleine said. "Is that not the lesson of the Tower Majestic?"

Eder chuckled at her stubborn wit. He should expect as much from his Celebrant. The hardstone that comprised the tower could not be worked, chipped, or cut by any tool known to man, and yet somehow the tower had split and fallen. Stories of why were more numerous than the stars, and Eder suspected all of them were wrong.

"Fair enough," he said. "But I know my limits. Hold faith in your Luminary."

The noises of civilization, even those of the night, such as the bawdy songs of taverns, the ripple of window curtains, fabrics drying on clotheslines, and the flutter of midnight birds nesting on rooftops, all came to silence here at the lowest portions of the Tower Majestic. A new sound replaced them: the roar of the waves below.

The lift slowed to a halt before a ledge. Two guards were there to receive them, standing at attention before a wooden gate sealing off the rest of the hardstone jut. One guard grabbed hold of the handrail to steady the platform, while the other offered his hand to Madeleine. She took it and hopped over the thin gap to the ledge. Eder crossed it himself, not needing or desiring any aid.

Once they were free of the lift, the first guard took a sand hourglass atop a nearby pedestal and flipped it. The largest and longest lifts were all moved by pulleys built on the tower's second-highest floor, known as the

Rafters. With such tremendous distance between floors, and so many different levers to pull, the various destinations used matching hourglasses to know when the lifts would be raised or lowered. Four minutes; that was the rule. No matter the destination, no matter the size of the lift, it would move again in four minutes.

"Greetings, Luminary," the first guard said. He was an older man with swaths of gray in his beard. Those who protected the cold cells were always the eldest of the kingdom's soldiers, battle worn and tested. He bowed and put his fist to his forehead. "May Father bless and keep you."

"And you as well, soldier," Eder said.

Another guard stood watch atop the gate, and seeing Eder, he quickly opened it. Together, Eder and Madeleine entered the encampment protecting the cells. Most of it was comprised of tents, the poles and fabric far easier to transport than planks of wood or heavy bricks of stone. To their right were bedrolls, and to their left, tables and chairs. Farther toward the edge of the jut were stacked crates of supplies.

Given the late hour, one would expect most soldiers to be asleep, but it was a full moon tonight, and they knew their Luminary would soon arrive. They stood at attention, their heads bowed and their right fists raised to their foreheads. Lantern light flickered off their steel armor. All of them wore the tabards of the Astral Kingdom, black cloth bearing the image of the broken Tower Majestic sewn with silver thread in the center.

"Praise be to the Luminary," their commander shouted as Eder passed.

"Praise be!" the soldiers echoed.

Eder walked among them, careful to keep his shoulders back and head held high. Among his brothers, he was not as beautiful as Sariel, nor as muscular and handsome as Faron. His dark hair he cut just above his shoulders and allowed much of it to fall across his face. A protective veil. Not handsome, not beautiful, but intense. Focused. Slow to anger, slow to smile. A soft jaw, a sharp nose, and eyes that would imprison if he allowed them to do so. Where he walked, people noticed and bowed low. Before he ever wore a crown, before he ever labeled himself a prophet, people sensed the radiance within him and trembled.

Stairs awaited at the far wall, and unlike most places throughout the tower, these were blocked off with a wooden barricade to prevent any arrivals from above. The only way was down, and waiting there was an elderly man wearing a thick black robe. It was rarely warm far at the bottom of the tower, where the sun was at its thinnest and the shadows their deepest.

"I bid you welcome, Mitra," said the man, a preacher named Glasga. While most preachers were assigned to the far corners of Kaus, specifically areas lacking a church and shepherd, Glasga was special. The people of the cells, and only those of the cells, were his to nurture and prepare. A difficult task, one that few would choose if given the chance. Glasga, however, had relished the challenge when Eder offered it to him.

"I hear there are nine ready for tonight?" Eder asked as they descended. The hardstone stairs were so wide ten men could walk them abreast, yet the trio kept close to the wall on their left. No railing protected the other side. It was also a good five strides from step to step, which birthed claims that the Etemen were, while not giants, extremely long-legged, portrayed to an almost comical degree when painters and storytellers attempted their imaginings of the Tower Majestic's original builders.

"Eight, I am afraid," Glasga said. He touched the balding portion of his head with his fingers. "Poor Desdemona perished this morning. The chill, I suppose. She could not endure the chill."

"Such a shame," Madeleine said without a hint of emotion.

"It is, but at least her soul was prepared," Glasga said. "In many ways, she was blessed, and her fate enviable. Is that not true, Mitra?"

Glasga always used Eder's currently chosen alias of "Mitra," unlike the rest of Kaus, which referred to him as Luminary, the title he had adopted when he merged his kingship over the Astral Kingdom with his rule over the Church of Stars. Given the importance, and secrecy, of the preacher's task, Eder allowed Glasga this minor form of familiarity. There was no hiding Madeleine's disgust, however, for she viewed it as a sign of disrespect.

"There is nothing enviable about their fates," Eder said, delivering the gentlest of admonishments. "Only joy in the cleansing of their souls. We can celebrate one while acknowledging the difficulty of the other."

The stairs did not reach the water far below, nor arrive at another enormous jut of hardstone. They simply ended. Hanging from them were the cold cells.

Given the impenetrable nature of hardstone, nails could not be used to secure ropes to the stairs. Instead enormous blocks of stone were placed near the edge, and it was to them the ropes were tied. At the end of those ropes were thick burlap blankets, secured from multiple holes so that while three sides of the cell curled up securely, a fourth would always remain open, facing the great expanse. Those kept within could see the emptiness, the darkness of the far side, and the waters of the ocean below.

When Eder came to power, the previous lord of the tower had used the cells as a form of punishment. Eder halted that on his very first day. He had far loftier plans in mind.

"Raise the first," he ordered.

"Of course, of course," said Glasga, and grabbed a metal hook resting on the floor. The hook was tied to a rope of enormous length, the end of which looped into the final step's lone structure: a hand-crank crane the size of a man. Glasga set the hook underneath one of the taut ropes holding an occupied cell, then walked to the crank. Slowly, amid a clatter of wood and clicking of gears, Glasga turned the wheel. The hook rose higher and higher with carefully measured speed and strength, bringing the cell up with it.

"Before you begin, I ask that you think of yourself," Madeleine said as they watched the cell rise. "If this first devout is too much for you, do not continue out of stubbornness or pride. The needs of both church and kingdom are so much more than one soul."

"Ah, but that's where you're wrong," Eder said. "What we do on these lonely, tiring nights will change the world. We shall shake the foundations of heaven and announce ourselves to Father." He smiled at her. "But only if I am strong enough. And I *am* strong enough. How could I not be, when so many hold me in their hearts and prayers?"

Glasga halted the turning of the crank at the arrival of the cell. It swung loosely, an arm's length from the final stair. Inside was a middle-aged man, fully naked, his head shaved and his body heavily tattooed.

Glasga administered those tattoos himself, back in his little hut filled with an exotic array of tools. They were a catalog of the man's worst sins, accumulated over dozens of past lives.

"What is the devout's name?" Eder asked as he approached the swaying cell.

"Atik," Glasga answered.

The man looked up, and upon seeing Eder, he began to weep.

"The moon is full," Atik said.

"It is," Eder said, and smiled.

"Am I ready? Tell me, are me and all my lives ready?"

Eder offered the man his hand. "Tonight, you shall be free of your past, but only if you hold faith in me, and in Father."

The devout accepted his aid, and he awkwardly climbed out of the burlap cell to stand naked before the three members of the church. Wordlessly, and still holding Atik's hand, Eder guided him to the final stair's edge, and the circle prepared there.

Eder had used melted silver to draw the lines with his own hands, enduring the burns to ensure each and every loop and curve matched his desires. They represented balance and order, and in its perfect center, a gap for the world of Kaus. Surrounding it were little droplets that were the stars of the sky, as well as a half circle for the moon. Eder had forever been fascinated by the midnight canopy, for he could not shake the feeling that it was *wrong*.

Oh, the stars moved. The sun rose in the east and set in the west. But though he could track the years, his heart refused to accept it. The math felt simplistic, the movements predictable and dull. Yet over centuries of watching, tracking, and counting, never did they falter or prove themselves false.

The stars granted him power, and yet they also felt like a lie. The contradiction grated on Eder's mind, even if his siblings professed no such similar sentiments.

"Stand in the circle's center," Eder commanded, and a shivering Atik obeyed. Glasga retreated, content to watch the fruition of his efforts from afar. Eder closed his eyes, gathering his strength. Every life, every soul, was precious, and he could not afford to be reckless.

"My knife," he commanded. Madeleine drew it from her belt and offered it to him. He took it, felt the metal hilt against his palm. His knife's familiarity granted him no comfort.

Eder drew in a long breath to gather himself, blew it out, and opened his eyes.

Radiance shone from where his irises should be. In their dark light, he saw Atik's soul. He saw the sins committed against the rules and desires of Father, and not only of this life. Atik's soul had been reborn, again and again, the sins of past lives stacked atop one another to form an oppressive weight that marred its pristine beauty.

But sins could be atoned for. It took faith. It took sacrifice. All sins, from all lives.

"Close your eyes, Atik," Eder said, his free hand wrapping around the trembling man's neck. He was so cold, so starved. He'd endured much over the past months since being declared a devout. Glasga had probed his dreams. He had plundered the memories of his past lives. Carefully, deliberately, the preacher compiled the sins of multiple lifetimes, and then together, preacher and devout, they performed the necessary penance.

At last, in preparation for this holy night, his soul was clean.

"You are free of any burden," Eder whispered so only Atik could hear. "You are light as a feather. You are pure as newly fallen snow. Beautiful, devout child of Father, you are beautiful."

The silver circle beneath them began to glow the fierce white of distant stars.

"You will be reborn no more. This sinful land will not reclaim you. It is to a new place you shall go. To a land free of strife and discord. To where no more sins may burden your soul. Beyond the sky, beyond the stars, awaits Father's paradise."

Atik's knees went weak, and he fell. Eder caught the weeping devout in an embrace, the man's cheek pressed against his breast. Tears wet the black fabric. Below them, the runic circle began to rotate, the silver flowing as if freshly melted yet refusing to break from its shape and order.

"Your journey is at its end, but only if you can be strong. Do you feel the power flowing through you? Do you feel the holy light ready to carry you?"

"I do," Atik said, his voice muffled by the robe.

Gently, lovingly, Eder separated them. He wiped away Atik's tears.

"You must do one thing," he said. "When the stars claim you, you must shout to them, do you understand? Shout with all your heart. Scream it. Howl it. That is all I ask, in payment for all I have done. Can you do that for me, Atik? Can you bear this burden?"

"I can. I can."

"Four words. Just four words. Promise me, Atik, or this will all be for naught."

Atik stared into Eder's eyes. He showed no fear of the swirling darkness and light within them.

"I promise."

"Then say them. 'Father, I am here.'"

Despite Atik's weakness, despite his nakedness, Eder saw him as the most noble of humans. This was their pinnacle, not titles and wealth and inherited lands. Not material gains. This strength. This belief.

"Father, I am here!"

Atik's lungs were weak, and his voice hoarse, but it felt like his words echoed louder than the roar of the distant waves below.

"Again," Eder said. "With a power to wake the heavens. Pierce the firmament!"

"Father, I am here!"

"Again!"

"Father, I am here!"

"Again!"

"Father—"

Eder sliced Atik's throat. Blood poured across his hands and wet the silver hilt of his knife. He grabbed Atik by the back of the neck, holding him still, as shock widened the man's eyes and his entire body trembled.

"Do not stop," Eder ordered. "Even without words. Even after death. Scream it to the heavens with your very soul. Father, I am here. *We* are *here*."

One push, and Atik toppled to the dark ocean below. The swirling of the silver circle halted in place, every moon and star as they once were. Eder stood within their celestial lines, gathering himself. His heart pounded against his ribs. When he looked up, the light of the heavens felt so very far away.

Celebrant Madeleine offered him a white rag, and he absently accepted it.

"My lord..." she began.

"The next," Eder said, interrupting her. "Bring me the next."

She swallowed hard and exchanged a glance with Preacher Glasga.

"As you wish, Luminary," she said.

Eder did not watch them detach the hook from the crane and set it to the next rope. The twisting of gears was a distant noise, one he could not focus upon. *Breathe steady. Wipe the blade clean.*

One devout purified. Seven more to follow, before the fall of the moon and the fading of the stars into daylight.

Chapter 4

SARIEL

Sariel carefully watched his brother's reaction to the tale, a hand resting on Redemption's hilt. He needed an ally, and while he loved Faron, he did not trust him. Sentimentality and idealization were both too strong in his heart.

"Luminary?" Faron said after a time. "The Astral Kingdom? This... No, he wouldn't. It isn't like him."

"Except it is," Sariel said, the past burning hot in his breast. "I stopped him once. This time, he succeeded."

Faron looked to him, and it was such a strange mix, that soft heart and handsome face upon a body so strong and muscled.

"Why didn't you prevent this?"

Sariel glared.

"You know damn well why. My hope was that he would come to his senses, but matters have only worsened as his church spreads. He's too strong now, too well protected inside his Tower Majestic. I need help. I need you."

"What of Aylah?" Faron asked. "I can't believe she would stand idly by while Eder broke one of our sacred vows."

"I haven't seen her for several decades," Sariel said. "And Eist has vanished into seclusion for twice as long. With you recovering, it left only Calluna and me, and she is no warrior. We both know that."

Faron picked up a nearby stone and tossed it into the fire. His frown deepened.

"Why would Eder seek to harm me?" he asked.

"He needs time," Sariel answered. "For what, I do not know, but I suspect he believed you would disapprove of what he has built."

"And what of you? Are you also hunted?"

The years flew by in Sariel's mind. Little nudges here and there, whispered words into the ears of royals about the dangers of the newly founded Church of Stars. It hadn't been enough. He'd used a soft touch when brutality was required.

"I have kept my machinations hidden," he said simply. "Eder does not know I plan against him."

"And just what are those plans of yours?"

Sariel grinned, and he felt a glimmer of the joy that sometimes awakened in him when in Faron's presence.

"I mean to kill him, break his kingdom, and end his sadistic religion."

His younger brother laughed. "Is that all?"

"It is a start. Will you aid me, or have you a hundred more questions to ask first?"

This was it. Sariel had spent the last decade learning the current politics of the far realms, and their various lords and ladies, in preparation for the coming war. And it would be a war. The Astral Kingdom reached its greedy fingers across the Sapphire Mountains, and at last, they would come back bloodied.

Sariel's chest tightened as he waited for an answer. His grip tightened on Redemption. No matter the decision, a hard road lay ahead of him, but at least he might not walk it alone. And if Faron refused, well...another twenty years or so recovering in a cave might do him good.

"I still wish to learn more," Faron said, breaking the silence. "But if what you told me is true, Eder has much to answer for. No crowns. No thrones. That was our vow. And if he is willing to murder me over it, then something vile has entered his heart. Yes, Sariel. I shall help you."

Sariel slowly exhaled and relaxed his fingers about his sword hilt.

"Head east from here, to the village of Clovelly," he said. "I trust you can convince a family there to shelter you as we prepare for our journey. I will follow you shortly after."

"Will you not come with me?"

He smiled at his brother.

"Forgive me, but there is business in this forest I must first attend."

●

Sariel needed no woodland training to track his prey, not with a faint line of radiance glittering gold in the midnight air. He followed it, slowly, steadily, his bone sword resting comfortably across his shoulder.

A mile later, he found the new camp of the preacher Russell.

"Faron?" the man asked, startling from his seat beside his fire. "Wait, you're not—"

Sariel slammed his sword straight through Russell's chest. The impact toppled the preacher off his feet, and he hit the ground in a clutter of leaves and a splash of blood. He screamed in pain, instinctively grabbing at the sword, only to flay the flesh of his fingers.

It was not lethal, not yet. Sariel had been careful with his aim. No quick death for one who would attempt to slay his family.

"I am not so kind as my brother," he said, grabbing the jar of insects from the preacher's hands. "Nor am I so forgiving."

One good shake set the bugs to swarming. He felt the radiance inside the jar, garish and golden. Vile. *Tainted.* One twist, and he removed the lid. Before any insects could escape, he ripped his sword free, flipped the jar, and pressed the rim against the gaping wound.

"We swore a vow," Sariel said as the insects swarmed the blood and crawled into flesh. "Radiance would never again be given to humanity."

Russell howled as the little creatures feasted.

"Your precious Luminary has broken that vow."

Sariel grabbed Russell by the throat to still his writhing. Cold anger iced over his mind, and he felt a subtle change come over his body. His irises would no longer be the striking silver that people remembered. They would be the pattern of stars across a darkened plane, swirling with glowing radiance. His call thundered into the earth, commanding the squirming, crawling things with a power they could not resist. He fed it with his anger. He shaped it with his fury.

"Tonight, you will suffer in his stead."

The worms were the first to arrive, crawling up from the soil. Ants came next, then the larger bugs, racing along the ground and over the leaves. Flies descended from the treetops by the dozens. They bit and dug, seeking wet, moist, and dark places to feast and lay their eggs. Russell thrashed and howled and pleaded for mercy, but Sariel would not give it.

Radiance did not belong in the hands of humanity.

Hours later, once Russell was dead and his corpse a decomposing mess of meat and insects, Sariel stood and offered the closest thing to a prayer he would give the preacher's soul.

"Be reborn a better man, for in this life, you were wretched."

Chapter 5

FARON

Faron paused at the edge of the forest and the start of the village. Its name was Clovelly, unchanged since the last time Faron had visited it some seventy years ago on the way to his pyre cave.

"Keep close to me, Iris."

The coyote softly whined. Two men approached, haggard and with callused hands. They lived by the sweat of their brow and the hardness of their spirits. Faron smiled easily at them.

"Hello there," he said, lifting a hand in greeting. He kept his sword sheathed. Drawing it would only spook them, and they were already wary, given how he towered over them in height. "I was told I could find lodging here for the night?"

"Told by who?" the first asked. He had a red beard that stretched from one ear, tucked underneath his chin, and then stretched back up to the other. There was only caution in his pale blue eyes.

"My brother Sariel."

"We don't want no wild dogs among us," the other man interrupted. His skin was deeply tanned from the sun, and his hair thin blond reeds. He pointed a long, chipped knife at Iris. "Or whatever that enormous bitch is."

"No offense to your pet, stranger," the first added with a quick glare at the other. "But the last thing we want is one of our kids bit, or our chickens eaten while we sleep."

Faron kept his voice calm and his smile pleasant.

"Understandable concerns, but Iris will behave, I promise." He glanced down at the coyote. "Won't you, Iris?"

In response, Iris flattened her ears, snorted at him, and then finally sat on her rear and lowered her gaze to the ground. The submissive act, seemingly unprompted, calmed the two men a little.

"Well trained, I'll admit," the bearded man said. He offered his hand. "Name's Willart Fairgrove. This here's my cousin, Billy. What brings you to Clovelly, stranger?"

"Did I not already say I wished for a warm bed for the night?"

"Lots of beds in lots of places," Willart said. "But there's not much to bring a man out here unless you're born here, or you're running from things done elsewhere."

In answer, Faron dipped his hand into the pouch Calluna left for him and withdrew a silver coin. The evening light flashed off its polished surface as he held it out between two fingers. Both men's eyes widened. Faron suspected by their reaction that this was worth far more than a night's stay in a cramped bedroom.

"I've a big heart, and a bigger mouth," Faron said. "Feed me and provide me a bed, and I'll talk until your ears ache for silence. Deal?"

"Deal," Willart said without the slightest hesitation. He snatched the coin and shoved it into his pocket. "I pray you don't expect much, stranger, but I can have my children share a bed for the night so you have one of your own." He looked him up and down. "Your feet might hang off the end, though."

"I promise I have had worse," Faron said, and laughed. "But please, call me stranger no longer. My name is Faron, and during my brief stay, I would hope you call me friend."

·

Perhaps the coin smoothed over matters, but Willart's family was eager to welcome him. His timing could not have been better. Supper was prepared and ready, and they gave him a seat at their long, carved wooden table. The home was a bit dim and stuffy, and an earthy smell hung in the air Faron doubted they could ever get rid of, but the food was delicious. A flank of deer meat, hunted from the forest. Willart's oldest son, Bartholomew, had felled it with his bow, a fact the father was greatly proud of. By the faint blush in Bartholomew's cheeks, Faron understood this was not the first time such praise had been heaped upon him.

They did not ask Faron where he came from, nor why he was there, both of which he appreciated greatly. Instead he offered a story, one from his past, of his travels westward. He did not mention it had happened more than three hundred years ago.

"Now, you'd think bandits would take one look at me and decide there were easier marks," he said, addressing the five at the table: Willart, his sunken-eyed but bright-smiling wife, and his three children, two sons and a daughter. "But these bandits, they weren't the smartest, and they surrounded me on that bridge, two behind me and two ahead."

"What'd you do?" the middle child asked. She was a spirited little thing, with hair as red as her father's. "Did you fight them?"

"Fight?" Faron asked. "Oh, I fought them, and bare-knuckled to boot. But before I did, I asked each of them if they knew how to swim. The ones who could, I tossed off the side of the bridge."

"And the ones who couldn't?" Willart asked.

Faron flashed him a grin.

"Broken wrists are another way to take a man out of a fight, though I suspect both those thieves wished they'd learned to swim instead."

Laughter all around, though Willart's was forced. Caution would be the norm for him. Faron was bigger and stronger than anyone in the village, and he carried sharpened steel. Faron didn't blame him, nor did he mind.

"So are you a mercenary?" Bartholomew asked. The eagerness in the question raised Faron's eyebrows.

"Do you hope that I am?" he asked in return.

"Ignore him," Willart said. "The boy's been hearing tales of the Bastard Princess of Doremy and it's got his head full of foolish ideas."

"It's not foolish," Bartholomew insisted. He leaned toward Faron, his green eyes alight with fables. "War's coming to Argylle. Isabelle's going to unite all the west, and when she does—"

"Nothing will change," the father interrupted. "Nothing ever does, not for people like us. You'd be throwing your life away for someone who wouldn't notice if you were dying at her feet. Isabelle might talk grand, but she's a princess, and no speeches are going to change that."

Bartholomew slumped in his chair, his face reddening from both embarrassment and anger.

"Nothing changes because we don't make them change," he muttered.

"Be silent," Willart said, harsh enough that the other members of the family flinched. Faron sensed an old argument here, one a long ways away from being resolved. "Go get your pa. It's his turn to eat."

The oldest son excused himself from the table and vanished through one of the curtained doorways. Faron's curiosity must have been evident, for the father leaned his elbows on the table and lowered his voice as he explained.

"My father is...not well. He gets confused sometimes, but even if he shouts or calls us by the wrong names, he means well. There's no menace in him, just the trials of age. Please, take no offense at his behavior."

Faron's smile softened. "You need not apologize for the ailments of others," he said, glad to have the awkwardness of the argument behind them. "What is his name?"

"He'll answer to Horace," Willart said, and there was no hiding the pain in his voice. "When he remembers it."

Bartholomew returned holding an older man's hand. He walked gingerly, with far too much care for someone barely into his sixties, by Faron's estimate.

"Something smells divine," Horace said. "Did Rosie cook again?"

"Barb cooked tonight like every night," Willart said, gesturing to an open seat near the crackling hearth that provided the bulk of the light since the sun set.

"We don't know who Rosie is," the middle child whispered beside Faron. The explanation was not necessary, but the girl couldn't know that. To Faron's eyes, blessed with radiance, Horace's soul was a twisted, bleeding wound.

"Well, tell Rosie she shouldn't be so lazy," Horace said, sitting before his prepared plate. He paused and grew visibly angry. "She...Barb, you didn't...Where is Rosie? Is she hiding? She should be helping you."

Barb patted his hand, not answering, just trying to soothe him.

"Your dinner's getting cold," she said. Horace muttered something, grabbed his fork, and began to eat, all the while mumbling incoherently.

"Can't say the same for my empty plate," Faron said, gesturing for emphasis. "Have you any more hidden in that pot over by the fireplace? A big man like me needs to eat if he wants to keep his size."

"For what you paid for your lodging?" Willart said, standing from the table. "We have more than enough to give you seconds."

•

Faron waited until the deep of night to leave his room. His every step was measured so the floorboards would not betray him. Most people assumed he was slow and clumsy given his size, but he could move with silence to rival even Calluna when he tried.

His room was at the farthest end of the short hall. Directly across from it was Horace's room, and after testing the door, he found it unlocked. Good. Quiet as a thief, he slipped inside and shut the door behind him.

To his surprise, Horace was awake. The older man sat on the edge of his bed, naked from the waist up. The curtain to his window was pulled back. Moonlight shone across his face as he bathed within it.

"Oh, hello there," he said, noticing Faron.

"Shh," Faron said, holding his finger to his lips. When he spoke, he kept his voice as a whisper. "Might I stay with you a moment, good sir?"

Horace shrugged in answer. He seemed uninterested in Faron's arrival, and much more focused on the moon. The midnight light seemed to give him comfort. In that, Faron felt a kinship.

"It's hard, isn't it?" he said, lowering to his knees before the bed. "To be buried in so many memories. All of them yours, and yet, some distant, unfamiliar."

Horace slowly turned his gaze. His body stiffened. He leaned away, suddenly frightened.

"Your eyes..." he whispered.

The stars of radiance shone brightly within them, for Faron must see to do his work. He put his hands on Horace's shoulders.

"Remain still," he whispered, "and hold faith in me."

There were many things Faron had learned during his centuries on Kaus, and one was the nature of a soul. Upon a human's death, their souls ascended heavenward, all their collected memories and emotions bundled together in a gleaming white orb so similar to the stars...but then they returned. They plummeted, unseen by all except the ever-living touched with radiance. The souls plunged into the bodies of the newly born, to experience life once more. Their faces would be new, their voices different, and their past forgotten.

Life after life, reborn, cyclical. It was precious, in a way, but sometimes the threads began to fray as human bodies aged and withered. Poor Horace was seeing his past lives. He was awash in memories, real memories, but not from this lifetime. Rosie was likely long dead, and perhaps had been for centuries.

Faron's hand gently stroked Horace's cheek. Radiance flowed through him, coursing into the older man's veins. It soothed the frayed strands. It eased away the cracks. It set right the memories, so that only this life would remain true within his mind.

Tears flowed down Horace's face. His lower lip quivered. When he spoke, it was a broken, confused whisper.

"I...I'm here. I don't...It's clear. Everything. It's clear. It's all clear."

Faron opened his arms, and Horace collapsed against him, silently weeping into Faron's shirt. Faron shushed him as he gently stroked the man's hair.

"Weep if you must, then sleep well," he said. "You have a family that loves you, and a life yet to live. Be present among them. That is my gift to you."

Horace went limp in his grasp, and he slumped back into his bed. Faron closed the window curtain, then left the room in darkness.

When he shut the door, the sound of weeping pierced through it into the hall.

·

The stars were still bright when Faron and Iris exited the Fairgrove home and walked the well-trod dirt path winding through the scattered buildings of Clovelly.

"Forgive our need for haste," he told the coyote as they left the village behind them. "But at least you had a taste of human hospitality. What did you think of it?"

Iris glanced at him, yawned, and then trotted a few steps ahead.

"Fine, fine," Faron said, and he laughed in the dim light. "Next time, I promise we will at least sleep until the dawn."

Faron glanced over his shoulder, just barely able to see Willart's home. The family would soon wake to start their chores, rebuild the hearth fire, and prepare water to boil. When Horace joined them and talked, they would realize the change that had come over him. As much as Faron wished to see that glorious moment, it was not worth the risk. Better to vanish in the morning hours. Better to be a wondrous stranger who changed their lives forever and then was never seen again.

The morning chill frosted Faron's breath as he walked. Perhaps he should have let Horace be. Sariel would come looking for Faron in Clovelly, and not find him.

Faron closed his eyes, imagined the morning the family would soon have, and then shook his head.

No. It was worth it. It always was. Sariel would just have to do a bit of tracking on his own. His brother had found him immediately upon his return from his decades-long slumber. He could find him again after a day or two of lazy travel along the dirt roads of the west.

"Hey, wait up, Iris," Faron said, clapping his hands and breaking into a jog. The coyote was up ahead, sniffing and sprinting about a nearby field. In search of breakfast, if he was to guess.

"Don't leave me behind. I'm hungry, too!"

Chapter 6

SARIEL

Sariel walked the road of Barkbent Town, ignoring the occasional glare. He had never been welcome here, merely tolerated. That was fine with him.

Faron would be received with open arms, he thought after a particularly vicious look from an old woman with graying hair wrapped in a blue bonnet. But hopefully Faron was a good thirty miles to the south, waiting for him at Clovelly. No doubt his brother had already made himself some friends. That had ever been his gift.

"Good day, miss," Sariel said to the old woman, trying to imagine how Faron would have managed it. Was it just his kind-hearted nature?

"Good day, Sariel," she responded, curt and quick as she continued with her business.

Sariel shifted Redemption across his shoulder and carried on. Enough pretending to be his brother. He had come to Barkbent for a reason, and it wasn't to win over old women in bonnets.

At the northernmost end of the small town was a home notable only because of how tiny it was compared to its neighbors. Sariel knocked on the door, waited a few seconds, and then knocked again when he heard no noise within.

"Not here," someone called from next door. It was a middle-aged woman named Agatha, gap-toothed and far too nosy. She stuck her head out her window. "Down to the creek, to do the wash."

"My thanks," Sariel said.

Not far to the east was a foot-trodden dirt path that led through the tall grass to a little bend of a creek. Sariel heard humming long before he reached it, and the sound made his heart ache. He knew that voice.

A young woman was at the creek, two baskets with her, one full of clothes, the other linen sheets. Her hair was tied back from her face and her dress rolled up above her knees so she could stand in the ankle-deep water. She sang softly to herself as she wrung out a sheet, hummed notes broken by the occasional word. Her hair was a dull brown, but her eyes a livelier shade of light blue to rival a summer sky.

"Hello, Tara," Sariel said. She startled, dropping the sheet and spinning about with a faint splash.

"Sariel," she said, blushing. "Warn a girl next time, would you?"

"I would, if the surprise were not worth the amusement."

She laughed, and the joy sent waves of emotions through Sariel's chest, some good, some terrible.

"So why have you come?" she asked. "Eager to help with my laundry? Oh, and Agatha's, too. I volunteered, don't worry, she didn't press me. The walk here's become too much for her old knees."

Sariel jammed his sword into the dirt to free up his arms and then sat by the edge of the creek, his dark coat folding over him.

"I came to say goodbye."

Tara grabbed the sheet she'd dropped, using it as an excuse to turn away from him.

"Oh. Does...No, it's wrong of me to ask, forgive me."

He knew what she was wondering. Tara's parents had died of disease five years ago, during a blight that had claimed almost one in ten people in Barkbent. It had come swiftly, vicious in its speed and deadliness, and ended only when Sariel provided iron-beech bark for them to boil for the sick to drink. He had left it in a simple basket on the town mayor's doorstop in the dead of night. Sariel did not want to be remembered, nor treated as the people's savior.

So far as Tara knew, Sariel was a friend of her father's, and ever since her parents' deaths, he had funded her stay in the little home she lived in, along with a small sum every month for food and clothing. Others in the town muttered sinister beliefs at his motivations. Sariel paid them no mind.

"If you are worried about your boarding, I am not abandoning you," he said. "I'll pay for another full year before I leave."

Tara scooped up the cleaned sheet and began wringing it out.

"I've been helping around Barkbent, I'll have you know. I still hope to one day repay you for all your kindness."

Sariel smiled softly at her. "If you do that, then it will have been a loan. Please, Tara. Let my kindness remain a kindness. You are worthy of it."

She plopped the sheet into the basket and grinned at him, her clothes wet, her feet muddy, and her hair a wild mess barely constrained by the band tying it back.

"Am I, now?" she asked with a laugh.

Sariel risked a brief flash of radiance in his eyes. To the soul beneath, and its layers upon layers of memories.

Before Tara, she had been Monica.

Before Monica, she had been Lily.

Before Lily, Rose. Before Rose, Amanda. Before Amanda, Ginnie.

Names after names. Lives after lives. Different faces. Different smiles. Centuries upon centuries of change, but that same soul, that same piercing link to his past. Moments from each and every one danced in Sariel's mind, visible if he reached out with his gift of radiance. Sariel felt his insides tremble, and he grabbed his sword.

"I must travel eastward with my brother," he said, standing. "I suspect it may be several years before I return. When I do, I hope to meet the good man lucky enough to have earned your affection."

"What if it ain't no man?" she asked. "What if it's a lass that stole my heart?"

Sariel ripped his sword free of the soft soil. "Then I pray she is equally worthy of it."

He turned to leave, but Tara was faster. She darted out of the water, crossed the grass, and wrapped her arms about him, her face pressed to his back.

"Stay safe, will you, Sariel?"

He turned, saw her looking up at him with a youth and life that threatened to pull his mind hundreds of years into the past, to his very earliest memories walking the land of Kaus. An even older face. The first name.

Isca.

Sariel hardened his jaw.

"I promise," he said, and brushed a bit of her wet hair away from her face. "Goodbye, Tara."

The path between the town and the creek was not long, but it still felt like forever as Sariel walked it, the distant sound of Tara's singing a spike to his heart.

•

Barkbent was just large enough, and near enough to the main roadway linking the iron-beech trade, that the town had a decently sized tavern with two rooms for rent. Sariel paid for one, found a seat by the fire in the commons area, and began the lengthy process of drowning himself in alcohol.

The late-night hours came. The commons area steadily filled with men darkly tanned by their work in the fields. What had been a quiet, somber evening turned raucous as the beer flowed and the first songs began. Sariel listened, his chest constricted and his mood foul.

Damn you, Eder, for all this nonsense, Sariel thought. He wanted nothing more than to spend the next few decades living unnoticed in the west. *Have we not all had our fill of building empires?*

As the night wore on, and Sariel started on his fourth glass, he noticed inquisitive glances from a nearby table. Four men, all farmers, he believed. Unlike the others in the commons, they were dour in mood and not prone to song. Sariel felt a sinking feeling in his stomach, but before he could leave, two of them stood from their chairs and approached.

"Sariel, right?" the younger of the two asked. He sported a mustache much too thin to be worth keeping, and an equally unimpressive stubble on his chin.

"It is," Sariel said, in no mood to banter. "Why come to me?"

The older one took a seat opposite Sariel at the table without asking. Like the youngster, he grew the hair out on his upper lip and chin, though thicker and grayer. He'd lost his left hand at some point, and he settled the rounded ball of his wrist at the end into his right palm. His eyes matched the dark color of the soil at the creek.

"Because no one carries a sword like that without knowing how to use it," he answered.

Sariel's dragon-bone sword leaned against his shoulder, the tip pressed into the floorboard. He glanced at it, then glared at the older man.

"Your name?"

"Strom."

"Listen well, Strom. I am no mercenary to be hired. Leave me in peace."

The younger man slammed his fists into the table.

"Then don't do it for money," he snapped, loud enough that other patrons nervously glanced his way. "Do it because it's the right thing to do."

Sariel's glare withered the man. Strom cleared his throat, equally displeased by the outburst.

"Rude as Mikel's outburst might be, you should know we are hard-pressed here in Barkbent. King Bentley lives a hundred miles away in Vendom and has appointed his son, Mortimer, to rule the southern half of Argylle in his stead. He is a brute, greedy in his taxes and a bully when it comes to any who might challenge his rule. We're lucky not to starve each year, but the day comes when we will not be so lucky."

Sariel knew of Bentley and Mortimer Casthe, of course. He'd looked into them over the past few years, to ensure neither would bother Tara here in Barkbent.

"I am no stranger to Argylle," he said. "Why tell me this?"

Mikel and Strom shared a glance. No one knew much about Sariel. Some thought him a trader, others a former knight or guard who had fled west. Sariel let them talk, so long as they also let him be.

"Because we thought you could help us," Strom said. "When hiding our coin didn't work, we started fighting back. Not much, just arrows from the trees on the forest pass, but we need to do better. Mortimer won't back down. We all know that, and we're not the only town looking to see him gone."

"War's coming," Mikel said. "And the Casthes are fools, provoking Princess Isabelle as they are. But if we act now, we can split off near half the kingdom and pledge ourselves to Isabelle's cause." He crossed his arms. "So will you help us? Or is that big sword of yours just for show?"

No hiding it now; other tables were listening in on the conversation. How many of these tired men were part of the growing desire for a fight? As if Isabelle Dior would treat them any better. Sariel knew of her, of course. All the west was awash in rumors of the golden-haired princess supposedly anointed by the goddess, Leliel. Nonsense, as far as Sariel was concerned. All these tiny little kingdoms were forever pecking at one another and forever conjuring reasons why they were virtuous and their enemies deplorable.

"My sword is my own, to be wielded as I desire it," he said.

"Hey, what's that sword made of anyway?" a man one table over asked. His nose and cheeks were bright red, and not from the sun. "We...we've seen it, you always got it with you, but we...we been guessing, and I got a bet. I say it's wood, painted wood."

Sariel hadn't thought his mood could worsen. He had been wrong. The entire commons room...this was no gathering of friends and family. This was a meeting. The men and women all turned to surround him.

"Not wood," Sariel said, glad for the excuse to grab Redemption by the hilt and pull it free so he could rest it across his shoulders. "Dragon bone, of a beast slain by my own hand."

"Bullshit," Mikel insisted. "No one's killed a dragon in over a hundred years."

Sariel gave his best smile. "I know."

Mikel scoffed at him. "So a liar *and* a coward."

"Please, we have no training among us," Strom said, trying to regain control of the conversation. "But you, you have the look of a man who has seen battle. You're also a stranger here, unknown to Mortimer. If you would kill him for us..."

Sariel interrupted, and his tone brooked no argument.

"No."

Mikel was in his face in a heartbeat.

"Mortimer is a wretch," he said. "A vicious, awful man who left us to die when the blight came. He taxes us within an inch of our lives but doesn't spare a split copper to buy iron-beech bark when we need it. You could do so much good with that sword of yours, thousands of lives in Argylle made better, and all for the cost of one life taken in return."

Sariel slowly stood. The collective breath of the crowd was held.

"One life," he said. "That is all you ask for, one life? Then I name my price. One of you must offer your own life, to die by my blade, in exchange for Mortimer's."

Shocked murmurs filled the commons.

"You must be joking," Strom said.

"A life for a life," Sariel said. "Is this not a fair trade?"

"No, it's fucking not," Mikel shouted. "All of us here, we are good people, while Mortimer...Don't you get it? The prince is an evil man, and all the little kingdoms would be better off with him gone."

A chorus of agreement. They brushed off Sariel like a paltry breeze. He locked his gaze on Mikel.

"Is that what you are?" he asked. "A good man?"

He moved before anyone could react, his left hand closing around Mikel's throat and slamming him against the wall. His right lifted his sword, keeping it pointed behind him so no one would dare interfere. Mikel squirmed, his hands clutching Sariel's wrist, but he could no more free himself than he could split a rock with his bare fingers.

Radiance swelled within Sariel's gaze, drawing out Mikel's memories, his life, and his sins. They paraded through Sariel's mind like half-remembered dreams.

"A good man, you tell yourself," Sariel said, a particular strain dominant among the parade. "A good man, as you creep outside Bethany's bedroom window. A good man, watching as the child sleeps. You haven't acted on your desires, not yet. You're too much of a coward, aren't you, Mikel? You're a coward, and so you touch yourself, and watch, and *imagine*."

Sariel's hand tightened as Mikel's face flushed red and his eyes widened with fury.

"The stars save us from good men like you."

The door to the tavern burst open and a young man stumbled inside. Blood dripped from his arm, which was poorly bandaged.

"Strom!" he shouted. "Please, you have to hide me!"

"Hide?" the older man asked. "Leliel help us, what did you do?"

Sariel's grip tightened on his sword, his attention not on the newcomer but the faint sound of hoofbeats from outside the tavern walls. The others couldn't hear them, not yet, but they soon would.

"I did what you told me," the injured man said. "Keep to the trees, use arrows, but they saw me, I don't know how, but they saw me, and they fired back with their crossbows."

Enough of this, thought Sariel. He dropped Mikel, the fool collapsing to the floorboards. He had sought solitude after bidding farewell to Tara, not this. Any hope of leaving was stopped by the three men in dirty chainmail pushing inside, bright blue-and-green tabards adorning their chests. The mark of Argylle. Mortimer's soldiers. All three had their swords drawn.

"Everyone on your knees," the lead one shouted. "On your knees, damn it!"

The panicked crowd hurried to obey. They had no weapons, no armor, and as much as they wished to stoke the fires of rebellion, it was much easier to do so at a quiet table overflowing with alcohol, and much harder when staring at naked steel. Even the bleeding man they chased dropped. He must have hoped the soldiers would not recognize him. A foolish hope. Only Sariel remained standing.

"There," one of the soldiers said, pointing toward the injured man. "There's the weasel who shot at us. I told you I saw him come in here."

Sariel strode for the door, not caring that they still blocked it.

"You have your man," he said. "Make way. I am not with them."

"No one leaves until I say they can leave," the first soldier snapped. He raised his sword. "And I don't recognize your face. You come here stirring up trouble for Prince Mortimer?"

Sariel tilted his head to one side.

"No trouble, unless you wish to make it."

Behind him, the instigator squealed as one of the three soldiers grabbed him by the injured arm. Angry mutters swept through the tavern, but no one dared resist. The soldier dragged the man along, smearing more blood on the floor and knocking tables aside. Meanwhile, the soldier blocking the door sneered at Sariel.

"I'm giving you to the count of three, stranger. Get down on your knees before I make you, and it won't be pretty. Got it? One…"

On "two," Sariel swept Redemption in a low, curving arc, slicing through the soldier's legs, severing them at the kneecaps. The soldier howled as he dropped, dragging the attention of the other two. One was behind Sariel, holding the injured man, the other in front, before the door. They both charged with their swords, flanking him. It was a powerful advantage and would have served them well against any other foe.

Not against Sariel. He planted both his feet, twisted his hips left, and swung his enormous blade in a single, swooping slash. The momentum twisted his waist to the right, adding power, adding speed.

One cut, and Redemption sliced the head off the first soldier and the arm off the second.

"Damn fools," Sariel said. A twist of his wrist, and he disemboweled the man with the missing arm, the sharp edge of dragon bone making a mockery of his protective chainmail. A brief silence followed, but upon realizing all three soldiers were dead, the tavern erupted in celebration, men and women who cowered on their knees not moments before now leaping up to cheer and holler.

Sariel shook the blood from his sword. It would not stain the bone, no matter how much was shed. Tired beyond measure, he looked to Strom.

"Three lives taken," he said, his voice nearly drowned out by the cacophony. "Consider it a kindness that I demand only one in return."

Strom's returned gaze was hard as steel. His was a spirit that could win a rebellion, if given time and men willing to fight for him.

"What you said about Mikel and Bethany," he asked. "Is that true?"

Sariel closed his eyes. Visions flashed through him, ones he held no desire to keep. Mikel, peering through Bethany's window. She looked ten years old, maybe eleven. Mikel's thoughts became Sariel's, and among the cowardice, he felt lust, and a stirring impatience. *Soon*, Mikel told himself as his hand stroked his crotch. *So very soon.*

Sariel opened his eyes.

"Yes," he said softly.

Strom straightened his spine and spoke with cold conviction.

"Do it."

Sariel spun, one foot planting and his upper body stretching into a thrust. The tip of his sword punched straight through Mikel's rib cage, puncturing his heart. The man died with his mouth open in shock, his bafflement erased only by brief pain before death took him.

Another swish of Sariel's sword, and the blood flowed off its edge to the floor, joining that of the three soldiers. Stark, sudden silence followed, unnerving in a commons so crowded with people.

"I'm leaving," Sariel said, fixing his black coat and then setting Redemption across his shoulders. He glared at the surrounding crowd. "Do not follow me."

This time, no one dared block the door.

•

Sariel walked the winding dirt road between the rolling hills to either side. It was hardly the first time he'd traveled beneath the stars. He favored it, if he was honest with himself, though it'd have been more pleasant if his stomach were not full of beer and his head clogged with memories of the fight. As dawn approached, he focused on a map of the region in his mind.

If Faron had followed Sariel's advice, he'd still be at Clovelly, which Sariel could reach by midday if he forfeited all sleep. Once together, they could better plan their coming war against the Astral Kingdom. The brewing skirmishes among the little kingdoms would hopefully work in their favor. Once people's blood was boiling, it would be a simple matter of choosing a champion and then shifting their goals toward something much grander than petty grudges and unsettled borders.

It'd be much easier, of course, if Faron or Sariel could lead these kingdoms themselves, but even the thought of it made the skin of his left
arm burn.

No crowns. No thrones. The unbreakable vow.

Sariel's isolation ended an hour after dawn. Four men on horses
approached, one of them flying a green banner sporting a blue raven.
Sariel's grip on his sword tightened.

"Greetings, traveler," one said as they halted beside him in the dirt
road. All four wore chainmail and blue-and-green tabards. Swords rattled
at their hips. "What brings you to the road so early?"

"I walked the night," Sariel said, keeping his tone dull and neutral.

"You'd walk these lands alone after dark?" asked the farthest back
of the four. He sported a large helmet whose opening at the front was
flanked by what appeared to be the spread wings of a raven. Unlike the
others, his chain was colored an obnoxious shade of blue. "Either you're
easy prey for bandits, or a bandit yourself."

"It's bandits that brings us here," the first soldier said, his hand drifting toward the hilt of his sword. "Do you know of them? There might be
a handsome reward for you."

Sariel ignored the question and instead eyed the man with the ridiculous helmet.

"Are you Prince Mortimer?" he asked.

The man straightened in his saddle. "So you know of me?"

Sariel's first swing severed the neck of the nearest soldier's horse and
then continued into the waist of the rider. The chainmail fared no better, parting before the sharpened edge of dragon bone to spill intestines
across the collapsing horse's corpse.

The other horses reared and startled, and the riders themselves froze,
overwhelmed with shock. They paid for their hesitation. Sariel's movements were perfect, fluid, his sword looping from the high arc of his first
swing to then curl around and plunge halfway up the hilt into the chest
of a second soldier. A twist of his wrist turned the blade sideways. He
planted his feet and swung, ripping Redemption out in one direction to
slam into a third soldier.

"Bandits!" Mortimer cried, nonsensical in his fear. His horse reared up from his panicked tug of the reins. Its hooves thrashed the air before Sariel, but he deftly sidestepped them, waiting for the opportune moment.

When the horse came back down, Sariel slid closer, gripped Redemption's hilt in both hands, and swung. The tip of his sword was all that reached Mortimer, but it was enough to cut underneath the wings of his helmet and open the flesh of his throat. The idiot gargled blood, clutching at his neck in a futile attempt to stop the bleeding. One more swing, and Sariel cut the straps of the saddle, dropping him. The freed horse sprinted away, joining the other two mounts that fled once their riders collapsed.

Mortimer hit the dirt and lay on his back. Blood leaked through the fingers of his gauntlets. His brown eyes widened in bafflement. His mouth opened and closed like a fish, forming words he had no breath to give voice to. Sariel jabbed the tip of his sword into that open mouth, ending it.

Silence returned to the morning. Only the faint beat of hooves marred it as the surviving three horses hurried away. Sariel shook the blood from Redemption and glared down at Mortimer's corpse. Frustration and anger built within him, directed solely at himself.

"Barely awake a day and you're already rubbing off on me," he muttered, knowing Faron would have eagerly agreed to help the townsfolk. Such foolishness was beneath Sariel…At least, that's what he told himself. The bodies said otherwise. No price. No payment. Tara was in greater danger now, too. King Bentley would hear of his son's death, and he would assume the worst about how it happened. The people of Barkbent would suffer. *Tara* would suffer.

Unless something happened to the King of Argylle.

"You better be waiting for me," he said to a distant Faron as he trudged toward Clovelly, his mind mapping out allegiances and territories. King Bentley lacked allies, and there were several nearby little kingdoms and queendoms already mustering armies for the expected war to come.

Perhaps Argylle might be in need of a little rebellion, after all.

Chapter 7

FARON

Rain came at midday, sudden and heavy. Faron and Iris huddled underneath a rare sycamore tree growing in the tall grass fields surrounding the road, attempting to wait out the storm, but after several hours, it was clear there would be no break anytime soon.

"It looks like we are sleeping under the stars tonight," Faron told Iris. The coyote whined at him, and he could practically hear her stomach rumble. He sat with his back against the sycamore, and when he closed his eyes, it did not take long to sense the groundhogs in the nearby fields. He stretched radiance toward one, stirring it from its lazy slumber and filling it with a sudden, panicked need to exit its burrow.

"That way," Faron said, opening his eyes and pointing. "If you don't mind a bit of mud, you will find your prey. I'll prepare a fire while you hunt."

Iris returned minutes later with the bleeding groundhog in her mouth. She plopped it down beside the fire he'd built in the shade of the tree, positioned so the thick trunk blocked the wind. Faron hovered over that fire protectively, using his coat to guard against the occasional raindrops.

"I knew you could do it," he said, grinning at her. The coyote's eyes narrowed, and she nudged the groundhog's body with her nose.

"Fine, yes, I helped a little. Just enough to make the creature stir and race about. You did the actual hunting."

He'd thought Iris unhappy with the nature of the hunt, but then she curled around behind him and shook to splatter him with a massive spray of water from her fur.

"Fine," he said, drawing a knife while grabbing the groundhog. "Next time, if the weather is poor, I'll make our dinner come to us and spare you the rain."

Iris plopped down beside the fire, its light flickering across her fur, and closed her eyes. There was no need to wake her once the groundhog was properly butchered and cooked. The smell was enough.

Faron made sure she got the larger portion.

•

The rain ended come nightfall, far too late to do any traveling. Faron appreciated the slowly growing gaps in the clouds nonetheless. They allowed the stars to shine through, lighting up the fields. The grass rolled like ocean waves in the wind, a beautiful sight to behold. He gently stroked Iris's fur as she slept contentedly beside him, and he let the hours pass. Sleep would come in time, but not yet.

Calluna was calling for him.

The heavy rains meant the dirt road cutting the little kingdom of Argylle north to south was an ankle-breaking mess. Faron abandoned his tree, careful not to rouse Iris, and then returned to that road. He walked among the puddles, his boots sinking into the mud. He looked into them, seeing his tired face, his brown coat, and the reflection of the clouded sky above.

Looked, until one was brightly lit by a clear field of stars, and it was not his face that looked back, but what appeared to be a girl with raven hair and deeply freckled nose and cheeks. Her eyes were black and silver, shimmering with radiance. Stars brighter and clearer than the ones in the sky above shone like diamonds within her irises.

"You're back," Calluna said. Her voice emerged slightly muffled from the water, as if she lurked just underneath the surface. "I'm...I'm happy you're back."

The angle to her visage was strange, as if she were actually peering down at him. It was the nature of her communication. Somewhere across the breadth of Kaus, Calluna huddled over still water. Ponds were her favorite choice, and he thought he saw little reeds blowing against her dark dress. It needn't be natural formations, though. She could seek him out with a bucket and some sewage, if she must.

"You don't sound all that happy," Faron said, and he smiled at her. "I pray the years have been kind to you."

Calluna leaned closer to the water's surface. She was sitting with her legs tucked against her chest and her arms wrapped around her shins. Her chin rested atop her knees.

"The years have been years," she said. "Long and lonely, as they always are."

Faron crouched before the puddle and studied his little sister's mannerisms, the way she picked at her dress, and how she refused to return his gaze.

"You're nervous," he said.

"No, I'm not."

"You are a terrible liar, Calluna. Always have been."

He grinned at her, trying to elevate her mood. She bit her lower lip, then looked away.

"Do the clothes fit you well?"

"Better than one could hope," Faron said, accepting her change of subject without protest. He leaned back a little to better show off his outfit. "The coat in particular is very nice. I'm impressed, the quality is much improved over these past decades. And it's worlds better than the fur coats they used to wear. Do you remember them?"

"I do," she said, and softly smiled. "The eastern kingdoms were atrocious, everyone covered in fur and fuzz and coats so heavy they looked like fat little animals. Thank the stars they've gotten better at spinning wool fibers. Now everyone wants to look sleek and long."

"Then I must enjoy it while I can!" Faron said, well aware that human fashion would forever ebb and flow, with the occasional dips into truly wild tributaries. His grin settled into a soft smile. Her nervousness worried him, and he had a suspicion he knew the cause.

"So how is Eder?" he asked.

Calluna flinched as if struck.

"Good, he's good," she said, refusing to meet his eye. "Keeping himself busy studying the skies."

Faron crossed his arms. "What did I say about your lying?"

Her gaze snapped in his direction. Her features hardened, her true strength washing away her shy demeanor.

"Then you know. Who told you? Was it Sariel?"

"It was."

"I should have known. Don't trust him, Faron. Don't ever trust him. He...he's bitter, he's angry, and he's ashamed of his own mistakes. Whatever he's told you, it was to win you over to his side."

"His side," Faron said softly. "Side of what, little sister?" She glared but did not answer. "Then you know. You know that what he's done cannot be forgiven. That neither his religion nor his kingdom can be allowed to stand."

All around Faron, in pools of water great and small, appeared a dozen matching visages of Calluna glaring at him. The water rippled, but not from the faint wind.

"Stay away, Faron," she said. "Stay west. Don't come to Racliffe. Don't come to the Tower Majestic."

"Why not?" Faron asked. "What is it you fear I will find?"

Her rage bled into sorrow. Calluna was ever driven by emotions, and they overwhelmed her completely. Tears trickled from her star-filled eyes even as her voice remained as hard as stone.

"We've spilled enough of each other's blood. Let Eder have his kingdom. It's what he deserves, after what Sariel did to him."

Faron crossed his arms. "We made our vows."

"Vows Eder never shared."

"Enough, Calluna! No crowns. No thrones. That is our law. Even if I were to forgive him for anointing himself a king, I have met one of his preachers. He has given radiance to humanity. I know you've seen it. I know you've witnessed their disgusting, tainted version of our gifts. For you to allow Eder to commit such a crime, to see it spread, and then *defend* him—"

"Stop!"

The scream burst from every puddle. Water sprayed with it. Faron endured the outburst. When the ripples stilled, only the largest puddle contained Calluna's visage. She stood, her hands clenched into fists at her sides. Mud caked the lower edge of her dress. The moon shone brightly above her, outlining her body in white.

"There's no saving you," she said, her voice colder than ice. "There's no saving *any* of you."

And then she was gone.

Chapter 8

FARON

Red smoke filled the air from the telltale burning of bloodthorn vines. Faron approached the crimson cloud, the road leading him northward toward a bark-harvesting camp. He eyed the cloud warily. That was a lot to burn at once. War was coming, and when there was war, there was a need for iron-beech bark, which, when boiled, could cure many mild ailments and dull the senses of those in pain.

"Stay close," he told Iris. The smoke was not deadly, but it could be deeply unpleasant to the eyes and throat. So far the cloud drifted lazily to the west, but if the wind changed, he wanted to be ready to aid the coyote immediately.

The cloud had thinned by the time he reached the camp. More than two hundred workers hurried about, thick gray cloths tied over the lower halves of their faces as feeble protection against the smoke. Iron-beech bark was highly prized, but to obtain it meant stripping away the bloodthorn vines that spiraled about the trees. The vines' thorns were sharp, and an errant touch could cause a man's skin to swell and turn purple. To stay safe, bark-strippers hacked those vines off with machetes, gathered them in piles, and then burned them, filling the sky with distinct crimson clouds.

A dozen Argylle soldiers camped near the road, lazily chatting while two remained on guard at the turnoff toward the camp and the iron-beech forest beyond. Their faces were also covered, except with blue cloth instead of gray.

"Move along, stranger," one of the soldiers said. He wore a blue-and-green tabard, the family crest of Casthe, if Faron remembered right. They'd ruled Argylle a good fifty years before Faron claimed himself upon a pyre. "If you're nervous about the cloud, don't be. The winds are steady and will carry it west."

"Not nervous, only curious," Faron said, giving them his friendliest smile. The man looked none too pleased by his arrival. His hand was twitchy, but then again, all the soldiers were on edge. The talk of war. It had to be.

"There's no bark here for sale," the soldier said. "You want some, you buy it through the guild like everybody else."

"I'm just wanting directions," Faron said, and he gestured farther up the road. "It has been some time since I traveled here. That way leads to Arbert's Crossing, yeah?"

The soldier gave him a curious look.

"No one's called it that for ages. You got yourself an old map, stranger?"

"Much too old, I'd wager," Faron said, laughing as if it were no bother. "What's the dingy old town called now?"

"Arbertown." The soldier sniffled and pulled at his own cloth covering his nose and mouth. "They've a good tavern, the Split Trunk. Fair owner, too. You could do worse than to spend a night there, and learn a bit more about the lands you're traveling."

"A good suggestion," Faron said, and he bowed low. "Thank you for the name, and the advice."

•

The Split Trunk was as welcoming as the soldier had promised. Faron rented himself a room and then claimed a seat in the commons. A gigantic kettle bubbled to his right, with enough stew to feed a hundred grown men. The smell of yellow beans, onions, and sliced boar meat awakened his stomach. Iris lay at his feet, looking miserable. Even though he'd bribed the tavern keeper to let her stay with him, that didn't change the foul looks patrons sent her way, nor remove her own discomfort at being inside a place so very human.

Come evening, workers from the iron-beech forest arrived in groups, and what had been a quiet room became awash in beer and song. Faron, never one to eat in solitude when given a choice, found himself a new seat at a square table with six boisterous young men.

"You see the size of that plume this morning?" a lively red-haired man said. "Donny nearly shit his trousers when the wind shifted."

"You're too mean to Donny," said another, also red-haired but with a bushy beard to boot and heavy discoloration across half his face, a permanent mark of an unfortunate tangle with bloodthorn vines.

"Donny's an ass," the first insisted. "He ain't working the forest like us, not really. He's here 'cause his family's got connections in the bark trade. Once Donny has a year of experience they'll call him back and get him set up with a proper job, all while pretending he 'earned' it."

Faron waved at the tavern keeper, then flashed another of Calluna's coins. Drinks all around for everyone at his table, to ensure the lips kept flapping. As much as he liked the company, he had ulterior motives. But first...

"You going to be all right, Iris?" he asked. The coyote had followed him to the new table and curled up underneath his chair. She poked her head up at him and snorted. In response, he lowered his bowl of stew, his third of the night, and set it beside her.

Enjoy, he mouthed, then turned back to the men as Iris first reluctantly, then greedily, tore into the chunks of boar meat that floated near the top.

"I wish I could stay here for days, but my travels keep me on the move," Faron told them. "Know you anything of the roads to the north, or perhaps those leading east?"

"Roads are roads," the scarred man said. "Maybe some bandits will bother you, but that's everywhere."

"I don't think that's what he means," the oldest-looking of the six said. His face was completely shaved and his hair cut short, a trait a lot of the bark-strippers shared. Though Faron doubted it happened often, he had heard stories of men getting bloodthorn vines snagged on their beards or unknowingly tangled into their hair.

"Everyone's talking of war," Faron said, deciding the men were properly liquored up. "And it's not something I want to get caught in."

The men exchanged glances.

"Then you might want to turn south instead," said the oldest. "Doremy's border isn't far from here, and there's no shortage of Princess Isabelle's people coming over from Luelle to spread tales of how much better it'd be if Argylle were to become part of her kingdom."

"What do you make of them?" Faron asked. "Forgive me, but I am new to the area and know little of this Isabelle."

"She's queen of Doremy in all but name," the scarred man said, then paused to finish the rest of his drink. "Supposedly the goddess blessed her in the cradle. That's what her people say, that she's been chosen."

"Sure, chosen," the oldest muttered. "Chosen to stir up trouble."

Faron drummed his fingers on the table. He needed an army if he and Sariel were to overthrow Eder's kingdom in the east. From what he'd gathered, this Isabelle sounded like the revolutionary sort. Perhaps that could be used to their advantage...

"Chosen?" Faron asked, exaggerating his incredulousness. "By the goddess? And what has Leliel supposedly chosen her to do?"

"Here we go again," one of the other workers said, standing. "I ain't listening to this shit, not after what I went through today."

Two of his friends went with him. Faron noted the reaction. Sentiment was divided, as should be expected in a border town. The others huddled closer, lowering their voices.

"You didn't hear this from me," the scarred man said. "But Isabelle's father, King Henri, is on his deathbed, and the moment he passes, the princess is going to declare war. Everyone says she's blessed by Leliel. Has the luck of the goddess, she does, and she's led her father's kingdom to prosperity while his health's declined over the years."

"Everyone says a lot of things that sound too good to be true," Faron said. "Blessed by the goddess? Come now, surely you three don't believe it?"

They exchanged glances.

"Is it really so strange?" the oldest asked. He rubbed his hands across his bald head, a nervous tic Faron had noticed over the course of the night. "We've heard that the Church of Stars has purged all of Leliel's believers from the east. Surely the goddess would not sit by and let her faithful suffer?"

"Isabelle's done good things, real good things," the scarred man agreed. "Including banishing all of the Luminary's preachers from her borders. We could do worse than to have Argylle join Doremy."

"I know I wouldn't miss King Bentley's rule," the third man muttered.

Faron crossed his arms, his mind racing. To have won over people in a potential enemy kingdom? Isabelle had to be something special. Not that he believed the goddess had blessed her, for he doubted the existence of the goddess at all. But if this woman's charisma was so strong, and the story built around her this powerfully appealing to the poor and destitute of the west...

Well. That spoke of potential. And if Isabelle professed such a strong attachment to Leliel, then Eder's wretched church would be a natural enemy.

"Let's say I wanted to know more of Isabelle," he said. "Where would I go?"

"The recruiters are always telling us to go to Luelle," said the scarred man.

"And where is that?"

The man gave the directions: follow a road many miles to the north before turning at a cross section and then traveling southeast. Faron mapped it in his head, then compared it to the geography he'd seen on the walk there.

"Why not just travel straight east?" he asked, confused. "There may not be a road, but I can hike the hills easy enough with just Iris and me, and save myself a full two days' travel."

"Nobody goes that way," the scarred man said. "Those are the faerie hills. If you value your life, you'll stick to the roads."

"I see," Faron said, hiding his curiosity. The faeries had moved this far west? He stood, careful not to move his chair until Iris was able to scoot out from underneath it. "Well, I should retire to my room. It was a pleasure to—"

He froze. There, by the door, a familiar young man stood nervously scanning the commons. Faron set his jaw and waved goodbye, not bothering to finish his sentence. He crossed the room, careful to keep his expression perfectly neutral. The young man, however, beamed with delight.

"Faron!"

"What are you doing here, Bartholomew?" he asked.

"Bart," he replied. "Bart's fine, and I'm here to find you."

Faron put his hand on the young man's shoulder as if the two were good friends and then guided him to the door. A snap of his fingers, and Iris followed, careful to keep at his heels. She'd learned quickly that the closer she kept to Faron inside human towns, the less likely anyone would accost her.

Once outside, Faron led Bart around the corner, away from the entrance, so they could talk in private. The day was late, the stars starting to peek out from behind the blue-black curtain. He tried to keep his frustration in check. This conversation, he knew exactly where it was headed.

"You're far from home," he said once they were alone. "Why?"

Bart crossed his arms, suddenly nervous. He must have anticipated a much different reaction to his arrival.

"I came after you because...because you did something to my pa, didn't you?"

Faron debated lying. He was good at it, when necessary, even if he disliked the habit.

"I did a good deed," he said, deciding Bart's mind was already made up and arguing would accomplish nothing. Better to appeal to his sense of honor. "And I would appreciate it if you told no one and let me continue with my life."

Bart nodded, his mouth twitching and twisting between worry and a youthful grin.

"Of course," he said. "Right. I will. But I thought...I just thought I should find you and thank you. It didn't seem right, you stealing off like a thief. Like you did something wrong."

Faron clasped the young man's shoulder and squeezed.

"I appreciate it," he said. He turned for the tavern entrance. "Now return home, before your family worries for you."

"Actually...I'm not going back home."

Faron froze.

Don't get involved. Leave it be, Faron. Leave it be.

Except he had to know, and of course he would get involved if he must. Bart was young and idealistic, which meant he was also capable of being very, very stupid.

"Why is that?" he asked, turning back around.

Bart stood up taller and puffed out his chest.

"I'm going to join Princess Isabelle's army."

Yup. Very, very stupid.

"War may be coming, but that doesn't mean you should seek it out," he said. "It's a hard business, and even those who survive in the flesh often die in the heart and mind."

Bart's confusion was plainly evident.

"I don't...I thought you'd support me. I thought you were already with her."

He arched an eyebrow. "Why would you think that?"

Bart's face flushed. "What you did to Pa, that was a miracle from Leliel. And they say Princess Isabelle performs miracles, too."

Faron fought down a groan. A connection he'd not anticipated, but one that made sense in hindsight. The people did not know of radiance. They knew only the goddess, and lately, the blasphemous Church of Stars.

"Listen to me, and listen well," he said, putting his hands on Bart's shoulders. He let a bit of radiance shine in his eyes, just a hint of starlight within the silver. "Return home. Return to your family. When war comes, lie low, and avoid recruiters. Live your lives. You need not be swept up into the bloody river that is soon to flood Kaus. Whatever riches and glory you think you'd earn, know that instead you would suffer marches, exhaustion, hunger, lice, chills, untended fevers, and the rot of flesh. Do you understand me, Bart?"

The young man's posture slumped. Though he tried to hide it, his lips quivered from barely held back tears.

"Will you avoid this war, too?" he asked. "Will you also go into hiding?"

Faron hugged the young man, and he again decided the truth would fare better than a lie.

"I shall do what I must, as I always have throughout my life. Farewell, Bartholomew."

He left him there and returned inside to the tavern keeper.

"I must sadly travel on," Faron told him. "Do not fret. The stars will keep me good company."

The tavern keeper reached underneath a counter for where he stored the paid coin, but Faron waved him off.

"Keep it," he said. "It was worth it for the meal alone."

When Faron exited, he saw no sign of Bart. He sighed with relief. Hopefully that meant the young man was headed home. War was coming, and thousands of lives would be lost. Faron held no illusions as to that. But the young man's family were poor folk on the edges of the world, forgotten and ignored by lords, kings, and queens. They need not bleed for those who barely knew they existed.

At least, that's what Faron told himself to ease the guilt growing in his breast.

War. Yet again, he would engulf Kaus in war.

Faron trudged east, following the road through Arbertown. At its end, he spotted a squat little structure, newly built compared to the surrounding homes. The light of dozens of candles shone through its windows. A middle-aged man with graying hair stood before its open door. Yellow and black stripes crossed his shirt, and he held a familiar staff, a jar of insects swinging from its top. The fireflies within lit up as brightly as the candles.

"Pleasant nights, stranger," the shepherd called out to Faron. "Would you be willing to sit for a while and listen to the wisdom of our Father? Perhaps there are burdens within you to cast aside, or wounds that my prayers may relieve you of?"

Faron's returned grin was all teeth.

"Not tonight," he said. He continued onward, past the end of the road to the rolling green beyond. The shepherd realized his destination and called out.

"Wait, stranger, that way lie the faerie hills. It isn't safe."

"Nowhere ever is," Faron called back, and continued onward, Iris bounding at his side.

Chapter 9

FARON

Iris whined, refusing to cross the rapid little stream. She would not even let her paws touch the water. Despite the late hour, the hills were clearly visible all around them. The grass seemed to shimmer with their own innate light.

"It will be safe, I promise," Faron said from the other side. It was no deeper than his heel and no wider than the length of his arm, but Iris was not afraid of the crossing itself. She feared what she sensed on the other side. He sensed it, too.

The stream marked the fairies' territory, as did the line of stubby blackwall mushrooms that grew on the eastern, and only the eastern, side.

Iris lowered her head, raised it, and then scooted toward the water before immediately retreating. Her paws wore a circle in the soft soil as she spun in place in her frustration. Faron crossed his arms, debating if he should carry her across, but then quickly dismissed the idea. He would not demean the coyote in such a manner.

"Do you trust me, Iris?" he asked.

The coyote paused to meet his gaze. He sensed her answer. Not yet a "yes," not quite a "no." Faron drew his sword and scraped away the mushrooms that formed a perimeter along the water, then knelt with his knees in the center of the stream and extended his arms to her.

"I have met their kind before," he said. "They will not harm you. At worst, they will pet your fur a bit too aggressively...and maybe see if you will play a game of fetch."

Her nose wrinkled. The lone thought was so strong he practically heard it in his mind.

Fetch?

"A game of retrieval," he said, and laughed. "Do not worry. I will not expect you to chase sticks for their amusement, nor mine."

Iris lowered her nose to the water, sniffed it a few more times, and then batted it with a paw. When she suffered no ill effects, she retreated a few paces, turned about, and then sprinted across the stream as if her heels were on fire. Faron winced as she splashed his face and chest with her passage.

"Fair enough," he said, and stood. He took in a long breath and then let it out slowly. If only he felt as confident as he sounded when speaking to Iris. True, he did not anticipate the fey would harm the coyote, for their love of nature was unmatched. But as for their ire? Well. It was not reserved for humanity alone.

Iris kept close when they resumed their walk following a naturally formed path where the hills touched. At least, it seemed natural, though Faron had his doubts. The grass was smooth and low, and rows of yellow and purple roses formed faint lines to either side of them.

As a test, Faron brushed one with his foot. The purple rose's petals burst like shattered glass, violet light wafting like smoke into the night sky. An unnatural rose, one of their own creation. Beautiful, he had to admit. He wondered what a full field of them might look like, and how lovely the eruption would be if Iris took a wild sprint through their center.

The hours passed, quiet and entrancing in their beauty. The hills broadened, the gaps between them growing, until they walked through the heart of a valley overwhelmed with flowers. It seemed Faron need not have to wonder. A rainbow of color exploded with their every movement. The air sparkled with light, shimmering, ephemeral, and shifting like smoke. The coyote's nerves eased over time, and twice he caught her playing with the flowers, purposefully nudging them with her nose or tail to make them dissolve.

They reached the first of the bushes near the center of the valley, black thorned and taller than Faron. They were clearly trimmed, and though they grew in a continuous line, it waved and curled like a serpent's tail. Little red fruits grew amid their blue leaves, the size of raspberries but perfectly spherical and swollen like cherries. Feyberries, to those who knew of them. Poisonous, even to Faron, but not lethal. Should one be willing to endure the stomachache and chills come morning, the berries promised wondrous dreams so vivid they felt like they lasted days.

Faron followed the bushes until finding a sudden gap. Within were more walls of bushes, curling and looping together to form a maze. Iris looked at it, looked at him, and then whined.

"I promise, the only way out of the valley is through that maze," Faron said. "Should we try to go around, we will find this maze waiting for us after every hill we crest. It's either turn back or go through, and so we go through."

Faron entered the maze, and he trusted Iris to follow. She did, but only after one last longing look behind them. He patted her head, and she did not recoil from his touch.

The entrance was sealed off, blue leaves and black thorns forming a wall.

Faron did not try to map the maze in his head, nor give any serious thought to its twists and turns. There was no solving a fey maze. Either they chose to let you out or you remained lost within it. Not forever, not unless you had committed a serious crime against the faeries. Just until you realized you were completely at their mercy...or they got bored.

Faron held no desire to wait that long. He walked until he found the heart of the maze, marked by a circle of gray mushrooms around a small patch of grass. He placed his sword and sheath just outside the ring and settled into its center on his knees. Iris sniffed at the mushrooms, then sneezed.

"Stay free of it," he ordered her. "This risk is my own."

She seemed all too happy to agree. The coyote plopped down, crossed her front paws, and then put her head upon them to watch. Faron pretended not to notice the nervousness in her eyes. He had to remain calm for what was to come. He bowed his head and rested his hands on his knees. A bit of exhaustion tugged at his eyelids, but he had many, many lifetimes of learning how to push through tired limbs and a need for sleep.

"A stranger, I come into your lands," Faron whispered, trusting the faeries to hear him. "A friend, I would leave them. Are you near, masters of bush and vine, flower and thorn?"

Iris whimpered. The grass rustled on a nonexistent wind. The light of the moon shone brilliant.

Faron opened his eyes, and he did not hide the radiance within them.

"There you are."

A dozen of the little creatures hovered in the air around him, unseen to any eye lacking the eternal blessing. Their wings buzzed like those of dragonflies, their faces insectoid, their eyes slanted and colored a solid red. Their bodies were long and lean, covered with chitin that shimmered all colors of the rainbow depending on the angle at which the moonlight struck them. Their feet dangled beneath them, dainty and three-toed. Little antennae poked out above their eyes, blue-white light glinting off the edges, as if they ended at tiny stars.

"You see us?" one of them asked. She pointed, her three fingers black and clawed. "How?"

"His eyes," another said, hovering closer. He scrunched his face unhappily. "Radiance. You are one of the cyclical, the eternal, the ever-living."

"I am," Faron said. "And though it has been many years since I met your kind, I am ever grateful to be in the presence of your beautiful valleys and flower-crowned hills."

"Flattering words," a third said. She was larger than the others, and her colors did not change with her flight. Instead she remained a regal purple from head to toe, all but her eyes, which blazed a red deeper than blood. "We listened to such words before, and it cost us dearly."

Iris barked and sat up, looking supremely confused. Two faeries hovered to either side of her, and though she looked, she could not find the source of the buzzing in her ears. Even their scent would be disguised, if they so wished it, for they were masters of deception. They possessed the power of radiance, but the manner in which they manifested it was unique, just as the abilities wielded by Faron and his siblings were unique to them, as the powers of prophecy were to the dragons and the manipulation of stone was to the elusive qiyan.

"But were those words from my mouth, or were they from the short-lived humans?" Faron asked, focusing his attention on the purple faerie. It marked her as the eldest, and the valley's grove-mother. The others would listen to her and honor her decisions.

The grove-mother hovered closer, her arms crossing over her chest.

"From the one named Mitra Gracegiver."

Faron failed to hide his disgust. Mitra, the alias taken by Eder during Faron's sleep.

"Mitra is my brother, whom I seek to punish for his transgressions," he said. "What crime did he commit upon you?"

The faeries began shouting in a sudden flurry.

"Banished us!"

"Tricked us!"

"Lied, and schemed, and killed us!"

The grove-mother lifted her arms, silencing them.

"He came to us and called us friend," she said. "But his words were poison, and his fingers scorpion stingers. His church declared us wretched. His soldiers came with fire, and sword, and heavy nets."

She lowered her head, and her voice became a whisper.

"They captured my friends. My family. Captured them and put them in jars."

Faron's stomach twisted at the thought. The sight of insects within Preacher Russell's jar had been vile enough. To place the mischievous but kindhearted fey within? To subject them to such torture, all to gift radiance to Eder's loyal followers?

Unforgivable.

"Do not trust him," the other faeries began arguing.

"He is like his brother."

"He will bring the nets again."

Faron denied the rage that boiled the blood in his veins. These faeries would not understand. They would think his fury directed toward them and not Eder. For these faeries to fear nets and jars...no wonder the people in Arbertown were so reluctant to approach the faerie valley. For centuries past, it had been a rite of passage to cross the mushroom-guarded rivers to steal a flower for a loved one, with the strength of your love supposedly deciding how long the flower lasted before dissolving into colored smoke. There had long been trade for feyberries across Kaus, too, but he suspected that, too, had come to an end.

Damn Mitra, for such cruelty.

"What is your name, grove-mother?" he asked when their cries subdued. The purple-chitin faerie hovered before him, deciding.

"Mae'lilia," she said. "Eldest of this village. Eighty years I have lived, yet never have I felt such hatred toward us before."

"The humans are turning worse," shouted a faerie.

"Much worse than the coyotes and dogs," a second added, this one sitting atop Iris's head; the coyote was very calmly allowing it to happen despite not understanding what was going on.

"Mae'lilia, I am Faron of the ever-living," he said. "I seek permission to pass through your maze, exit your valley, and continue my hunt to punish he who committed such terrible crimes against you."

The grove-mother stared at him in thought. The towering walls of thorn and leaf shook in a sudden wind.

"You wish to stop him," she said, her voice taking on a new tone. It was distant, faded, as if she were lost within a dream. Her eyes closed. Silver light sparked off her antennae. The fey's radiance granted them mastery over nature to make even Calluna jealous. It also allowed them to see a world known only to them, one in which time was frighteningly malleable.

"I do," he answered.

"And you will try. Oh, you will try, Faron, but there is no victory awaiting you. I see the sky breaking. The dragons speak true. Kaus will be consumed in a fire that does not burn. End, true end, comes for us all."

She opened her eyes. White crystals crinkled at the corners of them, the faerie equivalent of tears.

"You die, Faron. I cannot explain why, but my heart aches so terribly to witness it."

Faron rose from the circle of mushrooms. Mae'lilia fluttered her wings to keep equal height to his gaze.

"I have died before," Faron said, unafraid of her prophecy. "I will die again. Do not weep for me, grove-mother."

Iris barked. All the faeries had made themselves visible to her, and she stared at them wild-eyed. Dozens more appeared to join those in the heart of the maze, the little beings buzzing out from the bushes. The sky filled with red eyes glowing to match the stars in number.

"No," Mae'lilia said, her wings fluttering, lifting her higher. She spread her arms and looked to the east. "The dawn comes, and so I pass my judgment. You will stay, Faron of the cyclical. You will stay, sleeping away the day, and wandering the maze at night." She shook her head. "We suffered enough at Mitra's hand. You need not suffer, too."

The ring of mushrooms at Faron's feet erupted. Black dust rose like smoke, and when he breathed it in, the effects were immediate. The world grew hazy and his mind dulled. The faeries retreated into the blue leaves. He opened his mouth to protest, but his tongue felt clumsy and fat. His balance worsened, and he collapsed onto his side. His eyelids drooped.

The last thing he remembered before sleep taking him was Iris, gently licking his fingers.

•

A voice called his name. Movement. Rustling. Shaking. Someone was shaking him. Faron groaned, his eyes still squeezed shut. Why...why would someone wake him? Couldn't they tell he was tired? Sleep. He needed to sleep.

And then something sharp sliced across his arm. Its sting focused his mind. With great effort, he forced his eyes open, and he was not prepared for the face staring down at him.

"Bart?" he asked, bewildered.

"Oh, thank Leliel, you're awake," the young man said. He grinned, wide and playful, to hide the fear still clearly visible in his green eyes.

Faron groaned as he sat up, and he winced at the daylight. It felt extremely bright, though perhaps that was only due to the intense ache in his forehead. He glanced at his arm and saw a fresh line of blood dripping from where he'd been cut. Bart noticed it, too, and hurried to explain.

"I tried shaking and slapping you, but even that wasn't enough." He offered Faron his borrowed sword. "So I...I got desperate."

Faron took his sword, glad to feel its steel in his grip. The weapon was comforting, and he focused on it as he closed his eyes and summoned the innate radiance within him. Its cooling presence flowed through his limbs. The cut ceased its bleeding, and the ache in his mind eased. When he reopened his eyes, it was not so bright, either.

"What are you doing here?" he asked, now that he felt more himself.

"I barely know where 'here' is," Bart said, and he gestured to the maze of bushes. In the light of day, they seemed much less intimidating, the black of their bark and thorns now a dull brown, and their leaves a pallid green. "But I saw you enter, and when I circled around to the other side, you didn't come out. After a while, I decided to go in after you, and I'm glad I did."

Faron retrieved his sword belt and sheath, glad the faeries had left them when he passed out. While he buckled it, another thought came to him.

"Iris?" he said. "Where is Iris?"

Bart shrugged. "She wasn't here when I found you."

Faron frowned. Hopefully that meant the faeries chose to let her go, and not that they'd kept her as their plaything. Rubbing his eyes to push away the last of the sleep, he brought his attention to his unexpected savior.

"You still haven't answered my question," he said. "Why did you follow me in the first place? I thought you were returning home."

Bart blushed slightly and looked away.

"I was, I mean, I did plan to go, but just a few minutes on the road and...I couldn't, Faron. I couldn't. I want to fight. I want to help people, like you help people, so when the shepherd told me you walked east into the faerie hills, I went after you." He gestured to the now barren circle on the ground. "And I think you should be *thanking* me, not interrogating me."

Faron drew his sword. Bart flinched.

"Breathe easy," Faron said, lifting the sword and turning his attention east. The sun was high, and the faeries sleeping until the night resumed. If he and Bart were to escape the maze, now would be the time. But before he did...

"Bart, I want you to make me a promise," he said. He closed his eyes as he spoke. "You will witness wonders you cannot explain. You will see me accomplish feats by no rights any man or woman should perform. All I ask is that you speak of it to no one, not even myself. If you accept that, I will allow you to travel at my side."

Faron opened his eyes, and they shone with radiance so that he would know if the young man spoke truth or lie.

Bart took a frightened step backward, but he did not cower, and he did not lie.

"You have my word."

Faron nodded. Acceptable. That done, he turned his attention to the hedge wall. He had wandered this maze as a sign of respect to the faeries, but they had acted against him, and he would show them such courtesy no longer. He visualized the thick brush, the thorns, the fruit, and the leaves, saw them all in his mind's eye, and then demanded they part.

Silver light gleamed across his blade as he swung it in an overhead arc. Its edge cut through every branch, every leaf, and every vine. The wall parted, revealing the gently curving hills beyond. They were beautiful in the sunlight, the flowers swaying in a spring wind.

"Come," Faron said, sheathing his sword. "We must be free of these hills before nightfall."

The flowers did not burst with light at his passage, only shifted and swayed with a faint puff of pollen. Faron led the way, Bart keeping close. Just before crossing the first hill, he glanced behind and saw the opening he'd cut in the maze sealing over, the branches growing at a rapid, unnatural pace.

A loud bark stole his attention. He turned about and then beamed with relief.

"Iris!" he shouted as the coyote sprinted across the grass. He knelt and opened his arms to her. She did not slow in the slightest, instead barreling straight into him with enough force to knock him onto his rear. She rubbed her nose and face against his chin, soft little barks escaping her mouth in her excitement.

"All right, all right," Faron said, finally pushing her away. "It's good to see you, too, little coyote." She barked at him. "Sorry. Iris."

Another bark, quick and happy. Faron laughed.

"Let's go, Bart," he said as the coyote dashed back to the east. "Today, we race the sun."

Chapter 10

CALLUNA

At a little circular table, in the center of the moss-coated Kaleed Swamp, sat Calluna. There were four chairs. Calluna sat in the northernmost, her shoulders hunched and her head hanging low.

"I should talk to them, shouldn't I?" she asked the three occupying the other chairs.

One was a collection of twigs she'd tied with vines into the shape of a man, using dead ladybugs for eyes. Frederick. The second was puffy and huge, made of burlap sacks sewn together and stuffed with feathers, among other things, to make it huggable. That was Vance. The third was a frog who crouched unnaturally still in her chair. Susannah, the newest of her companions.

Susannah croaked once. Calluna frowned at her.

"But I don't *want* to talk to them," she grumbled. "They're stubborn and foolish; the men always are." She slumped farther. "I wish I could find Aylah. She would know how to stop this."

Her eyebrow twitched, and she glared at Vance. Eyeholes were cut into the face of the top sack, and she glared into them.

"Fine," she said. "If you think it's so important, I will."

She pushed from the table, clattering the tin teacups and plates. All empty. She rarely ate. Her companions, even less.

Calluna hiked up her dress as she walked, her bare, callused feet sinking into the swamp water so it might lap at the edges of her dress. She feared no bite or sting, for the little creatures knew their place. She walked until there was a break in the weeping oaks and their silvery blue leaves, which hung low and wide like spread hands. Dragonflies buzzed about. She dismissed them with a thought. So, too, did the mosquitoes and flies depart, chased away by a faint flash of silver that rolled from her hands. The water must be still.

"Sariel?" she whispered, closing her eyes. The stars above shone down upon her, and they were a comfort. Though she could not explain how or why, she felt their rays upon her skin, and it was cool and soothing. Another pulse of silver, and the distant bullfrogs quieted their croaking. Unnatural silence overcame the swamp. She felt herself falling, falling, the world swimming around her as her brother's face heightened in clarity within her mind.

She opened her eyes.

Sariel stared back at her from the dark water, a faint smile tugging at the corners of his mouth. Always a serious one, Sariel, but he held a soft spot in his heart for her. Knowing that always made her feel warm inside.

"I fear I know why you've sought me out," he said. The water rippled across his mouth, and it was from those ripples that his voice emerged.

"You found Faron before me," she said.

Sariel sighed. "What would you have told him if you found him first? To avoid me, and stay hidden and ignorant in the west?"

Calluna scrunched her nose.

"Anything would have been better than what you did. He's mad. You made him mad. Have we not had enough fighting between us? Must you force Kaus into another war?"

Sariel arced an eyebrow. "You cast blame at the wrong feet, Calluna. Eder put himself upon a throne, not I."

She hated how her brothers exuded such confidence. They never doubted themselves when they should. Sariel, though, was the worst.

"Fine," she said, throwing up her hands. "So what are you two planning? Will you come east and murder your brother?"

"Yes."

So simply. So casually. Calluna struck the water with her hand, banishing the image. She hated how angry it made her feel. How helpless. If only she had been the one to greet Faron, maybe then she could have set him on a different course.

She sniffled at the ripples.

"I miss you, Aylah," she whispered.

Every year for the past three decades, she had searched for her sister. With Faron, she would see the cave he'd burned within. For Eder, she'd see his home in the Tower Majestic. Sariel greeted her but hid his locations often, plotting as he traveled. But Aylah? Darkness. Only darkness. As for their last sibling, Eist, well...Eist had gone underground, and specifically asked beforehand that Calluna not seek them out. It was a promise she kept, as much as she hated it during the long, lonely years.

When the water calmed, Calluna closed her eyes once more. So be it. If this was their course, then she would ensure all was equal among them.

"Eder," she called out. Moments later, his pale face appeared. His smile was gentle, and his face partially hidden by waves of black hair cascading past his ears to frame the soft curve of his chin.

"Hello, Calluna," he said. "If only you would visit me in my tower. I would love to greet you properly and show you the wonders I have built."

The same invitation, year after year. She always refused. The Tower Majestic, and the nearby Racliffe, were both full of people. Too many people. Too many voices, and loud thoughts. Besides, she had spent more than enough years in the past scouring the tower and learning its mysteries.

Nervousness made her tremble, and so she blurted the truth out before she lost her nerve.

"Faron is awake."

Eder crossed his arms. His smile hardened.

"Later than I expected, if I were honest. Have you spoken with him?"

She nodded. "I have...as has Sariel."

No smile at all, just a tired sigh.

"I have not spoken with him since we last parted all those decades ago. I knew he would disapprove, but I also prayed he would not interfere. Did that change, Calluna? Has he merely been waiting for Faron to join him?"

It felt like Calluna need not speak a word. Eder saw things too clearly, and the siblings were all intimately familiar with one another's beliefs and motivations. But best to make sure. Say the painful truth out loud.

"They're coming to kill you."

Eder closed his eyes, and then when he reopened them, radiance shone brilliant within his irises.

"Let them try."

His face faded from the water. Calluna kicked it with her heel, but there was no heart to her protest. All she felt was loneliness deep within her chest. Stupid. She had been so stupid, hoping as she always did that once Faron was awake they could be a family again. But they hadn't been a family for centuries. Not since the shattering of the Anaon Kingdom.

But still, still, couldn't she hope? If only for a moment?

Calluna trudged back to her little table. Her three companions remained in their chairs. Her lower lip trembled, and she feared she would cry. Stars above, she was so lonely. How long had she lived in this swamp? Two decades? Three? Perhaps it was better to do as Faron did and let fire erase the passage of years.

A wave of her hand, and a dragonfly zigzagged through the air to hover above Susannah. A snap of her fingers, and the frog latched on to it with her tongue. Well. At least she could make her companions happy, if not her true family.

Calluna ignored her own chair and instead settled onto Vance's lap. All those feathers padded out the burlap sacks, making him so soft, so welcoming. She wrapped her arms around his waist and pressed her face against his chest. The burlap wrinkled.

"Maybe it's time," she whispered to the reawakened night. The insects returned, the bullfrogs croaked, and in the highest portions of the weeping oaks, gray bitterns and black-winged stilts called for mates. "Maybe I should go to them, be with them, and talk, really talk, really see..."

The idea of leaving her swamp terrified her, but stubbornness rose to match. Had it really been so long that she would fear the outer world? No. That settled it. She must travel the lands again, as she had for centuries prior.

She pulled back from Vance and smiled up at his burlap-sack face. He stared back through the holes, his blue eyes wide and bloodshot. Tears rolled down from them. They could not close. She had sliced off Vance's eyelids before sewing the burlap about him and filling it with feathers.

"What do you think?" she asked, and kissed his mouth. The bags and feathers crinkled inward, and she felt the curve of lips and hardness of teeth underneath. She held the kiss, painfully reminded of how long it had been since she last lay with another man or woman. Not since retiring to the swamp.

Her hand brushed Vance's crotch. Stupid of her. She'd sliced that part off, too, when she caught him trespassing.

"You're right," she said, hearing his answer. He need not speak, for his thoughts were open to her. Not that he *could* speak. Not after she'd finished her sewing. She stood and pushed him from his chair. He collapsed on his back, slowly sinking. Calluna watched the mud swallow him whole, its murky surface bubbling from his panicked exhalations.

A snap of her fingers, and Susannah fled into the swamp while Frederick burst into flame. Calluna watched the twigs burn, and strangely, she thought of Faron upon his pyre.

Decision made, excitement replaced her nervousness. The world was shifting back into motion. Her brothers would plot, plan, and scheme, but at least their paths were connected. There was still a chance things could be made right.

The bubbles stopped. The surface turned still.

A smile lit Calluna's face.

"We're leaving, Vance. We're leaving this swamp and returning to the world once more."

Part Two

BASTARD

Chapter 11

FARON

Faron and Bart arrived in Luelle by midday, having crossed the border from Argylle and into Doremy at some point among the faerie hills. Neither carried many supplies, but Calluna's coin quickly solved that.

"I cannot accept this," Bart had argued as the pair outfitted themselves with proper traveling packs, water canteens, and dried rations. Faron laughed off his concerns.

"You're with me now," he said. "Which means I'm responsible for you, through thick and thin."

The copious amount of coin had also been Faron's way of loosening the lips of the woman running the general store. She'd been wary when first meeting them, but after he'd plunked down a few heavy coins on her countertop, her dark eyes had sparkled.

"A bit extra, for you," he'd said. "If you could tell me where one goes if they are no friend of the Casthes."

Her directions took them down the busy main road, past rows upon rows of squat buildings carved from a nearby juniper forest. The iron-beech trade had done the town well, and it seemed Luelle was a common resting place for merchants come to buy wagons full of the bark. Rooms were plentiful, and Faron had a variety to choose from when outfitting for travel, a welcome fact given Bart's lack of…well, everything.

"Do you think they'll accept us?" Bart asked, tugging at the collar of his new coat. It was fine deer leather colored a deep brown and held shut with two bronze buckles. The young man was clearly unaccustomed to such finery. His boots were new as well, his old sheep-leather pair destined to break apart on him after only a few days of marching.

"They will," Faron said, unconcerned. No recruiter for an army would look at Faron's size and turn him down, and that was without any influence from radiance to sway his opinion.

Their destination was one of the town's two taverns, smaller and located near the northern end of the road, where the green grass and rolling hills resumed. The sign nailed above the door bore no name, just a crude drawing of a snarling dog.

"I think that means you'll be welcome," Faron said, grinning at Iris.

Her ears lowered, and she glared in a way only canines could.

With the day still young, the inside was quiet and empty. A barefoot girl hurried about, straightening chairs and sweeping with an ease that suggested a lifetime of practice. A middle-aged man sat by the dormant hearth, two pillows beneath him. His eyes were closed, but they opened at the sound of the door.

"Rooms are a half-copper per night," he said. "The bed's big, if you two are willing to share a room. There's enough space on the floor, too, if you'd rather it that way." His eyes narrowed as he noticed Iris keeping to Faron's side. "That's one big dog, stranger. Mayhap I should charge you for her, too."

"Coyote," Faron said, and flashed his most disarming grin. "And I was told those who prefer Doremy rule over Argylle would be welcome here. Is that true?"

The man rose from his pillows, sized Faron up and down, and then nodded. His eyes lingered on Faron's sheathed sword.

"Aye," he said. "Follow me. I suspect Tristan will want words with any man big as you who carries their own blade."

•

A small juniper forest grew along Luelle's southern edge, and within it was a camp of one hundred or so men and women. Sir Tristan was the one in charge, a grizzled-looking man with a split beard and eyes like icicles. Unlike most, he wore a fine chainmail shirt, and the sword he carried was worth more than what most in Luelle would earn in a year.

"Well, well, some new recruits," Tristan said, pacing before them. They stood inside his large tent, which was open on one side and surprisingly spacious. "But I fear your timing could not be worse."

Faron suspected something was amiss, though he knew not what. The entire camp buzzed with excitement. That so many were already dressed in padded armor, or the rare suit of chain, was another curiosity. Were they planning to march? If so, where?

"If you're in need of able bodies, I am here to help," Faron said.

Tristan pointed at Faron's sword. "You know how to use that thing?"

"I'm no stranger to battle, if that is your question."

Tristan crossed his arms and grunted.

"A mercenary, then. We do pay, but likely nothing close to what you're wanting. Princess Isabelle is not so wealthy as the eastern rulers." He frowned at Bart. "And what of you? Any training?"

Faron was quick to answer for him.

"He is my pupil," he said. He allowed a bit of radiance to leak into his words. "Consider him a squire, if the people of Doremy are familiar with the concept. He will be no bother to anyone at my side, and a valuable asset to a marching line."

Tristan's hard gaze softened.

"All right, if you're willing to obey orders, then I can use you, because right now I can't be picky. Ludwig will take care of you, get your names down, terms agreed, and some basic gear. Do it quickly. We have guests coming."

With that, they were shuffled out to a clearing of packed earth in the middle of a triangle of trees. Ludwig was an older man, his muttonchops grayer than the dark hair atop his head. Crates were packed up behind him, and Faron caught sight of short swords, round wooden shields, and rudimentary armor within.

"Tristan must be mad to take on newcomers today," Ludwig said, removing a cloth covering from a small chest and opening it up. He withdrew a few pieces of parchment, each cut no bigger than Faron's hand, as well as a capped inkwell and a feather quill.

"What's so special about today?" Bart asked.

Ludwig grinned yellow teeth. "Far be it from me to spoil the surprise. Give me your names."

Faron and Bart answered, and then nodded and agreed to every question that followed. This was far from Faron's first time joining an army or mercenary band. Pay rates were established, along with what would and would not be covered during their time serving in Doremy's army. Past an initial stipend, coin would be paid at the end of the year, provided they lived that long. When asked where to give that payment if they died, Bart told them of his family in Clovelly, whereas Faron just shrugged.

"If I'm dead, give it to Iris," he said.

Ludwig glanced at the coyote.

"I must admit, she's well behaved," he said. "Not the weirdest request I've heard, either. I'll add it."

When that was done, Ludwig opened the crates after sizing them up. He gave both some padded leather armor, having to scrounge a bit to find some he thought might fit Faron.

"Have you any experience with a sword?" he asked Bart.

"No," he admitted, his cheeks blushing a bit from embarrassment.

"Eh, you'll learn." Ludwig handed him a sword belt and sheathed short sword. "Have your friend teach you how to buckle it. Speaking of..." He turned to Faron. "That blade of yours looks nicer than anything I could offer."

"Perhaps," Faron said. "But I could use a sturdy shield."

"That I can do."

The shield was circular, strips of birch connected with linen and bone glue. Far smaller than Faron preferred, but it would do for now. Once outfitted, they were given prepared kits containing a bedroll, a tent, and some basic provisions, and then told where in the camp they'd be sleeping.

"Don't bother unpacking it," Ludwig said. "At least, not until you're told. Now get back to Tristan."

The pair crossed the camp, Faron's certainty growing that something was afoot. Two newcomers to a small camp should have earned curious glances, yet everyone was concerned with preparing their gear, tearing down their tents, and sharpening their swords. Another familiar sight in Faron's long, long life. They were preparing to march. The question was, to where?

When they found him, Tristan was locked in conversation with a towering man bigger than even Faron. He was bare-chested but for a simple sleeveless shirt, and his body bore numerous battle scars. His smile was wide, and his green eyes lively.

"…ain't enough time to train up whelps," he was saying as they approached. "They best be familiar with following orders…and worth the hassle."

"I pray you are not discussing my usefulness," Faron said, grabbing their attention.

The two turned, the big man crossing his arms and squinting.

"What's with the mutt?" he asked.

"A rude way to describe my friend Bart," Faron replied. "He's loyal and stays at my side better than Iris, but you shouldn't call him that to his face."

The stranger with Tristan froze a moment and then flashed a grin, ear to ear.

"You're a cocky bastard, aren't you?" he said. "Don't deny it. I've just met you, yet you jest as if we are the best of friends."

"If we are not the best of friends yet, I expect training and war to make it happen," Faron insisted.

The other man laughed.

"Yeah, cocky, and fearless. Good. That'll get you killed early, or make you one of our best fighters. Can't wait to find out which. At least you got the muscle to back yourself up." He gestured at Bart. "What about you, mutt?"

"Bart," the young man nervously corrected.

"Nope, mutt. And by your stammering, I'd say that's a 'no.' At least only one of you is greener than river moss."

Sir Tristan cleared his throat. "Faron, Bart, this is Alex Beaumont. He will be in charge of your training."

"I look forward to it," Faron said.

"Not as much as I do," Alex said, with an excited look that would have frightened lesser men.

A panicked soldier sprinted to the tent, interrupting them with his shouting.

"They're here," he cried. "The army, it's here!"

Tristan grew visibly nervous, while Alex just shrugged.

"Get 'em in line," the big man said. "Time to meet the bastard."

•

The hundred men and women gathered in the center of camp, forming ten-wide lines. A quick shout from Alex told Faron and Bart where to stand, a spot in the rearmost line along the left side. Faron caught those nearby shooting him confused glances. Someone so tall and strong as he would normally be on the front line, but Faron suspected such privilege would wait until Alex confirmed Faron actually knew how to swing a sword.

As for who the bastard could be, Faron had a guess. The rows upon rows of soldiers who marched into the camp only confirmed it. Half were in chain, half in padded leather, and all wore tabards dyed a deep yellow. This was no scouting force like he'd expected. It wasn't a full army, either, something more akin to a skirmishing force, numbering about a thousand in total. Perhaps Luelle was considered a potential target of attack should war break out between Doremy and Argylle?

And then he saw her, marching in the heart of the formation. She wore no helmet, so her blond hair hung low across her tabard to bunch up on her shoulders. Unlike the rest of the soldiers, she wore a full suit of plate, its surface shining a brilliant silver. A shield was strapped to her left arm, and at her side, a blade nestled within a black sheath trimmed with gold. Its hilt was similarly gold, that which was not wrapped in soft, dark leather. A white cloak flowed behind her, rippling from her passage.

The soldiers parted, making way for her to address the waiting camp. Faron's throat constricted, and he felt a sudden need to be closer to the front. This woman...

He had heard claims Princess Isabelle Dior had been blessed by the goddess. Heard, and not believed. But now he looked upon a face of striking beauty, and those eyes? Her irises seemed to glow, composed of gold more valuable than that which was filigreed into her sword hilt.

"Welcome, recruits of Luelle," Isabelle said to the hundred. Her voice was deeper than Faron expected, more commanding, too. This was not a woman who spent her life in delicacy. She did not wear that armor as if it were a costume, but as one familiar with its weight. Men and women stared at her, equally captivated, and Faron suspected whatever order she gave, they would obey without question. Her eyes swept the line, and when they settled on Faron, he swore he saw her momentarily stumble, and her gaze linger. She shook her head and quickly recovered.

"I am Princess Isabelle of Leyval," she said, slowly pacing before them, her shield arm at her side, the other resting upon the hilt of her sword. "Or the Bastard Princess, as some of you may have heard. It is the title the Casthes are all too eager to brand upon me, as if they whisper words I have not heard since I was a babe in a cradle."

She lifted her arms to either side, palms to the heavens.

"But I am graced with the goddess's blessing. It is *her* words that I cherish, and not the barbs of the violent and the cowardly. King Bentley is a pitiful man, fat on his stolen wealth from the iron-beech trade. Wealth he does not share with those who bend their backs and scar their hands to make his prosperity possible. But he insults more than the body. He insults the spirit. Argylle has embraced the blasphemous Church of Stars. He has welcomed their silver-tongued preachers and shepherds, and he helps build their ugly churches."

Her hands clenched. Fists now, shaking with rage.

"Leliel has rewarded them for their insolence. Word reached us not hours before arriving here. Prince Mortimer of Argylle is dead, slain by bandits of his own lands."

Gasps all around. For such a destabilizing event to happen to an enemy, and with war so close? Another proof of the luck of the goddess protecting Isabelle.

"Argylle condemns those who currently rule her," the princess continued. "Violence. Lawlessness. Her own people, here, among you, ready to make things right."

Her golden eyes swept the crowd, and Faron's insides tightened and his pulse quickened. How long had it been since he'd seen a woman so beautiful? Not since…since…

A face, a name, both threatening to return, but he fought them down, remembered the flames of the pyre Sariel had burned him upon. With his vision overwhelmed with fire, he watched Princess Isabelle draw her sword to end her speech.

"We are freedom, my friends. Freedom from the tyranny of the Casthes. Freedom from the vile faith of the east. Will you fight with me? Will you return to the homes you left, broken no longer, servants no longer, but instead free and radiant with the goddess's blessing?"

No hesitation. Every man and woman raised their arms and voices, crying out their acceptance. The hundreds of soldiers behind Isabelle joined in the chant, overwhelming it with a single name that the rest quickly took up.

Isabelle! Isabelle! Isabelle!

The Bastard Princess slashed the air with her sword. Her decree felt like it traveled for miles.

"Then, stand tall, warriors of Doremy, for this day, we go to war!"

•

From what Faron gathered while listening in on idle chatter, it was widely believed Isabelle would launch her war against King Bentley Casthe the moment her father died and she inherited the title of queen. That she would start early, and without any official declaration, could be seen as cowardly, conniving, or dishonorable. Yet he sensed no such judgment. The people feared the Church of Stars, and they adored their Bastard Princess. Whatever path she took, they would follow.

"I…I can't believe we're going," Bart said, sitting beside Faron as the army rested. They'd marched for hours, and all of them stank of sweat.

The young man was so red in the face the flush hid his freckles. A life on the farm had not prepared him for an army's long march. It had taken Faron's encouragement (and a subtle strengthening with radiance) to keep him going. "Not two days ago I was at home, thinking of what it'd be like to help free us from Bentley's tyranny. And now? To have met Princess Isabelle? To be marching back into Argylle, toward my home, with a sword in hand?"

"A sword you don't know how to use," Faron said, and put a hand on the young man's shoulder. Bart was excited. He was terrified. Most of all, he was stunned. He'd not lived through war. He didn't know how easily one could be swept up into its tide. Faron had tried to spare him this fate, but that ship had long sailed. Instead, Faron would keep him safe as best he could during the chaos of battle.

"It's going to be so much worse than you can imagine," he said softly. "Stay with me, always at my right side. Don't try to fight. You don't have the training, not yet. That will come, if you survive, but you must first survive."

Bart's pride was clearly wounded, but he accepted the suggestion.

"Alex might not approve," he said.

"Alex expects nothing of you, either, except death. Prove him wrong."

Trumpets sounded, resuming their march. Faron whistled, calling Iris from where she lay not far from them in the grass. The march did her old bones no favors, either, and she mostly skirted the edge of the troops instead of staying at Faron's side. Twice he was asked if she was an attack dog, and to simplify matters, Faron answered in the affirmative.

"Just keep her back unless Tristan wants her to join in the fight," one of them, a hulking woman missing one eye, snapped at him. "I don't want to die because some mutt trips my ankles."

"Hear that?" Faron had said, nudging Bart. "No tripping the fair lady."

As the army marched, Faron struck up conversations with those around him, relying on his charisma and the soldiers' excitement to open up their lips.

Their target was a fort to the west, one that guarded a bridge crossing the slender Wendway River. It was not expected to be well defended, for while King Bentley anticipated war, he still thought he had months to prepare, plus he wanted the bulk of his soldiers to remain with him at his capital in Vendom. It would be an easy victory, while simultaneously taking one of the two main crossings over the Wendway River that split off Argylle's lower third.

Isabelle's plan was to isolate a significant portion of her enemy's territory before he even knew a war had begun. A ruthless plan, and given the sentiment Faron had encountered when in Arbertown, one likely to work. If the people in southern Argylle saw Isabelle as a liberator, she might gain a groundswell of new recruits, all while stripping Bentley of potential conscripts.

And from what he gathered, this was not her main force. Three thousand more soldiers remained in her capital, more than enough to defend against a siege. Surprising, though, was that the princess would be willing to come so far to lead the fight herself. It inspired the soldiers, true, but it was a significant risk, one that improved Faron's opinion of her. She would not hide in a castle, safe and distant from the bloodshed she started. Resplendent in her armor, she would see it firsthand, if not fight in it herself.

Two hours later, they approached Wendway Fort from the south. Isabelle called a halt for everyone to rest while their trailing wagons caught up. Faron eyed the fort, curious about Isabelle's strategy. It was surrounded by a wooden palisade, the tops of the tree trunks sharpened into spikes. A large barricaded door blocked off the entrance. Two towers flanked it, and he spotted a handful of archers within each.

Isabelle lacked archers of her own, and though she outnumbered her foes tremendously, it would not take many men to hold a fort if the walls and door could not be breached.

"How are we getting through?" Faron asked one of Tristan's soldiers beside them. The hundred of them had been kept together and shuffled off to the rear of the marching formation, to serve as their own squad.

"Did you not see the wagons?" the soldier replied, and gestured toward the five covered wagons pulled by oxen stretched out behind them. "Isabelle came ready."

Sure enough, as the soldiers rested, the wagons arrived, and those within began their work. A thick tree trunk had been cut and brought in one of them, and as Faron watched, they began constructing a basic battering ram by nailing thick iron rods into its sides. Rudimentary, but likely enough for the meager fort. It was not their only plan, either. More of Isabelle's workers were busy nailing together two separate siege ladders. Between the three, Faron suspected they had enough ways to get soldiers over the walls.

The mood was tense yet jovial as the time passed. Soldiers stretched, checked their gear, and sparred with one another to loosen their muscles. Faron kept beside Bart, his eye on the fort. He thought those within might abandon their defenses and flee north, especially when so heavily outnumbered. Instead, he watched the numbers grow in the two watch towers as well as the walkways built along the inner side of the wall.

It seemed that Bentley had reinforced the fort after all...

"Stay here," he told both Bart and Iris, and then headed to the front. He ignored the dirty looks the professional soldiers gave him. Those who came south from Leyval with Isabelle would view Tristan's group as dead weight, and for the most part, they would be correct. A few dozen fighters with weeks to months of training would not compare to those who had spent years preparing for this war. It meant Faron would need to work to get himself into the thick of the fight, where he could truly make an impact.

Granted, there was also that battering ram.

Isabelle was deep in conversation at the front of the army, in clear view of the fort. A small group surrounded her. Loudest was a man with a deep scar disfiguring the left half of his face, leaving pale tissue upon his black skin from forehead to chin. His armor resembled Isabelle's, and from what Faron had gathered, his name was Oscar, and he was her marshal. Also with her was someone from the wagons, an engineer, Faron suspected, along with a few of her knights. Tristan was among them, too, though he kept quiet while the others talked.

Faron lurked at the edge of the group, waiting until Tristan noticed. The knight frowned, quietly excused himself, and then approached.

"Why are you not with the rest of my squadron?" he asked, keeping his voice low so the others did not overhear. His eyes were practically bulging from anger.

"The battering ram," Faron said. "I want on its crew."

Tristan looked taken aback.

"We...we are taking volunteers," he admitted. "But we've no covering for it, and there's more archers at the fort than we anticipated. The siege ladders will distract some of them, but it's going to be..." He paused, eyeing Faron with new respect. "Are you sure about this? We could use someone with your size anchoring it, true, but this will be dangerous work."

Faron grinned at him, a little silver flashing in his eyes to make sure the knight was amenable to the suggestion.

"I'm here to help where I'm needed most."

Tristan shrugged.

"So be it. I'll see if I can reserve you a spot. Now, back to my troops, soldier, and don't go wandering off again."

Faron accepted the dismissal and returned to Bart and Iris. They lingered separate from the rest of the squadron, Iris lying beside Bart and accepting his occasional pat across her head.

"I see you've warmed up to him faster than you did me," Faron told her as he sat on the trampled grass. The coyote's eyes were closed, and she did not open them, only let out a long, unimpressed snort.

Ten minutes later, Tristan returned, and after exchanging words with others of his squadron, pointing and gesturing about while giving orders, he joined the trio on the edge.

"Well?" Faron asked him.

"You're second crew," Tristan said.

"Second? Look at me, Tristan. I could carry the battering ram alone. Why not put me on that first crew, instead of the replacements?"

The other man hawked a glob and then spat.

"You want the truth, Faron? Two reasons. One, I don't know your mettle yet, and we can't afford anyone on that battering ram crew breaking and running the moment arrows start flying. And two..." He shrugged.

"I don't think Marshal Oscar expects too many of that initial crew to survive. I'd rather you ensure we finish than die in the initial volleys. So instead, you'll be protecting the ram as part of its shield wall. Consider yourself lucky to be even that close."

He then pointed to Bart.

"You, however, are on first crew."

Bart's eyes widened, and his skin visibly paled. "But you just said..."

"I know what I said. You're also no good with a sword, and every squadron was told to offer up members for first crew. I'm sending you, along with two others."

Faron stood, careful to keep his voice in check.

"What game are you playing, knight?" he asked.

Tristan shrugged, unimpressed.

"I told you, I don't know you yet, nor your true mettle. What I do know is that you care for the lad. You'll be his shield on the approach. You want him safe, then you keep at his side, and do your duty. That clear, soldier?"

Faron exchanged glances with Bart. The young man lurched to his feet, and he thudded a fist over his breast.

"I won't falter," he said. "And I won't be afraid. The gate will fall, I promise."

"I hope to Leliel it does," Tristan said, turning away. "Because otherwise we'll be retreating back to Doremy with our tails tucked between our legs and an ungodly number of arrows stuck in our hides."

Chapter 12

FARON

"I wish I had a bigger shield," Faron muttered as he stood beside the battering ram. The ram was crude, just a thick tree trunk with the front shaved down to a blunt point. Eight holes had been drilled into it and metal bars slid through to serve as handholds. No covering, no protection from arrows or oil. Sixteen men currently held it aloft, practicing basic orders.

"Heave!" shouted the knight in charge, and the men rushed forward ten steps to strike an invisible wall.

"Set!"

They pulled back, retreating another ten steps. The first half hour had been full of stumbles and miscounts, but it hadn't taken long for everyone to grow accustomed to the effort. Nothing spectacular, but cohesive enough to hit a big door with a big stick. Bart had taken to the practice as if it were his life's entire purpose, hanging on the commanding knight's every word. There was no doubting his dedication. Faron hoped his resolve would remain come the brutality of battle. As for Iris, she remained back at Faron's tent. A siege was no place for her, especially when she might be trampled by Doremy forces or catch an errant arrow.

"Attention!" the knight shouted, and the men set down the ram and turned. Faron joined the rest of the shield wall in forming a line, his arms crossed behind him. Princess Isabelle approached, her silver armor resplendent in the midday sun. Her marshal accompanied her, his expression dour.

"Is the ram ready?" he asked.

"I'd prefer we had another day or two to practice," the knight in charge said. "But yes, I think we are."

Isabelle circled the ram, quiet, her shoulders back and her head held high. Her gaze swept the first crew, judging them.

"Be brave," she said. "Make way the path to our victory, and know Leliel watches over you always."

Several men nodded, while others pressed their palms to their chests and lowered their heads, a sign of prayer to Leliel.

"Beloved be the goddess," Bart said, the only one to speak.

Isabelle smiled at him.

"Beloved be," she said, and turned to Marshal Oscar. The gentleness of her voice vanished. "Give the order. I want this fort claimed by the hour."

"It will be done," said Oscar, and then unhooked a small brass trumpet from his hip, lifted it to his lips, and gave the signal.

•

Faron marched beside Bart, the young man sweating as he helped carry the ram, positioned fifth back from the front and on the left side. They were just shy of the front line, following in Princess Isabelle's wake. Banners rippled in the wind, yellow fabric attached to high spears to announce her approach. The army marched wide, far beyond the width of the well-trodden road, to exaggerate their numbers.

Within Wendway Fort, the blue raven flew high from its walls.

"Be with me, Leliel, beloved goddess of dawn and dusk," Bart prayed as he walked. The words were hushed and quick, a litany against his growing panic as they neared the fort. Archers readied along the palisade, far more than Faron liked. "Be with me, Leliel, and look upon me with your golden eyes. Be with me, Leliel, so in my fear..."

The first of the arrows flew. It landed well short, a warning shot, but Bart saw it and paled.

Faron put a hand on Bart's shoulder, and he ignored the glares from the other members of the shield wall.

"So in my fear and weakness, I will be strong," he said, finishing the line. Faron held no faith in the goddess that humanity worshiped, but he knew well their prayers, their beliefs, and the Four Pleas that guided their doctrine.

A trumpet call. The pace increased, the space between them and the fort shrinking. Faron's pulse quickened. This was it. He grinned. Time to make his presence known.

Isabelle made way for the battering ram while soldiers parted on the right and left flanks for the two siege ladders. Faron readied his shield, and he positioned himself so his right hip was touching Bart's left. With his free hand, he grabbed the pole. His orders were to not lift, only use it to guide his steps to keep in line with Bart's...but no one need know that he aided young Bart in carrying his portion.

A second trumpet call. More shields raised. Shouts from knights, and the marshal. The charge had begun. The army rushed the fort in three prongs, soldiers meant to either climb the ladders or rush through the gate when it was broken.

In response came the arrows. Faron counted thirty archers in total, and they let loose a scattered volley. A far cry from some of the battles he'd participated in, but that did not remove the danger. Their aim was heavily focused on the ram. Faron lifted his shield and shifted so its surface broadly covered both him and Bart.

The arrows hit, thudding into dirt, smacking shields, and for one unlucky man, piercing through padded leather and into flesh. He didn't even scream, only collapsed, his mouth hitching, a lung punctured and filling with blood. The two men behind him stumbled as they trampled his corpse, but the ram continued moving.

"Fill!" their commanding knight shouted, and the soldier whose shield had failed to protect slung it over his back and grabbed the iron handhold. The ram, which had begun to list, righted.

"Heave!" the knight shouted.

"Leliel be my strength," Bart repeated as they sprinted the final distance. "Leliel be my strength, my guide, blessed be, blessed be..."

Another man in the front dropped, screaming as an arrow slipped past a raised shield to pierce his stomach. The rest trampled him, unable to stop, unable to slow. "*Heave,*" bellowed the knight, urging them onward. Just before the ram connected, Faron gripped the pole and added his own weight to it. It struck with a thunderous crack, wood splintering, metal bolts rattling. The wooden bar barricading the opposite end groaned from the impact. Close, but not enough.

"Set!" the knight shouted, his own shield raised high. Behind them, Isabelle and her soldiers halted, awaiting passage. Meanwhile, the ladders slammed down atop the spiked palisade, metal hooks latching into the wood. Soldiers hurried up them, shields raised over their heads against the arrows. Three locations to defend, stretching thin the fort's troops. Three locations, three skirmishes, three sources of screams as the dying began.

The ram retreated amid a hail of arrows. Another carrier fell, this the man who'd been a fill. Faron seethed. There should be a full squad of soldiers around them, baiting the arrows, all ready to replace any who fell. The ram also should have been on wheels and hung from chains. Everything about this assault bespoke an expectation of easy victory, and now they paid the price.

"Heave!"

An arrow struck Faron's shield and stuck into the wood. The ram surged forward, but slower, without quite as much distance to gain momentum. Its aim drifted, too, striking off-center. The door rattled, giant cracks splintering along its front. Whatever bar barricaded the other side threatened to break. One more good hit would do it. Faron could see through the cracks to the fort interior, and only a measly ten soldiers waited with swords and shields at the ready.

"Set!"

Faron bit back a curse, his shield weaving to intercept another arrow. Archers from all sides had shifted their aim to the ram, trusting the soldiers on the palisades to dislodge the ladders. Two more men holding the ram dropped, stalling it as fills rushed to grab the poles. Faron's head swung, watching, judging the archers, seeing whose aim was for Bart... and then he froze.

Just above the gate, he saw movement, and a hint of smoke.

"Oil!" he shouted, and grabbed Bart by the shoulder and flung him away.

Two Argylle soldiers lifted a pot over the gate. The first of it hit the center of the ram and splashed in all directions. Faron's face was still turning, his body moving from throwing Bart, when it struck. He saw it from the corner of his eye, saw black, and then saw nothing as the searing oil sprayed across the right half of his face.

Faron roared, pain overwhelming his senses as the boiling oil seared his flesh and sealed over his eye.

"Set," the knight shouted, but no one had been prepared for the oil. It coated the ram and even slicked the metal carry poles. Confusion reigned, men staggering away, confused, frightened, or wounded. The ram dropped, and when the knight in charge retreated, others followed him.

But not Faron.

Radiance bursting through his veins, he snarled like a savage animal and grabbed the front-most pole, the only one completely free of oil. An arrow thudded into the meat of his arm, but he ignored it. He set his feet, gripped the pole, and then howled his fury. Every muscle in his body flexed. Though the back end of the ram dragged in the dirt, the front rose high, and with a gigantic heave, he slammed it directly into the center of the gate.

The already weakened barricade snapped in half. The doors bowed inward, opening enough for a lone man to step through.

Faron dropped the ram and drew his sword. He didn't even bother retrieving his shield. The way was clear. No thoughts. No hesitation. Battle was in his veins, and it swept him away like a bloody tide.

Ten soldiers, readied and waiting. They raised their swords, thinking Faron outnumbered and mad from battle. And he was, but oh, how foolish they were to think they could slay him with a mere ten. Faron blasted into their center, his sword batting away strikes as if they were made by children. He lopped the head off the nearest soldier, then flung a second with his shoulder, knocking him into three of his fellows.

His vision compromised, he dared not remain still, nor abandon the offensive. He spun left, his sword striking the defending man's shield hard enough Faron could hear the bones in his arm snap. The shield dropped, and Faron plunged his sword straight into the man's chest. A twist, and he ripped his weapon free to bury it into the side of another Argylle soldier.

Something sharp sliced across his back. Damn it, his right eye; if he weren't blinded, he would have seen the approach...

He spun again, parrying a follow-up thrust meant to pierce his kidneys. His free hand grabbed the throat of the attacker, and he lifted him into the air with ease. His fingers crunched windpipe. His sword disemboweled intestines.

Another hit, again from his blind side. Stabbing pain, and this time, the blade went in deep. Faron screamed, swiping wildly, but he need not have panicked. His allies had finally arrived, and to his shock, it was Princess Isabelle herself who led the charge. Her shining sword punished the one who stabbed him, the blade's wickedly sharp edge easily parting the man's jerkin and crunching ribs to find his heart.

A wave of steel followed, the army sweeping into the fort. The arrows stopped, and through the blood pounding in Faron's ears, he heard the defenders shout their surrender.

"About time," he mumbled, grabbing and ripping the arrow out of his arm. His vision swam, that which remained. He put a hand to his lower back and was shocked by the amount of blood. Oh, it was deep, all right.

"Soldier?" Princess Isabelle asked, sheathing her sword and turning toward him.

"My lady," Faron said. He dropped to his knees and then collapsed, black nothingness taking him away.

Chapter 13

FARON

When Faron awoke, he was in a wide tent. It was a sight he recognized all too well: a battlefield surgeon's tent. He lay on blankets spread across the grass. His back hurt. His face hurt worse. Outside was dark, the tent's only light coming from a trio of candles burning in tin holders on a little stool nearby.

"Oh, you're awake." A woman's voice spoke to his right. He turned, his vision momentarily blurred from the movement. With his lone good eye, he surveyed the surgeon. She was a middle-aged woman, her red hair tightly bound into a bun to keep it from her face. The only thing more severe than the shape of her cheeks and jawline was the look in her eyes. She wore an apron, as if she were a butcher, only a butcher's apron would not contain quite so much blood.

"I am," Faron said, the words sluggish on his tongue.

"Consider me surprised. I'm Rowan, the one who stitched you up so you didn't bleed out the other half of your blood."

Faron closed his eyes and waited for his aching head to ease. He could heal himself immediately using radiance, but that would be tough to explain to an experienced surgeon. So instead he lay there, slowly letting feeling return to his limbs.

"You've probably figured it out already," Rowan continued, kneeling beside him. A surprising softness came over her gruff voice. "But you've permanently lost sight in your right eye. I'm sorry."

Faron cracked a grin.

"I've endured worse." He opened his other eye and glanced about. "Where is everyone else?"

"Oh, you get this tent all to yourself," Rowan said, rising to a stand. "A boon given to the One-Man Ram. That's what they're calling you, by the way. I hope you like the nickname, because you haven't the slightest hope of changing it."

Faron felt for the stitches in his back. Instead he touched only rough cloth, half soaked through.

"Don't be foolish," Rowan said, grabbing his wrist. Her other hand pressed his chest, forcing him to relax with gentle but unrelenting pressure. "Once you're up and about, I'll see if we can find you a hand-glass so you can survey my handiwork. For now, rest, and eat something, if you feel capable."

Arguing with this woman was like yelling at the moon to remain in the sky come the rise of the sun, and so he relented.

"How long was I out?" he asked, still trying to orient himself.

"Just a few hours. We're set up inside Wendway Fort. By the sound of it, we won't be marching for a few days, so you'll have opportunity to rest."

Good, that meant he had time to think. He did not fear for his recovery, but there were…complications that needed to be addressed. But how?

Rowan released her grip on him and retreated from the bed while wiping her hands on her apron.

"Now you're awake, let me see about getting you some water to drink," she said. "Stay here, and don't do anything foolish like getting up."

"Yes, ma'am."

She left him alone in the broad tent. It gave Faron a chance to shift his weight and, without fear of Rowan's disapproval, check the stitches in his side. His fingers slipped underneath the wrapping and then gently tested the threads. Tightly knit. The woman knew what she was doing. That spoke well for others in Isabelle's army, when their own time came to visit the surgeon's tent.

A bit of nervousness tightened his throat. Had Bart survived? He remembered tossing the lad aside to protect him from the oil before breaking through the door. Had he escaped? Or had an arrow taken him?

The flaps of the tent opened, interrupting his thoughts. In stepped Princess Isabelle, accompanied by an older gentleman in a warm-looking black coat and cap. Permanent frown lines marked his lips and forehead.

"Miss Rowan tells me you have recovered," Isabelle said, standing by the entrance. She'd shed her armor, though her sword remained buckled to her hip. She wore a fine set of black trousers, a loose white shirt with long sleeves, and a sapphire-studded necklace hanging low over her chest. Her hair was loosened, a golden curtain wrapping about her neck and shoulders. Just having her look upon him made Faron's stomach suddenly fill with butterflies. For what reason would the princess visit a mere soldier?

"That seems to be true," he said, and then gestured at his face. "Though we might need to discuss her opinions on what 'recovered' means."

She didn't flinch, didn't even twitch. If she were bothered by the ghastly burn sealing over his eye and scarring much of his cheek and chin, she did not show a hint of it.

"You live," she said. "It is more than could be said for others who fought this day."

Faron settled onto his blanket, his lone eye studying the woman. She fascinated him, and most maddeningly, he couldn't figure out why. There was something special about her, something that made her skin sparkle and add an otherworldly glow to those golden eyes of hers. Something like radiance. Something like the blessing of a goddess.

But that was absurd.

"Aye, you're right, I live," he said. "But since you have been so kind to grace me with your presence, might I ask a favor?"

Caution painted a guarded mask across her face.

"And what favor might that be?" she asked.

"Pray over my wounds, so the goddess may heal them."

"My lady's days will be long if she must petition the goddess for our soldiers' every scratch and bruise," the accompanying gentleman interrupted.

"This is hardly a scratch," Faron argued. "And surely my actions on the battlefield have earned the attempt?"

The cautious mask cracked. Isabelle smiled down at him, a sudden levity to her serious demeanor that made her seem all the more beautiful.

"Forgive Aubert his caution. He has been my family's adviser since I first learned to crawl, and he is rather protective of me."

"Does that protectiveness extend to the battlefield?"

Aubert's demeanor was carefully controlled, his voice as calm and smooth as a secret pond.

"I count numbers and track provisions. I do not man the battlefield, soldier, but I ensure we have food in the bellies and coin in the pockets of those who do fight. I shall let you decide which is more important to winning a war."

Despite his ribbing, Faron decided he liked this Aubert fellow. He was proud of his work, and there was no hiding his adoration of the princess.

"Forgive me," he said. "The pain has robbed me of my manners."

Isabelle knelt beside him and shifted her legs to get comfortable.

"Let me see if I may do something about that," she said, and settled her hands upon his face. He closed his eyes and listened to her pray.

"Beloved Leliel, this man has given much to your cause, and fought well in defense of your honor. Ease the suffering of his flesh. Make well his wounds, and grant him the strength to face these coming days. For your kindness, your mercy, and your love, I thank you."

Her hands retreated, but she did not leave. Her voice fell to a whisper, and when their eyes met, he felt himself held captive.

"Why are you here?" she asked softly. "What reason brings someone like you to my camp?"

The hairs on his neck stood on end. Surely she could not sense the radiance within him . . . right?

"Because the Astral Kingdom needs to be broken," he whispered back. "And I think you might be the one to do it."

Isabelle stood and did not acknowledge his answer.

"Some call you brave, and others, reckless, but no man in this camp doubts your strength, or the lives you saved breaking open the fort. I am glad to have you among my soldiers, Faron, and should you require anything else, do not hesitate to let me know."

"Bart," he said, closing his eyes. "Bartholomew Fairgrove is his full name. He was one of the initial crew for the ram, part of Sir Tristan's recruits. Did he survive?"

"I do not know," she answered. She glanced at her adviser. "But I shall have Aubert make sure you are sent an answer. Is he family?"

"A friend," Faron said. "Just a rare friend."

The princess and her adviser exited the tent. Faron did his best to relax. There was no reason to expect the worst. No reason to dwell on such dark thoughts as the time slowly passed.

The tent flap opened, and before he could sit up, Iris was atop him, licking the unburned portion of his face.

"Hey, hey, hey, now," Faron said, turning away from the slobber. "You act as if you haven't seen me in forever."

"True, but the past few hours have *felt* like forever," Bart said, entering the tent after Iris. The coyote retreated, allowing Faron to get a good luck at the young man. Not a scratch on him. Faron smiled. Excellent. Relief replaced the anxiety in his chest.

"You're well," he said while scratching Iris behind the ears. "That's good."

"All thanks to you." Bart sat on his haunches, his smile not lasting long. "Faron, you ... I'm sorry, your face, it's my fault. If you'd lifted your shield, if you'd protected yourself and—"

"No," Faron interrupted, his voice harsh enough that Iris flattened her ears and retreated beyond his reach. The coyote's reaction was enough to give Faron pause, and he fought to better control his words.

"No," he said again, and flashed his best smile. "I promised to take care of you, and I keep my promises. An eye? My face? Small prices to pay to save a life."

Bart looked ready to cry. He clenched his hands, unable to meet Faron's gaze.

"Thank you," he said. "I don't know how I'd do this without you."

"You'd find a way. Now, head on out of here. It's been a long day."

Bart stood, called Iris's name, and then exited the tent. Iris padded closer, giving him one last nudge against his arm with her forehead.

"I know," he said, patting her side. "I also promised to show you the world. I won't break that promise, either."

She left, and once alone, Faron snuffed out the last of the candles and sat on his blanket. Such matters always felt best done in darkness. He pressed his hands to his scarred face, his palms flat against the burns, and then called upon the innate magic within him.

"Make right the flesh," he whispered. "Return sight to that which is blind."

The power flowed through him, slowly and steadily. If given time, his wounds would heal on their own, even if he did not purposefully flood them with radiance to quicken the process. It was a tricky conundrum he'd often faced whenever he partook in human wars. During a lengthy campaign, it was hard to disguise the rate at which he healed. Even if someone lopped off a hand or leg, it would grow back within weeks. Whenever he suffered such terrible wounds, he normally had no choice but to desert and begin a new life with a new name somewhere far away from those who remembered him.

But not here. Not when he could shift attention onto another.

Silver light washed over his face, cleansing the scars. He blinked, and though the colors blurred and swam for a bit, his eyesight returned. He reached for his wounded back, then thought better of it. Isabelle had only prayed over his face, and that visible portion would be more than sufficient.

He slept.

•

Come morning, Faron awoke to Miss Rowan shaking his arm.

"Sleep later, eat now," she said. Faron rolled over from his stomach and onto his back, the thick blanket flopping off him. Rowan immediately retreated, the bowl of porridge dropping from her hands.

"Faron?" she asked.

Faron stood and gently touched his face, making a show of it. He then looked to her, not needing to say a word.

Still, this wasn't enough. He exited the tent, leaving her to stand shocked and still in her tent, whispering something inaudible to herself. He found himself in the center of the fort, new tents sprung up in rows to either side of him. Soldiers turned to greet him, and they all showed confusion or shock at his healed face. Only a scar remained, a long swath of pale skin to mark the burn's departure that would vanish completely in a few more days.

A crowd had begun to follow him by the time he arrived at the command tent. Isabelle was locked in discussion with her marshal but froze at the sight of him. She hid her shock well. Disturbingly well.

Faron approached her, well aware of how many eyes were upon them.

"Your prayers," he said, projecting his voice so all would hear. "Your kind touch. Princess Isabelle, you have worked miracles." Then, to the shocked onlookers: "Once blind, but now I see! Praise be the goddess, and her chosen!"

Princess Isabelle crossed the distance between them as cheers flooded the fort. Her golden eyes locked onto his, and they held him prisoner. His healing surely surprised her, yet she spoke as if everything were according to her desires.

"The goddess rewards those who give to her their all," she said. She drew her sword. The ringing of steel silenced the crowd. Faron lowered to his knees in response. "And she expects much from those whom she has blessed. Faron, yesterday, you were but a soldier, lacking even family or land name. I would bid you rise, and serve as my protector. Will you accept this? The honor, the privilege, and the responsibility?"

Faron bowed his head, needing to do so to hide his grin.

"I do," he said.

Her sword pressed against his shoulder.

"Then rise, child of Leliel, for I name you Faron Godsight, friend of Doremy and honorable warrior of her future queen."

Chapter 14

SARIEL

Within Arbertown, there was talk of war, and little else. Sariel failed to find his brother at either tavern, forcing him to speak with their keepers in hopes Faron had left an impression.

"You a mercenary?" the older man at the Split Trunk asked, his gaze lingering on Redemption resting across Sariel's shoulders.

"Just a traveler," Sariel answered. "I'm looking for my brother. His name is Faron. He has my face, only he's larger, and his hair is shorter."

The tavern keeper nodded.

"Aye, I did meet him. He paid for his room but then left without staying."

Sariel held back a groan. Of course Faron had not stayed in place and waited for Sariel to catch up to him. Ever impulsive, his softhearted brother.

"Know you where he went?"

The man scratched his face.

"I don't, sorry." He gestured to the crowded commons room, nearly every table full of rancorous young men and women drinking the night away. "You might ask around. His table was never shy for company when he was here. Might also check the church. Plenty of travelers like to give confessions prior to resuming their travels."

Sariel's mood darkened.

"Perhaps," he said, planning on doing no such thing. He made for the exit, then paused by the doorway to turn and rest his back against the wall. Ignoring the guarded glare of the tavern keeper, Sariel closed his eyes and let the radiance burn stronger within him. His hearing sharpened as his other senses faded away. The multitude of conversations washed over him, and he heard them sharp and clear.

His mind flitted through them like a moth, dipping in and out, seeking something useful. Minutes passed, and while most talk was dull and full of confused wondering over the future of the war, his efforts were finally rewarded as he overheard an argument among several men in the far corner.

I'm telling you, it's all nonsense. Just a lie to make her soldiers seem special.

But why lie about something like that? It don't make sense. That's why I think it's true.

You believe it because *the lie is so stupid? That makes even less sense.*

A third voice joined the first two.

The Bastard Princess is telling tales, no different than her healing the injured or hearing the voice of the goddess. The One-Man Ram supposedly lifted an entire tree trunk on his own. Do you really believe that? No one's that strong. No one.

Sariel opened his eyes. Oh, but there was one person who was that strong. It seemed like Faron was already making a name for himself. At least he had chosen his allies correctly. His brother might be acclimating to the changes since his slumber, but he'd been smart enough not to side with Argylle's foul king and his acceptance of Eder's church.

"So you've joined Princess Isabelle?" he wondered aloud. He'd never met the woman, only heard her outlandish claims of being chosen by the human goddess, Leliel. It was enough to dismiss her as either a charlatan or a madwoman. If Faron hadn't done the same, then he likely believed he could manipulate her into serving their cause.

Not a bad assumption, he admitted to himself as he left the tavern. Given her professed disdain for the Church of Stars, they wouldn't need much push to set her gaze eastward, toward the religion's beating heart within the Tower Majestic.

It would not be the first religious war to bathe the entirety of Kaus in flames.

•

It took little effort to locate Princess Isabelle's army. Everyone knew of Wendway Fort's fall. Sariel topped off his supplies, bit his tongue at the dramatically higher prices, and then started north. He questioned the occasional traveler, each time seeking to confirm the army's location and where they were expected to go when they moved out. He suspected northward, to pressure the Argylle midlands, but there was always the chance that Isabelle had left a small force to hold the river and then retreated east, back into Doremy.

Sariel barely stopped to rest, and when the distant fort finally came into view, the many cook fires and multitude of tents were enough to confirm the army remained within. The small fort could not contain all the people, and so dozens more tents were pitched in rows along the southern edge of the Wendway River. West of the road, he saw troops practicing drills and formations, the men and women caked with sweat from both the effort and the midday sun.

Where are you, Faron? Sariel wondered, scanning the drills. After so many lifetimes, he knew the methods Faron would use to win over the hearts of soldiers. He would give more effort than anyone but remain humble about his strength and size. He would not challenge any of his superiors, not until he had fought several battles, and the soldiers who fought alongside him realized his skill with a sword. Faron could dominate a battlefield, if given the chance. Once that happened, no soldier would choose a stubborn or incompetent superior over Faron.

One battle, and already his brother had a nickname. It would not be long before he marched at Princess Isabelle's side, trusted and revered in equal measure.

"Halt there, stranger," ordered a guard set to watch the road long before the rows of tents. He was a young man, his helmet resting in the grass instead of atop his head. "Passage across the river is blocked for now. You need to turn back."

"I don't seek passage," Sariel said. "I seek employment."

He glanced at the other soldier with him. The man was a little older, with a heavy black beard overhanging his jerkin. He sat in the grass, resting his legs and watching the exchange.

"You a mercenary?"

"At times," Sariel said. "But that is not why I am here. My brother has joined your forces, and I would accompany him on the battlefield."

"That so? Who's your brother?"

Sariel hated the title, but he said the foolish words anyway.

"I believe you know him as the One-Man Ram."

The younger soldier scoffed, but the older shaded his eyes with his hand and squinted.

"You do look a bit like him. All right. I'll accompany you in. I'm sure Sir Tristan would like a word with any blood relative of Faron's. You best not be lying, though. We won't take kindly to that." He stood and pointed. "Leave your sword here, though. I'm not letting you march through our tents while armed."

Sariel met the man's eye. Radiance flowed through his gaze and infused his reply.

"No."

The younger soldier reached for his sword, but the other merely shrugged, capitulating immediately.

"Fine. Follow me."

Sariel took stock of the camp as they walked the tents. The tents themselves were a bit cheap and would hardly endure a proper winter's cold. They'd do fine against a bit of rain, though. What weapons he saw were plain but acceptable, as were their shields. Sariel suspected a tight budget stretched effectively to form this army. No archers, he noted. Lack of time to train them, or was it the cost of bows and arrows the Bastard Princess could not afford? Easier to put padded leather on a man, stick a sword in his hand, and call him a warrior than to go through the lengthy process of teaching him to accurately judge height, draw distance, and wind.

Instead of going into the center of the tents, his guide took him to the far western edge, to a small clearing in the grass just before the palisade wall. To his surprise, a stone statue to Leliel had been carved there, about half the height of a man. She was depicted as a nude woman with four feathery wings stretching out her back, those wings curling around her body to hide her nakedness. Each wing bore four eyes along the bones, open and lidless. Her arms were held at her sides, her palms facing upward. Another pair of eyes opened at her wrists, these crudely carved so they more resembled gaping wounds. A wide square base below her feet allowed worshipers to leave flowers, the type and color of flower meant to signify the desired request, such as beardtongues for safety, or yellow rock jasmines for haste.

A man in chainmail knelt before the statue with his head bowed. His right hand rested upon her bare foot. In his left, he held a red orchid. Sariel's guide paused and waited respectfully. Curiosity got the better of Sariel, and he heightened his hearing to listen in on the softly whispered prayer.

"...placed into my hands, may I have the wisdom to know what is right, and what is just, so they may endure this coming war. May I be strong for them. May I be the teacher they deserve, and the firm hand they need, if they are to survive."

The man placed the flower upon the statue's feet and then stood. Upon seeing the pair waiting, his calm expression hardened and a frown tugged at his lips.

"Sir Tristan," the young man quickly said, thudding his fist against his breast in a salute. "I've brought someone who wishes to join us. His name is..." He paused, realizing he'd never asked. His face reddened. "He says he is Faron Godsight's brother."

Sariel's calm expression never changed, for he was too practiced at hiding his true thoughts, but the last name intrigued him immensely.

Godsight? What have you been up to in my absence, brother?

The knight crossed his arms, and there was no hiding his glare at Sariel's overly long dragon-bone sword.

"All right. Return to your post, Adam. I'll have a word with him."

The young soldier nodded and then hurried away. Sariel tilted his head to the side, analyzing the knight. Competent. Confident, but only in what he could control. His prayers revealed concern for his soldiers, but also fear about his ability to prepare them. Sariel suspected him a good man, though whether he remained one as the war progressed, he doubted. Good men died, or became terrible men, once bloodshed began and the consequences of every failure meant a field of corpses. Better to become heartless than mourn every life lost.

Or perhaps that was just Sariel's own opinions talking.

"Have you a name?" Tristan asked.

"Sariel," he answered. He dared not offer his family name, not when he didn't know what Faron might have chosen. And under no circumstances would he dare call himself Sariel Godsight.

"All right, Sariel. What's brought you here, to Princess Isabelle's army? Cause, coin, or family?"

Sariel analyzed what he had deduced of the man and debated a proper answer. He could influence the knight's decision with radiance, but that control would fade with time. If he wanted to join Faron without incident, he needed to convince Tristan properly.

Which meant the truth itself should be sufficient.

"King Bentley is a threat to those I hold dear to me," he said, thinking of Tara in Barkbent Town. "I want him gone. That I might fight alongside my brother in doing so is a boon."

Sir Tristan stared a moment and then grunted.

"I've heard worse reasons. Do you know how to fight?"

Sariel's lips curled into a half smile.

"I know how to kill."

"I suppose they're one and the same during war," Tristan said. "Follow me. I'll take you to Ludwig and get you enlisted. Welcome to Doremy's army, Sariel. I pray to Leliel you don't make me regret it."

•

Sariel signed his name, accepted a poorly fitted set of padded leather, and listened to a brief overview of how his days would go, where he would bunk, when he would be paid, and whom he would report to. By the time he finished, the drills had ended and the evening meal had been doled out among the camp. The mood was jovial, everyone's spirits buoyed by the fort's capture. Though there were several smaller fires about, a larger bonfire burned in the farthest southwest corner of the tent formations. It was there Sir Tristan's recruits gathered, circling the bonfire, and it was there Sariel finally caught up to his brother.

"I see you've done well without me," he said, approaching the flames and appreciating their heat against his skin. A dozen eyes turned his way. Faron glanced over his shoulder, saw him, and lurched to his feet. His smile was wider than the horizon.

"Sariel!" he said, throwing his arms around him. Sariel endured the hug like he would a sudden rainstorm.

"Everyone, this is my brother Sariel," Faron said when finished, and gestured to those gathered around the fire with wooden bowls in hand. "Sariel, these are my friends."

Of course you already have friends, thought Sariel as he endured the introductions. There was Alex, the green-eyed giant who would be in charge of Sariel's "training." A young freckled man with red hair named Bart. A cold-eyed woman named Rowan, a field surgeon, from what Sariel gathered. Several others, two spry and young brothers much too lively and optimistic to survive a war, and an older man, heavily scarred, who was clearly there for coin and nothing more. They were all from Argylle and had turned traitor to their homeland and joined the army of the Bastard Princess.

"Do you mind if we speak for a moment?" Sariel asked his brother. "In private?"

"Of course," Faron said, and led him away from the bonfire.

"You didn't wait for me in Clovelly," Sariel said once they had some space to talk.

"I had to keep on the move," Faron replied, offering nothing more than that. "I trusted you to find me, and you did."

"Yes, I did find you, already enlisted in an army, and apparently making a name for yourself...Ram."

His brother laughed.

"I didn't pick it. They named me while I was recovering from a bath of burning oil."

Sariel crossed his arms and glared.

"You chose our path without me," he said. "You chose Isabelle. Why?"

"What is there to say?" Faron asked, his mood turning somber. "She'll be an acceptable tool. She hates the Church of Stars and hates the east for spreading it. What more could we ask for?"

"Does she have the resources for victory? The potential support from nearby kings and queens to form an alliance? Who are her enemies? Who could stop her, once her ambitions grow beyond this little squabble with her neighbor?" When Faron did not answer, Sariel sighed and shook his head. "You don't know any of it, do you? As always, you trust your strength and charisma to be enough. And when it isn't, it will be up to me to pick up the pieces and make them fit."

Sariel turned to leave, but Faron grabbed his shoulder and held him still.

"You don't know her," he said. "You haven't seen the way people look at her. She will be enough. More than enough. Just have a little faith."

Sariel glanced over his shoulder and smirked. "In the goddess?"

Faron pushed him and flashed his widest, most handsome grin.

"In me."

Chapter 15

SARIEL

The wide field spread out before them, gently rolling down into a flower-blanketed valley. Not far to their left was the beginning of the Telbelt Forest and the road slicing through it that would lead to the next river crossing. In the distance approached Argylle's first legitimate attempt at defending her lands, a force of what appeared to be eight hundred soldiers. Outnumbered, they should have been running, but this defensive force, unlike the Doremy army, included what Sariel estimated to be nearly sixty mounted knights riding at the front.

"The knights are a problem," Sariel said. "They alone can turn this battle."

"I'm not afraid of them," Faron said, idly swinging his sword through the air to limber up. "Besides, rumors said they had a hundred, not sixty, so we're already better off than we anticipated."

"Bravado is not a defense against a mounted charge."

"True, but my sword is."

Sariel shrugged and dropped the matter. They would do what they must to secure victory, but he feared the losses would be too dramatic to continue the southern campaign. Princess Isabelle had left a token force to hold Wendway Fort and marched west, making for the second river crossing. With both taken, all of southern Argylle would be completely sealed.

It seemed King Bentley, or at least whoever was in charge of the small forces in the midlands, also understood that risk and had mustered what they could to intercept them on their way to the bridge.

"Look alive," Alex shouted, the big man surprisingly dashing in a suit of chainmail and an iron kettle hat. He walked before Sir Tristan's squadron, inspecting the soldiers. "I want us eager and ready if we get called to the front!"

Alex paused before Sariel, crossed his arms behind him, and then smirked.

"Too good for your armor?" he asked.

Sariel had refused to don the padded leather and instead wore his normal attire underneath his heavy black coat.

"Armor is necessary only if I am struck," he said simply.

"Cocky bastard. I pray we do get called to the front. I'm dying to see what that sword of yours can do…or can't."

The trainer had tried to convince Sariel to adopt a more traditional sword, insisting there would be no room on a battlefield to swing his giant, cumbersome weapon. Sariel had politely listened and then refused.

"Be glad you will gain such knowledge from a place of safety," Sariel said. "The same cannot be said for my foes."

"Of course," Alex said, unimpressed. "Just don't go stabbing your fellow soldiers with that oversized bit of bone." His attention then turned to Iris, who sat calmly at Faron's side. "Princess Isabelle herself has allowed the bitch to remain with you, but if she goes wild, or injures one of our own, I will not hesitate to put her down. Is that clear?"

Faron scratched Iris behind the ears.

"Don't worry about her," he said. "She knows who the enemy is."

Alex continued, checking the others. Sir Tristan's squadron was in the far left rear of the army, a little jut sticking out like an unwanted thumb. It was clear that Marshal Oscar held little faith in the Argylle recruits. The better-armed and -armored Doremy troops formed the front lines, stacked deep in the hope of better resisting the anticipated mounted charge.

"It's going to be hard to impress with your heroics so far from the front," Sariel told his brother. "Or do you plan to ignore orders and go charging the battle line anyway? That sounds like something the One-Man Ram would do."

Faron flinched at the name. "From the moment I heard them calling me that, I knew you'd never let me live it down."

"Then you know me well."

Trumpets sounded, a lone, long note. Not the order to march, but instead to prepare. Argylle's army had almost arrived.

"Do you think we'll be needed?" a young man beside Faron asked. Bart, if Sariel remembered correctly from the flurry of introductions. For reasons unknown, he stuck to Faron as if he were his own father.

"It all depends on how Isabelle handles the charge," Faron said, ruffling Bart's hair. "Just stay at my side if we do get called up. I'll make sure nothing happens to you."

Sir Tristan paced before his troops once Alex slipped into line not far from Sariel. His practiced eyes scanned those under his care, and he snapped at poor stances, improperly buckled sword belts, and a dozen other little things that might mean nothing, and might mean the difference between life and death.

He purposefully ignored Faron and Sariel. What that meant, good or ill, Sariel did not care to guess. His attention was on the front line.

The enemy army neared, the sound of hoofbeats and stomping boots growing louder. Doremy soldiers lifted their shields and braced. What few spearmen Isabelle commanded backed the second row, those spears peeking between shields in anticipation of the charge. Sariel watched, his eyes enhanced, so that he saw the distant battle as if he were a hawk circling overhead.

The Doremy soldiers might not have been the most impressively garbed and outfitted, but there was no questioning their training. They held firm against the charge with their shields raised high. They did not falter, nor did they break in fear as the sound of rattling armor and stomping hooves thundered across the grass.

The charge hit. Blows exchanged. Blood flowed. Sariel watched with bated breath, but the line did not crumble. The rest of the Argylle forces arrived, slamming into the Doremy front lines to prevent the knights from being swarmed. The battle began in earnest, and Sariel watched, captivated as always by the flow.

Most intriguing was Princess Isabelle herself. She did not hide with her marshal, watching from afar. The Bastard Princess fought in the heart of the conflict, two skilled knights guarding her flanks so the trio could press forward. Her armor shone brilliant in the daylight, and her sword cleaved through her enemies with strength shocking even to Sariel.

Aren't you a fascinating one? he thought as he watched her block a soldier's errant strike, bat the weapon aside, and then plunge her sword into his throat. She turned, shouted praise to Leliel, and then thrust once more at the nearest foe. Sariel's eyes narrowed, and he felt a squirming, wormlike worry grow in his chest. A faint golden light shimmered across her sword. Perhaps it was but a trick of the light…but then he saw it again when her sword punched through a soldier's armor as if it were straw.

What game are you playing, Princess?

With his senses heightened, the din of the battle was nearly overwhelming to his ears, but amid the cacophony he heard another sound, one strange and separate. From the west. From the forest.

Hoofbeats.

Sariel blinked away the radiance's blessing and grabbed Faron's shoulder.

"Riders in the woods!" he shouted.

Alex overheard and turned, his hand clutching the hilt of his sword tightly.

"Riders?" he asked.

Sariel rushed past him, ignoring everyone but Sir Tristan, who stood near their center, watching the conflict. When he saw Sariel, his glare could have curdled milk.

"What in Leliel's name are you…"

Sariel pointed past him with his sword.

"In the trees," he said, fibbing just enough so that he might be believed. "I saw riders in the trees. It's a flank!"

The knight looked to the greater forces to the north, then west to the trees. He hesitated only a moment, then began shouting his orders.

"Left pivot," he shouted, realigning them. The line turned, soldiers drawing swords and lifting shields amid the confusion. Faron joined Sariel's side, the two anchoring the new midpoint as the first of the riders emerged from the trees.

It seemed Argylle did have one hundred riders, after all. Forty mounted soldiers arrived, and now free of the forest, they whipped their horses into a charge. They were lightly armored, and their horses smaller and quicker than those crashing the front. Skirmishers, meant to hit and run. Sariel gripped his sword with both hands, the battle slowing, his senses and reflexes enhancing as radiance pounded through his blood.

Forty riders against one hundred infantry. Even with Tristan's squadron prepared for the charge, it would be a bloodbath. Once victorious, the skirmishers would hit the rear of Isabelle's army. In a battle so precariously balanced, the damage and chaos they sowed would trigger a panic.

Sariel and Faron exchanged glances, wordless in their agreement. Faron readied his shield, lifted his sword high over his head, and charged headlong at the riders. Sariel followed, ever the shadow to Faron's heroism. Sir Tristan hollered for them to fall back, to get in line, but neither listened.

Horses shifted, one rider seeking to cut Faron with a ride-by slash, while another sought to trample Sariel beneath his horse's hooves. Sariel planted his feet, and the world itself seemed to slow, his senses heightened and his speed unmatched.

He shifted left, his right foot dropping back to plant and his left foot digging in where he pivoted. Redemption thrust high, the dragon-bone tip easily piercing the hard leather armor the riders wore. The man cried out as the impact flung him from his saddle. Sariel continued the thrust as he shifted his weight from his left foot to his right, pirouetting into a slash at the next rider. The sharpened edge hacked right through the horse's shoulder, broke ribs, and then sliced off both saddle and the leg of its rider.

Faron was far less subtle. His shield leading, he flung his entire weight directly at the charging horse, which panicked at the sight and jumped, its hooves kicking wildly. Faron ducked underneath and thrust his sword straight into the horse's chest. The muscles of his arm bulged, and he cried out as he summoned all his strength. Despite the incredible momentum, Faron halted their charge, froze them momentarily in the air, and then flung them backward. The horse landed awkwardly, crushing the rider while bucking against the pain in its chest from the gaping wound Faron had delivered.

Riders raced past the brothers, but four pulled around, seeing the bloodshed and seeking vengeance. Between the distraction and the killings, Sariel hoped it would be enough for Sir Tristan's group to survive. He kept still, letting the riders come to him. He was not flashy like Faron. He did not barge into the thick of things, demanding all eyes turn his way. For Sariel, every battle, every war he'd lived through, was fought the same. A slow, inexorable certainty.

Where Sariel stood, foes died.

The first rider neared, convinced his height and speed would be enough. He wielded a heavy ax and swung it in a low arc for Sariel's chest. Sariel blocked it with ease, the ax's edge sharp but unable to break dragon bone. A twist of the wrist, and Sariel retaliated, slicing through the man's elbow. Ax and arm went flying, spraying blood as the rider howled. Barely moving, barely hinting at his awareness, Sariel curled low, a sword flashing overhead from a second rider.

Redemption lashed out, its reach unmatched. He carved a gash into the horse's side, cracking its ribs before slicing into the rider's groin and abdomen. The pained horse bucked and turned, tossing the dying man from the saddle.

Beside him, Faron absorbed a sword swing with his shield, his foe pulling back the reins so his horse remained near. Another swing, again into the shield. He was trying to beat Faron down and rely on his height advantage. It would never work. On the third try, Faron thrust his sword straight through the man's elbow, twisted the blade, and then wrenched it sideways, splitting the entire arm in half when the weapon tore free from the rider's fingers. The rider screamed at the pain, and he kicked the sides of his horse to flee.

But Iris leaped upon him, joining the fray alongside her master. The impact of her weight toppled the rider from his saddle, and once he was grounded, the coyote's teeth tore into his face and throat. Another rider, shocked at the sight, tried to stampede directly over Iris and trample her. A furious Faron blocked the way, his shield smashing the horse's skull in and his sword gutting the rider. The horse's momentum continued, and when it and Faron collided, it was the horse who staggered aside and collapsed.

Foes defeated, Sariel shook the blood from his blade and turned his attention to Sir Tristan's group. The riders had slammed into their center, but the hundred had walled up into a solid formation, able to react in time thanks to Sariel's warning. They also outnumbered their foes three to one. Blood flowed on both sides, a far cry from the chaos the skirmishers were meant to inflict.

The arrival was also noticed by the other nearby squadrons, reinforcements from the rear center rushing to join in. Sariel glanced to the front line and saw it holding strong. Princess Isabelle strode the center of the battle, a golden beacon in the chaos, both her sword and cloak stained with blood. As he watched, she slashed open one of the Argylle soldier's throats, pushed him away with her shield, and then lifted her sword to the sky while shouting the name of her goddess.

Yes, the front line would hold just fine.

"No hesitation," Faron said, joining Sariel's side. A bit of blood covered his face and chest from his own victories over the riders. He nodded at the skirmishers, still attempting to wade deeper into the three-stacked lines of Sir Tristan's group. "Deny them their retreat."

They sprinted together, crossing the space in a flash. Their foes were unprepared, their attention locked on the soldiers before them. Sariel and Faron tore into the riders, cutting down their horses and impaling any who sought to flee. Within seconds, it was over, the grass stained with blood and littered with corpses. The reinforcements arrived only in time to see the conflict's end.

Alex pushed to the front, his chainmail chipped at the breast and blood leaking over the left half of his face from a cut across his forehead. He gaped at the brothers.

"How?" he asked. Sariel flicked the blood from his sword, ensuring the trainer saw just how much covered his "oversized bit of bone." Their eyes met. Sariel said nothing, only smiled faintly.

Faron whistled for Iris to join his side, then adjusted his shield on his arm.

"Call us to the front," he said, also ignoring Alex's question. "Let us show you what we can do."

Sir Tristan joined them, his blade wet with blood. His expression was guarded and his mouth locked in a tight frown.

"Did you not hear their trumpets?" the knight asked. "There is no front."

Sure enough, the Argylle commander had sounded the retreat. The back lines fled, trailing after the dwindled remainder of their knights. Those unable to escape flung down their weapons in surrender, Princess Isabelle's soldiers already rounding them up.

Sariel rested Redemption across his shoulder and patted Faron's back.

"Do not worry," he said. "There is always another battle."

Chapter 16

EDER

Eder walked the quiet road of Bridgetop, his faithful Celebrant at his side. When the Tower Majestic cracked in a forgotten age, the upper half had fallen toward the nearby cliff. There it rested, wide and enormous, forming a bridge connecting the Tower Majestic to the grand city of Racliffe nestled against the rocky edge. Over time, homes had been built atop the gently curving surface, growing taller and more densely packed until it had become a full town in its own right.

"I'm getting worried about the reports I'm receiving from our more distant preachers," Madeleine said, walking stiffly beside him. Her black vest and trousers seemed to glow in the starlight. "Reception toward them has soured greatly with our recent annexations. The western people view the church as synonymous with the kingdom."

"They *are* synonymous," Eder said. "It is they who took too long to learn the obvious."

Madeleine glanced at a leaf of paper in her hand, scribbled with notes. A habit of hers, for it was much too dark for her to read it now.

"A mob in Cevenne hung one of our shepherds from the rafters of his church, then set fire to the building. We might want to delay sending out preachers until we can better assess where our faithful will be in the most danger."

Eder paused to admire a mural painted along a storefront, a lovely dance of stars across a blue backdrop. During the day, Bridgetop was a crowded bustle of trade, particularly with goods flowing into the Tower Majestic. Here at night, it was pleasantly calm, the waves crashing against the distant cliffs the only true noise. Taverns, gambling halls, and most other nightly activities were banned from Bridgetop.

Eder much preferred to traverse the expanse at night.

"Those who join the Voice of the Father know the risks they face," he said, referring to the branch of the church that dealt with sermonizing and proselytizing to the nations. "It is where people react with violence that we must focus our efforts. That violence reveals a fear in the heathens that our preachers carry wisdom, and that their brothers and sisters will be open to our words and the healing touch of our hands."

Madeleine hesitated. A patrol of two soldiers approached holding torches above their heads, and she waited until they were gone to speak.

"I suppose we could require the most threatening lands in the west to be voluntary assignments only."

Eder smiled at her. "If that is what you feel is necessary. But do not worry. I know my faithful. We will not be short of volunteers."

They resumed walking the half-mile stretch connecting the Tower Majestic to Racliffe. It always made Eder wish he could have seen the tower before its collapse, when it had been almost triple its current height. A finger of giants, rising out of the ocean to point accusatorily at the stars. Or perhaps Eder was assigning too much of his own biases to the image.

Eder paused beside a nearby home. There was but one road knifing through the center of Bridgetop, forcibly kept clear by law. All else was pushed up against it as closely as possible, the buildings stacked around and atop one another, layer after layer, with some even overhanging the edges on wooden platforms braced with ropes and propped up with wedge beams that connected far below.

This particular home had hung a long flower box underneath a window. Eder wondered how often the owner must fertilize the soil to allow the beautiful flowers blooming there to survive. Fresh water would be difficult, too, in these summer months. Not easy, or cheap, and yet the owner put in the effort to see it done. Eder's pale fingers brushed the petals of a thorned mistflower, their blue shade almost purple in the moonlight.

"A new age approaches," he said softly. "Should the world come crumbling down, would you stand with me, Madeleine? Would you accompany me to the end of all things?"

"Of course I would," his Celebrant said, much too quickly. He turned to her and let her see the radiance in his eyes. If she lied, he would know. The truth would not be denied him.

"Easy words," he said. "Spoken in confidence, not wisdom. You gave no thought to it, Celebrant, and so I ask you again. If the path I walk leads us to oblivion, would you still walk it with me?"

The blond woman crossed her hands behind her, and for a long while she met his gaze, unflinching. This was what he liked best about her, and why he had elevated her to his church's highest station. If pushed, she would set her mind to any task, any problem, and attack it more fiercely than starving dogs would a scared hare.

"I do not believe you lead us to anything but paradise," she said, breaking the silence. "But the change you bring, it has already led to war. Should its fires spread beyond our control, and the Astral Kingdom come tumbling down, I will still stand proudly beside you, my Luminary. This body is transient. Why cherish this life, when my soul shall go to Father's hands come its end?"

Eder picked the mistflower and twirled it, purposefully letting its thorns poke his thumb and forefinger until blood trickled down the stem.

"Not yet," he said. "This cycle of unending sin is not broken yet. But it will be, Madeleine. With your help, it all will be shattered, and humanity set free."

He clenched his fist, thorns cutting deep, his blood dripping to the hardstone street. The mistflower shifted in color, its blue petals darkening, turning black, and then suddenly blooming with light. Little stars burst from its petals, until it was like a night sky contained. He lifted it high above him as he silently addressed the heavens.

I know you are false, he told those distant stars. *And one day, I shall rip through you like the smothering curtain you are.*

Eder turned and tucked the mistflower into Madeleine's breast pocket. The shimmering light of the miniature stars had already begun to fade, becoming more like white pockets of color across petals now more a deep blue than black. Still, a beautiful sight. As he adjusted her vest, his hands briefly brushed across her breast. He caught her looking away from him and blushing.

There was no hiding her lust, not from his eyes. He was yet to grant her that desire. Perhaps he never would. The possibility tempted her. The potential tormented her. Lust, love, and loyalty blended together into a potent mix that made her, unquestionably, his. But for her to maintain that hope, there must always be whispers, hints, and words spoken that could mean one thing, or another entirely...

Eder leaned over Madeleine, so much taller than her, so much more overwhelming a presence. His lips brushed her ear. His warm breath teased her when he whispered.

"Should it be our fate, then let us together walk into oblivion, you and I."

She trembled before him.

"My Luminary," she whispered, unsure of what else to say.

Eder pulled back, and he adjusted the angle of the flower in her vest.

"Come," he said. "I would like to find Nem and be done with this business before the sun rises and the Hanging City wakes."

Though the Tower Majestic had cracked in half, and the upper cylinder fallen onto its side, it had remained very much intact all these unknown years later. This meant below Bridgetop was a second nest of homes and buildings built into the massive hollow space. Given the inability to drive a single nail into the surface of the hardstone, the town was a mess of beams and ropes, supported from platforms built along the lower floor of the tower along with crossbeams running along the surface of Bridgetop.

The two sections were distinct and yet inseparable, a symbiosis Eder greatly admired. A hollow cylinder cracked and lying sideways as a bridge, impenetrable to humanity's tools, and yet they had carved out homes above the churning waters of the sea. Collectively Bridgetop and Underbridge were known as the Hanging City, ruled over by Eder within the Tower Majestic as he did Racliffe across the way.

What had once been windows of the Tower Majestic were now entrances into Underbridge, and it was one such entrance Eder and Madeleine approached. A lone guard stood bored before the gap, which had been surrounded with homes on three sides. A bit of smoke drifted up through the opening from the eternal haze that blanketed Underbridge. The rope ladder down was nailed to the wall of one such home. The guard wore a plain gray tabard with five stars sewn in black, identifying him as lower in rank than the elite guards within the tower. Upon seeing Eder, he startled to a proper upright stance, the sleep vanishing from his eyes.

"Greetings, Luminary," he said, his voice cracking. The man was young. Eder wondered if he'd met him before.

"At ease," he said. "I pray your night has been pleasantly uneventful?"

"It has until your arrival, Your Excellence."

Eder gestured for Madeleine to go first and then followed her down the rope ladder. It wasn't far, just four feet or so before they set foot on a wooden platform that was the top of the mazelike scaffolding that made up Underbridge. From there, it was a series of ladders descending the platforms until reaching the actual bottom, where the largest of buildings were built upon the sturdy, unbreakable hardstone.

While certain delights might be illegal in Bridgetop, the same did not go for Underbridge. Smoke billowed from a hundred torches lighting up its streets. With every ladder they descended, they found a new layer of buildings, most windows open and lit with candles. Songs flowed from a nearby tavern. Not far away was a gambling hall, with two gruff-looking guards set at the front to keep out those lacking the proper amount of coin. Night women leaned at the entrances to the nearly infinite slender corridors and cracks between buildings, though they wisely covered themselves and slunk away when realizing who Eder was.

Eder accepted Underbridge like he accepted all other aspects of humanity's sinful nature. It was inevitable that imperfect beings would seek harmful indulgences. These vices were but tiny blots on the soul compared to the true sins of murder, betrayal, thievery, and false witness. So long as it helped suppress their worst desires, he would turn a blind eye in their direction.

Besides, when seeking to cleanse the sins of dozens of lifetimes, these little vices meant nothing. Once he perfected his methods to render souls completely and utterly clean, all else would fade away. It was a grand goal, perhaps impossible, but one day the whole world would be afforded the focus and attention of the cold cells, stripped of choice, free of temptation, and given purpose only in confessing their sins to loyal servants like Preacher Glasga.

But if Eder was correct about his guess as to the Tower Majestic's purpose, such lengthy and drastic methods might not be necessary.

"What brings us to such a...locale?" Madeleine asked. She despised Underbridge. As she did with most things, she preferred hard lines to define sin and acceptance. A blurred city of gray in the shadow of the Tower Majestic was a thumb in the eye of that desire. Eder did not like visiting, either, but for much different reasons.

"A matter has come to my attention that must be dealt with," Eder said. At last, they had descended their final ladder to the main road, and walked between towering multilayered stores, homes, whorehouses, and gambling halls. The air was blotted with smoke, and the sky a solid black surface without hint of stars or moon. Underbridge was a cave, and what little natural light it possessed came through the windows on the sides.

This was why Eder disliked visiting Underbridge. To be so thoroughly hidden from the stars set his skin to crawling. Instead, the guiding light was a series of oil lampposts unevenly spaced along both sides of the road, so that there were many gaps and deep shadows.

"And what matter is that?" she asked.

Eder smiled at a tubby old man sitting in a rocking chair at the front of a boisterous tavern. Lanterns lit the windows, and within drank a dozen men who would likely climb the ladders come daylight to haul crates and pull carts from Racliffe to the tower.

"Evening, shepherds," the man said. Madeleine opened her mouth to correct him, then closed it. The old man's eyes were milky white. That he could see at all was surprising.

"Why do you not drink within?" Eder asked, pausing.

"Too loud in there," the man said, adjusting the blanket across his body. "Too young. When they start to singing, I like to be a room away. Takes the edge off." He sniffed. "Could you spare a prayer for a believer, shepherd? Sleep has been hard to come by lately. Too many memories that won't leave me be."

Madeleine's eyes widened. A moment of prayer with the Luminary of the Church of Stars was a highly sought-after blessing, with dignitaries of the many little kingdoms throughout Kaus tithing exorbitant amounts of coin for the privilege.

"Such a request is—"

"No, Madeleine, it is all right," Eder interrupted. He stepped onto the porch and placed his hands upon the old man's wrinkled face. Milky eyes stared up at him, hazy and unfocused. Though the stars might be distant and covered, Eder could still feel their presence, just muted, and he called out to them. Their power would forever be his, radiant and limitless. It kissed his eyes, and he saw through the old man's flesh and bone to the soul beyond.

"You've seen much change in this one life, haven't you, Gerald?" Eder said. The old man's mouth dropped. He'd not revealed his name. Eder put his thumbs over the man's lips, shushing him.

"No, be silent," Eder said softly. "Let the song and music fade. There is only us, and your lives. All your lives, Gerald. When you were Langley and Savol and Tarry. You see them, too, don't you? You feel the weight of them as you sleep. You hear the laughter of loved ones you should have long visited in the starlit lands beyond this life."

Eder leaned closer.

"But we are denied them. Your soul should never be so heavy, and your memories never so twisted."

Radiance, visible even to the naked human eye, spun like silver threads from Eder's fingertips. It slid in through the man's eyes, ears, and nostrils, winding its way deep into the hidden soul burning within the organic matter that was his mind. Eder hissed as the memories struck him, now even stronger than before.

Know your place, he commanded, forcing them away. He ordered these past lives, putting them in their proper sequencing. But even as he did, he saw their many sins, affronts to the will of Father. They were so common and simple, Eder had witnessed them countless times before. Life after life, stacked one on top of the other, compounding the debt. The past parted, and Gerald's most recent life rose to the forefront. Again, Eder saw the sins. Lies spoken in greed. A spouse betrayed through infidelity. A friend's coin purse stolen after an argument.

That same friend, pushed from one of the platforms built along Underbridge's windows, to fall to the sea.

Eder's grip on the old man's face tightened, his wrinkled skin stretching as Eder's thumbs slid upward.

"How many years has it been?" he asked as the silver threads brightened. "How many nights have you lain awake in bed, remembering Roeb's screams?"

Gerald pushed the blanket aside, his bony hands shaking wildly. He couldn't reach out. Couldn't stop Eder from imposing his unbreakable will upon him. Eder clutched that wretched moment in this man's life and ripped it free like tearing a thread from a ball of yarn. Gerald screamed, but Eder's palms were over his mouth, muffling it, while his thumbs pressed into the milky eyeballs, rupturing them with a burst of silver light.

"You will remember," Eder whispered. "Every slow, agonizing second of your sin shall be your world. Every thought you felt, every fleeting doubt, all your guilt, your anger, the excitement of betrayal, they will burn forever bright in your chest. Your sight, I deny you. Let your murder be all you see."

Blood and fluid trickled down Eder's wrists. The silver departed. He pushed the elderly man away, setting his chair to rocking. Gerald gasped, weeping blood, and he held shaking hands in the air before him.

"Roeb," he murmured. "Roeb, look, over there, just keep looking. If only you'd listened. If you'd let me keep it." Sobs overcame the words. "I'm sorry. I'm so sorry."

Eder stepped away. Madeleine stood perfectly still, an offered cloth in hand. She kept it for when he must send the devouts to the stars. It was useful now. He took it, cleaned his hands, and gave it back. All the while, her face remained as perfectly still as a statue's. All the while, Gerald wept and cursed his murdered friend's name.

"Come," Eder said. "I have spent long enough in this star-hidden cave."

The rickety sign hanging by a lone screw read NEM'S PLACE, a meager explanation of a store that dealt in curiosities and relics. Tonics supposedly made of faerie wings, qiyan toenails, dragon entrails, and dryad hair filled his disheveled shelves. Many were lies, and Eder suspected Nem had hidden stock involving weeds and mushrooms that were illegal under his laws. He overlooked them, for there were none better at hunting down Etemen artifacts.

"Welcome, welcome," Nem said when Eder entered, Madeleine trailing just behind. He was a burly man, his hair curly and his muttonchops bushy and gray. He hurried around the counter and then dropped to one knee. "I am blessed as ever to be in your presence, my Luminary."

"Stand, Nem," Eder said, in no mood for any theatrics. "You requested a meeting, and so I have come. I pray it is with good reason?"

Nem licked his lips and grinned as he stood.

"The best reason," he said, and hurried back around the counter. He knelt and pulled up one of the floorboards, revealing a trapdoor. Eder watched, fighting against hope. Nem couldn't mean...

But then the man pulled out a stone object the size of his two fists and set it on the counter. Eder's pulse quickened.

"You found another?" he whispered. He'd scoured Racliffe, the Hanging City, and the Tower Majestic when he first took control. The claim had been a search for heretical material counter to Father. The truth of it had been a search for artifacts linked to the tower, scattered throughout cities dating back to the tower's initial collapse countless years ago.

Eder stroked the stone with his fingers, tracing the intricate runes carved upon its surface. All the while, Nem beamed with pride.

"I've had feelers for these since forever," he said. "But this one was in the closet of an old bag who finally passed last week. Her son found it when preparing to move his family in. I take it the same price as always will suffice?"

"Madeleine will send you triple," Eder said, cradling the hardstone against his chest like a child. "Thank you, Nem. May Father's gaze shine lovingly upon you."

"Hopefully not all the time," Nem said. "A man does like to have his privacy on occasion."

Eder ignored him while rushing out the door, Madeleine quickly at his heels.

"Luminary?" she asked, having to hurry to match his long strides.

"This is it," he said breathlessly. "This is the last runestone." He turned to her, stars glittering in his eyes, and he did not hide their burning radiance, so great was his excitement.

"At last, we can awaken the Tower Majestic."

Chapter 17

FARON

The Doremy army pitched tents after the battle, and come nightfall, the rains began. They started light at first, a patter across the tent fabric that helped lull Faron to sleep, but come morning, it was a miserable slog through the mud just to go anywhere.

"For once, I don't envy you your fur," Faron told Iris as he packed his belongings for the march. The coyote glared at him miserably, her fur sopping wet. It highlighted just how skinny she still was, even with the strength and growth Faron's blessing had granted her.

"Hey," Bart said, arriving holding two wooden bowls of porridge. He curled his body over them in an attempt to guard their contents from the rain. "Alex canceled all drills. So we have that good news at least."

Faron accepted the food and ate it greedily, not caring that "dull" was the kindest one could speak of its flavor.

"We have to march a dirt road through a forest amid a downpour," Faron said, and winked at the kid. "Expect that to be the *only* good news for the day."

Bart sought a dry spot to sit, found none, and so remained hunched as he dabbed his fingers into his own bowl.

"Faron," he said, suddenly quiet. "During the battle, I didn't...when everyone rushed the skirmishers, I didn't move. I couldn't. The fighting started, and I just…stood there."

Faron said nothing, only let the young man talk. This was something he needed to learn about himself, and fight through on his own.

"No one's said anything," he continued after a moment. "But I see the way some of them look at me now. They think I'm a coward. Or a dead man. Or maybe both."

He looked to Faron with eyes much too haunted for one so young.

"Is battle always like that? Will it ever get better?"

Faron could not count the number of times he had held this exact same conversation across the centuries. No words, no stories, and no lessons could ever prepare someone for the brutality of war. It was death and violence unleashed, and the cruel truth of one's mortality made manifest.

Well. Everyone *else's* mortality anyway.

"It will not get better," he answered softly. "War will ever be the same. What will change is *you*. It may sound impossible now, but you will grow numb to the pain and the blood. In time, even the fear of dying will become a familiar friend. The choice you face now is the same choice you will face in each and every battle. Will you cower before it? Or will you accept your fear, your uncertainty, and despite it all, fight for those you love, those you trust, and the ideals you hold true?"

Bart's fingers clutched the edges of his bowl so hard they began to turn white.

"I hate it," he said. "I *hate* being so scared."

Faron grabbed his shoulder and squeezed.

"Then fight with hate, if you must. This war is yours now. Do whatever it takes to see its end."

•

The trip through the Telbelt Forest was even worse than Faron had anticipated. The road knifing through the juniper trees was not well maintained, so at times it felt like they were battling overgrown brush as often as they were the deep pits of mud threatening to swallow up the wheels of the supply wagons. The army's mood remained high despite it all, a benefit of having won their first two battles.

Near midday, with them still in the heart of the woods, there came the order to halt.

"Hardly the friendliest of campgrounds," Sariel said, his coat firmly buckled and his back held to the wind. He'd tied his long hair into a ponytail to keep it from sticking to his face, granting him an even more severe look. Over the rain, wind, and rustle of the leaves, it was hard to even hear him.

Curious about the reason for their halt, Faron joined a trio of soldiers who had marched ahead of them. They were all Argylle recruits, though he recognized only one, a grizzled mercenary named Derek whose face bore a litany of scars.

"Did one of the wagons break?" Faron asked them.

"Nah," Derek said. He gestured farther up the road. "But the going's rough enough they're worried it'll happen."

"Are we supposed to pitch our tents atop this mud?" one of the soldiers with them asked. "Or will we be sleeping under the trees all night?"

Faron shrugged.

"We'll find out soon enough."

•

The order indeed came to pitch the army's tents upon a long stretch of the road. Faron did so without complaining, though he still wondered why exactly they had chosen this spot. It was only hours later, as night began to fall, that he heard the reason.

"Turns out there's some caves just off the path," Derek said. He'd joined Faron, Sariel, and Bart in huddling underneath the shelter offered by a cluster of enormous trees growing just off the road. Iris kept nearby, half buried underneath a thick set of brush.

"Caves?" Faron asked. "Why would they care about caves?"

"Caves mean shelter from all this rain," Derek said. "Sounds like the high and mighty will be sleeping well tonight. They even managed to get some fires going, the lucky bastards."

Faron exchanged a look with his brother, an unspoken conversation happening between them.

"It may mean nothing," Sariel said, pulling the collar of his coat higher around his neck. "Was the cave marked?"

"Marked?" Bart asked.

"By the qiyan."

The old mercenary scoffed. "I thought you had a better head on your shoulders than that. You actually believe in the qiyan?"

"That's like asking if you believe in rain or sunshine," Bart said. "There's a hole in a field north of Clovelly, and everyone knows you don't go near it. We even left the whole field fallow, just to be sure. You go into a qiyan cave, you don't come out. It's that simple."

Derek dismissed him with a wave.

"Everyone's so certain they exist, yet no one's seen a qiyan in ages. You know what I think? If you go unprepared into an unmapped cave in the middle of the field, you don't come back because you're dumb and got lost in the dark. Not because the qiyan came and ate you."

"The qiyan don't feast on human flesh," Sariel said, already sounding bored by the conversation.

"But they are territorial," Faron said, and stood. "Will you not come with me, Sariel?"

His brother slumped against the tree and closed his eyes.

"After a day spent marching through mud in the pouring rain, I am taking a well-deserved rest. If you want to warn people foolish enough to ignore qiyan markings, then go right ahead... if you can even make them listen."

Derek pulled out a pouch from his inner pocket, untied its drawstring, and dumped eleven dice into his palm.

"I'm not worrying about those who are warm and dry," he said. "Anyone up for a game of Wounds? What about you, Bart? You know how to play?"

"Play only if no coin is involved," Sariel said, his eyes still closed. "Otherwise Derek will swindle you."

"How could you say that?" Derek asked, sounding more curious than offended. "You don't even know me."

"I know Wounds players. Anyone who owns their own set of dice is not to be trusted."

The old mercenary laughed.

"Fine, fine, nothing at stake but some pride. And what say you, Sariel? Will you join us? Wounds plays better with three than two."

Faron groaned and stepped out from the cover of the trees.

"You're all worthless," he grumbled, and trudged through the mud. He passed soldiers doing their best to pitch tents. Their stakes easily sank into the ground, their grips weak and the tent interiors barely any drier than the outside.

The caves must not be marked, he thought as he found the path off the road. The juniper trees were thinner here, and he found several more tents pitched within their gaps. A couple of soldiers were placed on guard to form a perimeter, all of them looking tired and haggard. Behind them, the ground sloped suddenly and steeply, rising higher as cold gray stone pierced the earth to form craggy, broken points. Three cave openings awaited at the top, and the very sight of the unnatural rise set Faron's nerves afire. He need not even look to know these were qiyan caves.

"Damn fools," he muttered as he approached the perimeter. "How could they not know?"

All three caves looked to be filled with people. Smoke billowed out of them, with fires set just inside so they were sheltered from the rain. Faron ground his teeth. Did they think numbers would keep them safe?

"Halt there," one of the perimeter guards ordered at Faron's approach.

"I need to speak with Princess Isabelle," Faron said. "It is of the utmost importance."

The guard started to scoff, then hesitated. "You're the Ram, aren't you?"

Faron nodded. Well, the simplification definitely made the term more bearable.

"I am. Please let me through."

The guard glanced over his shoulder, looking visibly upset.

"I don't think I can," he said. "Orders are orders. No one is to come through without permission."

"Then get permission," Faron said, fighting for patience. As much as he wanted to storm in and call them all fools, he knew such rash, improper action would only get him threatened and ignored. "Tell whoever you must that Faron Godsight would have a word with Princess Isabelle, and if not her, whoever set up camp within the caves. And make haste!"

Faron added a flex of radiance into the word "haste," granting it power. The guard whistled over another soldier standing nearby.

"Wait here with Faron, will you?" he asked, and then hurried toward the caves without waiting for a reply. The second soldier shrugged, and he stood beside Faron looking miserable in the rain. His hair was long and tied so that it hung over his shoulder like a wet dog's tail.

"Something amiss?" the man asked, water dripping off his helmet in three thick streams.

"I pray not," Faron said, his attention focused past him. Perhaps he was being foolish. There truly were a lot of soldiers here. The qiyan might not risk a battle...

The first soldier returned, and he beckoned for Faron to follow.

"Princess Isabelle will grant you a moment of her time," he said. "Don't waste it."

Faron climbed the rise, inspecting the entrances of the caves as he neared. Sure enough, he found the markings carved into either side, three interlocking triangles, each one hanging below the other. Claimed by the qiyan. They never should have camped here.

The princess knelt beside one of the fires at the entrance of the third cave. Several bedrolls and soft blankets were beside her, drying in the heat. The woman's expression was carefully guarded as Faron approached. Aubert, her family adviser, was at her side. The old man looked miserable as he held his cap over the fire to dry it. Several knights sat with them or stood around looking agitated, and they did not disguise their disdain at Faron's arrival.

"Welcome to my humble little camp, Faron," Isabelle said as he dropped to one knee before her and bowed his head, as was expected of him. A bit of a twinkle lit her eyes. "Or should I call you the One-Man Ram?"

"Ram will suffice, if such nicknames must be used," Faron said, and stood. "Forgive my rush, but I bring warning. These are qiyan caves. They are not safe shelter, and even worse to sleep within. We must leave before all daylight is lost."

Isabelle's eyes narrowed. "You speak of the markings along the entrance."

"Fearful nonsense," one of the knights scoffed. "The qiyan have not bothered us for over a century."

"So you knew?" Faron asked, his bafflement growing along with his frustration.

"We did," Isabelle said. "But I thought them abandoned, and even if not, surely the qiyan would not protest if we use them as shelter from the rain."

"Qiyan tunnels are never abandoned," Faron said. Others glared at him, but Isabelle looked shaken by his words.

"Marshal Oscar shared this fear," Aubert pointed out.

"Where is the marshal now?" Faron asked.

"Farther inside the cave," Isabelle said, gesturing behind her. "He and several of his men took torches to check the cave's limits and ensure our safety. I thought that a fair compromise."

Faron clenched his fists. *Fools, fools, fools!*

"Call him back, now," he said, knowing he was crossing a line. Someone of his status should never speak to his princess thus. One of the knights reached for his sword, but Isabelle glared at him.

"I already have," she said. She hesitated. A hint of worry was added to her words. "He's been gone for much too long. I sent Firth to..."

A scream interrupted her. It contained one word, and it echoed through the stone to the cave entrance.

"Princess!"

Faron crossed his arms, biting down any comment he might make. Best to let this play out. A younger man came running, a torch in hand. His face was pale and his eyes wide with fear. Sweat ran slick across his neck and forehead.

"Princess!" he shouted again, his relief palpable at reaching the entrance. "The soldiers, they...they..."

Isabelle stood and grabbed his wrist. Her eyes bored into his. "Calm yourself, soldier. Breathe deep, and then tell me what you found."

The man obeyed, and when he at last recovered, he spoke steadily, but with haste.

"They were slain," he said. "I don't know what happened. Their weapons were drawn, and it looks like they fought a battle, but if they killed anything, I saw no other bodies."

"Everyone?" Isabelle asked. "What of Marshal Oscar? Did you see him among the bodies?"

The scout shook his head.

"No, my lady. I checked, too. I didn't want to leave anyone behind, but then I heard noises farther into the cave, and I...I..."

The princess hushed him with a word. All around her, knights drew their swords.

"Fetch us torches," one of them said. "We'll go and find the bastards responsible."

Faron closed his eyes and summoned radiance from the well within him. In this, he could not be ignored, and so he projected his power into a single word.

"No."

The knights froze in place, obeying as if the command came from the princess herself. The same, however, could not be said for Isabelle. She only tilted her head to one side.

"Why not?" she asked.

Faron closed the space between them, curious but unable to look into such a matter now. If Oscar was taken, then time was already running out.

"I have had dealings with the qiyan before," he said, revealing as much truth as he dared. "Please, put your trust in me. I will find Oscar, and if he is alive, I will bring him back safely. Anyone else you send inside will only join the ranks of the dead."

Isabelle stared at the dark tunnel leading deeper into the cave. Her frown tightened.

"You believe you can return him to me?" she asked. "Then swear it."

"I swear it."

"Then may Leliel's blessing be upon you, Godsight," she said. "Go, and bring me back my friend."

Faron had left his shield behind with the others, but at least he had his sword.

"A torch," he said, ignoring the grumbling of the knights. "Fetch me a torch. And find my brother Sariel. Tell him to follow me. He is the only other person I trust to navigate these caves and live."

More grumbling, but they obeyed. One of them thrust a torch at Faron, and he accepted it in his free hand. His other drew his sword.

"Be back soon, I promise," he said, winked at the princess, and then raced into the dark unknown.

Chapter 18

FARON

Faron waited until he was beyond sight of the entrance to snuff out his torch. He had no need of its light. Once surrounded by darkness, he let radiance swell within his eyes so that his surroundings appeared to glow as if bathed in soft starlight. A glance to his right, and he saw another set of triangles cut into the gray stone, these even larger than those at the entrance.

"What were you thinking?" he wondered aloud.

Stealth would be impossible here if the qiyan were alert for potential trespassers. They were master shapers of the stone, more at home within dark tunnels than any human was in wide grasslands. Faron ran as fast as he dared, for the ground was slick and his boots still caked with mud.

The tunnel never shifted or split. It was like a singular vein opened within the earth, slanted forever downward. As Faron moved, the cave walls shifted. What was once uneven smoothed out, worked to be an almost perfect semicircle. What had been gray stone shifted in color, darkening into a deep red. It sparkled in Faron's eyes somewhat akin to a gemstone. Rubystone, the qiyan called it.

The humans were madmen to have continued this far.

Another hundred feet past the transition, Faron found the bodies. The cave opened up slightly, the sides widening into an opening. Crumpled rubystone was scattered over the area. Soldiers lay in pools of blood, left wherever they died. Faron knelt beside one, inspecting his wounds. Clean cuts, razor-sharp. Faron suspected the qiyan had hidden within the walls and ambushed the soldiers from all sides as they passed.

Faron put his fingers to the cave floor, closed his eyes, and breathed steadily. He had to confirm before going farther, for his own life would now be in danger. His presence spread throughout the stone; it was like when he scattered his mind in search of food for Iris to hunt, only much slower and less efficient. Already he felt weaker, so deeply hidden from the stars.

Sure enough, he sensed a lone human presence farther down. Marshal Oscar, somehow still alive.

"Deeper in we go," Faron said, rising to his feet. "I did make a promise."

The tunnel widened, the rubystone taking on an even deeper shade of red and its carving all the more intricate. The qiyan had molded it so that it seemed to spiral and dance as he descended the depths. Should he have carried a torch, it no doubt would have looked even more wondrous with the flickering flame to dance throughout the swirls.

The downward slant of the cave floor evened out, and then the tunnel cut hard to the right. Around that turn was an enormous square room, its entrance marked with pillars cut from the rubystone itself. An obsidian table was set in the center of the room, its surface immaculately smooth. Marshal Oscar lay atop the table, his hands at his sides and his expression weirdly catatonic. His hair had been crudely cut, what was once neck length now closely hacked to the scalp. He was stripped from the waist up, and across his body glowed a dozen crimson runes.

Around him stood four qiyan.

Their skin was the dark gray color of the stone at the cavern entrance— at least, what portions that were skin. Across their chests, arms, and faces were patches of what appeared to be small interlocked gold scales. Their hair was long and matted to their bodies, crystalline and faintly translucent. It, too, shimmered a golden color. Their backs were hunched, and piercing through their leather robes were jagged growths of raw gold growing from their shoulders and spines. They were prepared for Faron's entrance, their red eyes shimmering in the darkness as they lifted weapons carved from rubystone.

"Another fool comes running to us," the eldest of the four said, for the growth upon his back was the largest. Unlike the others, he held only a knife, and kept it hovering above Oscar's breast. Runes matching those carved upon Oscar's body flared with light along the blade.

"A fool, perhaps, but one with good intentions," Faron said. He had never learned the qiyan language, nor did he need to. Radiance flowed across his tongue, molding his words so they would be understood, just as it ensured his ears could understand their slow, flowing speech.

The four startled, and they quickly exchanged glances.

"How?" one asked.

"I know you," the eldest said, and he turned and spat. The liquid came out red like blood. "You are not welcome here, immortal. Leave us."

"Gladly," Faron said, and then pointed. "But I am bringing him with me."

The eldest lowered the knife so its tip touched one of the runes. It flared brightly.

"Trespassers," he said. "We are right to take our payment."

"You have already claimed five lives."

"We want not their lives." The knife cut along the flesh, the tiniest groove to draw thin welts of blood to form a connecting line to the next rune. "We want the unworthy gift."

Faron stepped closer. The other three lifted their weapons, two swords and a spear.

"I wish for no more bloodshed," he said. "But I will not watch you commit murder. Retreat, qiyan. Spare him, and leave us in peace."

The knife lifted. Faron tensed.

"Warning was given," the elder said, and plunged the knife.

Faron crossed the space with his sword swinging, his large body turning to slide between the two nearest qiyan. The tip of his sword barely caught the knife on the downward trajectory, batting it aside so it slashed the obsidian table instead. He continued the weapon's momentum, but it struck the gold spires growing from the nearest qiyan's back and clanged off, knocking a dent into the gold and little else.

Faron pushed off the table with his knee, falling backward to avoid being gutted by the spear-wielder to his left. The other chased, rubystone sword slashing with the sharpened edge. Faron caught his balance with his right foot, then parried the hit. The qiyan was strong, but he did not fight like a warrior. None of them did. They were likely protectors of the nearest qiyan village, no different from farmers taking up arms to defend their land against bandits.

Faron's sword cut inward, expertly angled after the parry so his reaction would be far faster than the qiyan's. The tip pierced throat, then sank another few inches until striking the spine. Dark black blood flowed across the steel. Sorrow panged sharp in Faron's chest. Damn Isabelle, damn the qiyan, damn everyone involved, he wanted none of this!

He ripped the sword out and then flung himself at the spear-wielder. He dodged another thrust, then used his forearm to shove the spear away. His sword cut twice. The first struck the golden scales across the biceps and deflected off. The second went higher, along the collarbone and neck to open the qiyan's windpipe. He gargled blood, clutching at his throat as the light in his red eyes died.

Faron deflected another frantic strike, saw the elder readying his knife, and then vaulted over the table. The elder panicked, and he scurried around, walking with his upper back hunched and one leg limping. The other qiyan rushed to help him, slashing with wild strikes through the air. Faron crossed blades with him twice, then kicked, pushing him away. Undeterred, the qiyan lifted his sword overhead and charged, a guttural battle cry bellowing from his throat, one Faron's radiance need not translate for his mind.

One quick step forward, and Faron's sword was buried to the hilt in the qiyan's stomach. Blood, warm and sticky, flowed across his hand and wrist. Faron saw the qiyan gape, saw his sword fall from limp hands. He ripped his weapon free and then plunged it deep once more, this time to the heart.

The last thing he wanted was for the qiyan to suffer.

When Faron freed his blade, he turned to the elder, who cowered at the tunnel path leading toward the surface.

"No reinforcements," Faron said. "No sacrifices. If you wish to live, give me your promise. If so, I'll return to the surface with Oscar here and order the soldiers to move camp."

The elder's knife shook in the air before him. He was frightened. Uncertain.

"We would be fools to trust the words of a human," he said.

"And I am no human."

"Your whole family claims such, but we know the truth of you, immortals. You are more human than you would ever admit."

Faron lifted his sword. "Give me your answer, qiyan. My patience is ended."

The elder hesitated a moment longer and then lowered the blade.

"I—"

The sound of cracking stone filled the cave, and then Redemption emerged from the elder's chest, having broken through the golden growth on his back. The elder gasped, struggling to speak but unable to fill his lungs. Sariel ripped the blade free, and with it no longer supporting him, the elder collapsed on his stomach and then lay still.

A flick of his blade, and Sariel cast the black blood from the dragon bone.

"Must you always get involved?" he asked.

"They killed five men," Faron said, trying, and failing, not to be angry.

"And now four qiyan are dead. Well done." Sariel rested his sword across his shoulders and nodded at the obsidian table. "At least the marshal lives. Banish their magic so we can leave."

Arguing was pointless. Faron turned his attention to the marshal. The man had not moved since Faron's arrival, and unless one watched closely, it would seem like he did not even breathe. It was a potent paralysis and would last for days if it went unbroken.

Faron closed his eyes and hovered his hands over Oscar's body. He did not need his eyes open to see the runes glowing hot in his mind. Blood magic. Unique to the qiyan, so far as Faron knew. Another reason to avoid their caves. The days of qiyan raids upon the surface were long gone, but they still eagerly captured anyone foolish enough to trespass. Silver threads flowed from his open palms, latching on to the symbols. One by one, the red faded, becoming dried blood that flaked away on an unfelt wind.

When the last was gone, Oscar gasped in a deep breath and then lurched to a sit.

"Monsters!" he screamed.

"Easy there," Faron said, grabbing him by the wrists. In the pitch black, with neither Faron nor Sariel carrying a torch, the man would be completely clueless as to his surroundings. "It's me, Faron. My brother Sariel is with me. We've come to bring you back to the surface."

"Faron…" The marshal relaxed and no longer fought against the arms holding him. "The one Isabelle blessed with sight?"

"That's the one." Faron tucked his arms underneath Oscar so the man could lean against him. "Just walk with me, all right? And trust me to get us there."

"I'll try," Oscar said, unsteady on his feet. "But it feels like I am sick with the strongest ale imaginable."

Sariel went on ahead, not bothering to wait. Faron followed, the heavy thud of Oscar's boots the only sound. He kept a quick pace, muttering simple encouragements to the still-groggy Oscar. That grogginess would hopefully keep the man from realizing that Faron and Sariel were easily navigating the pitch black without the aid of a torch or lantern.

At last, they reached the surface, a score of soldiers nervously waiting. Upon seeing them, Isabelle pushed through the line and ran toward Oscar. Faron separated from the marshal, thinking Isabelle was to embrace him, but instead she slowed and clasped Oscar's hands in hers. Her wide smile lost a bit of its luster.

"Your hair," she said.

"Will grow back," Oscar said, and grinned at her even as he slumped to his knees. "Forgive me, Your Highness, but standing is…difficult."

Isabelle retreated, and immediately others were there to help Oscar up and bring him to Rowan for a look over. Faron suspected the fresh air would do him good, for it was anathema to the qiyan and their magic.

Sariel departed with nary a word. Isabelle glanced at him, then shook her head and turned her gaze to Faron. His insides warmed at the smile that stretched the gentle curve of her lips.

"Faron Godsight, you saved my dear friend, he who has watched over me since I was a child." She offered her hand. "Name any request, any boon, and it is yours."

Faron dropped to one knee, well aware that others were watching them, and took her hand in his.

"You have already graced me with prayers to return my sight," he said. "What deeds of mine will ever repay you for that miracle, Your Highness?"

He met her eyes, saw the intrigue within them, and her fierce intelligence studying his words.

"But if my lady would insist," he continued. "A kiss upon your fingers would be more than ample payment."

The tiniest bit of color flushed her neck.

"A payment granted," she said.

Faron bowed his head and pulled her hand closer, watching her all the while. Her very touch felt like lightning. The power in her voice, her ability to ignore his radiance-blessed orders . . . and her unmistakable beauty, they all left him wondering.

His mouth pressed against the curve of her fingers, slowly, softly, to ensure she felt the warmth of his lips upon her skin. Her eyes never left his, even when she called out the order to relocate camp.

Her hand, in his grasp, faintly trembled.

Chapter 19

SARIEL

I suppose this is all your doing," Sir Tristan said as he paused before Sariel and Faron in the middle of their squadron's formation. A wide field stretched out before them. Idyllic. Peaceful. Only the approaching army marred the beauty.

"We have found a place of honor upon the battlefield," Sariel said, not bothering to hide his sarcasm. "Why do you protest?"

The knight gestured to the Casthe army approaching on the other side of the field.

"Because as good as you two are, you're not enough to make up for what we face." He stepped closer and lowered his voice. "I expect the same effort from you as before. Otherwise, a lot of good but unprepared men and women are about to die, and yes, I do put that on your heads."

The knight left to check on the rest of the formation.

"He's right to be angry," Faron said, staring across the field as he scratched Iris's head.

"I do not care," Sariel said truthfully.

With how Sir Tristan's squadron had taken down the charging riders on their own, combined with the princess's growing interest in Faron since naming him Godsight, the whole group had been elevated to the front ranks, lining up not far from where Isabelle's own forma-tion marched in the heart of the army. Marshal Oscar walked beside her, his head freshly shaved to remove the mess the qiyan had made of his hair.

The lad Faron had befriended, Bart, said something Sariel could not hear. As Faron consoled him, Sariel directed his attention to the approaching army. After taking both river crossings, Isabelle had guided her forces northward, looting what supplies she needed from the vil-lages she passed while ordering that the people remain untouched. They would be her people soon, she insisted, and she did not desire to inspire hatred in their hearts.

Sariel doubted that did much to remove the sting of the stolen food, but it was an attempt, he supposed. They later met up with two thousand soldiers she had kept behind in Doremy, and together they made their way toward Vendom. At last, with nearly two-thirds of Argylle taken, King Bentley sent his own army to counter. Isabelle had the greater numbers, but Sariel frowned as his blessed vision granted him sight of the striped yellow-and-black shirts of men walking the front line, jars swaying from their staffs.

"An alliance born of desperation," Sariel muttered upon seeing preach-ers of the Church of Stars. Rumors had reached the army that King Bentley had pledged his kingdom's loyalty to the church in a bid for aid. A foolish ploy, in the long term, given the love the common folk showed Leliel, as well as their distrust toward the faith encroaching from Racliffe to the far east. But with Isabelle claiming herself Leliel's chosen, the church was a natural ally. The question now was how much use those preachers would serve in a battle.

"Do you see them?" Sariel asked. His brother spent a moment looking, then nodded.

"Foul users of stolen radiance," he said. "They'll be a problem."

"Which makes them *our* problem," Sariel said. "We can't let Eder's faithful stymie what little progress we have made."

Faron lifted his sword and shield as he stretched his arms and back.

"You worry over nothing," he said, and grinned at him. "Me and Iris could take this whole army on single-handedly. With you there, it'll be a breeze."

Beside him, Iris barked, and Sariel reluctantly grinned back at the beast. She was larger than ever, steadily growing in strength from the blessing his brother had given her.

"I'm not sure I trust Faron," he told the coyote. "Which means I must trust you instead to pick up his slack."

Trumpets sounded, their order for Isabelle's army to march drowning out Iris's excited bark. Immediately after, the big man, Alex, slid into formation to Sariel's right, his padded leather armor looking meager compared to his bulky frame. An enormous ax rested upon his shoulder.

"Hope you're able to repeat your earlier miracle," he grumbled over the rising din of rattling armor and weaponry. "Because otherwise we're all dead as shit."

Sariel flashed him a smile.

"I am not a maker of miracles, but I will kill the foes before me. When the bloodshed is ended, we shall see if it was enough."

Alex shuddered. "Such a coldhearted bastard you are."

The space between the armies shrank, and the nerves grew among Isabelle's forces. It was a good spot for a battle, Sariel admitted. A clear field outside the town of Greenberg, with thin, short brush easily trampled. No forests about, either, and few distant hills. There would be no ambushes, no tricks. A straight battle, which King Bentley must have believed his soldiers capable of winning.

Sariel adjusted Redemption across his shoulders, his grip on the smoothly carved hilt tightening. The preachers were the only unknown, and it was they who headed the enemy formation, their jars lifted high and their voices singing, audible even from afar.

Pallid light grew within the jars, gold and sickening. Sariel watched, analyzing the reaction, and then understood.

"Close your eyes!" he shouted, projecting his voice with a hint of radiance so hundreds of soldiers would hear him over the din. "Do not watch!"

In unison, the jars blazed with sudden, ferocious light. It washed over

Isabelle's army, and though its power was nothing compared to the radiance innate to Sariel, it was like a gut punch to those who did not turn away. Soldiers stumbled and staggered, and many vomited, unable to control their stomachs. Sariel shot a glance at Isabelle and was surprised to see her standing tall, her sword lifted above her as the light gathered for another barrage.

"The goddess is with us!" she bellowed. "Do not fear their evil!"

Another flash. More shouting and fearful cries, but this time the majority had cast their gazes to the dirt. A meager comfort, and a complete wreck of their organized march mere moments ago. Meanwhile, Bentley's army surged forward, accompanied by trumpet shouts and victorious battle chants. The ground vibrated beneath Sariel's feet. He readied his sword.

"Open me a path through their front line," Sariel told his brother, his attention locked on the preachers, who fell back toward the middle of the attacking army. "The radiance thieves are mine."

"Won't be easy," Faron said. "They're pretty spread out."

Sariel narrowed his eyes, his instincts taking over and his reflexes heightening.

"It won't matter."

More trumpets, these from Isabelle's side, giving the order to meet their enemy's charge. Faron and Iris took off like a shot, and Sariel trailed just behind them as their shadow. Together the three led the assault, the rest of Isabelle's army hurrying to keep up. A faint smile spread across Sariel's lips at the sudden uncertainty he saw on the faces of their foes. Two mad brothers and a coyote, racing ahead of their allies? Surely they had a suicide wish?

Faron struck his shield and sword together, bellowing a deep, wordless cry. No fear in them, only fear in the eyes of their foes, and then they slammed into the front line. Faron was an unstoppable bull, his strength fully unleashed. Soldiers were flung aside with every hit of his shield, toppling bodies into one another in a tangled mess of limbs. His sword cut quick and wild, denying his foes a chance to regroup or surround him. Iris kept close to his left, a shield sister without a shield. Her snarls brought hesitation, and those foolish enough to close the space found their blood on her teeth. When the pair should have been overwhelmed by sheer numbers, instead a wide space opened around them.

In that space, Sariel was a deadly shadow. Despite his speed, his movements were calm and controlled. Each slash of his long dragon-bone blade maximized both reach and efficiency in the slaughter. A twist here, and two soldiers died. A pivot there, and his sideways slash cut down three, their swords batted aside by his might and their armor crumbling against the impossible edge.

"Praise be to our Father!" a nearby preacher shouted, and that was Sariel's cue to advance. He sprinted past his brother, his movements a blur and Redemption hungry. The space Faron created led Sariel into the deeper lines, and he arrived at the same time as the rest of Isabelle's army. Amid that thunderous clash of steel, Sariel weaved and cut toward the first of the preachers. The man stroked the jar of insects, a song on his lips, and then came the disorientating flash.

It meant nothing to Sariel, a buzz within his mind that might have been a roar to others. Argylle soldiers tried to seal him off. They failed. Limbs flew. Blood flowed. Sariel drove his sword deep into the preacher's chest, turned the blade, and then tore it free, killing two more soldiers with the movement. Screams followed. Isabelle's army pushed inward, the Argylle front line crumbling and the back line hesitant and fractured by the two brothers' assault.

Sariel planted his feet and went to work, shattering weapons and cutting down any soldier foolish enough to challenge him. Bodies built around him, and then he was moving again, denying them a chance to gather themselves. Back into the space Faron opened, now crowded with Isabelle's soldiers to rally at his side. Beyond them, to another preacher.

The noise of the battle softened in Sariel's mind. He saw his foe, and he knew his purpose. Wielders of stolen radiance were dangerous and needed to die, without question, without mercy. With his dragon-bone blade, he would make right this wrong. His enemies swung their weapons at him, but they felt so slow, so weak. He batted aside frantic slashes, severed the limbs that held the weapons, and then pressed on.

The preacher saw Sariel's approach and panicked. The jar swung before him as he screamed out his faith to his beloved Father.

A ring of golden light burst from the hollow center of the jar and flew at Sariel like a disc. Sariel dodged aside, the swirling creation of radiance cutting a gash across his coat before continuing. He glanced behind him, saw it slice two Doremy soldiers in half. The death spurred Sariel on, for it was proof of all he believed. Such power should never be in human hands.

The preacher prayed for the creation of a second ring of light. Redemption opened his throat before he could finish that prayer. The jar hit the churned earth, and Sariel stomped it with his boot, shattering glass and freeing the insects. They buzzed up into the air, frantic in their sudden freedom. Sariel flashed a wave of unseen radiance into them, turning their ire toward the Argylle army, so that they buzzed and bit confused and frightened soldiers.

Goal completed, he retreated closer toward the Doremy line, batting aside panicked attempts to overrun him and killing several foolish enough to fall within reach of his sword. All the while, he looked for the next preacher. He found him facing off against Princess Isabelle and her most trusted contingent of soldiers. The princess herself led the way, her shield strong and her sword strikes skillful and well trained. The preacher raised his jar, the insects within swarming in circles so fast they were a black blur. He shouted out his love to Father, and golden light washed over her squad. Those beside her faltered, but not her. She blocked her foe's slash with her shield, gutted him with a thrust, and then lunged at the preacher.

The waves of light might not have meant much to her, but the sudden hands of gold that burst from the preacher's chest were another matter. They were ethereal and unnatural in size, six-fingered and grasping. They passed right through Isabelle's shield to grab her wrists, and she cried out at their touch.

"The fate of all heretics!" the preacher shouted, and readied a dagger from his belt.

Sariel tore a bloody swath through four soldiers, the shower of gore from their collapsing bodies the preacher's only warning before Sariel's dragon-bone blade punched through his throat, ending his triumphant cry. A twist, and he severed the spine, dropping him to the ground, his head connected to his body by a thin strip of muscle and skin.

The hands dissipated, freeing Isabelle. Their eyes met, and he had time to offer the faintest of smiles before her soldiers recovered and swarmed about her, forming a new shield wall. Not that it was necessary. Trumpets sounded from all directions, the Argylle army calling a retreat. With Faron, Sariel, and Iris wrecking the center, the line had bowed inward, and with it, the outer edges swept up and hit from two sides. Victory quickly followed.

A barking coyote stole his attention. Iris came bounding over, Faron calmly approaching behind her. Blood coated them both, none of it theirs.

"Another victory," Faron said as the Doremy army chased after stragglers and rounded up those who threw down their weapons to surrender. Sariel rested his sword across his shoulders, swept a bit of loose hair from his face, and smirked. He noticed Isabelle from the corner of his eye, watching him closely despite Marshal Oscar informing her of the state of their forces. His smirk grew, and he purposefully turned away.

"Was it ever in doubt?"

Chapter 20

FARON

After the victory at Greenberg, Isabelle's army spent the next week marching north, making its way toward the nation's capital of Vendom. What reports Faron overheard painted King Bentley as frightened and desperate, abandoning all outer lands and preparing the capital for a lengthy siege. So it was strange when, one morning, their marching orders directed them not north, but to the east.

"Did Bentley muster a real army after all?" Faron wondered aloud. He and his brother sat by a small campfire, freshly burning to ward off the morning chill. A faint few stars still lit up the pale sky.

"Or she fears an ambush on the main road," Sariel said. He shrugged. "It is too early for such pondering. If you're curious, go ask."

It would be a bit longer before the cooks arrived to dole out their porridge, so Faron shrugged and patted Iris on the back. The coyote slept beside him near the fire, and she opened a single eye at him to glare.

"Stay with Sariel," Faron said as he stood.

Iris snorted, closed her eye, and went back to sleep.

"I don't anticipate her being a bother," Sariel said as he added another few twigs he'd scrounged up to the fire.

Faron trudged through the quiet morning camp, nodding greetings at the few who were up and about. He thought about asking Alex, or perhaps Sir Tristan, but decided against it. Building a relationship with Princess Isabelle was key, and so he made for her tent instead.

No guards, just Isabelle already awake, packing maps and tokens from her table while two handmaidens gathered up her things from the small dressers they lugged around on wagons. Isabelle noticed his arrival and hesitated.

"Yes?" she asked.

Faron flashed her his grandest smile.

"Those of us who are awake are getting confusing orders," he said. "I thought I'd come hear clarification from Leliel's chosen herself."

It was very much a breach of both protocol and chain of command to come here directly, but he'd had her eye ever since his injury, and his rescue of Marshal Oscar had further indebted her to him. He fought off a smile. His kiss upon her hand had also gained her attention, for a very different reason.

"Sally, Trisha, a moment, please," she said, and the two women hurried out with quick, polite nods. Once they were alone, Isabelle gestured to a small, half-curled piece of paper remaining on the table.

"You get along well with my soldiers," she said, sounding both tired and bubbling with nervous energy. It was a strange mix, coming from someone who always seemed so regal and in control. "Perhaps you can help me decide."

Faron picked up the note and skimmed the message. It was short and to the point. Her father, King Henri Dior, had finally passed away after a yearslong illness. Isabelle was to return to Doremy's capital of Leyval to be coronated her nation's new queen. Faron set the note down, his mind racing.

"Decide what?" he asked.

Isabelle grabbed her sword belt from where it rested atop her dresser and began strapping it on.

"We will be putting a halt to our conquest and diverting our march for a visit to Leyval," she said. "Should I keep quiet the reason? The death of a king is always a tenuous moment for a kingdom, especially in wartime.

Do I make a show of mourning? Where now lies the path that best guides us to victory?"

Faron disliked her uncertainty, unbecoming of the woman he knew.

"*Are* you mourning?" he asked quietly.

Isabelle yanked the belt much too tightly and then held the leather in a quivering hand.

"No," she said. "I have mourned his passing for months now." She looked up at him. "I feel relief. I feel pride, for I shall be queen. What I do *not* feel is guilt for either emotion, Faron, but what of those who follow me? Will they understand?" She hesitated. "Aubert says they may view me as heartless and cruel if I do not mourn my father properly."

Faron crossed the room to lift her shield up from where it leaned against her bed. He held the polished steel out to her.

"I think your people love you," he said, and meant every word. "Take us to Leyval, and with all haste. Those who fight for their princess will fight all the harder for their queen."

•

"Beautiful," Bart said a week later when staring up at the walls of Leyval. "How could anyone think to conquer it?"

"Far bigger cities have fallen than this," Faron said as they marched toward the open gates, Iris close to his hip and looking nervous at the sheer number of people. "But can't say I would relish the attempt, either."

It had been close to a hundred years since Faron had visited Leyval, the capital city of Doremy, and he was impressed by its growth. The city was built up against the Warmwind Mountains, walled off with stone, and then ringed with seven towers. The towers were new, and the main portcullis significantly thicker and better reinforced than he remembered. Storming those walls would be unpleasant, and given the abundance of mountain springs that flowed from the Warmwinds' peaks into the city's many wells, a siege could drag out for a dangerously long time.

Sir Tristan's group marched near the front, matching the growing reputation Faron and Sariel had given them. The respect was welcome, though still far from what Faron desired. If he and Sariel were to influence the zealous Isabelle, he needed her to trust him fully and consider

him a confidant. Close, though, he was definitely close. That she had
invited him to join her table at the coronation feast was sign of that.

Faron grinned at the wide-eyed Bart as they passed through the portcullis and into city streets walled on either side with enormous pine buildings, their fronts waving little black strips of cloth as a sign of mourning.
Faron had declined that invitation to her table, of course. No one else
in Sir Tristan's group had been invited to join him, not even Sariel. He
needed Isabelle to understand they were all together. There would be no
plucking him out of his group of friends, whose loyalty he had carefully
cultivated like a gardener planting and watering a precious plot of land.

"You never visited anywhere outside Clovelly, did you?" Faron asked.

"No," Bart said, shaking his head. "This city is...Just look at it!"

"I could take you to a few places worth visiting," Derek said, listening
in from behind them. Faron glanced over his shoulder.

"Would they be places Bart's mother would approve of him visiting?"
he asked.

"Not any of the fun ones!" Derek said, and winked.

Bart blushed, but he stood tall and tried to hide his discomfort.

"Let's worry about the feast first, all right?" he said.

"Fair enough!" Faron said, clapping excitedly. "A feast, and a
coronation!"

•

Doremy's castle was far more elegant than one might expect to find,
given the squat, utilitarian look most of Leyval's homes bore. Its stone
walls were painted white, and its inner courtyard encapsulated not with
stone but with wide iron bars to allow even those passing by a glimpse of
the rows of eulmore trees surrounding carefully trimmed circles of fiery
blanketflowers.

Tables filled the courtyard, and in the left half the bulk of the army
sat with mugs in hand. Hundreds of city folk joined them on the right,
though plenty intermingled, with soldiers eager to tell stories of the multiple victories that had followed since the war began. The food was hardly
extravagant, mostly buttered clapbread, but the ale flowed freely, and
it did not take long for nearly everyone to be a bit red in the face. The

night ran deep, and the dozens of candles lit upon the tables started to dwindle low.

"It's a shame we won't get to witness the coronation," Rowan said, sitting on a little stool next to Faron. "I've never seen Isabelle in a dress. I bet she looks beautiful."

"You sure she's even wearing one?" Alex asked. The big man had joined their table and downed two enormous mugs already. He elbowed an annoyed Derek next to him as if he were about to tell the funniest joke. "I bet she'll take her vows in full plate. That's our Bastard Queen, ain't it?"

Faron looked to the castle. Its doors were open, granting a glimpse into the interior, where dozens more gathered, drinking and feasting from far more elegantly stocked tables. They were the nobility, and not just of Doremy. Rumors abounded that King Allan of Armane was in attendance. Some hundred years or so ago, Doremy and Armane had been one nation. With the king's arrival, hopes ran wild that, because of Allan's open hatred of King Bentley, he would be willing to unify the lands once more.

Inside, the three lords of Doremy would officially coronate Isabelle Dior Queen of Doremy. Outside, the soldiers would hear only a hint of the fanfare and the subsequent trumpet calls. A bit of a shame, but Faron was fine with that. At least he could drink and eat to his heart's content without upsetting some uptight noble. He grinned at Bart, Rowan, Alex, Derek, and then Iris sitting quietly underneath the table.

"Hungry?" he asked softly, tossing a bit of bread to her. She snatched it up and lay back down to chew. The coyote was nervous, but she leaned her weight against his leg, his presence comforting to her.

Faron smiled. Yes, the company was definitely better out here.

"Where's your brother off to?" Alex asked, stirring Faron from his thoughts.

In answer, Faron gestured to the far western edge of the surrounding iron fence. Sariel leaned against the fence, Redemption propped across his shoulders and his head turned low. If not for the tankard of ale he occasionally sipped from, one might believe he had nodded off.

"Lurking," Faron said. "It's what he does best."

"Not great at making friends, is he?" Derek asked. "Such a dour sod. Does he not know this is a celebration?"

"Oh, he knows." Faron drained the last of his current cup and lifted it high above his head to call for another. "He just doesn't care."

"Well, *I* care!" Derek insisted, and he lifted his own cup. "The king is dead. Long live the queen!"

"Long live the queen," others echoed, and Faron was all too happy to join in.

Not long after, trumpets sounded, and cheers roared from within the castle. Faron munched on a bit of bread and relished the noise. He had chosen well with Isabelle. Already a queen, and her longtime foe in the Casthe royal family was about to be ground underneath her heel. Most important of all, Faron sensed no desire in her to stop. The goddess called for her to cleanse Kaus of the Church of Stars, after all...

Those seated at the tables near the castle entrance hurried to stand, with others rising like a wave spreading toward the outer limits. Faron stood, curious, and saw the answer in Queen Isabelle walking the centerline path between the tables, flanked on one side by a finely dressed Marshal Oscar in resplendent plate. King Allan was on the other, decked in furs and with a beard stretched down to his stomach. Positioning the king in such a place of honor beside Isabelle was certainly no accident.

"She gonna give a speech?" Derek asked, stumbling as he tried to stand and nearly falling over, he was so badly intoxicated. Rowan snagged his wrist to steady him.

"If she does, you need to shush so we can hear it," she said. "And put that drink down, you oaf, before you vomit all over yourself."

"Yes, surgeon."

Faron was more than tall enough to see over the tables, though Bart climbed up on his own stool to join him. His eyes lit with a wonder that Faron envied. This whole ordeal had to feel like a dream to the young man. To go from a tiny village, to fighting in several victorious battles, and now to witnessing a queen's coronation? Better than he had any right to hope for.

Bart need not have bothered, for Isabelle herself climbed atop one of the tables, not waiting for those there to clear it. Alex had joked she would be wearing her armor, and though it was true, it had never looked so finely polished before. It was also dressed up with blue cloth that weaved through the creases, hanging in long strips near her legs as well as forming a cloak to trail behind her. The crown of Doremy rested on her head, thin and silver with a single canary tourmaline set across the front. Her sword was strapped to her thigh, and her shield rested comfortably on her left arm. The message was clear. Isabelle would be a warrior queen, and her reign one of conquest.

"People of Doremy!" she called out, and the crowd fell into a tense, eager silence. Faron pulsed a tiny amount of radiance to his eyes, just enough to ensure that he saw Isabelle as if she stood mere feet away. Her image now clearer, he spotted the little silver threads dangling from her hair, which, while still long, now bore multiple thin plaits from which dangled white ribbons. The sudden clarity of her, beautiful and armored, stole Faron's breath.

"I would give a message, not only to those of influence, land, or nobility," Isabelle continued. "I speak to those who toil the fields, who trim the gardens, and who sweat beside blistering ovens. I address not only the safe, the cloistered, and the elderly, but also the strong and brave who fight alongside me in a war for Doremy's rightful ascension. To those who live, and those who die, equal together in the arms of the goddess."

Faron's eyes widened. Something...something was amiss. Isabelle's words, they seemed to ripple the very air. All around her, faint gold sparks burst to life and then faded like fireflies. Could no one else see?

"Of Leliel's Four Pleas, the one I cherish most is the fourth and final," Isabelle continued. "'Be kind, my children, for you all belong in my arms.' Nothing more clearly reveals her love than this. All of you, no matter your birth, your blood, or your past. All of you, regardless of your failures, the life you have lived, the choices you have made, or the future you both fear and cherish. *All* of you belong. You deserve to be held. To be loved. To know the goddess smiles down upon you."

The crowd was starting to notice, too. The gold in her eyes shone as if there were lanterns behind her irises. She drew her sword and then stabbed it into the table before her.

"And the Church of Stars would deny you that love," she cried. "They would cast innumerable sins upon you, a dozen lifetimes of bleeding lashes, and call you wretched. They would demand blood, sacrifice, and repentance, all while insisting you are nothing, *nothing*, in the eyes of their cruel, judging Father. It cannot be allowed. I refuse. The people of Kaus shall not spend their lives with their souls enchained!"

Faron's heart was in his throat. The entire garden, and the thousands of people gathered within, were as silent as the grave. Even Iris had crawled out from underneath the table to watch, her ears raised and her nose sniffing the air. The crowd was enraptured, and rightly so. Lightning crackled across Isabelle's hands and the surface of her shield. With her every word, Faron saw a wave of gold light wash across the crowd.

Radiance. It was *radiance*.

"I have heard the call of my goddess," Isabelle shouted, her voice reaching a crescendo. "I have felt the touch of her hands. I know many of you disbelieve. I know many of you whisper, and wonder, but let this be the night that ends all doubts. Let this be the night where I am not alone in my blessing."

She lifted her arms. All the world froze.

"Let this be the night when Doremy hears Leliel's voice!"

Four ethereal wings burst from underneath her blue cloak, sparkling like scattered gold dust. They spread wide, ruffling with feathers. Lidless eyes blinked at the joints, mirroring those carved into the countless Leliel statues scattered throughout Kaus. Isabelle rose higher, and when she spoke, the radiance pouring off her tongue washed over the crowd in a tremendous wave that left Faron mesmerized. This...this matched power that even Eder might struggle to achieve.

"I am chosen, but I am not alone," she said. Her voice was deeper, and it seemed to thunder throughout the courtyard. Her eyes blazed, the whites completely vanished behind a shimmering sheen of gold. "I am blessed, but I am not the only one. I weep for my father's passing, and I rejoice for the legacy he has left me. I lament the ages passed, and I burn with desire to build a new age, one of unity and glory in a world that has known only fracture and chaos."

Higher. Higher. The wings fluttering in a sudden wind that billowed from all directions. Her legs dangled beneath her, and her hair whipped wildly as the crowd gazed up at her. Iris let loose a moon-song howl, aching in its cry. Its longing, its loss, felt so fitting, none even cast the coyote a second glance.

"Unity, my beloved!" Isabelle called to the last. "All of you, held safely within my arms."

Tears swelled in Faron's eyes. This wasn't the stolen radiance of the church's preachers and their loathsome jars. This was a gift unheard-of in all of Faron's lifetimes. Radiance, born within a human, and manifested in glory to the goddess.

A goddess Faron had never believed in.

Isabelle descended back to the table, and her wings shimmered away, scattering like dust upon the wind that slowly died. Her feet touched the wood. She pulled her sword free and held it overhead, as she herself wept, the golden glow of her eyes no longer hidden.

Never before believed, but now he wondered.

A lone voice pierced the sudden silence that followed, startling Faron from his thoughts. It was Bart, hollering with his hands cupped to the sides of his mouth.

"Goddess save the Queen!"

Marshal Oscar offered his hand to Isabelle so she might step down from the table, and he echoed the statement with his own deep voice.

"Goddess save the Queen!"

The crowd took up the cry, soldiers, commoners, and nobility alike. Faron joined in, the chant sweeping away his uncertainties and confusion. Radiance in a human...It couldn't be, and yet it was. A queen for all ages. A warrior to tear down the Astral Kingdom.

"I don't believe it," Rowan muttered beside Faron. "I...I mean, I did believe, in her, but I didn't expect...that gift. It was beautiful. So beautiful. Leliel, forgive me for ever doubting."

Faron took her hand and squeezed it, sympathizing with her shock. To see a human wielding radiance—

He froze, and a chill pierced his spine. A human with radiance. He looked to the iron fence, his throat tightening and his revelry slipping away into gnawing worry.

Sariel was nowhere to be found.

Chapter 21

SARIEL

The night was dark when Sariel vaulted over the gray brick of the walled garden, easily clearing the spikes along the top. He landed in a crouch, hidden behind a row of roses. Redemption weighed heavy across his shoulders.

It must be done.

The Warmwind Mountains' slopes were nothing like the grand spires that protruded from the earth at Spineridge, but what they lacked in beauty they made up for in survivability. Multiple streams flowed from within the stone to exit as various waterfalls. Most were channeled into communal wells and rivers, but not all. At the highest portion of the Leyval Castle grew the Walled Garden, its many trees and flowers watered by an isolated stream.

Guards patrolled every entrance, and two more stood chatting with each other at the crossroads in the garden's center. Sariel bypassed them with ease, his footfalls silent across the lush grass. He knew how to track the movements of a man's eye, how to distribute his weight, and how to keep low and quick, his body wrapped in his black coat, so that even crossing open grass he was but a half-glimpsed shadow.

Sariel would kill the guards if he must, but better to leave them alive.

The fewer the bodies, the longer it would take for people to notice a dead monarch.

At the innermost portion of the garden was a second wall, thinner and built of white marble imported from the nation of Kanth. No guards at this gate, thankfully. The sound of water roared steady and pleasant as Sariel pressed his back to the wall and glanced within.

Surrounded by the white wall was the initial source of the garden's water, exiting from a carefully worked opening in the mountain now made to resemble three doves in flight. The stream washed over their backs and wings before falling, distributing it into a wider spray as it fell to the little pool beneath. Sariel saw four women in the water, three of them handmaidens still partially dressed, doting on the fourth.

Sariel's eyes narrowed, and his heart quickened in his breast.

The newly crowned Queen Isabelle Dior, bathing after her coronation and the grand reveal of her blasphemous powers. Sariel pulled back and pressed against the wall, staring at the stars instead.

Radiance does not belong in the hands of humanity. It doesn't matter how. You swore a vow, Sariel. Do not falter. She is always replaceable.

His grip tightened on his sword, but before he could turn about, the queen called out an order to the attendants.

"Leave me."

He heard two of them exit the water, though a third tried to argue.

"Your Grace, are you sure it is wise to..."

"I said leave."

Sariel followed the wall farther from the gate until the distance was enough that he trusted the darkness and his coat to protect him. The three handmaidens departed, quietly whispering among themselves. Sariel was glad to see them go. He would shed no tears for them, but neither did he wish to kill them to hide his involvement.

Your desire for solitude is your undoing, he thought, and climbed the second gate to land in the soft grass beyond.

Isabelle remained in the water, directly underneath the great spray of the three doves. She crouched on a smooth, elevated stone, her back to him. Her arms wrapped about her knees. Her head bowed low. Sariel crept forward, each step silent upon the grass as he made his way toward the bathing pool's edge.

He stopped just shy of the water, frozen for a reason he did not understand.

Isabelle.

She was sobbing.

Her entire body shuddered beneath the water, and finally believing herself alone, she let loose deep, chest-wrenching cries. The water's spray pressed her blond hair wide across her back, a blanket that provided no comfort. The falls' roar was no match for her sorrow. It was almost savage, the way her sobs tore out of her throat, as if she was furious at her own tears. Yet it did not stop them, only made them sound all the more pained. Sariel felt something twist inside him, and he had to clench his teeth.

Radiance was for him and his siblings alone. Every time they had taught its use to humanity, it had ended in perversion and death. He saw the same inevitability in Eder's foul preachers and their insect jars. Isabelle's fate would be no different.

Only, who had taught it to her? And how did she wield it without any sort of focus?

Sariel stepped a single boot into the pool. The splash of water startled Isabelle, and she turned about, standing naked before him, the water cascading down about her. Her tears washed away beneath the flow, and when she spoke, her sorrow was gone, as was her fury. Only cold distrust remained.

"Sariel," she said. "Why are you here?"

No reason for him to talk. No reason for him to explain.

But he could not take another step into the water.

"Your coronation," he said. "I cannot forget it."

Isabelle stepped down from the stone and into the pool, submerging herself up to her waist. She did not try to hide her nakedness.

"No one there will," she said, slowly approaching him. "That was the point of it."

The only light came from the stars, and in its glow, her golden eyes seemed alive. Sariel knew it now, knew how she commanded the people so readily that they would offer her their lives. Radiance influenced her every word. It empowered her every touch. Even her physical features were tainted by it, her hair so lustrous, her smile bestowed with unnatural charisma. Beautiful, in every sense of the word.

And for it, she had to die.

"The light you wielded," he asked. "Who gifted it to you?"

Ever nearer, her approach silent, the water flowing across her muscled abdomen. Her frame was strong, resembling Sariel's much more than that of any of the handmaidens who had recently left, and yet she carried herself with surprising grace. Even naked before him, she moved with all the dignity in the world.

"The goddess, Leliel, granted it to me on the day my blood flowed and I became a woman."

He pointed his sword toward her. "You lie."

Her eyes narrowed, the golden sheen in them flaring. She grinned, exposing her teeth. It felt like the smile of a predator. It seemed impossible that this was the same woman who had wept, broken beneath the waterfall. She was *enjoying* this.

"Will you kill me, Sariel?"

"I would hear the truth from your lips."

Another step closer. Her voice lowered. No longer boastful, instead quiet, a volume appropriate for sharing secrets.

"Leliel blessed me in the womb. I was born as I am and have always known myself different."

Sariel blinked, radiance turning his eyes to stars as he met her gaze. It should have let him know whether she spoke the truth, and yet those golden orbs denied him. They, too, possessed a gift of radiance.

"Impossible," he said. "That power, it has been taught to humanity before, but never been born natural within them." Redemption shook ever so slightly in his grasp. "Whatever you are, it cannot be."

Isabelle closed the space so that his sword was now within reach. Her tone shifted again, keeping him off-balance. Gone was her soft whisper. What followed was worse. This...this was an accusation. He could feel disappointment in her every word.

"You fear me."

"Shouldn't I?"

She tilted her head so her neck pressed firmly against the edge of his blade.

"You wield a sword, and yet I do not fear you."

Sariel's mind spun and twisted like a windstorm. Their vows...even now, Sariel felt the itch from the tattoo on his arm, but it was subdued. They had sworn to never teach humanity how to wield radiance, but if she possessed it all on her own?

But that couldn't be.

In all the hundreds of years Sariel had walked the island of Kaus, humanity had never been born possessing the power he and his five siblings wielded. Whatever Isabelle was, she wasn't just a once-in-a-generation anomaly. She was once in a millennium.

Sariel pressed the sword tighter to her throat. The tiniest trickle of blood mixed with the water clinging to her skin to run down her collarbone to her breast. It would be so easy to kill her. So easy to end these questions and let the mystery die. He and Faron could start again. They could find a new leader to wage war against the Astral Kingdom.

But that leader would not possess a fraction of Isabelle's resolve. They would not be fearless, like her. They would not command the love of her fellows and the fear of her enemies, each emotion heightened by her radiance.

He tightened his grip on Redemption's hilt, shocked by his sudden revelation. Aylah. Isabelle looked like his sister Aylah, only with golden hair instead of his sibling's raven black. Was that why he hesitated? But how could that even be? What meaning was there in such a resemblance?

"My brother and I can ensure your victories, Isabelle," he said, his resolve breaking. "Your conquest will be absolute. But if given that power, what would you become?"

Isabelle's savage smile vanished. She took a single step forward, forcing Sariel to retreat lest his blade cut her. The distance between them shrank ever further. He could smell the oils the handmaidens had washed her with, blue roses and lavender. He saw the curves of her amid the muscle.

He felt his resolve weaken, even as her conviction swelled to match the roar of the waterfall.

"I would be a servant of my goddess, Sariel Godsight, as I have been all my life. My every rule and law shall be set by her hand as we exalt her upon high. With her guidance, my people shall blossom, and the Church of Stars be banished to the deepest corners where hide the roaches and vermin."

One final step. She reached out and cupped his cheek with her hand, cradling him with her touch as if he were beloved. His skin burned hot beneath her fingertips.

"Will you serve me true, Sariel? Will you be a blade to wield against my foes? Or will you be afraid of all that I am, and all that I may become?"

So easy, to take her life.

So easy, and yet impossible.

"I have seen so much more of this world than you can imagine," he whispered as he lowered his sword. "And yet never have I met one such as you. Where will your gifts lead you, Isabelle? Will they lead you to glory, or to misery and slaughter?"

She laughed. Just a little laugh, enough to curl the right corner of her mouth into a smile. Despite all his years, she spoke as if she were the one with true wisdom.

"There is always misery and slaughter amid others' glory. I only pray to Leliel that mine are worth the cost."

Chapter 22

FARON

When the celebrations were done and the alliance with Armane announced, Queen Isabelle led her people on a march straight for Argylle's capital. They were joined by King Allan's own soldiers, one thousand well-trained footmen to swell the ranks as they crossed gently sloping valleys into miles upon miles of flat farmland on their way to besiege the city of Vendom.

"How long do you think they will hold out?" Bart asked Faron as they set up tents. Behind them, soldiers dug latrine trenches, while to the west, a dozen more worked at the creation of a proper battering ram.

"I fear it may be weeks," Faron said, hammering in the final stake. "King Bentley has been pulling all his resources and soldiers into the capital in preparation for this siege. He may hope to wait us out and let hunger and disease take the lives his own fighters cannot."

The young man stood, his hands pushing against his lower back as he stretched.

"Can it really be that bad for us?" he asked. "I thought sieges were worse for the cities."

Faron held back a grimace. He'd seen more than a few, and from both sides.

"They are," he said. "But that doesn't make it pleasant for us, either. A lot of tedium. A lot of boredom. Scarce water, close quarters, and opportune chances for sickness to spread." He gestured to the battering ram being constructed. "I hope our queen decides to assault the walls instead."

It would not be a pleasant attack, but Faron had succeeded against worse. Vendom lacked a true castle, relying on the thick brick walls that surrounded the city to keep it safe. There were three entrances, one to the east, the west, and the south, with all three heavily fortified with soldiers, archers, and if the rumors Faron had heard were true, murder holes and boiling oil. In an age predating the Anaon Kingdom, it had once been capital of a magnificent nation. That glory had long since passed, the city having been razed in the earliest age of the Heartless King's rule and forced to rebuild from nothing.

Faron's tent finished, he opened up the little flap; Iris was already inside, having rested since it was only halfway secure.

"Stealing my bed already?" he asked the coyote. Iris yawned at him. "You know this is how I get fleas, right?"

That wasn't true, of course. A little flex of radiance kept Iris clean of all parasites, but she didn't know that.

"Faron," his brother called, and so he withdrew from the tent. Sariel approached, Redemption twirling in his fingers.

"Something the matter?"

Sariel gestured for Bart to join them.

"Orders coming in from Sir Tristan," he said. "Each squadron is to gather come nightfall for new orders, and prepare our weapons and armor beforehand."

Faron glanced at the distant city.

"A nighttime assault?" he asked. "Sure, we'd have surprise, but it's just as likely to end in disaster."

Sariel shrugged.

"I guess that will keep it interesting, won't it?"

●

Faron sat with Bart at his right and Iris at his feet, enjoying the warmth of the bonfire. Dozens of similar fires burned throughout the encamped army, filling the night sky with their smoke. The men and women muttered quietly to themselves as they waited. Once the night was deep and the sky full of stars, Sir Tristan arrived from his meeting with Queen Isabelle.

"I pray all of you are ready for a fight," he said.

"Gonna be hard to fight when we can't see," Derek said, and a few with him laughed. "I pity the fools pushing the battering ram in the dark."

"We won't need it," Tristan said. He pointed to the city. "Bentley was a fool to ally with the Church of Stars. He's made a lot of enemies, and they've been in contact with us since Isabelle's coronation. A group of men and women loyal to Leliel will overpower the guards at the southern entrance and open it for us. When we march tonight, we will enter the city unopposed."

Faron rubbed his chin as he thought. The numbers were significantly in their favor, and if they could bypass the walls? It would be a massacre.

"How trustworthy are these traitors to Vendom?" he asked.

"As trustworthy as traitors can be," Tristan said. "But if they fail, then we retreat, and at worst suffer the sting of a few arrows. If they do not? The city is ours, captured less than a day after our arrival."

"And what a victorious tale that would be," Faron said, and clapped his hands. Risky it might be, but it sounded infinitely better than waiting out a lengthy siege as the innocent people within the city walls starved. "When do we move out?"

"When the signal is given," Sir Tristan answered. "They will set fire to several buildings throughout the city to let us know when the way is open. So extinguish that bonfire, and prepare. We may stumble and trip over our own feet, but we've a city to capture and a king to behead."

•

Faron and Sariel stood at the head of their group, several thousand yards of trodden earth between them and the southern entrance into Vendom. They were still within the limits of the camp, hoping their gathering went unseen by the city soldiers. Iris slowly circled the pair, filled with anxious energy. The many soldiers around them fared little better.

"Have you a plan?" Sariel asked, keeping his voice low so no one would overhear.

"My plan is to cause as much chaos as I can," Faron said. Every squadron had soldiers assigned to them to light torches once they were inside the city. Sir Tristan was to guide them once inside, but Faron suspected his brother would break away to do his own thing if he so desired.

"If we separate, we could find and slay King Bentley," Sariel suggested. "He will be frightened and confused. It would not be difficult."

"I don't think stealing Isabelle's glory is the best way to go about this," Faron said, shrugging. "I'll stick with the rest of our soldiers. Someone needs to anchor our formation, especially someone who won't need a torch to see."

"As you wish," Sariel said, ending the debate.

"There!" Bart said behind Faron. He was the assigned torch holder of their group, and he pointed to the sky. "I see the smoke!"

Faron drew his sword and readied his shield.

"All right," he said, and looked to Sir Tristan for the order. "Are we good to go?"

The knight was staring to the side, looking for his own signal. Many of the camp's bonfires had been left to burn, and all at once, they were extinguished.

"We go," he said.

Faron and Sariel took point, having argued truthfully that they had good eyes for the night. Sir Tristan reluctantly agreed, likely thinking it just bluster. For the brothers, though, a field lit with stars was as clear as day, and they easily reached the road leading into the city and followed it. Iris trotted alongside them, careful to keep as silent as if she were hunting prey.

A glance over Faron's shoulder saw the rest of Isabelle's army awkwardly approaching the city. The formations were uneven and ragged, and plenty were bumping into one another. Isabelle waited near the back, uncharacteristic of her, but he trusted her to take to the front once they were inside the city and any pretense at stealth was abandoned.

The entrance was two thick oak doors, twice the height of a man and reinforced with iron. When Faron was some fifty feet away, they cracked open. Wood groaned as they swiveled outward, widening until two people could enter abreast. A woman with her face and hair covered in dark cloth stepped out, and she gestured for them to hurry.

"Praise be the goddess," she whispered as Faron and Sariel passed through.

"Praise be," Sariel whispered back, his voice dripping with sarcasm.

Four soldiers lay dead on the ground on the other side. When Faron glanced to the walls, he saw more than twenty men and women wielding swords, knives, and axes, all of them garbed in dark cloth. Blood dripped from the stones like a macabre rain over the city entrance. In the distance, a faint glow lit the rooftops from the fires Leliel's followers had set.

"The king grasped for power, and in doing so rotted from within," Sariel said.

"It's been a while since I heard your poetry."

"This is not poetry. It is the obvious. King Bentley is a damned fool."

Faron grinned. "Then it's good we're removing him from his throne."

Isabelle's army flooded through the gates as alarm bells rang, the city slowly awakening to both fires and the realization it was under attack. Along the walls, Argylle soldiers on patrol rushed to seal the entrance from both sides.

"Galag, get your soldiers up there to hold the gate," Marshal Oscar shouted as he led his own group through, Queen Isabelle in tow. "Pira, seal off the main road from the west. Don't let any reinforcements reach the Royal Manse."

Chaos spread in the dark, the army splintering as the first of many battles began along the walls. The Argylle soldiers were quickly outnumbered but pressed onward nonetheless, knowing that sealing the doors was their only hope of saving the city. Meanwhile squads rushed in all directions, some obeying shouted orders, some moving on their own. Screams followed, frightened and panicked as the populace hunkered down in their homes or fled for the outer walls.

We are here to liberate, not conquer, had been Isabelle's orders repeated throughout the camp leading up to the assault. A naïve hope, Faron suspected.

As for Sir Tristan's group, they accompanied Isabelle's on a straight march through the heart of Vendom. Faron was all too glad to take point, and he rushed ahead, Iris and Sariel at his heels. Smoke thickened, fires spreading unabated. The first defense Faron encountered was thirty men trying to form a battle line to defend the Royal Manse. Faron charged straight into them, a specter of the night they never saw coming. Swords fell from limp hands, shields dented inward, the bones of the arms holding them cracking. Iris leaped upon the nearest, her teeth opening the throat of a man so panicked he dropped his weapon and held his hands over his face in a futile attempt to save himself.

Sariel arrived last, his wide swings cutting open anyone foolish enough to stay. The rest flung down their arms and fled, so that when Isabelle arrived with her sword drawn, she had no one to face.

"Where are their soldiers?" she asked, sounding frustrated.

"Many will be on the walls," Oscar said. "Galag's soldiers can handle them. Our reports also said a large portion were bunked near the west wall. Pira should catch them unprepared. All that remain will be at the Royal Manse."

"I'll make sure to save you a few to murder, Your Highness," Sariel said, overhearing her complaints.

The queen flashed him a wicked smile. "How kind of you."

Onward, into the night, and into a city growing both brighter from torches and fires and yet darker and more clouded with smoke. Ahead loomed the Royal Manse, the seat of power for all of Argylle. Faron had been to it several times throughout his lives, having watched it first built centuries before. A beautiful three-story mansion held up with a dozen limestone pillars carved into the likeness of spiraling iron-beech trees. Dozens of triangular windows opened into every room, and they were filled with rare clear glass. A towering gate surrounded the premises, the top spiked and the bars decorated with iron roses.

Before that entrance gathered what was left of Argylle's defenders. Ninety footmen standing shoulder to shoulder, four rows deep. Three preachers of the church stood among their number with their lanterns held high.

"Hold faith in Father's mercy," one of them shouted as the Doremy army approached. "Stand strong, and believe in his protection."

Sickly gold light pulsed from all three lanterns, washing across the defenders. Their armor shimmered, and yellow dripped from their weapons like water. Despite being outnumbered, they stomped and cheered, eager for the battle.

"Drunk with radiance," Sariel muttered as they approached.

"Can you get to the preachers if I open the way?" Faron asked.

His brother feigned insult and lifted his dragon-bone blade. "Need you ask?"

"Show them no mercy!" Sir Tristan shouted, giving the order for their group to lead the charge. Faron sprinted with his shield up and ready, his legs pumping and his grin spreading. As much as he wished to spare the lives of these foolish humans, he could never deny the excitement he felt when diving into battle. There was always something thrilling about reveling in his pure, unchecked might.

Faron struck the center of their line like a mad bull, trampling the first man he contacted and blasting the soldier behind him to her back. His heel stomped on a throat, and then he was spinning, his sword lashing out at anyone foolish enough to test him. Only one man managed to block the hit, and his reward was Iris diving atop him, her teeth latching on to his lower jaw and her weight slamming him to the ground. Her snarl was bone-chilling, her shaking of his head back and forth vicious enough to snap the neck.

"Be gone, Doremy devils!" the nearest preacher shouted. A circle of light flashed from his jar, strong enough to make Faron's stomach perform loops. Before the preacher could continue his prayer, Sariel's sword plunged straight through his open mouth, turned sideways, and then ripped out his cheek. The preacher fell in a shower of gore, the brutality only increasing as Sariel spun through the mass of soldiers, a most lethal dancer. Redemption made a mockery of their armor. The blood flowed freely.

"Throw down your weapons," Isabelle shouted above the din. No one listened, and so she pushed through the battle line, her sword gleaming with light. She hacked and chopped, surprising her foes with her every strike. Faron fought his way to her side, blasting away Argylle soldiers as if they were children. Side by side with the queen, he became her shield, annihilating anyone who tried to attack her. Iris darted about in the thick of battle, keeping near his side and latching on to the limbs of fools who thought to catch him off guard.

All the while, Sariel slaughtered the left flank.

"Surrender!" Isabelle called again amid the screams of pain and clash of metal.

"Father protects us!" the final preacher shouted in response. He stood before the grand double doors of the mansion with his arms raised. Only a single line of soldiers guarded him, and Faron pressed into them, trying to halt whatever madness the preacher planned. "Father saves us!"

The preacher smashed the jar at his feet, and from it exploded a whirlwind of gold light and insect corpses. It encircled his body, teasing his clothes and spinning his hair, and then extended over the Argylle soldiers, reshaping, becoming an enormous pockmarked golden hand reaching out for the Doremy soldiers with six crooked fingers.

"Leliel denies your hate!" Isabelle thundered before Faron could react.

She lifted her shield and light pulsed off it, clearer and brighter than anything coming from the wretched jar. It rolled like a wave, crackling with fire, and struck the preacher's ethereal hand. The hand shattered like glass, the gold within it fizzling away. A gust of air followed, combined with an agonizing shriek like scraping metal. Soldiers on all sides grimaced and clutched at their ears.

Amid that cacophony, Sariel lunged ahead, plunging his sword deep into the preacher's chest to execute him.

The remaining Argylle soldiers dropped to their knees, forfeiting their weapons and pleading for mercy, which they were given. The way clear, Faron grabbed one of the long, ornate handles of the left door and tested it. It was barred on the other side, and he mentioned it to the queen, who had stepped to the front of her escorts.

"Good thing we brought a battering ram," Isabelle said, grinning at him.

Faron braced his legs, flexed his arms, and prepared himself. "Damn right, you did."

He screamed as all his might and innate gifts gathered together into one undeniable pull. The bar locking the interior snapped in half, and with a groan of wood, Faron wrenched the door halfway open.

"After you," he said, sweat trickling down his brow and neck.

The entrance room was open all the way to the ceiling, with winding stairs leading to the second and third floors to either side. Paintings of previous kings and queens lined the walls. Pillars painted over with thorns and flowers split the open space, and at the far end, standing before an ornate crimson throne, sword in hand and protected by four guards, was a haggard man in a crown.

"I am King Bentley Casthe of Argylle," he said as Isabelle steadily approached. He dropped to one knee, bowed his head, and lifted his sword. The guards with him did likewise. "I hereby surrender to you, Queen Isabelle Dior of Doremy, and ask that—"

One clean stroke, and she cut his head from his shoulders. His body crumpled to a bloody heap, the crown dislodging from his beheaded skull and rolling along the carpet before coming to a halt. The shocked soldiers pushed to their feet, screaming out wordless defiance. Sariel and Faron cut them down before they could bring their weapons to bear.

Between them, Isabelle stood over the corpse of the slain king. His blood dripped from her sword. The remaining Doremy soldiers lingered by the doors, uncertain if they should enter.

"Well done," Faron said, sheathing his blade. "The city is yours."

"But have you accomplished all you desired?" Sariel asked, Redemption resting across his shoulder. His silver eyes watched the queen closely, judging her ambitions, and if they must be pushed higher.

Isabelle lifted her sword and gazed upon its steel. Pure golden light shimmered across the blade, burning away the blood.

"No, Godsight brothers, this is not the limit of my desires," she said. She looked to them, her eyes alight with radiance. "This is only the beginning."

Part Three

HONOR

Chapter 23

CALLUNA

Calluna sat on the prince's bed, her fingers running through his dark red hair. He sat on the floor with his back to her, naked but for his loosely tied trousers. Silver spider threads of radiance stretched from her fingertips to all corners of his skull.

"All these warmongers," she lamented. "It's enough to ruin a lovely day."

"Yes, the day is quite lovely," the prince said. His name was Petr. He was handsome, if one liked the color red. His skin had a pinkish tint to it, and it blushed easily when she scratched it with her fingernails. Even his freckles were an unpleasant shade of orange.

Calluna flicked the back of his head with her forefinger.

"Shush, now. Wait for your questions."

She slid off the bed and bit her lower lip. Perhaps she was a bit cruel in her judgment of Petr's appearance. The freckles gave him a boyishness that was endearing, but the rest of him was quite muscled. She traced her fingertips along his biceps, enjoying the thrill it gave her. Petr watched, quiet, with a dumb smile on his face.

"Surely you would have heard of them by now," she said. "Two brothers, or perhaps not brothers, merely friends or acquaintances. Both dark-haired, and one wielding an enormous bone sword. They would be terrors on the battlefield and heroes for whomever they fight."

"That sounds like the Godsight brothers," Petr said. "They say Faron the Ram toppled an entire fort on his own. Fights with a wolf at his side, one half the size of a man. His brother is with him, and rumors claim he is so fearless, he wears no armor into battle."

Calluna smiled, and she patted him atop the head.

"That certainly sounds like them." *Faron didn't even use a false name,* she thought. *Did Sariel do the same?* "And who do these Godsight brothers fight for?"

Petr smiled up at her, so pleased to be helping. He hadn't a clue about the dozens of threads piercing his ears, mouth, and eyes to smother him with her will.

"Queen Isabelle Dior of Doremy."

Isabelle...Calluna had heard many rumors about her, mostly from the downtrodden populace. She doubted all of them. Petr, though, would be privy to far more accurate information. She spread her legs and sat atop him, her hands lacing tightly around his neck. She sucked in a hiss of air. Petr was currently...very happy with her.

"Tell me of Isabelle," she said. "I would learn of her. How strong is her army? How great are her chances for building a kingdom?"

"She claims she is blessed by the goddess, Leliel, to unite the realms," Petr said. He spoke as if lost in a dream. Which he was, for she was that dream. "My father calls her the Bastard Queen and insists she is unworthy of the throne she inherited months ago. Her armies are strong, though. Queen Sillia swore loyalty after King Bentley's death at Vendom. The three realms, Armane, Argylle, and Rudou, all became one Doremy."

"She sounds dangerous, then."

Petr shook his head.

"My father did not believe so. He thought she would be defeated when she turned her eye to the Blue Rivers Alliance."

Calluna shifted her weight again, the motion pressing his crotch against hers. She clenched her teeth and groaned. Heat was building between her thighs, bothersome in its urgency.

"But she wasn't defeated, was she?"

"Forez has already surrendered," Petr said. He reached up to touch her face, and she slapped his hand back down. His smile never shifted in the slightest at the rejection. "My father is amenable, too, if we can remain vassals to Doremy. Bastard blood or not, we will bend the knee if it spares our homeland from pillaging. King Murta is the only one holding the alliance together."

Calluna stopped pretending not to be enjoying herself. She pressed her weight down, impressed by how firm the prince felt. The pressure was a delight, but still, a far cry from what she had begun to crave.

"Then Isabelle is the tool my brothers have chosen," she said, standing. "And it seems they chose well."

Which left just one recourse. If Isabelle was her brothers' tool to wage war against Eder, then Isabelle would have to die. It was that simple. She smiled. Killing a single human should be easy enough. Sariel and Faron would eventually find a new stooge, but that could take years. Maybe during that time, she could talk some sense into them.

She patted Petr's face.

"You've done well," she said, and the way he beamed sent a tremble through her. "Now, let's see if we can scrape a little more use out of you."

She hiked her dress up above her hips, then undid the laces of his trousers. When he was free, she took him in her hand and then slowly, carefully guided him into her. Her legs locked about his waist, and she groaned at a sudden wave of pleasure.

"Too long," she muttered. "Thirty years too long."

She rocked her hips, slowly grinding against him while using her own grip about his neck to occasionally lift herself ever so slightly. Petr's breathing grew rapid, his exhalations sometimes released as groans.

"Am I beautiful?" she asked him as she lashed threads into him. They pulsed from her hands into the back of his neck. She kissed along his chest, leaving sparkling silver dangling into his spine and rib cage. More. More. She wanted more of herself inside him. Her thoughts. Her emotions. He would feel *everything*.

"So beautiful," he said with what breath he could spare. His eyes spread wide. His mouth quivered. She kissed it, then bit his lower lip to help her focus. She felt him stiffen within her, his climax approaching. She rocked faster, her eyes imprisoning his. Her legs locked about his waist, squeezing. Her vision went white, and radiance burst about her eyes.

Everything, she pounded everything through those threads into the prince. When he looked at her, he did not see a rather plain-looking woman with long black hair, a button nose, and chin and cheeks so curved and small she was often mistaken for a child. Instead he saw his whole world. He *loved* her, more than himself, more than life itself. To even gaze upon her overwhelmed his heart. Her every touch lit him with fire. He stared at her as if she were a goddess of the heavens, and oh, how good it felt.

If only one of her siblings would look at her like that.

"Sariel," she moaned, imagining his face there, his long dark hair wrapped between her fingers. Her legs went weak. She felt Petr flexing inside her, but his orgasm was an afterthought. Her teeth released his lower lip, and she tasted blood on her tongue. Not entirely unpleasant. She slowly slid her weight against him, enjoying those last few waves of pleasure, and then stood on unsteady legs.

He looked up at her with glazed eyes. An empty smile covered his face.

"I love you," he said, and most assuredly meant it.

Calluna wanted nothing more than to rip each and every thread of radiance from his body. It suddenly made her skin crawl, to be so close to him. This red-haired fob was not her majestic, timeless brother. He was no blinding beacon of radiance able to match hers. He was a stupid lord with a limp, wet prick who had taken her into his room thinking she was a naïve farm girl thrilled by the thought of a fun time with the eldest prince of Etne.

"I should have resisted," she said, kissing his nose. "But I'll keep my word. I said you'd enjoy the sunshine, didn't I?"

He nodded at her. "The day is quite lovely."

She pulsed her will into him even fiercer than when she had fucked him.

"Then go enjoy that sunlight, Petr. It's waiting for you right out that window."

Calluna lowered her skirt and slipped out the bedroom door. They were in a high tower of the castle, and several dozen steps were between her and the outside. She encountered an older servant on the way down, who gave her a strange, pitying look.

"I pray you are well?" the woman asked, looking her over. Calluna wondered what she was looking for. Stains? Evidence of bruises?

"Better than Petr," she said, and giggled.

Once outside, she passed by the stunned crowd gathered around Petr's broken body, unknown and unnoticed as she ever was.

Chapter 24

SARIEL

Much of their travels had been spent in small tents on hard ground, so it was a welcome relief, even to a seasoned traveler like Sariel, to relax inside a warm, crowded tavern. It was one of many within the city of Lontaine, whose mayor had opened its gates and welcomed Isabelle's army upon the announcement that their king, Yarrick, had allied with Doremy in the war against the Blue Rivers Alliance.

"Hey, now, there's a fine piece!" someone shouted, reaching past the bar to where a five-stringed lute hung from the wall. The tavern keeper, an older man half buried in a bushy white beard and hair, protested futilely. The entire tavern was overrun with Sir Tristan's squadron, which had ballooned to several hundred in size as Queen Isabelle's trust in them grew. Having so many in such a space, and with how freely the ale flowed, created noise that was worse than a battlefield.

"Here's to hoping King Murta sees reason like King Yarrick did," Faron said, seated at one of the round tables. Sariel lurked behind him, leaning against the wall. Several friends surrounded Faron, while underneath the table, Iris slept atop his feet, rousing only to eat the occasional scraps tossed her way. "I wouldn't mind a few more feasts like this."

Sariel closed his eyes, holding back his chuckle. Yes, Faron would ever be at home in such crowded environs. As much as Sariel enjoyed the comforts, he'd be just fine once out and about again. An army rarely afforded privacy, but one could at least find some measure of solitude within a tent.

The sound of horrid, tortured strings ruined his thinking. He looked over to see one of the soldiers rubbing his fingers across the lute, some half-remembered song escaping his lips. Meanwhile the tavern keeper looked on, flushed and upset but still hesitant to make demands of the soldiers practically drowning him in coin.

Sariel leaned Redemption against the wall and then pushed through the crowd.

"Cease this," he said, yanking the lute away from the man. "You insult our host and the instrument both."

The soldier started to protest, saw the serious look in Sariel's eye, and then immediately reconsidered.

"Yeah, sure," he muttered, escaping with his drink.

"Many thanks," the old tavern keeper said. Sariel went to offer it back to the proprietor but then hesitated. A twinge tightened in his chest, coupled with a subtle longing.

"Might I play?" he asked instead.

The tavern keeper licked his lips. The instrument seemed a family heirloom, and not cheap to fix if damaged.

"Do you know how?"

He smiled at the man. "I shall let you be the judge."

Sariel returned to Faron's table. Bart quickly darted to his feet and offered his seat.

"What are you going to play?" the freckled man asked as Sariel sat down and properly positioned the lute on his lap. One benefit of endless lives had been his mastering of a variety of instruments, the lute being one of them. His fingers tested the strings. Well tuned. The tavern keeper's care was apparent.

"An old favorite, I suspect," Faron said, and nudged the surgeon Rowan sitting beside him with an elbow and a wink.

Sariel closed his eyes, his strumming growing louder. Fingers limber, he began to play. The notes rose from the lute, joining the din of the crowded tavern. It was doubtful anyone beyond their table could hear them. The song was slow, its somber tone the opposite of the raucous crowd. Sariel did not care. This was solely for him.

"*Shadows fall upon you as you lie down to rest,*" he began to sing. His soft voice flowed like water. "*The moon rises, the light fades, and when I speak your name, you do not hear. You do not hear.*"

He strummed harder, falling deeper into the flow. It had been many years since he'd sung this song, and it opened a wound within him that was always so much deeper than he anticipated.

"*Your wrinkled hands in mine, I hold you, I cherish you, and I sing you songs of old. None clasp my soul as you do. I will not leave, not until your end. Not until our end.*"

Faster now. He closed his eyes, the old notes returning to him. He sang of memories, some true, some false. A woman named Isca, with a beautiful smile and sky-blue eyes. A wedding underneath violet eulmore leaves. Travels across the realm, hands held at the cliffs of Aberdi, and love made before the falls of Twinsides. A time before wrinkled hands.

"*And wherever you go, I shall follow,*" he continued. He felt his insides shudder. "*One life with you is not enough. Not ever enough.*"

The woman named Isca was reborn as Elena. Emerald eyes instead of sky blue, but still the same warmth, the same love. It had been decades since Sariel wrote the song, and still it hurt to remember.

"*And young once more, we shall dance,*" he sang, momentarily opening his eyes. The tavern had fallen silent. All listened, enraptured. His fingers moved with expert precision, drawing life from the strings to cast it into the air. He had not meant to do so, but radiance shimmered unseen upon the strings, and it reverberated within the lyrics, adding to the spell.

"*We shall dance, and sing, and sing. Isca, I loved you. Elena, I love you still. Wherever you go, I shall follow. One life is not enough. Not ever enough.*"

The tempo increased, though his melancholy never eased. This was the part that had given the song popularity and allowed it to endure for centuries since he first sang it while standing over the freshly dug earth of Elena's grave. A barrage of names. A pain of a hundred lifetimes, made universal to all who listened.

"Isca and Elena. Mildred and Tara. Agnes, Ginnie, and Haley."

His fingers strummed harder, and the unseen waves of radiance pulsed throughout the crowd. They would not know it, would not understand it, but Sariel's memories were carried on those waves. The moments spent with his beloved entered their minds, a casual smile, a wine-soaked laugh, one of their simple homes, built of sod and sticks. These images would flit in through the ears of all who listened, unknown, little thieves carrying Sariel's melancholy.

"Amanda, Rose, Camille, and Lily."

Life after life, spent in love, always doomed to age and dust and starting all over again. Sariel sang, eyes closed, momentarily vulnerable as the weight of the past carried him down.

"Each face, each name, new and yet known, I am here. I am waiting, waiting, waiting, for you."

The tempo slowed again, each brush of the strings releasing the power of a thunder strike in the silent tavern. Every note struck silver, and he gave it his blessing.

"The moon rises. The shadow falls. Every grave. Every pair of wrinkled hands. I will hold you, as the light fades. As the light fades. As the light must ever, and forever, fade."

One last strum. The note hung in the air, and then the spell broke. A few dozen clapped awkwardly, uncertain of what had just transpired but knowing it was something special. Others looked away to hide the wiping of their eyes, and some guzzled down their drinks with renewed fervor. Sariel took in a deep breath, his insides feeling like he had sprinted a half dozen miles.

"That was...exceptional," Rowan said. She leaned against Faron's side, her head resting on his shoulder. "I can't believe I have never heard it before."

"It's an old song," Faron said. He patted her hand, which was resting atop his knee. His smile was gentle. "Old, but a good one."

"My pa used to sing 'Isca,'" Bart said, staring at the lute as if it were magic. "The names weren't all the same, though."

"Every singer chooses the names," Sariel said, rising from his seat. "Tonight, I chose mine."

He returned the lute to the tavern keeper, who accepted it graciously.

"Might you sing more?" the man asked. "Something a bit more jovial, perhaps?"

"Forgive me," Sariel said, and he dipped his head. "I have but one song within me this night."

He exited the tavern. His cramped room, shared with Bart and Faron, was not sufficient. He sought privacy. He sought the company of the stars, and the stars alone. The din of the tavern faded behind him, and he walked Lontaine's streets, Redemption resting across his back and shoulders.

The night was deep, the homes he passed through quiet and dark. He walked until reaching the thin stone wall surrounding the city. Once he easily scrambled up, he sat with his legs hanging over the side, and he rested his sword across his lap. No guards were nearby. At last, he was alone.

"Am I right to leave you, Tara?" he asked the stars. "Are you better never knowing who I am? Who we were?"

A dozen funeral ceremonies flashed through his mind. A body, sometimes burned, sometimes buried, and sometimes entombed. The names changed. The faces differed. The grief forever remained the same.

"Damn it all, Sariel," he muttered to himself. "You're no better than Faron."

He sat on the wall until the stars faded, the sun rose, and he could drown his memories beneath the rote activities of the day.

Chapter 25

CALLUNA

The next week was a blur of dirt roads and odorous towns as Calluna traveled the steadily flattening hills more and more covered with potato and cabbage fields. With each step, her nervousness grew. It was one thing to flash a smile at a dumb prince and rely on his lust to obtain the privacy she needed. Trying to seduce a queen in the middle of her conquest was another...especially when two of her brothers would be nearby.

Isabelle will dance as your puppet, she told herself as she approached the sprawling military camp fifty miles outside the city of Lontaine. It filled an entire valley, tents and boots flattening the grass and ruining what beauty the tranquil landscape had once possessed. Now it was carved with latrine ditches and tent spikes. What grass endured was devoured by their horses and the oxen pulling their supply wagons. *You will play and then toss her away, like all the rest.*

Calluna walked among the throng of bodies, unnoticed because she chose to be unnoticed. She was such a little thing compared to them, plainly dressed and with her dagger hidden. It was easy to overlook her. She had a hundred lifetimes of practice, and a flicker of radiance at those who cast her sideways glances was enough to make them turn away.

Banners flew above the tents, and she compared them to the

information Petr had given her. Most were the same as when she first vanished into her swamp, family heirs clinging to traditions, though a few were upstart nobles or newly enthroned kings and queens, such as Rudou. All of them unified by Sariel and Faron. The people might believe Isabelle responsible, but they were all fooled.

Calluna walked without thinking, letting her feet guide her. She'd find Isabelle in time. She had to be patient. Best she fully take in the layout of the camp before making a move. That was the excuse she told herself anyway. The truth of it was beyond denial when she approached a small roaring fire and a cluster of men and women seated around it.

"This is bullshit," an older man with a heavily scarred face said while pointing at a cluster of dice on a small wooden board before him. "There's no way you knew I had axes waiting for the clash."

"But why else would you have rerolled your swords?" a young freckled man at the opposite side of the board asked.

Calluna used the nearby tent to hide her arrival. She peered around the fabric, her heart leaping into her throat.

"Because *you* were trying for swords," the scarred man grumbled. He pointed an accusatory finger past the young man. "You've been teaching him, haven't you, Faron?"

Her brother laughed, the enormous mug in his hand splashing a bit of its contents as he slapped his knee.

"Sorry, Derek, but I'm a poor Wounds player myself. If Bart's winning, it's because he's better than you."

Bart blushed hard enough to hide his freckles.

"Our marches are so long and boring," he said. "I've nothing else to think about but our previous games, and things I wanted to try instead."

"You spend your whole marches thinking about dice?" Derek asked. "Leliel help me, you're dull as ditchwater."

The blushing intensified.

"What *should* I be thinking about?" he asked.

"Besides one foot in front of the other?" Derek shrugged. "How you're going to spend your pay come the next town, for example...or maybe what color hair your next lady will have."

Faron pointed at the dice board. "You're stalling, Derek. Roll your remaining dice so we can all watch the dull little farm boy humiliate your ass."

Laughter all around, and Faron at the center of it. Calluna watched, her fingernails digging into the tent fabric. Jealousy burned hot in her chest. That could never be her. She'd tried. She once spent years alongside Faron fighting in some pointless war, trying to smile the way he smiled, to encourage those who needed encouraging, and to use her radiance to give strength to those whose willpower faltered.

It didn't suit her. She'd ended each day exhausted, and though men and women were all too eager to share her bed, she'd denied them, craving solitude instead. There was just something about Faron. While these social inanities drained energy from Calluna's mind, he seemed to grow on them like a fire constantly fed new kindling.

"That's what I thought," Faron said after the final roll. He scooped up four of the dice and clattered them about in his palm. "But now my honor's been assailed! If you think I've been helping Bart, then let's show how well that would work. Two against two, Bart and me against you and...whoever else is willing to endure the misery of having you as a partner."

Bart grabbed a die from Faron's hand.

"He'll probably have to pay like he always does his partners."

The entire group froze in shock, their mouths dropping open.

"Damn, the kid found his balls," a red-haired woman said, smacking him across the back as howls of laughter erupted throughout the group. This time it was Derek who blushed a bit of red. "And I'll be your partner, no payment required. Consider it my obligation as a surgeon to help the wounded."

"I don't pay for my women," Derek grumbled, scooping up two of the dice. He sounded honestly offended.

"I don't pay for mine, either," the woman said. "But I suspect they say yes to me as often as they say no to you."

Faron cleared the board, his grin stretching from ear to ear as he handed over two of the dice to the surgeon.

"The man's already bleeding, Rowan. You don't need to twist the knife."

Calluna turned her back to the group and crouched within the tent, her arms crossed over her knees. She listened as the dice rolled and the banter flowed, little pokes at someone's skill or cleverness. She drank in their joy and camaraderie like a parasite, but it did not feed her. Instead it darkened her mood and left an aching hole in her chest that pulsed with sadness. She fed upon a thing she would forever want and could never have.

Robbed of whatever joy she felt upon seeing her brother, Calluna departed the campfire for new environs. She had her mission, after all. Using the many banners to guide her, she sought out the heart of the Doremy camp.

Where is Sariel? she wondered as she walked. Usually the brothers kept together in camps, with Sariel quiet and lurking, content to be in his brother's presence in a way Calluna was not. A need to see him gripped her, but it must wait. Once Isabelle was dead, there would be time. Assuming he forgave her.

Calluna clenched her hands tightly, digging her fingernails into the soft skin of her palms. Sariel would forgive her for killing Isabelle. He always did. He was good that way, no matter how often he insisted that he was the coldest and cruelest of the six.

The highest hill contained the largest tent. A peculiar flag waved from its center pole, a new banner for a new Doremy empire. Sewn in black over a yellow background was a pair of wings enveloping an upturned sword, a lidless eye serving as its cross guard. Calluna climbed the hill, needing to expend a bit more radiance to ensure no eyes lingered on her. This had to be Queen Isabelle's tent. There were even posted guards forming a little circle around the tent. Getting past them would be more difficult, for they were actively searching for interlopers. More difficult, but hardly a challenge. She smiled at the nearest guard as she approached. Bending simple humans to her will would forever be easy to her.

"Hello," she said, smiling brightly at the soldier. "Are you hungry?"

The man tilted his head, confused by the question. He didn't answer immediately, either, Calluna's radiance already starting to seep into him. Not the deep threads, not yet. She needed to touch him first. Just hints of it, wafting off her like rays of the moon. Enough to unsettle him, make him pliable.

"Supper won't be for several hours," he answered. "I barely choked down the morning porridge, though, so I could certainly eat. Why, are you a baker, miss?"

Before she could answer, a couple exited the tent. Her eyes widened, and she positioned herself so the soldier's bulky frame blocked her from view.

Sariel, and with him, a silver-armored, blond-haired woman who matched Petr's description of the Bastard Queen.

"We must reinforce our numbers with spearmen," Sariel was saying. "Our swords will not suffice against a cavalry charge of the size King Murta can bring upon us."

"You say that as if I may snap my fingers and conjure said spears into existence," the woman said, shaking her head. "I'm looking into where I can purchase more, but for now, Queen Sillia's two hundred will have to suffice."

The soldier Calluna hid behind tapped her on the shoulder.

"Miss?" he said, still trying to be polite.

Calluna shoved her hand against his mouth, and she spiked a dozen threads of radiance straight into him.

"Shhh," she whispered, peering around his shoulder to watch Isabelle and Sariel pass by. The way they walked, the way they talked...there was a familiarity there Calluna immediately hated. The two respected each other. Why? What did her brother see in that woman?

No. Calluna licked her lips. She was being unkind. The way Isabelle carried herself, the way her hair seemed to sparkle in the daylight, her body strong with muscle, her smile warm but measured...

"I have a present for the queen," Calluna told the soldier. She withdrew her hand but did not withdraw her control. Her eyes flooded with stars as she exerted her influence to its fullest. "But it has to be a surprise. No telling anyone, all right?"

For her siblings, control exerted upon others would fade the moment they broke their concentration. Not so with Calluna. She didn't know if it was a gift unique to her, or a talent born of hundreds of years of practice, but the commands she gave others would remain upon them, sometimes for years.

"Of course," the man said, and he smiled at her. "Isabelle's working herself ragged leading Leliel's army. She deserves a reward for that effort."

"Right," Calluna said, and laughed as if he'd just said the funniest thing. "But no one can know, so could you please go distract your friend over there? I'd hate to ruin the surprise."

"Yeah, of course, good thinking."

The soldier waved at her and then trudged to the other nearby soldier watching the entrance, striking up a conversation. Calluna hurried past them through the open flaps of the enormous tent.

The furnishing was what a queen could expect of an army on the move. A simple bed with fine, sturdy sheets. A table containing multiple maps and leaflets of paper with notes and figures. A small dresser containing a handful of outfits. All of it could be quickly loaded onto a wagon come morning.

Calluna approached the bed, nervousness mixing with a perverse thrill in her mind. Sariel had been alone with her. Did that mean...?

She buried her face in the sheets and inhaled deeply. No, no scent of sex. No sweat, no semen, just a bit of dust and a hint of lavender soap. Calluna was shocked by the strength of her relief...as well as a tiny hint of disappointment. Whoever this Bastard Queen was, she didn't deserve her immortal brother's adoration. But to have been so close, to lie upon the same bed they had lain upon, to smell the proof of their lust...

"What are you doing?"

Calluna spun about, clutching the blanket as if she had been caught nude. Isabelle stood in the tent entrance, her hand resting on the hilt of her sword. Not drawn, for now. Her golden eyes narrowed into a glare.

"My things are not to be rifled through, little thief."

"I'm no thief," Calluna said, better observing Isabelle now that they were so close. Stars help her, she was beautiful. There was something almost unnatural about the perfect curve of her chin, the swell of her breasts, and the thick flow of her hair. It unnerved Calluna. No. Worse. It frightened her, which was baffling.

"A trespasser, at the least," Isabelle said. She stepped aside from the entrance. "I will show mercy and let you leave, so long as you let my guards search you thoroughly."

Calluna slowly approached the queen. Her shoulders hunched, and she took little, uncertain steps. She knew how to make herself seem young and small. Her confidence steadily returned. What reason had she to be frightened of this woman? It didn't matter that she was a queen, or that she wielded a sword. Everyone danced once Calluna lashed them with her radiant threads.

"Yes, yes, thank you, Your Grace," she said, pretending to be demure. Meanwhile, heat built in her abdomen. She stared at Isabelle's figure, imagining her on her knees and stripped naked. Calluna's fingers twitched and curled. Surely Sariel desired her, but if Calluna had her body first, experienced what her brother had not...there was power in that. A message beyond merely delaying the intended war against Eder.

"You are most kind," Calluna continued. The weight of her hidden dagger felt heavy against her thigh. Not yet. Not until the end. She stepped closer. Closer. When but a few feet away, she dropped to her knees, bowed her head, and lifted her hands.

"Please, will you accept my penance?" she asked. Her voice trembled, and she added a flash of silver to each word. "I...I only sought to meet she whom the goddess has chosen."

She stared at the dirt, waiting, trusting.

Isabelle's hands closed about hers.

"Give me your name, child, and I will pray it tonight when I retire to my bed."

Calluna looked up and locked eyes with the woman.

"I am no child," she said. Threads of radiance, so thick and bright they were visible to the human eye, spiked through Isabelle's palms. They swirled like cast spider silk, wrapping about her wrists and elbows, and then came even more, crawling like tentacles, working toward her face and neck. Calluna let the stars shine full in her eyes as she issued her commands.

"You will make not a sound," she said. "You will not run. You will obey."

The threads swirled higher, Calluna's will pulsing through them, reaching greedily for Isabelle's heart and mind. Her pulse raced with excitement. Petr would be nothing compared to this woman. To see her kneel, to see her obedient, feeling the warmth of her breath and the softness of her tongue...

"I will not."

Calluna's entire mind tore in half. The threads recoiled. Golden light shone from Isabelle's eyes, matching the silver from the stars within Calluna's. The queen pulled her hands free, and she retreated a step while drawing her sword. The ringing of steel echoed in Calluna's ears.

"I don't know who you are," she said, the sword unsteady in her grasp. She sounded shaken, and uncertain, but still very much in control. "But I obey only my goddess."

Calluna sprinted past her, out the tent and past the two guards. She didn't understand. She didn't understand. No one could resist her, no one had ever resisted her, the only ones who could deny her threads were her own siblings, she knew because she had *tried*, just once, she had tried, and Sariel had been so furious...

Tears streamed down her face as she descended the hill. A nightmare awaited her at the bottom. Faron, climbing up, apparently to meet with the queen. He froze in place, shocked to see her as she stumbled mid-run.

"Calluna?" he asked.

"Apprehend her!" Isabelle shouted from up high. Faron glanced between her and the queen, and then he knew. He knew. Anger and disappointment formed a cruel mask over her kind brother's face.

"You never should have come here, Calluna," he said, reaching for his sword.

"*Stop!*" she screamed at him, all her power flooding into the cry to create a shock wave of confusion and hesitation that sent soldiers tumbling to their knees. Not her brother, of course. And somehow, not the queen.

But Calluna was faster than either of them, and she sprinted through the camp, weaving and ducking past baffled soldiers and scattered tents. She ran, and ran, and ran. Failed. She had failed. War would come, and now her brothers knew what she had tried. They would be watching for her now. Ready for her.

Calluna fled to the wilds, hating Faron, hating Sariel, hating herself and her tears, flowing without end.

Chapter 26

FARON

Fifty miles past the border of Vivarai, the group gathered around a map, the tent filled with frowning faces and heavy concentration.

"I cannot imagine this slipup is intentional," Marshal Oscar said. "We must take advantage, lest our war drag on needlessly for months."

Sir Tristan leaned back and crossed his arms over his chest. He was among several other squadron leaders, all brought in to offer their advice on how to react to the latest scouting reports. Also with them was vassal King Allan of Armane, the burly man a mixture of splint armor and fur, and whose ax had earned him a fine reputation among the soldiers. Beside him stood Queen Sillia's son, Druss, sent in her stead. He was clever but young, and deferred to Allan often when it came time to discuss plans.

There was no reason for Faron to be among such a group, but he accompanied Tristan anyway, and endured their glares.

"Intentional or not, we cannot risk overstepping ourselves," Tristan said. "What seems like a blessing may become a curse if we find ourselves with an entire mounted host charging into our backs."

Queen Isabelle stood on the opposite side of the map, and she gestured to the pieces.

"We have a day to react, maybe less, if our scouts were off on their estimations. The question is, how do we best respond?"

Faron peered over Sir Tristan's shoulder to observe the pieces. The current problem had been a weakness in Isabelle's army since the beginning, which was her total lack of mounted units. The Blue Rivers Alliance, on the other hand, had an estimated two hundred trained knights serving King Jehan of Etne, and another four hundred serving King Murta of Vivarai. The Etne knights had split off from the main army, and week after week picked opportune moments to charge in and assault Isabelle's army as it sprawled out across the miles on their march toward Murta's seat of power at Lossleaf Castle.

In response, Isabelle had tightened her ranks and flooded the surrounding lands with advance scouts, but this slowed their progress to a crawl. Food was growing scarce, and meanwhile King Murta's coalition refused to engage in a full-fledged battle. They only skirmished, letting their few archers pepper the Doremy lines before withdrawing, their retreat protected by yet another rear charge from Etne's knights.

It was bleeding them dry, but finally came a bit of good news; Etne's forces had, in an attempt to flank Doremy's troops, misjudged distances and separated significantly from King Murta's grander force. The question was, what did they do to take advantage of that mistake?

"We should rush King Murta's forces with all haste," one of the other squadron leaders insisted. "With our numbers advantage, our victory will be assured."

Marshal Oscar judged the distance and shook his head.

"We will arrive haggard and tired, and these hills make for tiresome travel as it is. I don't like it. And should we call for a retreat, and Etne's knights arrive, the losses will be devastating."

"We may not have a choice," Isabelle argued. "We need this fight. We're on their land, among their people. They can outlast us and outsupply us. If we lay siege to Lossleaf Castle without first crushing their army, we may find ourselves completely surrounded."

Faron had not a good measure of King Murta yet, but he'd seen enough of the knights' charges to judge the tactics of Etne's king, Jehan. He was patient, lurking until he found what he deemed moments of weakness, but upon seeing one, he would attack with all-out aggression to maximize the damage. A person like that could be baited…

"Then make them seek out the fight," Faron said. The squadron leaders turned his way, many not bothering to hide their disdain.

"And how, pray tell, do we do that?" asked one of them.

Faron pushed through until he could reach the figures on the map representing the armies.

"We see Etne's separation from the rest as a weakness to exploit," he said. "But what if we make them think it is to their own advantage?"

He took Isabelle's squadrons and spread them out in a line, purposefully positioning Sir Tristan's the farthest west, closest to the errant knights. Doing so placed them at a nearby forest's edge. He knew the terrain well from his lifetimes of travel, and a secondary plan was already forming in his mind.

"We spread out on our march," he continued. "Make it look like we're tired, and careless in our attempts to hunt and forage. Most importantly, we fool King Jehan into thinking we do not know the location of his forces." He tapped the forest. "And it is here we prepare for the knights. Jehan will think we are exposed on the western flank and send in another charge."

"While also informing King Murta of our thinly spread lines and his planned attack," Marshal Oscar said, following through the logic. "Murta will almost certainly pivot to hit from the east at the same time."

"How does that help us?" Isabelle asked Faron directly.

Faron slid more pieces east, leaving Sir Tristan's behind.

"Because we're ready for the attacks on both sides. It will take time for riders to cross the distance between King Murta and King Jehan, and during that time, we will reposition and use the hills to disguise our movements. Only Sir Tristan's shall remain behind, and we will be enough to occupy Jehan while everyone else fights the real battle."

"This may bait Murta into a fight along the east, perhaps here at Oswind's Crossing," Oscar said, tapping the map. "But there still remains the threat of Etne's knights. If they break Sir Tristan's squadron, they can still flank us unimpeded."

Faron grinned, and he projected an aura of utmost confidence. It would win over all present by the sheer influence of the radiance he projected...all but Isabelle.

"Hold faith in me and my fellows," he said. "We will not break."

Isabelle bit her lower lip as she stared at the map. All others there fell silent.

"We've whittled Etne's numbers, but they still possess some two hundred knights," she said. "And though you'll have a slight edge in number, you will lack the advantage of horses. It would be a miracle for you to fight them to a standstill, let alone win."

Her golden eyes met his silver, and his smile hardened.

"We will not break," he repeated, quieter and more assured. "You will have your miracle."

The queen matched him smile for smile.

"We are an army of miracles," she said. "Let it be done."

•

"A lot is riding on this idea of yours, Faron," Sir Tristan said as he fiddled with the straps of his armor. "The thinnest of margins separates a planned retreat from a real one."

"Would you rather fight Etne's riders on the open plains?" Faron asked. "Have a little faith."

"My faith is in Leliel and in Isabelle, not you."

"Fair enough," Faron said. "But I'm the one here with you, not them, so at least give me a little confidence."

The knight laughed. "We're doing your bullshit plan. What more do you want from me?"

Sir Tristan's squadron had been reinforced with two hundred soldiers from another squadron, pushing its numbers up to five hundred in total. They formed a battle line five deep in front of the forest. In the distance were King Jehan's two hundred knights, riding in full view toward them. The ground seemed to tremble with their approach. With their armor and momentum, they would run straight through Tristan's lines with ease, and both sides knew it. Far behind them marched another four hundred Etne footmen, seemingly forgotten in the charge.

"Steady," Tristan shouted. "On my command, we move as one!"

Faron adjusted his kite shield on his arm. It was much larger and more finely made than his old one, and with Doremy's new winged sword standard painted across its front. It had been a gift from Queen Isabelle, to celebrate his role in the battles leading up to the conquering of Argylle. The sword was newer as well, and had opened many throats over these past few months. It wasn't as sharp as Redemption, granted, but neither was anything else.

"Hope you're having fun, brother," he muttered to himself. Faron couldn't stay with Isabelle after proposing his plan, but neither did he like the idea of the queen fighting alone on the battlefield. So Sariel stayed behind to be her shadow and protect her while Faron dealt with the knights.

The distance closed between the two forces. Soldiers fidgeted nervously. Iris growled beside him, keeping near his leg as she watched the approach. Sir Tristan waited, and waited, wanting the Etne soldiers to be fully committed.

"Retreat!"

The five hundred turned tail and sprinted into the forest. The trees were thin and spaced wide apart, with little underbrush to trip a man or horse. Faron led the way, Iris at his heels, as they crossed the few hundred feet to reach a shallow creek. The water was barely enough to wet one's ankles when crossing. It would scare no riders, and that was entirely the point. The creek's rapid flow would, however, be enough to hide the traps placed within.

Faron had led the practice for several hours that morning, whipping soldiers into a frenzy and then sending them sprinting across the water from various angles and starting positions. Each time, they were to look for little sticks propped up along the stream's edge, just high enough to be noticeable. They marked the safe paths. That training paid off as the hundreds of fleeing soldiers filtered into smaller lines when sprinting across the water. There were a dozen safe paths, enough to ensure the fleeing soldiers could cross in a timely manner without alerting the chasing knights.

"Hold steady!" Sir Tristan shouted, pointing, directing, and even shoving soldiers into line as he rushed along the newly created front on the opposite side of the creek. "This day is ours!"

The ground shook with the approach of the riders. They barely slowed from their chase through the thin trees. Neither the creek nor the line of Doremy soldiers would give them pause. With their numbers, their horses, and their momentum, they had every reason to believe they would stampede to a crushing victory.

"Almost here!" Bart shouted from up above Faron. He'd been waiting there since this morning, perched on a heavy branch with a bow in hand. Twenty other hunters were with him, their goal to bring down riders who happened to unknowingly use the safe paths across the creek.

"Stay beside me, Iris," Faron whispered, kneeling down beside the coyote. "I don't want you trampled underfoot."

Water splashed as the horses reached the creek, their hooves scraping the smooth stones. And then the first hit the traps.

Faron had guided their creation, modeling them after bear traps that had been common several hundred years ago, before the switch to the preferred iron-teeth style. They were flat boards adorned with small but stubby spikes, dozens of them laid out along the bottom of the creek, half buried in gray mud and pebbles. The lead horse let out a horrific shriek as spikes pierced its hooves. Balance ruined, it collapsed forward, the impact twisting its neck awkwardly to one side. The rider suffered worse, his head striking the ground before the horse's body trapped his lower leg and thigh underneath.

The same horror played out for hundreds of feet in all directions. The knights came in rows, and those not in the lead found their path strewn with collapsed horses and thrown riders. Blood painted the creek red.

"For Doremy!" Faron bellowed, sprinting out from the trees. This was his plan, his victory, and he would lead the charge into the mad chaos. First blood, however, would not be his. An arrow from Bart shot overhead and pierced the neck of the closest knight, the first of a salvo from the twenty hunters. Faron thrust his sword into the man's gut for good measure, then flung him from his horse. A second knight leaped over the trampled body, his sword swinging a long, low arc in an attempt to slice Faron open from waist to chin. Faron's shield blocked it with ease, and then his own counter took the man's arm off at the elbow.

The horse's momentum continued, but Faron dug in his feet and roared out his fury. He would not be moved. The horse crashed into him as if he were a stone statue and then stumbled away, only to be overwhelmed in the sudden wave of Doremy soldiers rushing the creek.

The knights, already outnumbered, suddenly found themselves swarmed with swords and spears. Those whose horses were lame or wounded were the first to die, and then came the second rows, disjointed and lacking momentum. Faron tore into them, blasting his way from knight to knight with speed to rival even Sariel. His shield smashed aside any attempts to slow him. His sword hacked off legs and thrust into ribs and abdomens. All the while, arrows flew overhead, the hunters easily finding targets with their height advantage.

"Fall back!" one of the enemy knights called. Faron didn't see any markings on him to signify that he had that authority, but then again, given the copious number of dead, such a leader might not even remain. Several others took up the call, but the one who gave the initial order would not live to enact it. Iris flung herself onto him, easily clearing the height of the horse with her powerful legs and tremendous size. Her jaw snapped tight about his face, and her momentum whipped him sideways in the saddle. His neck broke, and bloody chunks of his face tore free, trapped tightly within Iris's teeth.

The knights turned about and retreated from the creek and out of the forest. They left behind dozens of corpses. A quick survey had Faron estimating at least eighty knights dead, if not more.

"It's not over yet," he shouted, sensing relief sweeping through the Doremy soldiers. "Get back and ready for the footmen!"

He shouldn't have been giving the order. That was Sir Tristan's responsibility...but where was the knight? Faron scanned up and down the line, not finding him.

"Come on, form ranks," Alex said, the giant man barreling through the troops and echoing Faron's demands. It seemed he had appointed himself in charge. "The day is not won yet."

Faron stared at the thin forest ahead, to see if he could glimpse any approaching soldiers and judge how much time he had, but saw nothing.

"Bart?" he asked, calling up to the tree behind him.

"I don't see anyone," the young man shouted back.

Faron's frown deepened. What was going on? Even with the ambush, their numbers would be mostly equal once the four hundred footmen arrived. Had they spooked King Jehan that badly?

"Wait here, girl," he said, patting Iris's side. "I'll be back in a moment. Protect Bart in the meantime, yeah?"

Iris licked a bit of blood from her face, then yipped at him. Close enough to a "yes" for Faron. He dashed along the line, scanning bodies as much as he did survivors. If Sir Tristan had perished in the assault, chain of command would pass on to Alex, his second-in-command. It'd be best to know that now, before the footmen arrived...

If the footmen arrived. Faron's worry grew. Had they misinterpreted Etne's tactics?

At the far southern end of the line, Faron finally found Sir Tristan. He stood behind the rest of his soldiers, talking with a mounted rider bearing Rudou colors.

Faron held no rank, and no sway here, but he had to know.

"What's going on?" he asked, projecting radiance into his voice so they would struggle to resist answering. Sir Tristan turned, a bit of blood staining his beard. Worry tainted his blue eyes.

"King Jehan has retreated," he said. "And the fighting at Oswind's Crossing has halted completely. King Murta is calling for an armistice."

Faron furrowed his brow.

"Isn't that good news?" he asked. "Why the dire faces?"

Sir Tristan glanced at the rider, a young man who looked pale from fear.

"Because this is no ordinary peace, but a matter of desperation," said the knight. "Word from southern Argylle has reached us of ruined villages and great swaths of burning fields."

"Raiders?" Faron asked.

Sir Tristan shook his head, and he clutched his sword tightly as the messenger turned his horse about and rode for the distant army.

"No," said the knight. "A dragon."

Chapter 27

SARIEL

Y ou called for me, Your Highness?" Sariel asked, stepping into Isabelle's tent. The queen leaned back in her chair to study him. She
wore her traveling attire, boots caked with dirt and yellow shirt stained
with sweat. Not long from now, she would meet with the two kings of
the Blue Rivers Alliance, and Sariel suspected she was making a point in
keeping dressed for travel and war.

"Indeed," Isabelle said, folding her hands together and leaning forward. "Marshal Oscar has no training in fighting dragons, and my advisers lack any materials on the matter other than vague stories of conquest
from the days of the Anaon Kingdom." She arched an eyebrow. "But
you . . . you and your brother are mercenaries from afar, with backgrounds
unknown. You are mysteries to me, and every time I test you, you reveal
yourselves more knowledgeable than you have any right to be."

Sariel crossed his arms. "This sounds more like an accusation than a
compliment."

"It is a statement of fact," she said, and smirked. "If I wished to make
accusations, I would remind you of your behavior at a certain waterfall in
Leyval. Instead, I would point to your sword, also carved of dragon bone,
and say that my desperation leads me to you. Have you any wisdom to

impart about dragons, if not fighting them, then at least on their behavior, and what might drive one beyond its borders and into the north?"

Sariel approached, his eye on the table before her. Set up on it was a map of Etne and the nearby Vivarai, showing their forests, rivers, and villages. Painted wooden pieces marked the locations of the various armies currently mustered, and among them, a red block representing the last sighting of the rampaging dragon.

"The western lands have united against dragons many times before in their history," Sariel said. "Even before the dragon-defense pact was signed. Numbers are very much our greatest strength, as is our tenacity. We must give chase and be relentless, until the dragon is forced into battle."

Isabelle gave him an incredulous look. "How do we force a battle with a creature that can take flight at any moment?"

Sariel grabbed the various pieces representing armies and started moving them about the map, positioning them on all sides of the dragon's red block.

"Dragons can indeed fly, but it is slow, taxing, and tires them quickly," he said. "If this dragon is truly rampaging, assaulting all in its path, then it is already stressing its body and expending much of the flame from its belly. When it sees an army approaching, it will indeed take flight, but only to gain a mile of two of separation so it may resume crawling."

He showed this by moving the block, and then in turn had two of the armies on either side close in further.

"So we stay spread out at first, each army separate, almost daring the dragon to fight us. But it won't. A rampaging dragon has lost most control of its mind, and reacts on instinct. It seeks easy blood, and easy meat. A battle against a human army is neither."

"But what if the dragon does decide to fight?" she asked.

In response, Sariel took the other pieces and had them converge.

"Then we respond," he said. "But trust me, the dragon will try to fly away. It won't be foolish, nor risk its life for no reason. It will fly, trying to avoid us, and so we keep spread out, keep chasing, until..."

He shifted the pieces again so the dragon was surrounded on all sides.

"If the dragon continues to fly, it will tire itself and be vulnerable when landing for a rest," he said. "Once it realizes the trap is set, and multiple forces chase from all sides preventing it from easy escape, that is when it will land, and be a savage monster against the first army it encounters in hopes of breaking through."

He had the dragon's piece knock over the army ahead of it, but then pressed the remaining two into contact.

"But while that assault is happening, the remaining armies arrive to reinforce. Losses are guaranteed, Isabelle, make no mistake on that, but a methodical, strategic chase covering multiple directions will be the best method. If the dragon is cunning, it might slip from the trap between chasing armies, but an outer ring of scouts with horns should form a wide enough net to alert everyone and allow us to pivot so we are always on the chase."

Isabelle pinched her lower lip between her fingers, silently absorbing the strategy.

"All right," she said at last. "This was very helpful, thank you."

"Wait," he said, before she might dismiss him. "Might I suggest a different course of action first?"

Her studious gaze shifted into caution. "Which is?"

Sariel shrugged.

"Attempt to speak with the dragon. It does not rampage without reason. Granted, that reason might not allow any potential solutions for peace. But as with any war, we should first seek to avoid violence."

"Avoid violence?" She shook her head. "Multiple villages in Argylle, full of innocent lives under my direct care, were murdered. My people have been *feasted upon*, Sariel. There is no room for peace, only retribution. The dead demand it."

Sariel's patience thinned at the rebuke. To have the woman listen so readily to his strategy, but then brush him off when suggesting an alternative to war...

"As you wish, Your Highness," he said. "At your leave?"

"No," she said, surprising him. She pushed off from the table and reached for her sword belt hanging from the back of her chair. "You're coming with me, and bring your sword."

•

Sariel suspected a gathering of such esteem had not happened on Kaus in years. The chosen spot was a shrine to Leliel, open-aired and surrounded with stone pillars weathered by centuries of storm and wind. Most importantly, it was in clear view of every waiting army.

Isabelle arrived first. Along with Sariel and her marshal, Oscar, she was accompanied by King Allan of Armane and Prince Druss of Rudou, as well as the newly surrendered King Yarrick of Forez, once the third member of the Blue Rivers Alliance. It wasn't hard to see the symbolism there. It was a message that those who bent the knee could still maintain power, and respect, as vassals to Doremy. Behind them, banners waved from their respective forces.

King Murta of Vivarai led the procession from the east. They were all dressed for war, but with far more splendor than Queen Isabelle. Murta was at the midpoint of his life, and while he might have been muscular once, he had a bit of a belly and a face swollen from far too many nights drowning in wine. His armor shone with silver, that which wasn't hidden behind green sashes. With Murta was King Jehan of Etne, as well as a gaggle of lords from the smaller realms each had united. Their own armies waited to the east, filling the distant valley with their banners.

"We meet at last, Bastard Queen," Murta said, and sniffed. "And I see you brought the beaten dog with his tail tucked between his legs, too."

King Yarrick's face lit up with rage, and he clenched his jaw to prevent from speaking. Sariel had met him only once, a proud man of stocky build and a face like a horse. He had yet to decide if the man surrendered early out of wisdom or cowardice.

"Did you think King Yarrick would be hanging from a noose?" Isabelle asked, forgoing a welcome. "I seek a united Kaus to push back against the Astral Kingdom's conquest. Yarrick is an ally now, as will be all who properly bend the knee."

The words were not truly for Murta, but for those accompanying him. King Murta's alliance was held together with fraying threads, and Isabelle wasted no time picking at them.

"Spare me the lofty lies," Murta said. "Let us deal with the dragon."

A table was set in the center of the temple, containing a map similar to the one in Isabelle's tent. Pieces representing the various kings' and queens' armies were marked and painted, but not yet placed. Sariel suspected they were left for their own leaders to position as a sign of respect.

"Are we certain of the dragon's location?" asked Jehan. He sniffed as if allergic to the map. "These creatures are supposedly capable of traveling great distances if they so wish."

"I have had scouts tracking its position ever since Siltborough burned," Isabelle said. She pointed to the little red cube that represented the dragon. "It is there, or close enough as to not matter for our discussion. What matters now is if the kingdoms of Doremy, Etne, and Vivarai are willing to honor the ages-old pact of dragon defense."

King Murta crossed his arms, his scowl deepening.

"And who would lead this defense?" he asked. "You?"

"A council formed among us," she replied, with more restraint than Sariel could have managed. "Which is what we are here to do. With each passing day, the dragon's destruction spreads, and hundreds lose their lives."

"Yes, a very convenient destruction," Murta mumbled.

"Are you implying that I summoned a dragon?" Isabelle asked.

Murta scoffed at her.

"I imply it is a wonder bandits have not stolen everything you hold dear, you are so incompetent in defending your realm. I find it insulting that we will be expected to carry the burden you cannot."

Isabelle leaned against the map table, her golden eyes piercing Murta's.

"Are you saying you will abandon your duties to Kaus?" she asked.

"My duty is to defend my people," he argued. "And if I believe their lives are better spent within my borders than dying because of your incompetence, then yes."

Sariel scanned the others, judging temperaments. King Jehan would follow Murta's decision; that much was clear. The other lords and ladies sworn to the two looked less certain. They feared the dragon, and they did not trust Vivarai to protect them.

The question was, Did Isabelle sense it, too, and could she use it to her advantage?

"Your borders," Isabelle said, and she traced her finger along the map to Vivarai. "Retreat if you must, King Murta, but let me spin you two tales. One is where you hide within Vivarai's borders, while my brave men and women slaughter a red dragon. I will be the dragon slayer and have proven myself capable of defeating the mightiest of foes. What then of your allies? I wonder who they will feel safest with…a dragon slayer or a coward?"

King Murta's face turned beet red, but when he opened his mouth to speak, Isabelle interrupted him with an almost primal cry.

"I am not done."

Her words rippled over the crowd. Murmurs and whispers turned to dead silence. Sariel shivered. Her words…they carried the coercive power of radiance.

"There is a second tale, one where you get your limp-willed wish, and my fellows and I are destroyed by the dragon." She took the dragon's red cube and shoved it straight east into Vivarai. "Its carnage will continue, and its flight already carries it toward your borders. Will your forces, far fewer than ours united, be able to defeat that which defeated mine? No, Murta, they will fall. Your people will suffer dragon fire. Their villages will burn, and their sons and daughters, *eaten*."

Her words carried farther, beyond the vale. A deadly promise. An inviolable truth.

"And while your people suffer, I shall ensure all of Kaus hears of your cowardice. The dying shall know you failed to protect them. The destitute and broken will know they were abandoned. Have you the wisdom to envision what happens next? Kaus's history is filled with graves of nobility who lost the love and trust of their people…and I know of what love you garner, and it is *nothing* compared to mine."

Isabelle stepped away from the map table, and it seemed all the world could breathe again. King Murta stammered something unintelligible as he adjusted his collar underneath his metal breastplate.

"You spin pointless tales that carry not a hint of truth," he said, trying, and failing, to match the power of her voice. "Not once have I denied my loyalty to the defense pact. My fears are that you would use this opportunity to benefit yourself, or worse, seek unearned glory. I will grant you neither. The peace between us shall last until three days after the death of the dragon. As for our combined forces, we shall each remain in charge of those loyal to us, and while we will listen to the advice of our fellow kings and queens, we will accept no orders from them."

"You only reiterate the established rules of the pact," Isabelle said, unimpressed. "But I accept such terms, if hearing me say so will put you at ease."

"It does," King Yarrick said, trying to lower the meeting's tensions. "The question is, if we are to unite against this dragon, how shall we go about it?"

"I have a plan," Isabelle said, and looked to the others. "If you are willing to hear it."

Murta waved for her to begin, and so she did. Sariel listened, with mild interest at first, then more focused as what she described deviated from his own explanations of how a chase against a dragon would proceed.

"The three chasing armies will suffer the brunt of the battle," Isabelle lied as she moved the pieces. "We will endure these skirmishes, for there will always be losses when dealing with a dragon. But this keeps the dragon on the move, tiring it from flight, until at last it realizes it is trapped on all sides. That is when it will land, and the final army rides in to seize the kill."

"My knights will lead the charge," King Murta said, grabbing his own piece and positioning it last. "You said yourself the dragon flies toward Vivarai. Have your and Jehan's armies corral it toward me, where I shall wait. When the wounded beast lands, it shall face a cavalry charge unmatched by all the kingdoms of the west. We shall bury its red scales in horses and steel."

"Agreed," Isabelle said, so quickly it raised King Murta's suspicions.

"This will only work if your forces do not break during the chase," he said. "Can I trust in the bravery of Doremy?"

"As much as you can trust the honor of Vivarai," Isabelle said, and smiled. "It is a plan. Appoint one of your advisers to be part of the pact council, so we can best coordinate our movements, and then send them to my camp before nightfall. Until then, farewell, all of you, and may Leliel watch over and guide your steps."

With that, she and her retinue exited the shrine. Sariel marched behind the queen, uncertain why she had asked him to accompany her. When she halted in the empty vale midway between the shrine and her waiting army farther uphill, he suspected he was about to find out.

"Spread word of our plans," Isabelle told King Yarrick. "The rest of you, prepare your armies to march. For now, I would speak with my friend."

The others cast wary looks in Sariel's direction but obeyed.

"You lied," Sariel said once they were alone. It wasn't an accusation, nor was he upset about the fact, just curious. Isabelle glanced over her shoulder at the shrine, where a lone priestess of Leliel was busy sweeping up the clutter.

"King Murta is a coward to the last," she said. "He thinks to watch us throw our armies at the dragon, weakening it until his own troops can swoop in to claim the victory."

"And so he unknowingly faces the worst of the assault," Sariel said. "I am impressed, Your Highness. A threat to all the realm appears, and you wield it as a weapon against your greatest rival. So very opportunistic of you."

"Either way, the dragon dies," she said. "If Murta had any bravery, he would have volunteered to lead one of the corralling armies. He has no one but himself to blame for the deaths that follow."

She hesitated.

"No one else to blame," she repeated, and cast a curious gaze in Sariel's direction. "I brought you with me for a reason, Sariel. What do you think of King Murta and his alliance?"

Sariel drummed his fingers along Redemption's hilt, thinking.

"He clings to power like a babe does to his mother's breast. He cannot imagine a life without it. His people are nothing to him, and his alliance, weak and breaking. The war is ours, in a few weeks if we are aggressive, a few months if we are careful."

"Months," Isabelle said. "And how many more battles would that take?

How many more good men and women would die to carry us to a victory already assured?"

Sariel arched an eyebrow in her direction.

"Isabelle?" he asked, curious about where this was leading.

She looked about, as if to confirm they were alone. Armies surrounded them on all sides, but there in that vale, they were as isolated as one could hope for.

"How far are you willing to go to secure my reign?" she asked. "What lines are you willing to cross to dethrone Mitra and destroy the Church of Stars?"

Sariel's guard immediately rose against such a question.

"I will do all that I must to break the Astral Kingdom," he said, offering nothing more than that.

"Then I have a request of you, Sariel Godsight, if you would obey your queen."

"I will gladly accompany you on your assault against the dragon, if that is your concern," he said, still uncertain of her plans.

Isabelle shook her head.

"No," she said, glancing once more to the shrine and the eastward-retreating kings beyond. "You will not battle the dragon at all, for I have need of you elsewhere."

Chapter 28

FARON

Horses were few in number in the Doremy army, but a pair had been loaned to Faron and Isabelle to ride ahead as they chased the rampaging red dragon.

"It's tiring," Faron said, watching the monstrous creature fly ahead of the marching army.

"How can you tell?" Isabelle asked beside him.

"See how it sags?" he said, pointing. "Its belly is nearly touching the trees. No doubt it understands we will not leave it be, and once it sees Murta's army, it will descend with all its fury."

The queen watched, nodding absently as the dragon bobbed over another cluster of trees. Etne's geography was mostly shallow hills covered with stubby grass, and what red oaks that grew were clustered together in small bunches, their crimson leaves fluttering at the dragon's passage. Across those hills marched the Doremy army, having chased the dragon eastward from Argylle for two days. King Yarrick and Queen Sillia's smaller forces approached together from the northwest, their banners high and just barely visible in the distance. King Jehan occupied the southwest, visible to Faron only if he blessed his eyes with radiance. Together, the three armies funneled the dragon westward, toward

Vivarai's border and the waiting King Murta.

Faron shuffled uneasily atop his horse as Isabelle watched the three armies march.

"Why am I here?" he asked, breaking the silence.

"Because I would not go chasing a dragon without an escort," she said, not looking at him.

"You evade the question. Why am I the escort?"

At last her golden eyes turned. They pierced him in a way he found strangely exciting, even as it unnerved him.

"I have known you were special since the moment I saw you, Faron Godsight," she said. "And everything you and your brother have done since then only confirms my suspicions."

Faron grunted. He knew she was blessed with radiance, though he could not begin to guess how. Could she sense his and Sariel's unique nature?

"Where is Sariel anyway?" he asked, the mention of his brother souring his mood. "I have not seen him since he accompanied you to the shrine for your meeting with Murta's alliance."

"Your brother disagreed with my plan. He believed we should communicate with the dragon before attacking it, and when I refused, he departed, saying he had more important business elsewhere."

That certainly sounded like Sariel, except for the part where he'd left without telling Faron goodbye.

"I must admit, in a fight against a dragon, I wish he was with us," he said.

Isabelle narrowed her eyes and watched the dragon fly. "So do I."

They trotted onward, staying several hundred yards ahead of the marching Doremy army, the bulk of which was spread out for nearly half a mile in distance. Multiple times, the dragon had turned about to belch fire, and even landed once to devour a trio of soldiers, but then flew off before the army could gather. Such hit-and-run tactics must be endured, Faron had coached Isabelle. Small losses in the lead-up to a true battle.

The pair reached the apex of the next gentle hill, and beyond spilled a valley beautiful in its sheer size. It stretched for several miles, the grass lush from the gentle river flowing through it that marked Vivarai's west-ern border. Four thousand soldiers formed ranks at the water's edge, a collection of minor lords' and ladies' forces combined with Vivarai's. Behind them were Murta's four hundred vaunted knights. Upon seeing them, the furious dragon roared with such power, it seemed to shake the very air.

"You can hear its madness," Faron said when the roar ended. "The rampage is at its fullest. Order your soldiers to sprint, or there will not be an army left to save."

"As if that would be such a tragedy," Isabelle said. "No, Faron. My soldiers shall preserve their energy. If you are right, the dragon will not leave until all its foes are broken. We need not hurry."

Faron stared at the queen, his mouth dropping open.

"You gamble with the fate of the realm," he said.

"It is no gamble," she said, and she meant every word. "With Leliel at my side, the dragon shall die." Another glance of her golden eyes. "Will you stay by your queen when she challenges the beast?"

Faron turned his attention to the dragon and its dive toward Vivarai's soldiers.

"To the very end," he said, wishing he did not sound so bitter as he watched the battle unfold.

Fire belched in gigantic plumes from the dragon's mouth, washing over dozens of screaming soldiers and charring their skin within their armor. Into that chaos it landed, making a mockery of the Vivarai battle lines as it clawed and thrashed at anyone within reach. It was small for a dragon, though Faron doubted that gave any comfort to the panicked soldiers. It was thrice the height of a man, and from head to tail, perhaps two hundred feet in length. Its scales were a brilliant crimson, and they easily withstood the first sword strikes it suffered as it waded through the line toward the river.

Trumpets sounded from the south. King Jehan had spotted the attack and was urging his soldiers to sprint to close the distance. Isabelle watched them from her perch atop the hill, judging their pace, and then unhooked her own trumpet from her belt.

"I thought we were waiting?" Faron asked.

"I would have us arrive exactly as Etne does," she said. "My ire is for Vivarai alone."

She lifted the trumpet and blew two quick notes. Marshal Oscar heard and echoed it with his own, giving the order for haste. To the northwest, Yarrick's trumpets answered, closing in the trap.

Isabelle put away her trumpet, drew her sword, and readied her shield from off her back.

"I shall lead the charge," she said. "Will you be my shadow, as Sariel is yours?"

Faron grinned, unable to deny the excitement he felt. Even among all his lives, a battle against a dragon was a rare thing.

"Shine bright, my queen," he said. "And you need never fear losing your shadow."

The two dismounted from their horses, for they could not trust the beasts' reactions when faced with such a terrifying foe. On foot, they rushed the battle as it began in earnest. King Murta's knights thundered across the valley, meeting the dragon in charge as promised. They held their curved swords high and their shields before them, and against any other foe, they might have been a fearsome prospect.

The dragon, however, cared little for their horses and their speed. It spun on them, fire blasting from its mouth in a great torrent. The flame struck the center of the knights' formation, annihilating a third before they could cross the space. More horses reared about and panicked, ignoring the riders' tugging of their reins to flee the dragon. Their formation broke, and numbering half of their initial charge, the knights reached the dragon, riding alongside its flank as they swiped with their swords. The curved blades slid along the scales, drawing not a single drop of blood.

Damn fools should have brought spears, Faron thought as the dragon spun in place, its tail lashing out to knock a dozen men and their horses to the ground. Vivarai soldiers pressed on, encouraged by their commanders, who continually blew the signal to charge on their trumpets. They fought well, but their numbers were not enough. Faron watched the carnage unfold, and he hardened his heart against it.

Whether they die by our hand or a dragon's, they are dead all the same, he told himself, wishing he could believe it.

By the time the armies of Doremy, Forez, and Etne arrived, Murta's forces were in tatters, his knights in retreat, and his footmen reduced in number by half. Many threw down their arms and fled, wading through the river into Vivarai. A shameful display, not that Faron blamed them. None there had been alive since the last time a dragon had rampaged through Kaus. They never could have anticipated the savagery they would face.

Faron and Isabelle slowed their run so the rest of her army could catch up with them, and then together they pressed as a swell against the dragon, colliding at the same time as the other two armies. The dragon twisted and snapped in all directions, losing focus with each passing moment. Each bite and claw claimed lives, but the four armies pressed with unmatched tenacity. Spears slid upward into flesh. Swords chipped away at the red scales, scratching their surfaces and stripping them of their shine. The casualties would be terrible once counted, but there was no other path to victory.

Faron sprinted to the side of the dragon's neck, weaving through the bodies and relying on the distraction of the melee. He sheathed his sword to free up a hand and then leaped, kicking off the dragon's shoulder to vault higher. He caught the top of its neck and then quickly pulled himself up. Once precariously balanced, he drew his sword and turned his attention to the dragon's head. Punching through the scales along its neck and forehead would harm it, but he had more significant damage in mind. He took three steps to gain momentum and then lunged off the neck and into the air, his sword raised high above him for a thrust.

"Dragon!" he shouted, forcing every bit of his power into the cry. Commanding a dragon was impossible, even for those blessed with radiance like him and his siblings, but influence could be very temporarily exerted. The dragon turned, a yellow serpentine eye focusing on him as he flew, and into the center of its black pupil Faron plunged his blade.

The dragon howled, and it slammed its eye shut, the thick eyelid trapping Faron's sword and hands within. He put his feet to the dragon's face, braced his legs, and kicked to rip his sword free. He fell the short distance to the ground, rolled to absorb the impact, and then came up with weapons at the ready. The dragon howled, a deep rumble mixed with the faintest serpentine hiss. Blood seeped from its wounded eye, and fire leaked between its teeth.

"That's right, keep your eye on me!" Faron shouted at the furious creature. He knew, buried deep beneath the rampage, there burned a fierce intellect. It would recognize what he was, what he truly was, and seek to end him as its greatest threat.

Fire swelled within its open maw. Faron grinned. Perhaps it recognized him, perhaps not, but it most certainly wanted him dead. It opened its jaws wide and breathed out its flame, a spout dozens of feet wide. Avoiding it was impossible. His armor would mean nothing against it.

"Faron!" Isabelle screamed, hesitating just underneath the dragon's throat.

Faron dropped to his knees, closed his eyes, and trusted the only power in all of Kaus worth trusting. A shield of radiance shimmered around him, sparkling translucent silver. He focused his mind upon it, hardening it, giving it strength to deny the flame. The dragon's fire washed over him, and he felt no heat. The shield creaked and groaned in his mind like cracking glass, but it did not break.

The fire ceased, and he disbanded the shield before the last of the smoke from the charred grass blew away, to reveal himself unharmed.

"Leliel is with me!" he shouted to the dragon, knowing this moment, and his survival, would be retold for years to come. "Your fire is nothing!"

The beast roared in defiance, which shifted to pain as Isabelle thrust her sword into the base of its neck, her blade sliding up and underneath scales to carve the soft flesh underneath. Soldiers swarmed the dragon's body, hacking into its legs, its sides, and even its tail. Many more rushed to join Isabelle, refusing to let her fight alone. The little nicks and cuts only added to the dragon's ferocity, and it rose into the air, fire swelling in its throat.

Faron sprinted underneath the neck, legs pumping, shield rising. Two soldiers unknowingly barred his way, but he flung them aside to crash into Isabelle. His shield positioned between them and the dragon, he flooded his body with radiance as the fire exploded from the dragon's mouth to wash over them. Men and women screamed, blackening to bone and ash before the barrage, but not Faron and Isabelle. She was safe in his arms. Their eyes met for the briefest moment, and he sensed her questions, but she kept them silent.

The fire faded. The two separated, and Faron readied his sword, but his chance to attack never came. The dragon's front leg swiped across him, carving a deep groove into his shield when he blocked. The impact sent him rolling, and he went limp to minimize the damage. He came up to his knees, his attention snapping back to the queen.

The dragon bore down on Isabelle, its teeth eager to crush her. Panic spiked in Faron's breast, but he fought it down. This was it. This was the moment. The creature was bloodied and weakened, but if the kill was to be hers, she must take it on her own. He had to trust her to survive. To succeed.

"I am the blade of the goddess!" Isabelle screamed. "I am her light!"

Wings burst from her back as they had during her coronation, and they carried her into the air to meet the jaws of the dragon. Light flared brilliant from every inch of her armor. Her sword rose high, and across its blade shimmered a beam of gold so bright, it was blinding.

The dragon hesitated, its good eye turning away from that light, and that moment spelled its doom. Isabelle screamed, a wordless, primal cry of triumph heard throughout the entire battlefield, and then swung her sword. An arcing beam of light flashed off the steel, twice the size of her meager sword, and flew through the air. It struck the dragon's throat, and against that golden power, its scales crumpled inward. Flesh separated. Blood flowed.

The dragon cried out, that winded shriek lacking the power of its earlier roars. Its wings flapped wildly, unable to lift it. Its legs thrashed, but the frantic flailing passed harmlessly above a perfectly still Isabelle. The dragon toppled to one side, its eye bulging, its mouth opening and closing like a dying fish, and then collapsed completely. Its head struck the dirt, mere feet away from the queen, and it lay still.

Silence followed, the air electric, and then the cheers sounded from the crowds. Faron sheathed his sword and approached the queen, knowing they must capitalize on this moment before it was too late. He sprinted past her to the dragon's head, climbed up halfway, and then turned about while hanging there.

"Come, my lady," he said, and offered her his hand.

Isabelle startled as if waking from a dream. Her wings were gone, as was the light that had enveloped her. Realizing what he wanted, she nodded and accepted. With his help, she climbed atop the head of the slain beast. The height made her visible to all four armies, and she lifted her sword high above her head while shouting at the top of her lungs.

"The dragon is slain!"

The soldiers cheered, clapped, and stomped their boots to create a din that matched even the dragon's mightiest roar. Faron let it echo for a brief moment before pooling radiance in his throat and projecting his voice so it boomed above the rest.

"Dragon slayer! Dragon slayer!"

The Doremy forces took up the chant first, then Forez, and then even Etne and Vivarai.

"Dragon slayer! Dragon slayer!"

Isabelle slowly lowered her sword, and she looked down at Faron. The sunlight caught in her hair. Her cloak billowed in the wind and smoke from the dwindling fires of the dragon's breath. Blood, dragon blood, stained her clothes, her armor, and even her face, but it only added to the image. And then she smiled at him.

"All hail my queen," Faron said, even though no one would hear him, not even her. His heart was aflutter. It felt like a confession.

"All hail Isabelle the dragon slayer."

Chapter 29

FARON

Faron waited until the night was deep to leave his tent. He crossed the grass, memories of the day's battle hovering like phantoms in the corners of his eyes. So much death, and all for one creature's fury. Such destruction demanded answers, and he would have them.

"Faron?" a soldier guarding the corpse said, quickly saluting with a fist against his chest. "Is something amiss?"

Faron had insisted to Isabelle that she place guards around the corpse, lest it be looted. Once carved, nearly every part of a dragon's carcass could be sold for a tidy sum that her army desperately needed. He had also told her dragon corpses were exceedingly dangerous, with the fire they belched potentially erupting at any point, and therefore they should camp a safe distance away. All of it a ruse so he might have his midnight meeting.

"I'm having trouble sleeping," he said. "Consider all of you relieved. I'll make sure no one comes to clip a few dragon toenails to sell at market."

The soldier looked uncertain, and he glanced to the man with him, who shrugged.

"It'll be fine," Faron said with a bit of radiance for emphasis. The two immediately caved, and they called for a third soldier to join them.

"As you wish," one said as the three left.

Now alone, Faron approached the dragon's head. Its red scales had taken on a purple hue in the starlight. They were beautiful, and if Faron allowed it, they would soon adorn many a ring and amulet across the continent of Kaus.

"Dragons have ever looked upon these human lands with disdain," Faron said as he sat before the head. Its good eye was open and still. No flies buzzed about, nor any carrion creatures or insects. Death had not yet come for the dragon, and its innate magic kept it protected. He spoke without any of the jovial attitude he'd shown the guards. Such a magnificent beast deserved solemnity, not the charisma he exuded to win over the humans around him.

"So why now did you descend upon us with such hatred?"

Faron closed his eyes and reached out, his fingers gently touching the scales of the dragon's nose. His breathing slowed. As he had when he called Iris to him, he let his presence flow, but this time, not into the earth. Instead, it plunged into the dragon's corpse, and the secret beating heart within. Two hearts, a second even deeper within the rib cage. The dragon was not yet dead.

A spark in his mind. The connection was made. The dragon's name floated over him, vaguely familiar, for each of these creatures was as old as Kaus itself: Teldrass.

Faron opened his eyes to see faint blue light shimmer across the scales.

Would you torment me even after my demise, ever-living?

The voice sounded within Faron's mind, slow and imposing. It echoed as if spoken from everywhere, and if it had been real, the ground would have shaken from its depth.

"I would speak, now that you are not overtaken by your fury," Faron whispered.

Fury? The dragon laughed. *No, it was not fury. To admit as much causes me great shame, ever-living, but it is desperation that drove me here. Desperation, and fear.*

"Fear?" Faron asked. "What could possibly strike fear into the heart of an immortal dragon?"

The blue light swirled across the scales, growing in depth. It would not be long now.

Our dreams are haunted. The end comes. Even for us, the immortal. Even for you, the ever-living.

Faron's throat tightened. The fey mother, Mae'lilia, had spoken similarly.

"Then your dreams are false," he said. "No power can break that which binds my family to Kaus."

Teldrass laughed, slow and mocking.

You think yourselves eternal. We remember when humanity emerged from the dust. We remember when you ever-living first knelt before us, blinding in your radiance. It is dull now. The stars weaken. The false moon soothes no longer. We dream of three suns, gold, sapphire, and crimson, all rising for the final dawn. The sky shall rip apart and weep burning tears, bringing forth our end. Bringing forth FINALITY.

Faron shuddered, his insides constricting. The prophecy of dragons was rare. Never did they lie. Never were they wrong.

"And so you attacked us?" he asked. "Why?"

The red drained from the dragon's scales, which began to pulse the cold color of the moon.

Your kingdoms bring about ruin guided by a pale hand. My fellows retreat south, flying for land promised yet unseen. I stayed. I swore to resist. To burn your kingdoms and spare our realm. I failed, and so I, too, will flee.

Faron stood, and he drew his sword.

"Whose pale hand?" he asked. "Tell me, dragon."

Enough, ever-living. I have gifted you far more than you deserve.

"No!" Faron pointed his sword toward the dragon's corpse. "Give me a name. Refuse me, and I shall pry open your ribs and thrust my sword into your true heart, denying you your rebirth."

As your brothers once did to Asruma?

Faron flinched, hating to be compared to Eder and Sariel. Together, they had slain Asruma centuries prior, when the black dragon rampaged across the southwest lands of Kaus, killing thousands. When his brothers defeated Asruma, they had burned every part of its body, carved apart its bones, and pierced Asruma's second heart, ensuring the dragon's true death.

"If you speak true, then all the world is in danger," he said. "Against such a threat, yes, Teldrass, I would do the same."

And so you would echo their unforgivable sin.

Faron walked around the body, his impatience growing. He found the specific rib, slid the tip of his sword underneath one of the scales, and then pressed the sword halfway to the hilt into the dragon's flesh.

"A name," he said. "I will hear a name."

You are not ready.

He pressed the sword deeper.

"A name, or you will not be reborn within your egg."

You are not worthy.

"A name, dragon! A name, or death claims you!"

It is you, *Faron Godsight. You who shall tear open the sky and bring about the end of three worlds.*

Faron staggered as if from a blow. The words echoed in his mind, over and over, for he could not believe them. It couldn't be. It made no sense.

"You are wrong," he said.

Your denial is meaningless. Leave me to my rebirth, ever-living, if you are capable of such kindness. This fate is writ into the stars themselves.

Faron sheathed his sword. He swallowed what felt like glass shards lodged in his throat.

"Farewell, Teldrass. When you hatch, may you find your prophecy in ruin, and the world turning as it ever has and ever will."

The scales dissolved into pale light and drifted skyward like cast-off embers. Meat and bone followed, the entire dragon corpse becoming luminescent. Wind blew from the north, sudden and fierce. The glowing trail surged southward, fading away like dust. Miles upon miles away, safely hidden within the land of dragons, Teldrass's essence would travel to the egg it had already laid. The dormant egg would quicken. A decade from now, the dragon would be reborn, its cycle begun anew, but its memories and wisdom intact.

Nothing but a great splatter of blood remained of the slain dragon. Faron stood before that emptiness, his hands shaking at his sides.

"It can't be," he whispered. "I would never. I would *never.*"

He returned to the camp, wanting nothing more than solitude. It was not given. To his surprise, a lone rider arrived at the camp, and though he was cloaked, there was no disguising the dragon-bone blade propped across his shoulder. Faron's mood, already dire, somehow worsened.

Sariel passed his horse off to one of the guards at the camp entrance and then made a straight line for Isabelle's tent. Faron cut him off half-way there.

"Hey," he said. "Where were you?"

Sariel tried to brush past him without answering. Faron stepped in front, his hand pressing against Sariel's chest. His anger tumbled out of him, adding unintended fire to his words.

"I asked where were you, Sariel. Why did you abandon us when we needed you most?"

"Is the dragon dead?"

Faron flinched, angry at the answer he must give. "Yes."

Sariel pushed him away. "Then you did not need me."

The dismissal burned his insides further.

It is you, *Faron Godsight.*

"You can't keep doing this," he said. His words accosted Sariel's back as his brother walked on. "You have to be with us, and commit, Sariel. No half measures if we're to win. How can I trust you, if you won't give this war your all?"

Sariel froze. His head curled over his shoulder. The midnight sky burned in his eyes, fierce with light.

"Watch your tongue, brother," he said, and his words could freeze rivers. "For you know all that I am capable of, and all that I should not be. The dragon is dead. Let it die."

Faron had no argument left to give, only confused anger and frustration, and so he watched in silence as his brother adjusted his sword, turned away, and entered uninvited into Queen Isabelle's darkened tent.

Chapter 30

SARIEL

The tent was dark, lacking even a candle, but Isabelle was still awake when Sariel slipped inside. He knew she would be. She'd be awaiting his return.

"Sariel?" she asked, sitting up in her bed. He saw her every curve, saw her hair fall across her face and neck, in desperate need of brushing. She wore only a long, thick shift that exposed her muscular arms. Her golden eyes seemed to glow in the night, visible without any need of his radiance.

Sariel did not answer. He walked to her bed, flipped his sword, and then jammed the blade into the soil so it would remain standing. Isabelle reached for a little dresser positioned beside her bed and pulled out a tin holder and candle. She did not seek out a tinderbox, but instead lit it with a brush of her thumb and forefinger, sparking it with a flash of her golden radiance. Somehow the light only made the room seem smaller, her features that much harsher.

"Is it done?" she asked.

Sariel met that golden gaze. "It is."

She set the tin down, brushed a bit of hair away from her face, and then met his gaze. Her will was iron. There was no relief in her voice. No joy, either. Just satisfaction.

"Then you have done well. You have my gratitude, Sariel."

Images flashed through Sariel's mind. Brutal ones, caked with blood.

"Gratitude," he whispered. "I do not want your gratitude."

His right hand was around her throat before she could move. His left grabbed the wrist of the hand reaching for the dagger she kept with her when she slept. His fingers constricted, holding her there, as her eyes bulged. She wasn't panicking, not yet, but she was close.

"Who are you?" he asked her, his voice a whisper. "Who are you truly?"

He relaxed his grip enough so that she might answer.

"I am your queen."

"But you want to be more than a queen. You want to be empress. You want all of Kaus united under your banner. Do not deny it. You reek of ambition."

Her smile was all teeth when she answered.

"Yes, Sariel, I will be empress. Leliel has promised me a throne."

"Enough!" He slammed her to the bed, his weight atop her, his hand still on her throat. Their faces were so close, their noses nearly touched. He peered deep into those golden eyes, seeking the truth within them, and the explanation for radiance so powerful.

"The goddess doesn't exist," he whispered into the dark. "Leliel is a lie. You have been promised nothing. Tell those fables to the populace to win their support, but do not dare tell them to *me*."

She rose, her back and shoulders straining, so that her lips could press to his ear.

"I don't care what you believe, Sariel, so long as you serve."

Sariel felt keenly aware of her every movement beneath him. Her legs, wrapped about his. Her free hand, pressed to his chest, not pushing him away, nor drawing him closer, but spreading her incredible warmth through him. That gaze, indomitable to the last.

His fingers left her throat, and he withdrew from the bed. His heart hammered within his chest, and it felt like he had been holding his breath.

"What I did tonight," he said, glancing at Redemption. Forever free of the stain of any blood it shed. If only Sariel could say the same of himself.

"I have to know it was worth it. I have to believe it will lead to a future worth embracing. I will not put you upon a throne to be a tyrant or a monster, Isabelle. Mitra's crimes are many, but I know he believes himself righteous. That is what drives him, even if it is to places he should never go. You, though?"

He turned back to her.

"You, I trust not."

Isabelle stood, and though she wore such meager garments, she held her head proud and regal. Her voice hardened. No more whispering.

"I will destroy the church that would laden our people with lifetimes of sins. I will unite the little kingdoms that have slaughtered countless generations with petty wars born of greed and personal vendettas. I will bring about a peace, and prosperity, that benefit all of Kaus's people, not just her lords, kings, and queens. A land of justice and mercy. That is what I will create."

Sariel shook his head. "The Heartless King sought to do the same, and we all know his final legacy."

"My legacy will not be one of slaughter and cruelty."

Sariel ripped his sword free of the dirt.

"Will it not?" he asked, and moved for the exit.

"Wait."

He stopped. That he did upset him greatly. Redemption's hilt gently turned within his grasp. He glared at Isabelle, but that glare did not last. Radiance blazed like fire within her irises, her power let loose for him, and only him, to see. Golden threads floated like mist from the corners of her eyes. The darkness retreated from her, and when she spoke, his chest constricted.

"Twice now you have threatened my life for fear of what I am," she said. Her voice burned across Sariel like wildfire. Her fists clenched, and faint lightning arced across her knuckles. "Do not let there be a third."

He wanted to challenge her, to deny her the right to possess the radiance she commanded. The words died in his throat. No matter her faults, they were a pittance compared to his. He wanted out. He wanted to be free of her. And so he gave her his promise so he might leave.

"There won't be," he said. "Should I fear what you are, and what you are becoming, you will be dead, and I, long vanished."

She smiled. Wide. Playful. Like a predator. Her words haunted him long after his departure.

"Do you truly think me so easy to kill?"

Chapter 31

FARON

Do you think we'll get to participate in the feast this time?" Bart asked as they marched the road through the forest on their way to King Murta's castle.

"What do you mean, 'this time'?" Faron asked with a laugh. "I remember you getting quite drunk at Queen Isabelle's coronation."

The young man blushed.

"That wasn't a feast, not really. That was a bit of buttered bread and all the beer we could drink."

Bart jumped as Derek thumped a hand on his shoulder from behind.

"For lowly soldiers like us, that *is* a feast," he said, grinning down at Bart. "What say you, a game of Wounds once we get ourselves seated at a table? It's always more fun to play with proper drinks. We might even have some coin to gamble with!"

"Remember what I told you," Faron said, nudging Derek away from the young man. "No gambling unless you want to lose it all."

"I don't remember Bart struggling to win our last few games," Rowan chipped in. The surgeon was never far from Tristan's group once free of her duties. Faron need not wonder why. He caught her sideways glances in his direction, and sometimes even returned them. On lonely nights, he pondered sneaking over to her tent but so far had resisted the temptation.

"It's one thing to play for pride, another for coin," he said. "Trust me."

"I don't want to gamble," Bart insisted. "I just want to eat something nicer than what I could have had when hunting back at home. That's all."

"I'll raise a glass to that," Derek said, and began describing the most succulent cuts of deer he would prefer. Faron laughed, agreeing that all of it sounded divine. The miles vanished as Murta's castle finally appeared in the distance.

"Do you think it'll last?" Rowan asked, walking alongside Faron, her voice lowered so the others would not overhear. "I know the armistice is only for three days, but for King Murta to play host despite the losses he suffered..."

"He might be hoping for peace," Faron said. "A celebratory feast would be a good time to ask."

"I hope so," Rowan said. "I know Leliel commands Isabelle to conquer the Astral Kingdom. I know a lot of war is lurking ahead of us. But it... it'd be nice to have a few weeks of peace. To rest up and pretend the island is not at war."

She stumbled on a stone, and Faron reached out to steady her. Their eyes met, and Faron smiled, truly noticing for the first time the deep red of her hair and the way portions of her bangs had escaped the tie of her ponytail to curl around her forehead. His insides warmed. Perhaps tonight could be a celebration in more ways than one.

"My parents live in Rudou," she said, as if there had been no spark between them. "Queen Sillia's surrender spared them the plague of war, and so far our battles have remained within Blue River's territory. If peace came, then they'd never have to worry about invasion should the winds turn against us. They wouldn't have to see..."

She trailed off. Faron sympathized. The horrors of battle were brutal, and as a surgeon, she would have seen the worst of it up close.

"That's all up to Murta," he said. "He could also bend the knee, swear allegiance to Doremy, and keep his crown. If he is smart, he'll do it. Surely even his people would understand him bowing to the newly named dragon slayer."

The procession of soldiers trailed on for several miles, with the various nobility clustered around King Murta and Queen Isabelle at the lead. Faron and the rest of his group were not far behind, granted permission to march near the front in honor of their role in slaying the dragon. Well, Faron's role, he knew, but it was best to extend the honor to everyone.

It was that proximity that allowed him to see the sudden shock on King Murta's face when he arrived at Lossleaf Castle's drawbridge and it did not open.

"Franco!" King Murta shouted at the edge of the thin, empty ditch that surrounded the castle's western side. "Are you blind? Lower the bridge so we might entertain our guests!"

Nothing happened. Murmurs of confusion spread.

"Excuse me," Faron whispered to Rowan, and then pressed forward. Marshal Oscar saw his approach and frowned, but he also knew the role Faron had played in slaying the dragon and allowed it.

"Is something amiss, my queen?" he whispered.

"We shall find out," Isabelle said coldly as she stared at the strangely dormant castle. No soldiers walked the walls. No servants moved within the windows. It was unnatural. With so many marching toward Lossleaf Castle, runners should have warned the castellan and servants within to prepare for their arrival. To be greeted with silence...

Unease spread as more time passed. A group of Murta's men finally crossed the ditch and, with the help of some rope and hooks, climbed inside through one of the lowest windows. Long minutes passed as the various nobles whispered gossip among themselves. Only Isabelle abstained. She watched the castle with a steady gaze, to the point where Faron and Oscar shifted uncomfortably beside her.

Suddenly the drawbridge began to descend.

"At last," Murta said, clearly feigning relief. Sweat trickled down his neck, and he tugged at the collar of his fine lavender coat. "There better be a damn good..."

The words died in his mouth. His two scouts stood waiting on the other side of the drawbridge.

One held a woman's corpse.

The other held the corpse of a child.

"Sandra?" Murta said, taking a single, unsteady step forward. "Willis?"

He sprinted, his coat flapping behind him. He slid to a halt at the edge of the drawbridge, his legs going weak and his entire body collapsing to his knees. The scouts laid the bodies before him and whispered something Faron could not hear. Murta's response, though, was a clear shock through the group of nobles.

"*Everyone?*" the king asked. "It...but that can't..."

With the drawbridge lowered, Faron could see into the courtyard beyond. Several bodies lay still upon the grass. All of them bore similar wounds. Long, deep cuts across their throats and chests. Faron thought of the many servants and guards living and working within a castle to keep it functional, as well as serve the slain queen and prince, and feared to know their sum.

With his senses enhanced, he also heard the whispering of the scouts to their king.

"While some coin was taken, it wasn't much, and most rooms have been left untouched. If they're raiders, they're unlike any I've encountered."

Murta buried his face in his slain wife's hair, wetting it with his tears.

"Sandra," he moaned, ignoring the scout. "Why, why Sandra? Why take her from me?"

The murmurs among the nobility grew louder as realization dawned upon the lot.

"The whole castle, taken and killed?" Marshal Oscar said beside Faron. "That would take numbers and coordination few bandit raiders possess. Why strike here, and not at any of the lesser-guarded villages nearby?"

A valid question, and Faron feared the answer.

Queen Isabelle crossed the space to the drawbridge. Conversations dimmed, the nobility eager to hear her words as she addressed the weeping king.

"You have my heartfelt sympathies, King Murta," she said. "But I have the bellies of my men to worry about. We will depart for Vendom and leave you privacy to dwell on your grief."

Murta looked up, a bit of blood and his wife's hair sticking to his face.

"That is your sympathy?" he asked. "That is your kindness? This... this was your doing."

Her voice deepened, each word cutting like a knife.

"I am not the one incapable of defending my realm. It is you who had bandits steal everything you hold dear. Do not cast your guilt my way."

The callous echo of Murta's words lit a new fire within him. He burst to his feet, his teeth bared like a feral animal as he pointed and spat.

"Liar!" he shouted. "Their blood is on your hands!"

Isabelle's expression, already cold, turned more brutal than a winter blizzard.

"My soldiers and I rode straight into dragon fire," she said. "With all the west watching, I cut open its red-scaled throat. I sympathize with your grief, King Murta, but do not dare insult my honor, nor the bravery of those who fought alongside me."

She turned away and shouted orders to her marshal.

"We move out," she said, and cast a glance to the other gathered vassals. "And we move quickly. We have three days to make ready for war."

Faron saw the way faces paled at her warning. Where once those lords and petty kings had looked upon Isabelle with anger or rivalry, they now gazed in horror. None desired to face Doremy in battle. King Murta had been the one holding them together, but his army was decimated by the dragon, and his castle slaughtered. Come three days, there would be no war, only surrender.

Murta knew it, too, but he held no proof for his accusations. Faron suspected it wouldn't matter even if he did. He was a man who used power to manipulate and control those beneath him. Now broken, he would be quickly abandoned. The king returned to the corpses of his wife and son and collapsed.

"Sandra," he said, gently stroking her hair. Tears fell, his sobs undignified. "Willis... I'm sorry. I'm so sorry."

Faron turned away from the sight, and he refused to look Isabelle's way. He couldn't shake his growing dread.

My soldiers and I rode straight into dragon fire, Isabelle had claimed, but that wasn't true. One particular soldier had been notably absent. Faron pushed back through the ranks, his insides twisting.

"What's going on?" Bart asked as Faron passed them by.

"We're marching out," he said, offering no further explanation than that. His rage was growing, and he did not wish to unleash it unfairly upon his friends. He pushed onward at a jog, passing through King Murta's men to reach the rest of Isabelle's. Somehow rumors traveled faster, and confusion and unease reigned. Some even readied their weapons, fearing a battle would break out despite the armistice.

Faron ignored the uncertain looks and fearful questions. He had but one destination in mind. One person he must confront.

For you know all that I am capable of, and all that I should not be.

Sariel lurked at the far back of the army, leaning against a juniper growing alongside the worn dirt road. His head was bowed, and his eyes closed, as if he were asleep. Faron grabbed him by the shirt and pulled him close. His brother's eyes snapped open. No, not asleep. Just waiting.

"Careful, brother," Sariel said softly. "Others are watching."

The fire in Faron's belly grew hotter.

"What did you do?" he asked, having to fight to keep his voice down.

"I did as commanded."

"An entire castle?" Faron asked, not wanting to believe. "You murdered not just the queen, but their soldiers, their servants, their families…"

Sariel leaned in close, his words only for Faron, and not the nearby soldiers pretending, poorly, to ignore the confrontation.

"You let your love of humanity blind you to the larger picture," he said. "The blood of those few will spare us a war against many. Not just the losses in battle, but the starvation and disease that follow. No pillaged villages. No lengthy sieges. I *saved* lives, Faron. Just not in the honorable way you prefer."

"War is war, as humans will ever wage it," Faron hissed back. "But you murdered innocents. Children, Sariel? Have you no heart, that you would murder *children*?"

That finally lit a fire within Sariel. His brother smacked his hand away and then shoved him. Faron stumbled a step and reached for his sword.

Redemption was ever near, resting on Sariel's shoulders, and the hand holding the carved hilt clenched in a white-knuckle grip.

"What truly bothers you so?" Sariel asked, again in that deep, maddeningly calm whisper. "That these supposed innocents died...or that it was your precious Isabelle who gave the order?"

Faron flinched as if struck. Sariel saw and grinned, the light behind his eyes so brilliant and cruel.

"As I thought. I pray tonight cleanses you of whatever delusions you hold toward Leliel's supposed champion. Now you see her for who she is."

"And who is that?" he asked softly.

Sariel pressed his shoulder to Faron's, and he spoke with an air of frightening finality.

"The future empress of Kaus, and the blade that will sever the head from the Church of Stars."

Part Four

BLOOD

Chapter 32

FARON

During the Heartless King's reign, the Unity of Leliel had been broken, and its temples and priests stripped of land, title, and the right to practice. In return, the priests had fled west, as far as they could from the Tower Majestic. Despite the centuries, the damage had never been undone. The temples were mostly isolated from one another, little deviations in dogma sprouting like weeds throughout the little kingdoms.

If there was a true successor to the Unity of Leliel, it was in Cevenne, deep in the midlands of Kaus. There ruled the Council of Worship, a collection of five priests who regulated the temples scattered across a third of the continent. Their influence could not be denied, and it was for that reason, six months into her island-spanning campaign, Isabelle and a large portion of her army camped outside the affluent city.

"Have you a plan if the council rejects your claims?" Faron asked as they approached the city gates. They were a small group, Isabelle, Faron, her adviser, Aubert, and a handful of armed soldiers.

"How could they, given who and what I am?" Isabelle asked.

"People are stubborn, stupid, and weak to pride and arrogance," Faron answered. "I assure you, the council has shown plenty of all four throughout its existence."

"When appealing to matters of faith, one can never be certain," Aubert said in agreement. "But having the truth on one's side certainly helps."

"As does having already conquered more than half the continent," Faron added with a chuckle.

The gates opened, and soldiers bowed low in respect to the visiting queen. A priest robed in white greeted them. He was a kindly-looking older man, a bit on the heavy side, and like many who lived in the midlands, his skin was a deep shade of black. What white hair remained around the sides of his head was carefully trimmed. A winged eye hung from a silver chain around his neck. His robe was tied with a black sash, and a series of bells tied with blue thread hung from it, the number signifying the priest's rank within the council's established hierarchy. Five bells. A member of the council, not just a representative. They softly chimed with his movements, the sound pleasant.

"Greetings, Queen Isabelle Dior of Doremy," the priest said, clasping his hands before him and bowing. "My name is Reglia, humble member of the Council of Worship, and I shall be your escort to our temple."

"I am honored to have a member of the council come all this way to greet me," Isabelle said.

"A little walk does this old body good," Reglia said, and he smiled. It was far less pleasant than the tinkling of the bells. The priest was sharp, and his trust in Isabelle was forced. "But I must confess, I am eager to meet with someone supposedly so blessed by our beloved goddess."

He hid it well, but Faron sensed the emphasis on the word "supposedly." The priest had come not to greet, but to judge. Faron held back a chuckle. Oh, how great a surprise all these priests had waiting for them.

"And I am happy to meet with you," Isabelle said, walking alongside Reglia as they passed by the homes built of the nearby salwood trees. "I suspect there is much you have heard of me, not all of it true."

"Oh, based on the stories that have reached our fair city, I suspect much about your exploits has been exaggerated."

"Have they now?" Isabelle asked.

"Indeed," Reglia said, and winked. "For you are not eight foot tall and sporting wings. At least, not yet."

The queen laughed. "Give me time."

Cevenne was bisected by the Verdon River running north to south, while also being the closest major city to the road that led through the Sapphire Mountains that isolated the eastern coast. As such, it had become a major hub of trade from all four corners of Kaus, and that wealth showed. Compared to the more simplistic structures in cities like Leyval and Vendom, even the smaller homes here sported little flourishes in design, windows curling near the tops and bottoms, doors carved with decorative birds and felines, and a plethora of wind chimes hanging from seemingly every house. Cevenne was sometimes called the City of Winds, for it seemed there was always a breeze blowing in from some corner of the plains.

They next passed through a market, city guards quick to join their group and clear a path. The smells of roasting chicken and cracked pepper rumbled Faron's stomach, and he was tempted to abandon all the coming politics to instead feast. It would surely be a more enjoyable use of his time. Instead he ignored his stomach and kept with the group as they arrived at the Cevenne Temple.

It had been decades since Faron had last seen the temple, and little about it had changed. It was a lovely mix of white stone painted blue, open-aired and lined with imposing pillars whose surfaces were carved with the names of priests who had lived and died spreading Leliel's grace. A grand statue of Leliel herself awaited at the top of the stone steps leading into the temple, her arms spread wide and the eyes upon her wrists gazing out upon the city. Her face was blindfolded. The six wings stretching from her back were bound with rope and chain. It was a reminder of the days of the Anaon Kingdom and the persecution the faithful had endured.

At her feet, written on four stone tablets, were the Four Pleas, the words supposedly given to her beloved on the day of humanity's creation and the goddess's subsequent departure from the lands of Kaus. "Offer love when tempted with hatred. Show compassion when treating the broken. Be joyful when those around you fall to despair. Be kind, my children, for you all belong in my arms."

As long-lived as Faron and his siblings were, he did not recall the moment of humanity's creation, nor hearing the voice of the goddess. So far as Faron was concerned, the Four Pleas were simple, basic concepts asking for humanity to be less awful toward one another, but as usual, they managed to fail miserably no matter how faithfully they served the goddess.

Given its open structure, there were few walls, and instead many blue curtains fluttering about to segment the structure into various "rooms." At the apparent entrance, a priest demanded that all who would enter surrender their weapons. The soldiers remained outside, while Isabelle and Faron reluctantly handed over their swords. They then traveled deeper inside, down a hallway formed almost entirely of thick curtains, which ended at an entrance whose curtains were black.

"Within is the temple heart," Reglia said. "It is there we will discuss your conquest. I pray you show proper respect and remain silent if you are not addressing our members."

As with all parts of the temple, there was no ceiling, only open sky. The room was surprisingly large, made up of pillars forming a perfect circle, the gaps between them filled with black curtains. In the center were five chairs, the wood polished, the cushions crimson, and the backs and arms decorated with little gold and silver wings. All five chairs were empty, but that would not last for long. Already one of the other curtains pulled back, and robed members of the faith slipped inside.

"Stand within the heart of the circle," Reglia ordered Isabelle. The queen nodded and obeyed. Faron started to follow, but the priest held out his hand.

"Our laws decree only the council may be seated within the temple heart," Reglia told Faron and Aubert. His eyes twinkled. "Seated, I would point out. Thankfully, there is no law about standing and observing by the door."

And so the pair waited near the entrance, bystanders to Isabelle's meeting with the five members of the council surrounding her in their ornate chairs.

"Her belief is unassailable," Aubert said softly beside Faron as they watched the five members take their seats. "Will that aid her or harm her, I wonder."

Faron held full trust in Isabelle's abilities. Her words were gifted with radiance, granting them power. Of course, Aubert would not know or understand that.

"Our queen is quite convincing," he told the adviser. "And besides, as you put it best, the truth is on our side."

Once the five members of the council were ready, one of them, a tanned man whose head was fully covered with a blue cloth lined with silver threads like spiderwebs, lifted his hands to signify he would speak first.

"Welcome, Queen Isabelle," he said. "We have watched Doremy's conquest with great interest, for even when you were but a princess, grand claims reached our ears of your supposed blessing. At first, we scoffed, but with each subsequent victory of yours, and your slaying of a rampaging dragon, we have now begun to wonder."

"But conquest does not mean sanctification," the lone priestess of the five said. She looked the oldest, her head wrapped in an ornate bonnet and her neck positively drenched in silver chains containing wings and eyes. "That is why we have called you here, to judge the truth of your claims."

"And how will that be done?" Isabelle asked. "Will you pray to Leliel and demand she answer?"

"We have our methods," the first priest said.

"Oh, I'm sure you do," Isabelle said, slowly turning in place. "But none that matter. If you cannot hear her voice, then you are in no position to judge me, she who has felt the very touch of the goddess."

"I see we are not here to make friends," Aubert whispered beside Faron.

Insulted glares and mutters from the five. Faron smirked. If they expected Isabelle to grovel before them and kiss their feet in hopes of receiving their blessing, they were sorely mistaken.

"What is it you want?" Reglia asked, his voice slicing through the noise. "We are all guided by our desires. Yours, however, frighten us. You claim it is the goddess's will you serve. What, then, does the goddess require? Tell us her will, we who have spent all our lives studying it and praying for it to occupy our hearts and minds?"

Isabelle pulled back her shoulders and stood tall before them.

"The goddess must rule Kaus, for it is her creation, and we her beloved children. Yet belief in her is threatened by the Church of Stars, and the Astral Kingdom, which would reenact the crimes committed upon us during the reign of the Heartless King. Grant me your blessing, Council, and I shall form Leliel's Protectorate, a union of all little kingdoms under one banner, whose faith in the goddess shall be unquestioned, and whose purpose is forever defined as a servant to her holy will."

The five priests were stunned by the grandeur of her desires. Some were shocked, others openly aghast.

"You would anoint yourself empress?" one asked.

"We are not meant to sway the fate of thrones," the blue-headed priest insisted.

"We have watched Doremy swallow up the west," a third priest shouted. "You move in greed disguised as faithfulness to our goddess of peace."

Isabelle let them ramble for a few seconds before she clenched her fists and bellowed out her response.

"I shall have silence!"

The words rolled like thunder across them, radiance threading her cry into a command, golden and undeniable. The priests rocked in their chairs, eyes wide and uncertain.

"Greed, you call it, as those who trust in me march their feet to bone and bleed out upon the battlefield," she continued, slowly turning in place to meet each of their gazes in turn. "It is not greed, priests. It is necessity. Are you deaf and blind to the fate our beloved suffer within the Astral Kingdom? Mitra Gracegiver burns our temples. He banishes our priests and priestesses. His preachers and shepherds spread west like wildfire, and if left unchecked, they will consume us all with a hollow, wretched faith in their sin-obsessed Father."

Reglia was the first to overcome the command, and he leaned forward in his chair.

"We have sought ways to counter him," he said. "But why should it be you, Isabelle? Why should we grant you unprecedented power to build your protectorate?"

"Because I have been chosen by the goddess to lead her people."

The five were calmer now than before, but they still showed great distrust at such a claim, and the lone woman dismissed her entirely.

"History is rife with charlatans and liars who would claim the goddess has given them her blessing," she said. "Why are you any different?"

Isabelle lifted her arms and tilted her head. Faron smiled at the sight. There it was, the dwelling power within her. This was how it should have been from the start. No exchanging of words. Just Isabelle's truth, and the undeniable blessing she possessed. Gold light crackled across her arms like lightning. Her irises shone as if lanterns burned behind them.

"Because *I am*."

The four ethereal wings burst from her back, golden and translucent. Brilliant light swirled about her like a dress. Her feet rose off the ground, and she rose before them, her hair fluttering in a silent wind. Though she had surrendered her sword, she held her hand aloft, and when her fingers closed, she held a gleaming blade that looked capable of piercing the heavens.

"Since the moment I lay in the cradle, I have lived with the goddess's power within me," she told the stunned council. "And no man or woman can deny the truth I know. I shall sit upon a throne to reign all of Kaus. It is not greed, pride, or vanity that shall put me there. It is fate."

"The stories," Reglia said breathlessly. "We thought them lies and exaggerations."

Isabelle lowered herself to the ground. The blade vanished from her grip, and her wings faded away like brilliant smoke. Only the glow in her eyes remained, golden and beautiful.

"I am truth, followers of Leliel. Foes of the goddess await, and I shall lead the assault against them. Abandon your fear. Believe not in limitations and defeat. Believe in Leliel. Believe in *me*. The protectorate shall march upon Racliffe, and by my hand, the Luminary shall be broken and his church cast like refuse to the sea."

•

The council had the trio depart for a cozy waiting space decorated with standing statues of deceased priests and priestesses among the many wicker chairs. Reglia was the one who came to them with the news, the deliberations lasting less than an hour.

"Thank you for your patience," he said as he joined them in the curtained room. "Not only in waiting for our decisions, but also for our stubbornness and doubt to your claims."

"I ask for much," Isabelle said. "Reluctance is to be expected. But tell me, what is the council's decision?"

The priest crossed his arms and spoke firmly, as if reciting a religious decree.

"We of the Council of Worship acknowledge Queen Isabelle's unprecedented status as chosen of the goddess. In the name of saving our faithful from the evils of the Astral Kingdom, we will grant our blessing, as well as our financial support, to the creation of Leliel's Protectorate." He paused, a bit of his guarded nature returning. "With the belief that, in her desire to serve the goddess, the queen shall consult with the Council of Worship and always put the needs of the faithful above her own."

Faron fought down his chuckle. He should have guessed. The council sought power should Kaus be unified as Isabelle desired. Perhaps they even thought they would be a safeguard against potential tyranny.

"Thank you," Isabelle said, and she gestured to Aubert. "My family adviser here is familiar with the status of my army's logistics, and well-versed in my plans for the protectorate. He will help with its establishment, and the council's role within it."

"I am eager to be of aid," Aubert said, bowing low.

"We shall start immediately," Reglia said. "Time is of the essence. Mitra has been strangely dormant in responding to your wars across the little kingdoms, but I suspect he will finally awaken when he hears of the birth of Leliel's Protectorate. On the bright side, our decree will grant you legitimacy, and it may ease the fears of those yet to bend the knee to your rule."

"If it avoids bloodshed, then all the better," said Isabelle.

Faron clapped his hands, glad for this business to be concluded.

"All right, let's head back to our army, share the good news, and then prepare to march," he said, and then turned to Reglia. "Thank you for the escort to the temple. May we meet again soon."

"Oh, I suspect it will be much sooner than you expect," Reglia said, and he bowed low to hide his much-too-pleased smile. "For I am coming with you."

Chapter 33

EDER

Eder ascended one of the lifts to the top of the Tower Majestic. Madeleine did not accompany him. The apex of what remained of the tower was for Eder and Eder alone.

"Luminary!" the nearby liftmaster said when Eder arrived at what was known as the rafters. The dozens of liftmasters cranking the levers and turning the sand hourglasses cried out his name. Those who could dropped to their knees, while those who couldn't bowed their heads in respect. The night was dark, and so they were illuminated in the glow of dozens of lanterns stationed equidistant throughout the floor.

"At ease, my friends," Eder said, smiling at them. They were strong men, bare-chested despite the cold wind that blew through the tower at all times. This floor was not a true hardstone floor, but one constructed over decades, hundreds of crisscrossed wooden beams and a veritable jungle of ropes to suspend an octagonal platform. All across it were gaps for ropes and chains, along with cranks to turn the many pulleys and gears for the tower's lifts. They were true machinery allowing civilization to blossom within the ancient structure, tucked away and unseen. If not for them, traveling across the many floors would take dramatically longer, and the transporting of goods be near impossible.

The boards groaned beneath Eder as he walked a center path, gently touching the foreheads of liftmasters who approached him for a blessing. Ever since occupying the Tower Majestic, he had made sure the liftmasters were treated with the utmost respect. If he was to keep his secrets, he needed them to be loyal.

"Going to the Final Ascent?" one asked when Eder approached. He stood before three different pulleys, each one with an hourglass timer marking when to begin its ascent or descent. At this lift, unlike the others, two armed soldiers stood guard with him, silent and serious.

"I am."

Behind the soldiers was a roped-off platform. Unlike the few platforms that led all the way up to the rafters, this was the only one that progressed even higher, to the true top of the broken tower. Eder stepped onto the platform, turned about, and then addressed the soldiers.

"I shall signal when I am finished," he said as his platform began to ascend.

It was not far, twenty feet or so, to reach the final stretch of hardstone that jutted out from the tower walls. This was the Final Ascent, space reserved for Eder's eyes alone.

The platform halted just shy of the hardstone, hovering over the deep pit that ran through the Tower Majestic's center. Eder stepped off onto the small platform. High above, the tower ended, granting a beautiful display of the stars. Eder stared up at them, compelled to whisper.

"What secrets do you hide behind your lustrous curtain?"

Shaking his head, he turned his attention to the relics of the Etemen.

This collection was his pride and joy, salvaged from both the Hanging City and the tower itself. In one corner, a bookshelf contained what writing remained of the Etemen people. Much of it was nonsensical, but it was within those tomes that Eder had discovered the runes he used to send the souls of the devouts to the heavens. That knowledge was just the beginning of his great work.

Dominating the center of the Final Ascent were the runestones of the

Etemen. They varied in height, somewhere between one and two feet tall, and were composed solely of unbreakable hardstone. They curled and looped into one another, pale gray, bearing markings that should have been impossible. No iron or steel chisel could even dent hardstone, and yet these runestones were covered in great swaths of intricate swirls and markings.

The stones spiraled inward, wide at first, rarely connecting, but then growing taller and more tightly intertwined as they curled inward. To walk among them was dizzying. To see the starlight reflected off them set Eder's nerves on edge. This was a thing that should not be, and yet he craved knowledge of it above all else. The lines of silver he drew for the devouts were but a pitiful facsimile of their grandeur.

Eder walked to the center, where the only other structure remained. It was an elevated pedestal roughly Eder's size. The sides were sculpted to look like a multitude of hands rising. Six-fingered, as Eder assumed the Etemen to have possessed. Those hands reached and reached, the fingers and palms coming together to form a basin at the very top. An empty basin. His ultimate mockery, this altar of hands.

Even when Eder placed the final runestone obtained from Nem, the runes never came to life. The magic of the Final Ascent remained dormant. Whatever they needed, it was missing from that pedestal.

Eder paused before it, letting the sight of those hands burn into his mind. He had searched, oh, how he had searched. Soldiers had torn apart both Underbridge and Bridgetop alike. Every floor of the Tower Majestic was swept clean. Nothing. Despite slowly piecing the runestones together over decades, linking the heavy stones into their proper place on the floor, he had failed to find the key that brought it to life.

"To come so close," he said, resting his hand upon the basin. "Did the sea swallow the key? Will the water lock away its secrets, denying me, as my brothers come marching to destroy all I have built?"

A voice startled him from behind.

"But what is it you have built, Eder?"

Eder slowly turned. He recognized that voice...

"Calluna?"

His little sister squatted beside the bookshelf, her shoulders hunched, her arms crossed behind her, and her head tilted so her hair hid much of her face. When he called her name, she glanced up at him, her dark eyes burning into his. Tears filled them.

"Hello, Eder."

Eder rushed across the space, careful not to trip over the runestones, and then knelt before her. He spread his arms, and she eagerly fell into them, her small self cuddling against his chest. He wrapped her in an embrace, her face pressed to his chest, and his lips upon the top of her head.

"Dearest Calluna," he whispered as he held her. "Where have you been?"

"With Faron," she said, her voice soft and trembling. "And Sariel."

Eder was glad she could not see his frustration. He knew well their plans. There was no preventing the stories of the Bastard Queen from crossing the Sapphire Mountains and reaching the ears of those living in Racliffe. Upon conquering the Blue Rivers Alliance and winning over the Council of Worship, she had declared Doremy Leliel's Protectorate. All churches dedicated to Father were destroyed, and the faithful ordered to repent or be banished forever. Multiple little kingdoms had pledged allegiance, and many others had been quickly conquered and added to the protectorate. There was no hiding Isabelle's aims any longer. She was coming for the Tower Majestic.

And pulling her strings were his two brothers. Isabelle was their dutiful puppet, building the army they themselves could not. Two-thirds of the west was united under the protectorate's banner, with only King Silvein and his allies still holding out in the more isolated, mountainous regions known as the Crowning. It was only a matter of time until they, too, folded against the growing crusade.

"How fare my brothers?" he asked, working to keep his tone light. Best to pretend he knew none of that with Calluna.

"They're mad at me, Eder," she said, sniffling. "They're mad I tried to kill Isabelle and stop this stupid war."

Eder stroked her hair.

"Precious one, killing her would stop nothing. They will have this war.

Even if you had succeeded, they would have found another puppet to put in Isabelle's place."

Calluna leaned away from him. Her tears were dried, her weakness now safely hidden.

"I don't understand," she said. "I never have. You knew they would protest, and yet you built this kingdom anyway. You spread your faith. You claimed the tower. Why, Eder? What is worth so much animosity between us?"

Eder gestured to the runes.

"Wisdom, my sister. The only true pursuit. The skies are false. I know it. I feel it in my bones. With the Etemen runes, I can finally pierce them and shout out my protest to Father." He sighed. "If only I could find the final key."

Calluna slowly separated herself from him, and when she stood, she wiped a bit of dust from her dress. Her voice hardened, as did her expression. Growing duller. Colder.

"What if I gave you the key?"

Eder's breath caught in his throat.

"Do not tease me, Calluna," he said, once capable of responding.

His sister crossed her arms and stared at the spiraling runes.

"Follow me," she said. "And I will show you."

•

They rode lift after lift, steadily descending each and every time. Calluna refused to explain where they were going until there was but one location left: the final step leading to the small military encampment, and beyond it, the cold cells.

Eder escorted Calluna through the camp, his presence ensuring soldiers said not a word about the strange woman's arrival. When descending the final steps, he expected Glasga to be awake, but it seemed the hour was so late even he had ceased questioning his devouts and gone to bed. There were eight hanging from the ropes, purifying their souls for the next full moon.

Calluna stopped at the very edge. She saw the ropes of the cold cells, frowned, and then peered over into the dark.

"People are alive in there?" she asked, seeing the wrapped canvases swaying. She turned, her glare accusatory. "How could you? After what Sariel—"

Eder felt those memories claw at his mind, threatening to return. He pushed them away.

"I do what I must," he said, interrupting her. "This place is...sacred. I do not know if you feel it, but I do. We are close to Father here."

Calluna stood, wiped at her dress, and then walked along the edge and its cavernous drop.

"No, not Father," she said. "But we are close. You believe Father is in the heavens, and so you climb ever higher to reach him. But the Etemen? I think they believed the opposite. Their god lived beneath the sea."

She stopped at the silver markings he had formed for the ritual. He thought she would protest, especially if she realized their purpose, but instead she stood in their very center and turned about so her back was facing the edge. Cold wind blew across her, teasing her hair and the hem of her dress. She crossed her arms behind her, a bit of shyness returning.

"You just want your knowledge, right?" she asked.

"I seek to pierce the veil separating us from Father," Eder said. "All else has been the means needed to accomplish that goal."

"So if you succeed, then you don't need to fight Faron and Sariel? You won't need your kingdom, your faith, or your tower?"

"I cannot say, little one, for we dabble in realms beyond us all. What might I learn? How might I change? In what ways will Father guide or command me? It is unknown, all of it. I promise I seek no war. I desire no violence. Beyond that, you must trust me to do what I believe is right."

Calluna clutched the sides of her dress, thinking. For a long moment, the only sound was the distant crashing of the waves.

"I trust you, Eder," she said. "I always have. It's why I let you do this for so long. And I...I'm going to trust you again. But only if you trust me, too."

Eder smiled softly at her.

"Among us all, you are the purest, Calluna, and the most true. I would put my life in your hands, if you would but ask."

Calluna withdrew a knife from her dress pocket and held it to her palm.

"Then I do ask," she said, and sliced her flesh. Blood poured, and she clenched the wounded hand so it collected into a single stream. The blood dripped to the center of the silver runes and splashed upon them. Calluna moved her fist about, painting them all.

"Your little silver is drawn across what once remained," she said, her voice taking on a strange, dreamlike tone. "It is carved, so softly, so thinly, you did not see. But you feel it. You chase after it, as you draw your own spirals."

She knelt down, not caring that her blood was staining her dress. She pressed her bleeding palm to the center of the runes and then began to swirl it about as if she were a painter seeking to cover a canvas. The blood smeared across the silver, banishing it...and then revealing beneath it similar runes and markings. Blue light sparkled across them, illuminating the dark. It was as if the blood awakened them.

"How?" Eder asked, excitement racing through his veins.

"After the shattering, I came here," she said, and stood, her work apparently finished. Light washed over the lower half of her body from the blazing runes. "The Tower Majestic defeated me once, Eder, and so I swore I would learn its secrets. *All* its secrets, even the ones it would hide most deeply. It took years, but I won."

She lifted her arms. Her eyes sparkled. The runic circle blazed with light.

"Fly with me, Eder, to the tower's truth."

And then she tilted backward to fall headfirst to the water below.

"Calluna!"

Eder dashed forward, too slow to stop her. His hand grabbed air. He peered over the edge, tormented with the thought of watching her plummet...only he saw no sign of her. Even with his radiance-blessed eyes, which lit the deep dark with starlight, he could not see her.

"Calluna?"

He glanced to the runes and saw their light fading. The blood she had spilled cracked and burned away into dust, leaving a ruin of his original silver designs. The waves crashed and broke against the Tower Majestic's sides. Laughing. Mocking.

"I said I would trust you," he said, and drew his own knife. One cut, and blood dripped from his hand to the runes. "But it is a monstrous recovery, even for us, to endure years of being feasted upon by creatures of the sea. I pray you are right. And if not..."

He grimaced as the runes shone once more with light.

"If not, then hopefully Faron and Sariel drag our corpses from the water sometime this next decade."

Eder smeared his blood, just as Calluna had, to ensure each and every mark and line flared with silver light. It was so familiar an act, akin to preparing the devouts for their sacrifice, he suspected he had been imitating this Etemen ritual without ever realizing it.

When finished, he turned, his back to the edge, and spread his arms.

"Fly," he whispered, and let himself fall.

The world turned and shifted, the terrible height of the Tower Majestic stretching on and on above his feet as he fell headfirst. Wind blew against his robes and hair. The roar of the ocean neared. He closed his eyes.

Water washed over him, but it was not the cruel impact that should have broken his neck, nor was it shockingly cold, but instead pleasantly warm. His descent slowed. Not suddenly, but gently. His weight returned, and weirdly, it felt like he had righted himself. The sound of the waves faded, and at last, he found the courage to open his eyes.

Eder stood upon the ocean. No, not upon the ocean. *Beneath* the ocean. His feet pressed to the surface as if he were a spider clinging to a ceiling, yet the change felt natural. It felt right. He could see a faint outline of the final step in the distance, as well as the eight devouts hanging from the edge.

"How is this possible?" he asked. Though surrounded by water, he breathed in open air. His voice was muffled, but only as if he had a bit of cotton stuck in his mouth. "Above" him was the seabed, brown stone smoothed over countless years. Faint blue light shimmered through the water, lighting the way as if he walked in broad daylight.

Calluna waited for him a few steps away, a playful grin on her face. Her hair floated wild about her.

"Come on," she said. Her voice entered his mind as if spoken from all around him. "It isn't far."

Eder walked along the underside of the surface, the water somehow firm below his feet. As much as he told himself the ocean floor was above his head, it still felt like it was a cave ceiling instead. As a test, he blew out a long whistle of air, expecting to see bubbles. Instead, there was nothing.

"I've been down here for an hour once," Calluna called over her shoulder. "After that, my head started to feel light. I wouldn't try for longer. I think that's when the air finally goes away."

Given everything, Eder held no sense of direction, and so he followed Calluna toward one of the tower walls. As it neared, he expected to find the immaculately smooth hardstone surface down here, same as above. It was, for much of it... but Calluna led him to a strange little jut, sharp and jagged, like several pyramids broken and pieced back together unequally. In its center was a door, or a gap left to serve as one.

"What is within?" Eder asked, trying, and failing, to control his excitement.

"What the Etemen tried so hard to hide," Calluna said. "And everything you claim to seek."

Remarkably little remained of the Tower Majestic's original builders. Even the name, Etemen, had been given to them thousands of years prior by the humans who first settled the tower, their word for "ancients," which had clung and remained as the human language shifted and changed. They had no diagrams, no stories, and no statues, just the pedestal in the Final Ascent and a small collection of books filled with nigh-untranslatable runes.

Never did Eder expect them to appear so... plain. A hundred colorless statues filled this underwater building, all of them carved so they knelt with their arms lifted toward the ceiling. They were six-fingered, not five, and none of them sported any hair. Little ridges marked their skulls, faint and almost like a series of waves. Their noses were sharp, their mouths open wide in a way that unsettled his stomach.

They were not human, but they resembled humans closely. Even their robes looked familiar, and were buckled with sashes carved with incredible attention to detail so that they seemed to ripple and flow within the water.

All one hundred faced the center of what certainly felt like a temple. Within was another pedestal matching the one upon the Final Ascent. And resting upon it...

"The key," Eder whispered, unable to believe it.

It was a bowl, shaped like a half sphere, its sides a dizzying maze of runic lines and circles. At first he thought it made of hardstone, but its surface was too shiny, its color too reminiscent of silver. Eder touched the sides, feeling the lines beneath his fingers. It was warm, and the contact made his insides tighten and his heart pound in his chest.

"Here," he said. "Right here." He turned to Calluna. "Why did you never reveal this to me?"

Calluna pointed to the ceiling.

"Look," she said. "And see."

The floor was barren, as were the curving walls. The statues and the key had stolen his attention, but now he looked to the ceiling, he saw it was a grand mosaic formed of tens of thousands of tiny colored stones. It depicted the key, held in the pedestal, while bright sunlight shone through the windows of the Tower Majestic. Two Etemen garbed in deep blue robes stood before the bowl, knives in hand. In their grasp, they held a man whose neck was cut and whose blood filled the bowl.

That man looked exactly like Sariel.

"I don't understand," Eder said, humbled by the sight. "The Etemen, they were gone from Kaus long before us, or the humans. We...we couldn't have been here."

"Couldn't we?" Calluna asked. "With each death, we remember less. With every year that passes, the limits of what we remember fade deeper into fog. When did we first arrive? We don't know. Were we children? Perhaps, but not in a time any of us remembers. What if we did walk among the Etemen? Maybe they loved us. Maybe they hated us. I do not know which, but I do know one thing, Eder." She pointed to the bowl that was the key to the entire device. "It needs our blood. Radiance-blessed blood.

That is why I left it here. That is why I feared it. What good could come from such a thing?"

Eder pulled the key from the pedestal. The metal felt like squirming worms beneath his fingers, but he did not care. At last he would solve the riddle of the tower and confirm his theories of the purpose of the runestones.

"Thank you," he said, turning to Calluna, only to discover she was gone. There were only the statues of the long-dead Etemen, their arms raised toward the now-empty pedestal, their mouths open in prayer.

Prayer, or perhaps wailing.

Eder carried the key out, walking along the water's undersurface. Instinct had him return to where he fell, and sure enough, he found a collection of runes glowing upon the water's surface. Eder stood in their center, clutching the key to his chest, and waited.

The sea gave way below his feet, and he fell. The world righted itself, and a great splash of water washed over him and forced his eyes closed. He gasped, then retched, suddenly heaving out a tremendous amount of water from his stomach and lungs. His legs went weak, and he dropped to his knees. Hardstone greeted them, leaving bruises.

Weak and breathless, Eder opened his eyes. He knelt upon the runic circle, now just scattered dust that had once been blood. Below, swinging from ropes, slept the devouts in their cold cells.

"Thank you," Eder said, the key safely cradled in his arms. Cold water dripped from his face and clothes, and he shivered. "I will never forget this kindness, dear sister. When we hear Father's words, and the lies of this world crumble around us, I will repay your faith tenfold."

Chapter 34

SARIEL

Sariel and Faron stood at Isabelle's right hand, Aubert to her left, as the diplomat from Kanth bowed low before her. Reglia hovered not far away, silently watching as he always did these meetings. They gathered in the center of the Doremy camp, tents packed tightly together alongside the small stretch of forest marking Kanth's border.

"I am honored to meet you at last, Queen Isabelle," the diplomat said. He was a small man, and strangely dressed in a thick black coat that seemed to swallow his entire body. His hair was covered in a scarf, his boots tall, his hands fully enveloped in gloves. Only his eyes were visible, pale and yellow. Sariel did not remember such a style being common in Kanth, but then again, he had not been there in many years. "It gives me great pleasure to bring news of peace and prosperity instead of war."

Sariel was careful to hide his surprise. With the bulk of western Kaus unified, either folded directly into Doremy or united within Leliel's Protectorate, they had marched their army northward, across the plains of Vivarai to the mountainous reaches of Kaus's spine known as the Crowning. Of the three main kingdoms, two were vassals, Queen Lythia of Perche and King Salo of Valois. Both were ruled by the largest of the three, the kingdom of Kanth. Their control over the Crowning Mountains and the gold and silver within granted them enviable prosperity, while the deep forests surrounding their lands formed a natural wall against invasion.

So if they were willing to join the war effort against the Astral Kingdom, that would be the last piece falling into place, and the invasion of the east would be ready to begin.

"I do not seek peace," Isabelle told the diplomat. "I seek Leliel's rightful return to her exalted place, and that Mitra Gracegiver be cast down from his throne of lies."

The diplomat offered her a scroll.

"To which His Majesty King Laurence Silvein the Second is willing to pledge substantial resources."

Sariel stared at the scroll, immediate distrust sinking into his belly. Something about this diplomat was off, and not just in his garb. There was an aura about him...Unsettling. Hinting of radiance, but how could that be? Had the people of Kanth pledged to the Astral Kingdom in secret and learned forbidden ways from Eder?

Isabelle accepted the scroll, unfurled it, and skimmed the numbers before handing it to Aubert. Sariel glanced sideways at it, a tiny hint of radiance sharpening his eyes.

King Laurence was offering, while not soldiers, a tremendous amount of gold and silver from his nation's coffers to fund the war effort, along with pledges of troops from both Perche and Valois to march in their stead. In return, they would be considered part of Leliel's Protectorate, although King Laurence would remain sovereign over his lands, and Perche and Valois his dutiful vassals.

A fair offer, in Sariel's eyes, especially as it avoided the potentially costly march through Frostlash's blue pines to lay siege to the Grand Castle of Kanth. Which was why there was no hiding Sariel's surprise when Isabelle rejected it outright.

"From those who possess much, much must be expected in return," she said, tossing the scroll to the dirt. "And what I need more than coin are bodies. In return for King Laurence submitting reign of his kingdom over to Leliel's Protectorate, and supplementing the wealth he has already offered, he will deliver to our armies half of his standing forces. In addition, he will forfeit both his vassal states directly to Doremy, to become part of our glorious lands."

The diplomat's eyes bulged, and despite his well-practiced composure, he sputtered a moment before he could respond. Aubert nearly matched his expression behind Isabelle.

"Such terms are unreasonable in the extreme," the diplomat said. "I come seeking to avoid bloodshed, and—"

"You come so your king may waggle a coin in front of my face and pray I am distracted by it as a toddler would be," she said. "You have heard my terms."

"Terms I reject outright, without need of consultation with my king, for they are egregious to the last."

Isabelle dismissed the diplomat with a wave of her hand.

"Then we have our answer, and you yours. Leave us, diplomat, and come not again unless you are ready to properly bend the knee."

•

Later that night, Sariel paused at the entrance to Isabelle's tent. Two guards were stationed before it, as there always were since his return from Lossleaf Castle. He fought back a smirk. As if they could stop him.

"I would speak with Queen Isabelle," he told them.

"A moment," one said, and then slipped inside. He emerged a moment later, whispered something to his fellow guard, and then gestured behind him.

"She'll see you," he said, and then the pair wandered away. It seemed Isabelle would ensure them their privacy. He appreciated it. Pretending not to notice the increased beat of his heart, he slipped inside the tent.

Isabelle sat in a chair before her little dresser, slowly combing her hair. She wore her travel attire despite the late hour. It seemed she held no expectations for sleep.

"Yet again you arrive late to my tent," she said, not looking at him. "Is this your promised third time, Sariel?"

He jabbed Redemption into the ground and then crossed his arms.

"I would hear an explanation," he said. "You are no fool, Isabelle. Your eye has ever been on your goal. Yet this baffles me. King Laurence's offer was reasonable. Your counteroffer was not."

Isabelle set her brush upon the table with a soft thud. He caught the faintest glimpse of her reflection in the mirror. She looked shaken, possibly even trembling.

"You sound like Aubert," she said coldly. "Representatives of both Perche and Valois have confided they are willing to join Leliel's Protectorate. They only fear King Laurence and his retaliation. Something is amiss in Kanth, they insist, and they plead with me to remove Laurence from his throne. Once we do, they will both bend their knees in obedience."

"They would also bend the knee if you accepted Laurence's proposal," Sariel said. "To my eyes, you seek war with Kanth even more than you desire to unite Kaus and sit upon an empress's throne. That isn't the Isabelle I know."

She turned to glare at him. Raw, seething anger overwhelmed her voice.

"Then you do not know me," she said. "Yes, I seek to unite Kaus, but crushing the Grand Castle of Kanth has ever been one of my goals."

"Is it?" he asked, intrigued. He remembered the faint aura of wrongness wafting off Kanth's diplomat, that hint of radiance, and wondered if Isabelle knew things he did not. "Will you explain why, or must I make assumptions and guesses?"

Isabelle looked away. Her fingers drummed the top of her dresser. "Not a word of this may leave my tent."

Sariel slowly sat upon the edge of her bed and folded his hands. "You have my promise."

The queen stood and paced before him, her fingers twitching and her steps quick and light. She looked filled to the brim with energy. No wonder she had not made an attempt at sleep. Her pacing slowed, then stopped. Whatever internal debate she held, it was intense, and he thought she might change her mind and order him to leave. Instead she resumed her pacing and quickly blurted out her truth.

"I am not my father's bastard."

Sariel lifted an eyebrow. "I see why this is not to leave your tent."

She smiled briefly, a hint of amusement amid her anger and excitement. It warmed his insides.

"And I am a fool to trust you with this knowledge, Sariel, but perhaps I yearn to be a fool after a lifetime of studying and plotting. I do not know the identity of my father by blood, only my mother. Her name was Eliza, and she was a lowly servant of the Grand Castle."

A "bastard," her opponents freely called her, but it seemed even that link to noble blood was false. Perhaps she *was* a fool to tell him this.

"Are you certain?" he asked.

"All this was told to me by King Henri long after he adopted me in secret," she said. "I hold no reason to believe he lied. He was a friend of King Laurence, but he claims that the man changed over the years. Became something...darker, and stranger. Age left him, and his youth returned. My adoptive father...Henri...he traveled there less often, and at his final visit, he was appalled by the sinful depravities taking place within the Grand Castle's halls."

Her mood shifted, cooling like embers thrown from a fire.

"I will not repeat the horrors, but they were many, Sariel. Even my father would not deign to tell me them all. The people of Kanth are twisted and vile, influenced by the sins of their king. My father said he feared for his life, but before he could leave...I was born."

She closed her eyes.

"Henri said I was meant to be sacrificed, Sariel. Sacrificed, and my blood drank at a feast. And so he saved me. Just a meager child of servants, but he smuggled me out nonetheless, and at great risk to himself."

It did not take much for Sariel to piece the rest together.

"And when he returned home with you, he claimed you as his bastard daughter."

"He had no child of his own," Isabelle said, nodding. "I suppose his kindness also served himself, if you view it in such a way. I choose not to do so. He never spared me the truth, even if he lied to the rest of the world. I grew up listening to stories of the Grand Castle of Kanth and the blasphemies within. Blasphemy, he insisted, that they wielded through blood and sacrifice. Blasphemy, that the Church of Stars repeats with their wretched jars and prayers to the false Father."

She sighed, a weak smile pulling at her lips to hide the hurt the next words caused her.

"Blasphemy, he said, when the light first leaked from my eyes on my thirteenth year."

Sariel frowned at the discovery of yet another lie.

"At your coronation ceremony you said your father declared your gifts from the goddess."

"An easy lie to make, when Henri lies in a grave," she said. "No, Sariel, I experienced them far sooner, and when my father found out, he made it clear they were born of the sins of Kanth. He bade me never reveal what I could do. It was a burden I was to bear, secret and foul. And I did. I did. For years, I pleaded with Leliel to take away this light. I prayed for her to cleanse my blood, for it was a curse, a vile curse. My father, he never doubted, not after what he saw in Kanth. Not even on his death-bed. That is why I had to wait. That is why I could not reveal myself, my true self, until he lay cold in his coffin."

She lifted a hand, and from within her palm a golden thread of radiance rose. It swirled, the light sparkling as if composed of a thousand grains of sand, and then spread about, becoming a winged sword, the cross-guard eye blinking once. A clench of her fist, and it scattered, gold dust fading into nothing. The tent fell once more to darkness.

"Was he wrong?" she said, so softly, he wondered if she truly wished for him to hear. "I don't know. Perhaps I am a monster, a most beautiful, gilded monster."

Sariel remembered his sword upon her throat as she stood naked before him, the waterfall roaring behind her. He remembered his desire to name her a monster for wielding the radiance within her. It seemed he was no better than a foolish human king.

"Damn any who would hold you responsible for the nature of your birth," he said, and though he left it unspoken, he considered himself among them. "It is no curse, Isabelle. It is a blessing. You are a miracle upon this land, and I would see no man or woman denigrate your worth."

"Miracle," she whispered. Her expression was as stiff as iron, and yet tears slipped down her face. "No, Sariel, I am no worker of miracles. Leliel does not speak to me. I have prayed to her each and every night of my life, but not once has she deigned to answer. I have lied to my people. I have lied to my kingdom. I am not gifted by the heavens. I am not chosen by the goddess."

She lifted shaking hands. Resolve washed away her sorrow. Anger spiked fire into her tired eyes.

"I am the daughter of servants, and cursed with evil blood, but it will be enough. *I* will be enough. Leliel may not speak to me, not yet, but I will deliver to her a world beholden to her beauty and free of those who would cast her aside. The Church of Stars will burn, and Mitra Gracegiver scream out his repentance from the streets of Racliffe for daring to banish our goddess."

She closed her eyes, finally at peace.

"And at long last, I will hear her voice, for how then could she refuse me?"

Sariel stared at this powerful enigma of a woman. By all rights, he should call her delusional for destroying so much in the name of the goddess. She was a liar, a usurper, and she was manipulating her people's faith into unifying Kaus behind her cause, all in hopes that she would hear a whisper from the divine.

But that strength of hers, that fierceness, it could topple mountains and move the stars. Even the unbreakable Tower Majestic might crack when she struck it with her fist. Sariel could not have asked for a more worthy champion to bring his brother low. Nor could he deny the hope he felt when he listened to her speeches. The promises she made, they were so akin to those of the Heartless King, and yet, and yet...

He reached out to her, his fingertips gently brushing the sides of her face. His forefinger traced the last of her tears, pushing it away. The gold of her eyes shone bright, and it soothed away his uncertainties.

"We shall march upon Castle Kanth come the dawn," he said. "It will be a hard trek through the Frostlash Forest, with many opportunities to slow our progress and ambush our forces, but I am confident we can reach it by the end of the week. Once there, we shall crush King Laurence, tear open the castle's walls, and reveal to the world the depravities your father witnessed. Whatever the sins of your birth, they shall be atoned for, and at last, the entirety of the west unified under your banner."

Isabelle grabbed his hand and held it against her, forcing his palm to cup her cheek. She did not smile with her lips, but the radiance in her eyes glowed ever brighter.

"Thank you, Sariel."

Her skin was so soft. His thumb brushed her mouth, felt the warmth of her breath, felt the gentle curve of her lips. He leaned closer, saw her lips part, heard her hold her breath. All the world turned unreal, this moment isolated, a potential hope he had never considered. If he would but lean a little closer, if he would close his eyes and give in to the softness underneath his fingertips...

Their lips touched, not even a kiss, just a furtive meeting, and then he forced himself away.

"I should rest," he said, yanking his sword free of the dirt. "We have a long day ahead of us."

Isabelle's arms fell to her sides. Her fingers curled the fabric of her trousers within her fists.

"Do not tell Faron any of this," she said. "I know you are close to your brother, so please understand, I do not make this request lightly."

"You would have me lie?"

"Faron's dedication to me is strong, and his heart, so kind. I fear how he may react if he learned the truth of Leliel's promise. Please. Consider doing so for his sake, if not mine."

Sariel pushed open the flaps of her tent.

"I will not lie to him," he said after a long moment. "But for you, I will remain silent. Consider that the best I may give."

Chapter 35

FARON

N o wonder all the people fled Kanth," Derek said, slapping at the red gnat biting his neck. "I'd leave, too, if I had to deal with these little shits every day."

Isabelle's army camped in the heart of the Frostlash Forest, which formed a perimeter around the capital, the ostentatiously named Grand Castle of Kanth. The forest was not so cold as the name might suggest, not with it still in early fall, but instead the cool tones of the blue pines, their needle tips shifting from green to blue halfway through, added a strange wonder to the passage. After a few hours in, the swarms of red gnats had arrived, smaller than flies but far more aggressive as they filled their bulbous little bellies with blood. Faron had hoped they would be chased off by the smoke from the campfires, but that seemed not to be the case.

The red gnats left him and Sariel alone, of course, for they could dismiss them with a thought. Given everyone else's misery, Faron worried even that minor privilege might be noticed and commented on...

"My ma told me about red gnats," he said, scrambling for a lie. "The smoke makes them angrier at first, but just because they know they need to leave."

"I hope you're right," Rowan said, sitting beside him in the grass. She leaned against him, content to be near, as she had ever since he offered her a stay in his tent one night several weeks prior. Their lovemaking was pleasant enough, and she a warm body to hold as he slipped into sleep. "Because I've never seen gnats this large, or this vicious."

"They're rare," Sariel said, huddled underneath a blanket with his back to a blue pine. His eyes were closed, as if he was trying to sleep. Iris slept beside him, on just a tiny sliver of the blanket. It had taken time, but the coyote had slowly warmed up to his brother's standoffish demeanor. "But I've seen worse. If you hate these, never travel the swamps of Kaleed."

Faron tossed another log onto the fire, using the motion to hide the closing of his eyes and summoning of his radiance. He spread his command of nature through the air, directing it solely upon the swarm of red gnats.

Begone from here.

That done, he sat back, clapped his hands, and then wrapped an arm around Rowan.

"See?" he said as the buzzing swarm started to disperse. "Just needed enough smoke."

"I hope the bastards had their fill," Derek muttered, watching them go.

Their conversation halted at the howling of a wolf pack hunting in the nearby forest. Faron was surprised by just how close they sounded, having thought they would be frightened off by the sheer size and noise of the encroaching army.

"Not to say the gnats aren't terrible," Rowan said when the howls ended. "But I don't believe a few bugs could empty out those dozens of villages we passed through. Faron, you're close with Isabelle. Did she tell you where the people went? Something they don't want us common soldiers and surgeons to know?"

Faron shook his head.

"Nothing," he said. "Everywhere is just...barren, and far too soon for it to be a response to our invasion."

Nearly every village along the western half of Kanth they'd encountered was abandoned. They faced no resistance whatsoever on their march to lay siege to the capital, either. Isabelle's best guess was a plague of some sort, yet no news of it had ever spread beyond the kingdom's border.

Kanth is much weaker than we ever anticipated, she had said as they investigated yet another abandoned town. *No wonder they wished to give us coin instead of soldiers.*

Perhaps the rot of the castle had spread to the commoners, Sariel had suggested. He and Isabelle had exchanged a look, but when Faron asked about it, he was given no explanation. The secrecy upset him, but he let it die. Whatever the truth, he was certain they would discover it upon arriving at the Grand Castle. At least the lack of defense had kept the vassal kingdoms out of the war, too, both seeming content to let Kanth fall to Leliel's Protectorate.

"Shit," Derek suddenly blurted. "I just realized Bart's stuck out there. Poor guy. No smoke to save him on his hunt. He's gonna come back covered in a thousand bug bites, if he comes back at all."

Faron's call had gone out for at least a mile, likely saving Bart from the bites as well, but there was no way to explain that to Derek.

"Smoke travels far," Sariel said, his eyes still closed. "I suspect he'll be fine."

A fine enough excuse, which Faron was thankful for. Rowan nestled her head against his chest, and he slumped a bit, getting more comfortable before the fire. They'd retire soon, and he drifted his hand lower to her waist. His fingers slipped just underneath her shirt, brushing across her skin. She shivered, and he fought back an amused smile. No matter how many lovers he had taken, he never tired of the way he could make a woman tremble at his touch, or how the slightest spark of radiance pulsed from his fingertips or tongue could—

"Faron!"

Bart crashed through the trees and underbrush to stumble into their camp. His quiver hung empty from his back, and his bow was loose in his hands. His neck was covered with bites, and his eyes wide with fear.

"Something amiss?" Faron asked, withdrawing his hand from Rowan's waist.

Bart stammered a moment, unable to form words. His face was pale, and he constantly glanced over his shoulder to the stretch of woods he came from.

"I don't...I don't know who else to tell," he said once he composed himself. "While I was hunting, I saw a wolf, and it...it saw me, and so I shot it with an arrow, and it didn't go down. It charged my tree, trying to climb, so I shot another, and another, until it died."

Faron put his hands atop Bart's shoulders and squeezed tightly.

"Get yourself together, lad, it's just a wolf," he said.

"But it's not!" Bart shouted. He looked on the verge of tears. "It fled before it died, so I went to check, to make sure, and it... You won't believe me, none of you will, but you have to, Faron. You have to. It's not a wolf. I don't know what it is, but it's not a wolf. It's not anything."

Sariel was beside them before Faron even registered he had moved.

"Show us," his brother said, Redemption ready atop his shoulder. "I would see this strange wolf that troubles you so."

Bart glanced between them, uncertain.

"Be brave, now," Faron said, and he used his innate gifts to add power to the words. "You can do this."

The effect was immediate. Bart's grip on his bow relaxed, and he nodded in the affirmative.

"All right," he said. "I'll show you. It's...it's probably nothing, right? I just spooked myself in a strange forest."

"I pray it is so," Sariel said.

They started to leave, and Iris hopped up from Sariel's blanket to follow.

"No," Sariel said, surprising Faron. "Remain here, Iris. This is not for you to witness."

A strange request, but one the coyote followed. Faron's frown deepened. His brother knew something. Why was he keeping secrets?

"Lead on," he said, putting his hand on Bart's shoulder while doing his best to not let it bother him. "We're with you."

The location wasn't far into the woods. Bart had found a tree with a suitably high perch where he could wait in hopes of a deer wandering by, or, worst case, a few squirrels. The underbrush was thick, and Faron stomped through it, glad he need not fear the bite of a snake or sting of a spider.

The confidence Faron inspired with his radiance faded from Bart the closer they came to the hunting spot.

"There," Bart said, halting in his tracks. "It died over there, past those bushes."

Sariel pulled his sword from his shoulders, and Faron was surprised by how he twirled it in his grasp. It was a rare sign his brother was nervous, but why would he be so concerned by a strange wolf?

"Stay here," Faron said, following Sariel. Together they pushed through the slender bushes.

The wolf lay collapsed on its stomach, its legs splayed wide at awkward angles. Six arrows were sunk into its gray fur. Faron saw nothing wrong at first, but his instincts cried out a warning. He realized it when he looked to the paws. They were too long, and curled like human fingers.

"What strangeness is this?" Sariel asked as he lowered Redemption toward the beast. Its eyes were open in death, and they were a yellow color Faron strongly disliked. The dragon-bone tip tucked underneath the jaw and lifted the head. Immediately they both froze.

Underneath that wolf jaw, where its throat should be, was a second face, human, also frozen in death. A pink tongue hung swollen from its mouth. Blue eyes stared into nowhere.

"Heavens help us," Sariel muttered, and flipped the entire corpse over.

Six human arms sprouted from the rib cage, and they curled inward like a spider in death. They were small and chubby, like those of a newborn. The fur across the belly was thin, pale, and resembled goose down more than wolf's fur. Where the wolf's crotch should have been was a spider's stinger.

"Burn it," Faron said, fighting through his shock. "Whatever that is, it should not be."

Sariel summoned blue flame in his palm and dropped it upon the corpse. The fire swarmed, catching easily. Faron felt no relief until the bulk of it was blackened and charred.

"Isabelle told me of rumors shared by her father," Sariel said as they watched. "Rumors that Kanth is a place of horrors, and home to monsters."

"He was not wrong," Faron said. He kept his voice low as a change swept over him. His kindness and jovial attitude vanished, the centuries of age returning to weigh upon him. He studied the slain beast, his stomach twisting at what he saw. "You sense it, too, don't you?"

Sariel slowly nodded.

"I do. They are tainted with radiance. I sensed the same with Kanth's diplomat, though nothing quite so severe."

Another set of howls from a nearby wolf pack interrupted their vigil. Sariel and Faron exchanged a look, their eyes wide.

"Back to the camp, now!" Faron shouted as they sprinted through the brush. Plans raced through his mind. They needed patrols, thrice as many as they had now, before anyone considered sleeping. Their camp needed to be more tightly constricted, the less to guard over. Perhaps they should flee the forest entirely and leave the Grand Castle to rot deep against the Crowning Mountains.

Screams from ahead. Faron drew his sword, leaving Bart behind to crash through the brush.

Panicked soldiers scrambled about, some for weapons, some in search of the threat, and others in sheer terror. Against any other ambush they might have reacted accordingly, but these monsters had them frightened deep to their core.

One such monster crouched atop a screaming Rowan, paw-like hands pressing down on her chest. Its wolf head reared up to howl, while underneath, the human face drooled with teeth steadily growing in size and sharpness. It bore no spider stinger, but instead a scorpion tail, its stinger vibrating. Iris snarled and barked at it, but the scorpion tail had her frightened, and she knew not how or when to strike.

Faron blasted past them into the clearing and sliced the monster's tail off, then grabbed it by the scruff of the neck and heaved it into the air. Six little arms writhed underneath its belly, and the human face howled in a mindless rage. Faron spiked it to the ground, then jammed his sword directly into its stomach. A twist, a slash, and he opened the wolf from chest to crotch, spilling blood and intestines upon the dirt.

"Faron," Rowan said, her eyes wide in shock. "What...what was..."

He couldn't answer her, couldn't stay to protect her. Shouts echoed up and down the camp, matched by the snarls and howls of wolves that were not wolves.

"Take the front," Sariel shouted to Faron, shaking blood from his sword after beheading his own target. "I'll protect the rear."

The brothers split, each traveling in a different direction. Faron barreled through frightened troops and past cook fires in search of battle. The screams guided him. The next creature he found slain, the corpse beside a trio of dead soldiers, all three with their faces purple and their bodies punctured by the dead wolf's stinger. Several more soldiers stood over them, in shock, or weeping at the loss.

"Move," Faron shouted at them, his voice a roar never used upon them, only his foes, and it shocked them into movement. "Secure the camp, damn you!"

More screams, these from a battle still in progress. Faron found one such wolf fully surrounded, the soldiers keeping a wide berth as they penned it in. It snapped and snarled at them, and though it lacked any stinger, its neck was overly long, and it moved like a serpent as it bit, seeking openings. Faron pushed through, fearing no venom it might produce.

It leaped at him, mouth open, dripping fangs seeking his throat. He greeted it with his sword, plunging it deep into its neck and then slamming it to the ground.

"Do you not see?" he shouted to the others as he ripped his sword free. "It bleeds and dies like any other beast."

More howls all around them, as if in defiance of his cry.

"Set up defense lines along the road until we have the camp secured," he continued, and then pointed to the body. "And someone burn that damned thing."

The next bunch of tents contained frightened men and women shouting at one another, along with two more bodies. He ordered them burned upon his arrival, but they paid him no heed. Their attention was locked on the trees.

Faron looked to the blue-pine branches and saw it, another strange wolf-thing. It lurked within the needles; four vulture wings sprouted from its spine. Its head was tilted to the moon, and the human face watched them with horrifying intelligence.

"It hasn't moved," a woman beside Faron said. "It just watched as the others attacked, as they…they…"

She need not finish the sentence. Faron could see the nearby bodies.

"Are you afraid?" Faron shouted while twirling his sword in a display meant to grab the monster's attention. "Come down, you wretched thing. Come and die like the others."

The human face opened its mouth. Its lips twisted. Its tongue slithered out like a snake's.

"Die?" it asked, and then leaped from the trees. Faron held his ground, and when the beast was in reach, he swung with all his strength, his blade cutting the thing in twain. Its two halves split, and its gore splashed across Faron. As the blood sizzled against him, audibly hissing, he felt the undeniable tinge of tainted radiance burn across his skin.

Whatever was happening in Kanth, it was deeply, deeply wrong.

"See!" he shouted, pretending he felt none of those feelings. "Fight them, brethren! Fight them, sisters!" He rushed ahead, to where soldiers were already recovering and stabbing at the horrid beasts.

"Take up your swords, and fight!"

•

By the time the camp was secured and the wolf corpses burned, they counted forty of the twisted not-wolves. Reglia oversaw the burying of the dead, praying to Leliel for guidance and mercy. Afterward, Faron and Sariel were summoned to Isabelle's command tent. Marshals, lieutenants, and the like were there, arguing logistics and morale, and she dismissed them all.

"I'm glad you're here," she said once the others departed. "I need someone to tell me I am not insane."

"There is madness here, but it is not yours," Sariel said. "Why call for my brother and me?"

She paced the small tent, her arms crossed behind her.

"My past is tied to this place," she said at last, and glanced at Sariel.

"And now I see the horrors of Kanth made real, I would hear your opinions on the matter."

"And why would our opinions rank above those of your advisers?" Faron asked. Not that he minded, for this was the type of trust he'd always sought to build with her, but he couldn't shake the feeling there was more happening beyond his understanding.

"Because you possess knowledge my advisers do not," she said, much too harshly. "Do not play the fool, either of you. Oscar tells me you were the first to encounter these beasts, so speak plainly. I am willing to listen, if you are willing to offer the truth."

Faron struggled for an appropriate response. This did not feel like the proper time to reveal their own ever-living nature, so how might they explain their familiarity with radiance, or that these bizarre wolf-things were changed by it?

"There is a strange magic in this land," Sariel said before Faron could attempt his own explanation. "And as unbelievable as it may sound, it is akin to that which has blessed you."

"You would call these things a blessing of Leliel?" Isabelle asked, the color draining from her face. "You would mark me akin to those... monsters?"

"No," Faron said, pushing to her side while glaring at Sariel. "They do not compare. Yours is proper, and controlled within you. What we saw, it is wild, rabid, and wrong."

Isabelle did not look comforted.

"Aubert refused to admit the possibility, so I will ask you instead," she said. "Those things, were they first wolves, or were they people?"

Faron slowly exhaled. Best he be the one to break such news.

"I fear they were never wolves," he said. "If I were to wager, they are some of the people who went missing from the outlying villages."

"Never wolves," Isabelle muttered. "And yet I am different. I am... proper. I am controlled."

Faron hated how his every word was being taken wrong, but before he could try again, she turned away from them both.

"Aubert wishes for us to flee this goddess-forsaken forest, declare the whole of Kanth desolate, and instead focus on rallying the remainder of the free nations into the protectorate so we might invade the Astral Kingdom. Many of my vassal kings and queens seek the same." She shook her head. "I refused. We must see this to its end. Come dawn, we march for Castle Kanth."

The queen turned back to them, exerting clear effort to remain calm and stoic.

"Marshal Oscar fears soldiers will desert my cause if we continue deeper into the Frostlash. What of you two? Will you stay with me unto the very end?"

Faron drew his sword, knelt, and laid the blade across his knee.

"I will never leave your side," he said. "My life is yours, my queen."

After a moment, Sariel dropped to one knee as well. Redemption remained across his shoulder.

"Even if you ordered our army to abandon the forest, I would march ahead," he said. "I must see this nightmare put to an end."

Isabelle put a hand to her breast and bowed to them in turn.

"Thank you, Godsight brothers. Come our arrival at the Grand Castle, there is a task I would ask of you, and I can think of no others I trust more to carry it through."

Faron beamed, thrilled to hear such trust placed upon him. This was it. They were confidants now. Come the invasion against the Astral Kingdom, they would now always have her ear.

"Whatever you wish," he said, and bowed again.

Sariel stood, far less impressed.

"You should address your people," he told Isabelle. "They are frightened, and it would do them good to hear your words. If they are to face what nightmares await, they must believe the goddess is with them."

"There will be more of those creatures?" she asked.

Sariel did not answer before departing the tent. Faron stood, and after sheathing his sword, he offered his hands to his queen. She took them reluctantly, and he felt her fingers tremble within his grasp. So strong, when she must be, but so frightened now. He looked into her golden eyes and spoke the painful truth.

"A perversion hangs like a pall over the countryside. These beasts were but a taste of what is to come. Whatever awaits us at the heart of Kanth shall be so much worse. We will face monsters, true monsters, the type of which this world has never seen."

He stepped closer, his presence overwhelming her, his dark eyes holding her captive.

"But know this, my queen. I am always here to slay your monsters."

Chapter 36

FARON

Several hundred feet of barren, rocky land separated the Frostlash Forest and the sudden, sharp rise of the Crowning Mountains. Nestled against those gray spires loomed the Grand Castle of Kanth. Its walls were steep, its spires tall and pointed. Stained glass covered the windows, and across the front fluttered an enormous crimson banner. Embroidered in gold was the Silvein royal crest, a mining pick whose handle morphed into the shape of a blue-pine tree.

And fully surrounding the castle walls was an entire second city.

"I think we found Kanth's survivors," Faron said. His tone was grim and had been since they discovered the foul creatures tainted with radiance.

"But why here?" Sariel asked as Isabelle ordered her army to halt at the forest's edge. The entire way they had battled strange beasts, which thankfully never posed much of a threat when confronted by prepared soldiers. This strange town, however, built of dilapidated homes, hastily and poorly constructed, gave Isabelle pause.

"It's like half the nation packed up and moved to live beside the castle, and built what shelter they could," Faron said.

Iris whined at his feet, and he patted her head.

"Don't worry," he said. "I won't make you go anywhere near there if you do not wish it."

Faron and Sariel closed their eyes and then reopened them with the faint light of stars glowing within. With vision significantly enhanced, they observed this strange town.

Most homes were barely more than cut boards placed in vaguely square and triangular shapes. Faron caught sight of a small well, so a village had likely existed here before it swelled to such gargantuan size. People milled about the gaps between buildings, while others peered out from windows and doors. At least fifteen thousand people, Faron guessed, if not more.

All of them shone with the faint light of radiance.

"They are tainted," Sariel said.

Faron wished he could disagree.

"How badly, though?" he asked. "They still seem human."

"For now."

It did not take long to confirm such fears. The people's flesh was extremely pale, far beyond what might be justified by their environs. Many sported little feathers in their hair, while others walked on legs that resembled tree bark. The more he looked, the more things Faron saw wrong. Necks that stretched a bit too far. Children hanging upside down from windows with no visible way to support themselves. And then there were the guards patrolling the place. All of them bore a second set of arms underneath their first. They were gloved and wrapped in cloth to hide their flesh, but Faron suspected it would look anything but human.

"Come with me," Sariel said, dismissing the blessing from his eyes. "We must speak with the queen."

As expected, Isabelle was busy in her command tent, fielding questions of logistics, where to position armies, where to dig latrine trenches, and of course, what to do with the strange, sprawling town. Isabelle noted the brothers' arrival but let the conversations play out for several more minutes before interrupting.

"I have a task I must discuss with the Godsight brothers," she told those with her. "Please, give me a moment with them."

Plenty of grumbling, but at least the leaders were getting used to it at this point. Faron entered the tent and crossed his arms.

"We are here," he said.

Isabelle's shoulders sagged now they were alone, and she did not even pretend to smile.

"I trust you have looked out upon Stone's Refuge?" she asked.

"You mean the town about the castle?"

"Indeed. My father said it was a small place of maybe a thousand workers, servants, and traders. Clearly it has swelled far beyond its original size." She hesitated. "Tell me, is it as dire as you feared?"

"Worse," Sariel said. "I suspect each and every person here has been claimed by the curse that has overtaken Kanth."

"So they're beasts, too, like those that assaulted us in the woods?"

"Akin to them," Faron said. "But not quite. They don't seem as far gone, but it is only a matter of time."

"And should you wonder, they cannot be saved," Sariel added. "There are but two fates awaiting them. Either they die by our hands, or they become creatures as strange and twisted as those we have already faced."

Isabelle approached the far side of her tent, and she peeled back one of the flaps. Beyond was the castle, and the surrounding town.

"You speak so callously about thousands of lives," she said. "As if ending them would be such a simple thing."

"Their lives are already ended," Faron said, trying to break the news as gently as he could. "They are suffering, Isabelle. These forms they take, you saw them. It is unnatural and causes them great pain."

Isabelle closed the flap. Resolve hardened in her gaze.

"I know. But I do not wish to ever make such a decision callously. They are citizens of a sovereign nation, even if I would see them join my protectorate instead of remaining yoked to the Silvein family."

As difficult as the future loomed, Faron was heartened by her hesitation. Monsters, these people were monsters, and yet she still cared. He could not have chosen a better queen to rule Kaus once the Astral Kingdom fell.

"Some would see your compassion as a virtue," Sariel said, and he pointedly glanced Faron's way. "But do not let it become a chink in your armor. This must be done, and my sword is ready to lead the culling."

"No," she said, shaking her head. "There is a task I would have you complete, if you are willing. You two are my best fighters, and more importantly, you seem the least disturbed by the horrors around us."

She cast a wary gaze Faron's way.

"There are things I must admit to you, Faron. I was born here, in Kanth, not in Doremy. My adoptive father smuggled me out of the castle when I was a babe, and he has long warned me of the depravity of King Laurence and Queen Alise. He also told me of the hidden tunnel he used to escape the castle. I would have you two use that same tunnel while my army distracts those within by burning Stone's Refuge."

"You would have us enter alone?" Faron asked.

"I would," she said. "If outside is any indication, I fear what is within those castle walls. I...I would spare my soldiers those sights. You need not conquer the entire castle on your own, only judge the status within. If it is beyond salvation, then I will not bother with a siege. By your judgment, I will burn the castle to the ground and leave Kanth a barren land of ash and graves."

"And what of your vengeance against King and Queen Silvein?" Sariel asked softly.

"Will I not have found it?" Isabelle asked. "Just so long as they are dead, I will know peace. Do not think me so bloodthirsty as to need it done by my hands."

"I am willing," Faron said, and looked to his brother despite knowing the answer already. No other sibling was as ruthless in removing radiance's touch from humanity.

"So be it," Sariel said. "These monsters must have their end. Where is this hidden entrance?"

•

The army of the protectorate marched upon Stone's Refuge. Hundreds among their ranks carried torches. With blade they would slay the defenders. With fire they would cleanse the corruption.

Faron, Sariel, and Iris kept to the road leading to the drawbridge, their destination close to the castle walls. They watched from afar as the forces reached the outer edges of the swollen, dilapidated town. If Kanth possessed an army, it was either isolated within the castle or a pitiful fraction of what it was rumored to have once possessed. A few hundred guards came rushing to form a wall, and they were a disturbing sight, their extra limbs flailing and waving about.

Isabelle kept the march steady and controlled. Her army formed an unbroken wall of swords and shields. No one would escape the purge.

The battle ended in moments. The torches reached the first homes. Amid the smoke and fire, the inhabitants screamed and fled. They were as gruesome a sight as Faron had feared.

"What happened here?" he wondered as Stone's Refuge steadily burned.

"I am hoping to find that answer inside," Sariel said. "They've passed by the crypt. Let's go."

Faron knelt down beside Iris, and he gently put his hand atop one of her shoulders.

"Stay free of all this," he told her. "The castle is no place for you, nor is that needed purge. Wait out here, all right?"

The coyote glanced behind her at the swelling fires and whined.

"I know," he said, and scratched behind her ear. "I don't like it, either."

As requested, she stayed behind on the road. Alone, the brothers headed into the thickening smoke, collapsing homes, and corpse-choked streets of Stone's Refuge. It was not hard to find their destination. Most of the buildings were cut from the nearby blue pines, and so the stone crypt stood out among them, as did the copper statue of Leliel atop it, her wings spread high and her hands wide, the eyes upon her wrists forever open.

"Sneaking alone into a castle," Faron said, unable to keep the bitterness from his voice as they paused at the entrance. "Does it remind you of Lossleaf?"

"Do you still resent me for that?" Sariel asked.

"I don't know," Faron answered truthfully. "But I have no desire to see it done again."

"And yet here we are," Sariel said as they watched the destruction of Stone's Refuge all around them. "Rumors will spread of Isabelle's cruelty, and of her burning thousands of innocent people who came to the Grand Castle in search of safety. It will not matter if we insist they were monsters. No one will believe the truth. The people will assume it a lie meant to wash away the sin of Isabelle's cruelty."

"It needs to be done," Faron said. "And so we do it. Let the rumors fly. Once Kanth falls, all that remains are scattered little nations, and they will bend the knee rather than face Isabelle's armies. The protectorate is ready. Eder's kingdom will fall."

Sariel shook his head.

"For once, I hope you are right, Faron. Now let us be done with this odious task. I want to be gone from this nation as soon as I can. There is a foul air to this place, and it burns my lungs."

The two traveled to the far end of the crypt, needing no torch or lantern with their blessed sight. There they found the marked coffin, its lid made of heavy stone. Faron pulled it aside, exposing a deep drop and a ladder bolted to the edge.

"After you," he said, and grinned at Sariel.

His brother tilted Redemption vertically so it might fit, then hopped down, holding on to one side of the ladder so he might slide to the bottom. Faron dropped after, not even bothering with the ladder. He landed with a thud in a pitch-black tunnel of worked stone. The ceiling was low, so that both of them had to bend over to walk.

At least it's not a crawl, Faron thought as they traversed the tunnel to the castle. It suddenly widened, the worked stone becoming a more naturally formed cavern. Water dripped along the walls, leaks from natural rivers running down from the mountains. He stretched his shoulders, glad to stand, and then followed his brother.

The cavern curled to the right but also forked straight ahead with a human-made tunnel fortified with bricks. The two chose that direction, following it for a few moments more before it abruptly ended at an iron ladder.

"Are you ready?" Sariel asked.

"Ready for anything," Faron confirmed. "So what's the plan? Kill the king and queen and then leave? Or just scout like Isabelle desired?"

"I would take the measure of the castle," Sariel answered. "Beyond that, I do not know. Our vows compel us, though, do they not? Each and every one of these deviant humans reeks of stolen radiance. The people within the castle will be no better than those in the town outside."

"If we must, then we keep our vows," Faron said. "Better us than the soldiers outside seeing these... things."

Sariel climbed up the ladder with his left hand, his sword held tightly against his body with his right.

"They will see enough horrors tonight," he admitted. "Perhaps it is a kindness if we spare them more."

Sariel emerged first, Faron after, the ladder ending in an extremely cramped room barely big enough to fit both of them. All four walls were bare stone. Sariel tested the wall in front of him, and with enough force, it rotated slightly, creating a gap he could slide through. The pair exited, stepping out into the end of a long corridor.

To either side of them were prison cells.

"Heavens have mercy," Faron whispered.

The people were trapped in darkness, without torch or lantern. There were at least a hundred of them, cramped within a mere eight cells, so that many leaned with limbs pushed through the bars for space. They were stripped of clothing, and their heads shaven. Faron approached one of the cells, dreading to confirm his fears.

Radiance. All of them pulsed with radiance, faint but there. Tainting them.

"Why?" he whispered, the word unheard by the prisoners over the sounds of their own snoring, whimpering, and crying. But the more he looked, the more he feared he understood. Nearly all of them were missing a limb, be it an arm or a leg.

"Why torture their prisoners in such a way?" Sariel asked, his voice soft and low.

"Because this isn't a prison," Faron said. "It's a feed pen."

Stars burned in Sariel's eyes, and he lifted his sword.

"Then this is a mercy."

The lock on the cell shattered at the strength of dragon bone. Sariel entered the first cell, Redemption slashing with precision. Screams followed, and blood flowed across the stone floor. Faron watched, his heart sinking into his stomach. These people. These poor people.

With the dungeon so dark, the others could not see, but they could hear the slaughter, and they shouted fearfully within their cells. Faron drew his sword, and he told himself to be strong. Their suffering would end. The radiance that pulsed through their veins would corrupt them no longer. He shattered a lock and went to work.

Blind, they could not fight back. Cramped together, they could not move or flee. They died, and their blood soaked the stones.

At last, all was silent.

Sariel stood in the center of the passage, Redemption resting across his shoulder. He seemed incapable of moving as he looked upon the destruction they had wrought.

"Need we see any more?" he asked the dreadful quiet. "Anyone who would do such a thing deserves to burn."

"I know," Faron said, breathing through his mouth instead of his nostrils to take the edge off the horrid stink. "But then we would not have our answers."

He approached the door at the far end of the passage. Its window was covered with a slab of metal, and when he checked, he found it was barred from the outside. Faron lowered his shoulder and smashed through, emerging into another dark corridor.

"No guards," he muttered, glancing in either direction. "How long has Kanth been rotting from within?"

"Long enough," Sariel said, following him. "Which way leads out of this dungeon?"

"That way, I believe," Faron said, pointing to his left, where he saw curling steps at the far end. "But... wait. Do you not sense it?"

"I sense radiance seeping from the very walls," Sariel said. "It is suffocating. What do you sense?"

Faron closed his eyes, forcing himself to focus. He was no Calluna.

Detecting the telltale shine of radiance was no easy feat to his mind, but it was still a gift he occasionally used.

"This way," he said, ignoring the stairs leading up and out of the dungeon. "Just…trust me, all right?"

Another set of stairs awaited around the turn, and at the bottom of them, another corridor leading to a single door. Two guards stood before it, and they startled at the sight of the brothers. Their faces were hidden behind helmets, but there was no hiding the second set of arms growing from their backs as they lifted their swords and axes.

Faron charged both of them, unafraid of their clumsy skill. He blocked an ax strike, then flung the soldier against the wall with a swing of his arms. A whimper escaped the helmet at the collision, which Faron ended with a thrust underneath the helmet into an exposed throat lined with garishly white scales. The second guard howled, the noise, reminiscent of the screech of a bird, shivering Faron's spine, and he was glad when Sariel ended it with a single slash of Redemption.

The soldiers taken care of, Faron checked the door they guarded. The top of it had once borne a barred opening, but it was sealed over with planks of wood. Faron tried it, found it locked, and then returned to the corpses to find the key.

There, he thought, withdrawing it from a pocket. The key was strangely ornate, its handle encrusted with rubies and sapphires. He slipped it into the keyhole, turned it, and then pushed the door open. Light slipped into the windowless cell, falling upon a face so familiar, Faron's jaw dropped. The key slipped from his numb fingers. Behind him, Sariel gasped, shocked and horrified in equal measure.

Faron took a single hesitant step forward, his mind reeling. A lone word formed on his lips as his heart broke at the sight of a naked woman hanging from chains in the deep depths of Castle Kanth.

"Aylah?"

Chapter 37

SARIEL

Sariel stood frozen in horror before the pitch-black cell. A thousand curses appeared and died in his mind, each one angrier than the last. His shock imprisoned him as Faron rushed to their sister's side.

"Aylah," he said again, hesitating before her. He spoke as if her name would resurrect her. "Aylah, we're here. We're here for you."

Their sister hung from the ceiling by two sets of chains, one holding her arms, the other her ankles. She swung above the ground, like a hog set to butcher. She was naked, exposing a terrifying number of scars across her body. The words of the vow they had sworn centuries ago were visible in the shape of blackened blisters across her left arm. Even worse were the scabbed wounds on her throat, angry and red.

Sariel's horror magnified. He and his siblings did not scar, for the healing magic of radiance was too strong. For Aylah to be so beaten, so marked, then those wounds had to have been inflicted each and every day upon her…

"Faron?" she groaned, lifting her head. Her eyes fluttered open, her eyelids heavy. When she spoke, she sounded intoxicated. "Is that you?"

"Yes, it's me," Faron said, grabbing the manacles around her wrists. He fumbled at them, searching for a way to open them. "A key, a key, do you see a key?"

"Catch her," Sariel said, stepping close, his paralysis finally ended. One swing, with all his fury swept into it, shattered the chains. Faron caught his sister's fall. She leaned against him, burying her face in his chest. Her hair, once as beautiful and black as the midnight sky, was a pale shade of gray and brittle as it wrapped about her to hide her face.

Sariel turned to the table alongside the lightless cell. A seemingly endless array of cutting instruments filled it, knives and daggers of all sick shapes and edges. What frightened him most were the dozen silver and gold cups and the deep red stains within them.

"What happened here?" he asked.

"Now is not the time," Faron snapped.

"They drank," Aylah said, ignoring him. She curled tighter against Faron, so weak and pitiful. "They cut me and then they...they drank."

Sariel needed to hear nothing more. He clutched Redemption with a grip to make his fingers ache. The entire world around him swam red with his rage.

"Get her out of here," he said.

"Where are you going?" Faron asked.

"I said out!" Sariel shouted. His teeth were bared. His self-control wavered on the edge of a knife. His brother stood and cradled Aylah in his arms as if she were a child. She likely weighed as much as one. Faron hesitated, perhaps to argue, perhaps not. He relented in the end.

"Do what you must," he said, and pushed past him to exit the cell.

In his absence, Sariel walked to the middle of the cell and stood where Aylah had hung. He looked to the stone floor. It was caked red, and when he scraped it with the tip of his sword, it was nearly an inch thick. So much blood, and spilled for how long? Aylah had been missing for decades. Had she spent each and every one of them here, in the pits of the Grand Castle of Kanth?

The knowledge gave him the rage he craved. He didn't want to think. He didn't want to doubt. Such crimes inflicted upon his sister deserved only one fate, no matter the level of involvement.

The entire castle would die.

Sariel burst out of the cell at a full sprint. The world narrowed around him. Colors drained. Up the stairs. Out of the dungeon and into the castle proper. He saw bleak halls, cold stone, and portraits of dead humans without love or joy in the remembrance. The curtains were the color of his sister's dried blood. He crossed the hall, searching for life. Searching for victims.

Two servant women were the first, their skin marble white and their eyes pink like a rabbit's. They saw him and fled. He ran them down, hacking both in half with a single swing of his sword. Stepping over their corpses, he kicked the nearest door open. A man cowered on the bed, his lower half bulbous, two legs becoming four, each short and ending with a silver scorpion tail. Two women were with him, their mouths fanged and their skin sparkling like gold. Their hair had fallen out, and little feathers replaced it. They hissed at Sariel like angered vipers.

Sariel impaled the first that charged at him, ripped Redemption out her side, and then cut the head off the second. The man howled, but he could not move from the bed.

"Angelica!" he cried. "Beatrice! You...you killed them!"

One thrust, and dragon bone punched through the man's open mouth to tear out the back of his head. Blood sprayed across the bedsheets.

Not enough.

Never enough.

Another room. Another. Servants. Families with little children, spiked with quills and with three faces upon their skulls, not one. Sariel butchered them all.

The hall took him to the castle entrance, its grand doors locked and barred against the coming invasion. A chain was attached to a pulley to lift the bar, and he cut it, ensuring no one could escape. Still unsatisfied, he grabbed several paintings, as well as a nearby dresser, and piled them near the doors. A raise of his clenched fist, and he summoned blue flame within his palm.

"Smoke and fire are better than any of you deserve," he whispered as he set the pile aflame. "Pray that it finds you before I do."

To the stairs, and the higher floors. Two pale-skinned soldiers were there to stop him, and he gutted them with ease. Their clawed hands could not hold their swords correctly. Another door. Another slain monster, this a woman whose entire lower half was a brilliant white-and-gold serpentine tail. Door by door. Room by room. Locks shattered with a kick of his heel. Throats bled with lone cuts of his dragon-bone blade. Their fine silks, gold rings, and silver necklaces were no armor against his fury.

One hall finished, he returned to the entrance. In the grand foyer, three women were panicking before the flames, seeking a way out. Sariel leaped upon them from the upper floor, his momentum strong enough to impale the nearest all the way up to the hilt when he landed. She flailed, blood pouring across his sword to the carpet.

Sariel ignored her pained thrashing, ignored the fearful screams from the other two women, whose six eyes were bloodshot and wide with fear. He watched the blood pool and witnessed it burning with stars. Radiance. The blood of these wretched people bore the faint signs of sickly golden radiance.

There was no doubting where it came from. Where it was *stolen* from.

"You drank of her," Sariel said, swinging without removing the first body. The heads collided, bones snapping. The third fled, but he chased her down, Redemption's long reach carving her open from shoulder blade to hip. She collapsed, her intestines spilling out, and from within the pink ropes of flesh burst a dozen red gnats, buzzing and swirling wildly.

A glare from Sariel, and they burst into flame, ruined by his own seething radiance.

Back to the stairs. To the third floor. Higher. Cleansing the rooms. Butchering the nobility of Kanth. He began setting fire to the radiance-twisted corpses. No one needed to see the monstrosities within. They deserved no burial, no grave, and no headstones. A man with the head of a goat bleated furiously at him, and Sariel severed it in turn, grabbed his collapsing corpse, and burst it into flames with a thought. A woman with him shrieked, turned, and leaped through the stained glass window. Feathers covered her arms, and thin flaps of flesh connected her elbows to her hips. Perhaps she thought she could fly.

Sariel glanced out the window, saw her corpse lying amid shards of broken glass.

She could not.

The next room. The next. With his sword, he bled the monsters dry. With his sword, he reclaimed the gift they had stolen from his sister. His beloved sister. With every swing, he saw her hanging naked from the chains. With every kill, he imagined the blood flowing from the scars across her neck, pooling into decadent cups and goblets stained red. There was no fixing this. No redeeming this. Fire was the only cleansing that would suffice.

The fourth floor. More guards, looking fearsome in their silver armor and red tassels. They wielded slender short swords, and they stood fearful before a set of wide doors. Their skin was pale. All of them lacked eyes. All of them had too many arms. They clicked their tongues, and Sariel suspected them still capable of seeing him.

Sariel charged into them, the reach of his blade and strength of his swings making a mockery of their meager human training. Their armor parted against the dragon-bone edge. Their blood flowed, black as the night, radiance sparkling in it like sickly golden stars. Sariel kicked open the door they guarded, revealing a long, cramped dining hall.

A crowned woman crouched atop the table. Her crimson dress was torn in multiple places, making room for the six pairs of wings that sprouted from her back. Their feathers mixed white and gold near the top but transitioned to a deep crimson by the bottom set. Goat horns grew from her forehead. A second pair of reptilian eyes opened above her human ones, the irises of all four a pale shade of red. Her hands were clawed and coated in blood, for a human corpse lay open before her, a twisted image with its legs bent backward and arms tucked underneath so it might fit upon a silver platter.

"Greetings, Queen of Kanth," Sariel said, leaping atop the table to join her. "Have I interrupted your feast?"

Queen Alise grinned at him, a strip of muscle still between her teeth.

"You," she said, standing to her full height. Her wings spread to their fullest extent. Her voice was deep, and it sounded as if four women spoke at once. "I see you for what you are. You're like our dear Aylah, aren't you?"

Sariel approached, Redemption at the ready.

"Did she tell you of us?" he asked.

"She murmured your names when she was at her weakest. Which are you? Faron? Eist? Sariel?"

Sariel closed the distance between them with a leap, his sword plunging for her chest. Alise caught the blade with her scaled hands, her claws latching tightly about it to prevent herself from being impaled.

"Do not speak our names with your defiled tongue," Sariel said, and twisted the hilt. The dragon-bone edge scraped the queen's claws and opened gashes across her hands. Blood, white like milk, splashed to the table. If the pain caused her distress, she gave no sign. Instead she spread her wings and beat them to rise into the air. A second pair of arms emerged from within her dress, the flesh rough and brown like bark. Vines grew from her fingernails and wrapped about her wrists, encasing them in thorns.

"Defiled?" she asked. "I am beautiful, immortal one! Look upon me and witness the light of creation."

She spread her four arms in opposite directions, and before her swirled a golden ring of tainted radiance. It crackled with lightning, and peering through it sickened Sariel and left him dizzy. The queen laughed, and as much as he hated it, Sariel could not deny the joy he felt in hearing that laughter. She pulsed with a desire to be loved. Her voice was crystalline, perfect, radiant, incomparable...

Sariel sliced his own arm, using the pain to focus his mind. As his blood flowed, Alise stared and licked her lips.

"I have always wondered," she said, her four arms twirling the golden ring so the reality within it wobbled and threatened to break. "Will you taste the same as her?"

Tentacles burst from within the ring, each one coated with white scales and intermittent gold thorns. Sariel retreated, his sword lashing back and forth, cutting the tentacles in half. The pieces collapsed to the table and writhed as they dissolved into smoke, leaving behind only puddles of white liquid akin to Alise's blood. The fourth he failed to stop in time, and it slammed into him. He rolled off the table, jarring his left shoulder hard upon the stone floor.

Instinct had him halt his momentum to leap aside, but his timing was still wrong. More tentacles beat against him, bruising him and opening shallow cuts across his arms and back. Sariel came up swinging, cutting free one last tentacle. More blood coated the ground, white from the tentacles and red from where the thorns had opened up a gash on his chest, thin but painful.

The tentacles retreated into the center of the ring, which then broke apart into buzzing golden fireflies. Alise gasped, sweat trickling down her face and neck from the exertion. Her wings beat harder, lifting her to the ceiling.

"It matters not the size of your armies or the death of our people," she said, her vine-laced hands clapping. "We can always rebuild. My husband and I are eternal."

"Eternal?" Sariel said, descending into a prepared stance. "No, Alise, you are not eternal. You are not of the blood of my family. When my sword opens your throat, you will die and stay dead. If I could, I would burn your soul so even it would not be reborn, you are so wretched."

Alise licked her lips. "Breaking you shall be divine."

The vines extended as they shot like arrows from her second arms. Sariel lifted Redemption, thinking to deflect, but they were never aimed at him. The vines wrapped about his sword, curling around again and again as their grip tightened. Sariel pulled, matching the queen strength for strength. He was careful with the direction, applying all the force upon the blunted side so he would not cut the vines. Alise used all four arms to pull those vines, uncaring that the thorns pierced the scales of her hands and dripped pale blood upon them. Her wings beat, adding to the power so she might disarm him.

Sariel held firm, forcing her to commit, to lift with all her strength, and then he reversed the force, leaping into the air. The vines catapulted him upward, and this time he did twist the sword and swing, cutting through the vines with ease. Alise screamed and slashed at him with her claws as his momentum carried him higher. He spun, dragon bone slicing off fingers, and then the last of his momentum ended with him at a hover directly before the queen.

One thrust, and he plunged Redemption into her chest, piercing her heart.

Her dying scream rattled the walls as they both fell, Sariel pulling the hilt closer and rotating so her body was beneath him. She landed upon the table, and he slammed down atop her, his knees crushing her abdomen as his sword punctured flesh, wood, and even the stone of the floor as it was buried all the way up to the hilt.

The queen's wings flopped wide and went limp, and her scream ended with a wet gurgle. Red blood mixed with the white, forming a milky pink substance that sickened Sariel's stomach.

"Queen of Theft, I name you," Sariel said, needing both hands to yank his sword free. That done, he extended his right fist and summoned his fire. "May you die nameless and forgotten."

He opened his palm, and from it dropped blue flame. It landed atop the corpse and immediately set it alight. The fire quickly spread, the spilled blood volatile as oil.

Sariel stretched, testing the limits of his body. He was coated in his own blood, and his bruises ached, but no injury was significant enough to prevent him from battling. No pain would compare to the disgust he felt at seeing what Alise had become.

"One left," he said, exiting the room as, behind him, the fire spread from the table to the curtains and paintings, blackening them and coating the ceiling with smoke.

More stairs. Another floor. He kept going. Nothing would stop the cleansing. Sariel felt guided, for now he had met the queen, he knew the odious sensation of their ultimate corruption. In the highest tower of Castle Kanth loomed a presence like a thorn in Sariel's mind, and he climbed the stone stairway toward it. His dread grew with every step. Only his rage kept him climbing.

The room was small, perhaps six feet wide in total. King Laurence stood at the far end, gazing out upon the burning remnants of Stone's

Refuge. All around him were scattered tomes and broken tables, the study room torn apart in a past tantrum.

"Your queen purges my people like a vermin infestation," he said, his back to Sariel. His words rumbled, as if each syllable were voiced by grinding stone. "Were they truly so terrifying? Does the slightest change frighten you so greatly?"

Sariel lifted Redemption for a killing thrust. There was barely enough space to do so in the cramped tower.

"Kneel, and I will limit your suffering," he said. "It is better than you deserve."

Laurence chuckled. He wore his finest, a crimson tunic trimmed with gold, black trousers and boots, and a fine leather belt that held his sword. His crown rested upon a head of thick, curly black hair. That he could seem so...normal upset Sariel in a way Alise did not.

"Kneel?" the king asked, and turned. "No, immortal one, I will not bend my knee to anyone, not even you."

His eyes were solid white, and within them sparkled stars, golden and vibrant. He smiled, and his teeth were fanged.

"You intrude upon my castle, and so to you, I say, *kneel*."

Sariel's right leg gave out. His knee hit the ground, and with it, a spike of pain amid a deluge of horror. He should be impervious to commands born of radiance. No one, not even his siblings, could force their will upon him. To be commanded by a *human*...

"Aylah told me of your lives," Laurence said, his arms crossed behind him as he remained by the window. "Death cannot claim you. Your gift, and your curse. You think it makes you special. You think it makes you superior. But you are like us, immortal one. You are the culmination of your muscle, bone, guts, and veins, and yes, your blood. Your precious blood."

The king approached, the golden stars in his eyes shining so brightly they burned their image into Sariel's sight. A strange mist wafted from their edges, and it, too, sparkled like gold dust.

"Your eternal dance is no different than our own reincarnations. You are just blessed to remember them."

He uncrossed his arms and held them before him. Like Alise's, they were coated with white serpentine scales. Unlike hers, they remained human in shape. No claws, just silver fingernails. They reached for him eagerly. Hungrily.

"But you are lambs before us lions." He knelt before Sariel, his smile growing. And growing. "You are stars, and we are the sun."

His mouth opened, the bones of his jaw unhinging. His teeth swirled in a circle, rows upon rows about a gaping gullet. The mouth of a leech. A scarred strip of flesh that resembled a tongue waggled in its center as he spoke.

"We are the future, and you, the past."

The teeth sank into Sariel's neck. Flesh parted. His blood flowed. Amid that helplessness, Sariel focused on his rage. He remembered Aylah's emaciated figure, the brokenness in her voice, and the scars upon her throat. He remembered Faron on a pyre, surrendering once more to death to blunt the pain of loss. He remembered the tattoos on his arm, and the vows he swore one shameful night almost four centuries ago.

He did not fight the flow of his blood. He gave it freely.

Radiance was many things. A mastery over nature. A mending of flesh. A view of the world stripped of lies. It was truth, and creation itself, but it could also be something else. Something pure.

Fire.

"Drink," Sariel said, and used every last shred of his draining strength to command the radiance within his blood. "Taste of your superiority."

His blood burst into blue flame. Laurence writhed, his teeth sinking in deeper, but Sariel would not be stopped. The fire burned hotter, seething with all of Sariel's contempt and rage. The king's flesh bubbled and peeled. His teeth unlatched, and he howled as smoke belched from that gaping hole in his face. The blood was burning him, even within his belly.

Sariel slowly stood as the control over him faded. He held his bleeding neck with his free hand, stanching the flow with his fingers as he glared at the king.

"You will suffer," he seethed. "You will burn. And when you are reborn, you will have nothing, *nothing*, left of the power you stole."

So much blood had spilled across Laurence's face and neck that it burned away his human flesh, revealing the true scales underneath. His hair charred. His crown melted. His legs were feathered, not scaled, and they burned all the faster. Sariel thrust his sword straight into the king's open mouth, piercing the space between the writhing teeth to pin him to the wall.

"I have seen the color of your soul," he said. "When you are reborn, I will find you, Laurence, and I will murder you again. You and your wife will never know peace. I'll tear the memories from your soul so you remember this moment. You'll relive this burning before you die, again, and again, and again."

Sariel slid closer, and he pulled his hand from his neck to paint Laurence's forehead with another stripe of burning blood. Fire seared the scales to reach the soft flesh underneath. Stars swarmed in Sariel's eyes, dark and silver. The proper, untainted hue.

"And I will enjoy it. Every. Single. Time."

He ripped Redemption free, cut the head from the king, and then left the body to burn to ash in the inferno consuming the wretched pyre that was once the Grand Castle of Kanth.

Chapter 38

AYLAH

Aylah huddled half buried in blankets atop a little nest of pillows in the center of the broad tent. Beside her was a cold bowl of porridge, untouched. She had no appetite. There was a fire in her mind, and it held no room for basic necessities.

"...malnourished to the extreme," she heard a woman outside her tent tell some unseen guest. Her name was Rowan. She'd introduced herself to Aylah as the surgeon in charge of the medic tent. They had set it up in preparation for a battle, only there had been no battle, just slaughter, brutal slaughter, as Faron carried her out of the tunnel.

"Her body shows...she's been tortured. Cut. Scraped. Her skin is so pale, I fear the poor woman has not seen sunlight in years."

"Thirty years," Aylah whispered. Even in that deep pit of darkness, she had sensed the rise of the moon. It had been faint at first, a distant hum in her mind, but then the years crawled along, her blood bled, and its unseen light became her only succor. Each time she had counted those moonrises she was awake for. Sometimes she slept through them. Sometimes she had been dead.

Laurence's annual rituals, though, ensured she never lost track. The winter solstice. The summer harvest. Feasting and drinking, so much drinking, so much...so much...

"Is it all right if we speak with her?" a familiar voice asked, one that warmed Aylah's heart.

"She needs to rest, Faron."

Another voice, as pleasant as rain across desert sands.

"She is our sister, Rowan. Make way, and give us our privacy."

The surgeon relented. The flaps opened, and Aylah winced and looked away. It was night, but the light burned anyway. What cruelty, that she would dream of seeing the stars only for their gentle silver light to be too much for her sensitive eyes.

The flaps closed, returning them to darkness. They all possessed their radiance, though, and in that soothing light she looked upon her brothers and fought for words.

"I waited," she said. "So long, I waited."

Faron collapsed to his knees before her, his big arms wrapping around her. The warmth of him washed over Aylah, even through the blankets. She felt an impulse to cry but could not. She had not shed tears in years.

"I'm so glad to have you back," Faron said. He hugged her gently, as if afraid to break her. He'd never embraced her in such a way before. She used to be as strong as him, equally broad-shouldered and skilled with a sword. To be treated like a porcelain doll...

Aylah pushed aside her blankets, returned his embrace, and buried her face in his chest. She let herself fall into him. Every part of her, her mind, her thoughts, her feelings, all of it clinging to her brother so that her bitterness, and her brokenness, would not rob her of the joy she deserved. Her beloved brothers had saved her. She would not judge them now.

"I'm glad, too," she whispered into his shirt.

Faron's embrace did not end. Instead he shifted to sit beside her on the pillows, and she gladly leaned against him, his arm around her and her face resting gently against his chest. Sariel sat across from them, Redemption resting across his shoulders. No blood on it. Aylah wished there was blood. It would do her good to see proof of the Silveins' executions. Instead, it was her brother's body that was visibly battered and bruised from the tribulations within the castle.

"Calluna searched for you often," Sariel said. "Every time, she saw only darkness. It left us with questions, and nowhere to search."

"It is my own fault," Aylah said. She closed her eyes. "I foolishly told the royal family I was gifted my power through the sun and stars, and so they imprisoned me in darkness."

She felt Faron stiffen, his anger radiating off him in tangible waves.

"The bastards," he muttered. "How dare they. How *dare* they!"

She traced shaking fingers across his chest.

"It doesn't matter," she said. "They're dead. They're dead."

Sariel set his sword down across his lap, careful with the movements. His eyes never left hers.

"You have endured much," he said. "Are you capable of telling your tale, or should we accept only the comfort of your presence?"

It was so strange, to think of it in the past already. Her entire life, for thirty years, had been dominated by an interminably horrid procession of cruelties and torture…and yet now it was past. She was free of it, at least in body. Her mind was another story.

"I will tell what I can tell," she said, deciding she owed them that much. Perhaps in the telling, it would become…distant to her. The pain lessened, when shared among family instead of her own to bear.

"It all started with a simple mistake, one we often foolishly make. I was wandering the northern lands and stumbled upon a yearly feast held by King Laurence. The food was fine, the music lovely, and so I participated. Unnamed. Unknown. But then one of his servants fell ill, someone who Laurence had known since he was a child, and he was distraught."

Aylah had relived this moment incessantly in her mind, each and every time, pretending she had let the old woman die. A thousand different reasons justified it, a thousand different ways in which she had been a fool.

"I healed her," she continued. "And worse, I did not flee unnoticed in the night. I was swept up in the drinking, singing, and feasting, and the king's praise was so effusive, so joyous, I thought I would be safe. I claimed it was no miracle, just a bit of prayer to the goddess; that was my excuse. Only Laurence did not believe me."

She still remembered the sound of her door bursting open, armed soldiers descending upon her while she lay half naked in her bed, sleeping away the effects of the wine.

"Laurence captured me," she said. "He sought an explanation for my healing, and I...They hadn't hurt me yet, you two must understand. Even then, it seemed he would be reasonable. He was frightened of our gifts, as humans often are. I told him only pieces of the truth, that my hands could heal, and as best I knew, the stars had gifted me that blessing since the day I was born. I did not tell him how long ago I was born, or of the centuries we have walked these lands. I thought if he believed I was special, he would assign me a role within his kingdom. Once free of his dungeon, I could plot my escape."

Aylah's hand clenched tightly, bunching the fabric of Faron's shirt within her fist.

"Instead, he chained me in the deepest, darkest pit of his castle. He demanded I give him my gifts, and I told him truly, I could do no such thing. I endured his beatings and his knives. He would kill me one day, I was certain of it. Once dead, he need only dispose of me somewhere I could recover, preferably in a grave outside his castle. It would not be the first time I clawed myself free from the soil."

Faron embraced her again, and he kissed her forehead.

"You don't need to tell us if you're not ready," he insisted. "Sariel and I can wait."

"No," she said, harsher than she intended. "I have to do this. I have to be free of it. Once you both know, once the knowledge is yours, then I... then it won't be mine alone. Do you understand?"

Perhaps they did, perhaps they didn't, but both brothers nodded in the affirmative.

Aylah took a moment to gather her thoughts. She had always prided herself on being the strongest in their family, the most consistent, and the most mature. When conflict arose between them, as it often did, she was the mediator. Sometimes it meant a stern discussion. Sometimes it meant brandishing a sword. She considered both finely honed skills within her repertoire. Surely she could be strong now. She could discuss these matters with the cold distance they deserved.

"Laurence's wife, Alise, was the one who first had the idea," she said. "She was convinced my gifts flowed within my blood, and when Laurence tired from years of silence, he let her do with me as she wished. She...bled me, day after day, little cuts so she might fill herself a glass. And then she drank."

Faron's disgust was evident, while Sariel looked ready to dig up their corpses so he might murder them anew.

"It did nothing at first, though she claimed it added to her beauty. But then, over time, it did. I saw it. I watched the change. Little scars faded from her body. The stretch marks from birthing her son, gone. She never fell ill. Once Laurence accepted this, he joined Alise in her drinking."

What had been private bleedings at Alise's hands became something more. At first, it was a ritual between the couple, and many times they fucked in her presence, drunk from the consumption of her radiance-blessed blood. It only demeaned her further, listening to them rut, as the flesh of her left arm blistered and peeled. Radiance was not to be given to humanity, but they were taking it, *taking* it from her, and the cruel magic of the vow punished her nonetheless. Their son was next to join in the feeding, becoming golden, otherworldly, and beloved by the people. His own wife soon accompanied them, the four taking turns with the knife.

And then, one day, Aylah died. They knew it, too, and yet kept her there. Perhaps they debated what to do with her. Perhaps they planned to wring out what blood they could from her corpse and then devour her meat and bones. The problem was, the death had come from simple blood loss, an easy malady for her body to fix. She awoke a mere day later.

When Alise discovered Aylah was breathing, things became so much worse.

The bleedings intensified. The rest of Laurence's family partook. Then came lords and ladies, brought into the secret collective they dubbed the blood-blessed. They performed the cuttings in the dark, fearful to lose the power they gained. It changed them further, but as the change came, they realized the rest of the populace would not understand... unless they, too, became drunk on the blood.

She heard them discuss their plans. Pouring pails of her blood into wells. Administering little sips to newborn babes. The population of the Grand Castle and its surrounding Stone's Refuge swelled, while the outer realms were steadily abandoned. Kanth became a nation obsessed with crimson life, so that they drank not only of her own radiance-blessed blood but of that of the young, the beautiful, and the foreign. They even drank of each other, further twisting and corrupting the radiance within them.

What were once blisters on her arm became terrible burns and searing pain to match the carving of their knives. A full kingdom blessed with radiance, and it was her fault, her fault, even when she argued with herself that her consent was denied, her blood taken, her radiance stolen.

When alone, Aylah had wept and pleaded for Calluna to find her, before yet another death stole her for a spell.

She looked to her brothers. Her head hurt and her heart ached beyond measure—telling all this was too much. She should have known freedom wouldn't come so easily. Even knowing the entire castle was slain, she felt their phantoms lingering over her. In time, she would recount the bizarre, quasi-religious rituals the royal family developed, and the prayers they spoke as their knives opened her veins. Of how only Laurence and Alise were allowed to put their lips upon her, and drink from the blessed source, for fear of tainting her body and the blood within.

Their favorite was to cut her lip, and with their kiss, feed their gluttony.

"Soon everyone drank," Aylah said at last. "And it changed them, too. They shared it. First with the castle, then the nearest towns. Then the kingdom."

"We saw proof of this on our travel here," Faron said. "Whole villages were vacant. Many assaulted us as fiends, corrupted and vile."

"Our blood is poison to those born without radiance's touch," Sariel said. He shook his head. "But it is a strange poison, almost akin to an addiction. Those closest to the Grand Castle, who could constantly partake, staved off its effects the longest, enjoyed our stolen blessings even as it changed them within. Those far out weren't given enough. Their bodies craved what they had tasted and lost. They devoured animals, then strangers, and then each other..."

"To feed an entire kingdom," Faron said, his voice soft and in shock. "Aylah, you poor, poor thing."

As much as she desired their comfort, she could bear no such pity.

"Enough," she snapped. "I am your sister, born and blessed equal to you both. I am no broken thing." She gestured about her. "And you have equal explanations to give, for you appear to march at the forefront of an army. Where are Eder, Calluna, and Eist?"

Sariel stood, his mood darkening. He probably thought he hid it well, but he could never disguise his true thoughts from her.

"Tomorrow," he said. "Rest tonight, and enjoy the returned comforts of your freedom."

He exited Rowan's tent. Faron gave her one last hug and then separated himself as well.

"If you need anything, anything at all, you call for me," he said, smiling at her. "For at least a few weeks, you can consider me your personal servant."

"Appreciated but unnecessary," she said, and forced a return smile. "Now go, so I can sleep, and on padded pillows instead of hanging from chains."

He winced at the mention of her imprisonment environs.

"Of course," he said, and left.

Aylah looked to her wrists, and the deep marks left upon them. *Instead of hanging from chains*, said so casually, as if what she had endured was a harmless thing to mention. Her scars would fade. What bones of hers were broken would mend and return to their proper shape. The strength within her would grow, and her blood, replenish. Soon no proof would remain upon her body of her torture and imprisonment.

She closed her eyes.

Her body.

Just her body.

She pushed to a stand, endured the dizziness, and then approached the flap opposite where Rowan lurked outside. With shaking hands, she pried it open a crack and then slipped outside.

The night was deep, the stars vibrant above her. The camp was enormous, and the light of their dwindling campfires a searing pain to her vision. She turned away from them and focused only on the stars. They, too, burned, but if she could endure decades of knives, she could endure this blessed heat. This silver scarring.

Tears trickled down her face as she looked upon the glorious expanse of stars. So grand and distant, she felt she could fall into them if she stared long enough. The grandeur was a balm for a mind locked in a small, dark cell.

Laurence was dead.

Alise was dead.

"I'm not there," she whispered to those distant stars. "Not anymore."

She dropped the blankets wrapped about herself. Underneath was only a rough shift Rowan had given her upon her arrival at the camp. Even that was too much. She stripped it away. She stood naked once more, but this time of her own choosing.

The light of the stars was gentle upon her skin, blessed and life-giving. Aylah lifted her left hand to the sky, her trembling fingers lovingly stroking the image of the moon that had given her strength in her suffering. A cool wind blew across the blisters of her left arm, already beginning to heal in the wake of Kanth's utter destruction.

"I'm not there," she insisted, and this time, she felt like she might believe it. The deep scars across her arms, chest, and throat shimmered in the pale light. "I'm free."

Aylah clenched her fists, finally feeling like her old self. Feeling strong and in control.

And allowing herself to feel, for the very first time, savage, jealous rage at being robbed of her rightful vengeance against King and Queen Silvein. Two murders that were hers. Two murders, stolen by Sariel.

"What joys have you left me, brother?" she asked the night, but the stars held no answer.

Chapter 39

CALLUNA

Calluna was very good at hiding when she desired to go unseen. Avoiding the soldiers patrolling the Tower Majestic was child's play. Not even those born and raised within the ancient edifice could compare, for she had spent nearly five decades scouring the tower before discovering the underwater temple.

Only one person's eye could find her, and he spotted her with ease as he walked the rafters toward the guarded lift near the center.

"It's all right, Calluna," Eder said, his back to her. "You're welcome at my side."

Calluna slipped out from behind one of the cranks. The liftmaster nearby startled, his eyes wide and his mouth dropping open. She'd been so close, she could have reached out and touched him if she so wished.

"If you don't mind," she said, and reluctantly joined Eder's side. She'd hoped to watch from afar, as she had the past few weeks as Eder prepared. Those preparations, though, had finally reached their end.

For good or ill, Eder would activate the ancient machinery of the Tower Majestic.

"Of course I do not mind," he said as the pair stepped onto the lift.

"Without you, I'd have never discovered the key. It is only right that you accompany me."

The Final Ascent was much the same as it had been, only now each and every runestone shimmered with a pale silver light. Eder had spent the days and nights cutting his arm, dripping his blood into a small bowl, and then using a brush to paint across the swirls and lines. Each rune. Each mark. It had taken him days, and a shocking amount of blood, but with every crimson brushstroke he brought life back to the ancient device.

It now hummed with power, deep and unpleasant. Calluna felt it in her teeth, and she hated it.

"Do you know what will happen?" she asked.

"I know what I believe will happen," Eder said as they exited the lift. "This device was the grand achievement of the Etemen, and the entire purpose of this tower. At last, we pierce the veil. With everything set, I need only trigger the catalyst."

"The key," Calluna murmured.

"And my blood," Eder confirmed.

Despite the confusing mess of runes, there was a single straight path piercing through them directly to the pedestal in the center. Calluna followed Eder there, her fingers twitching and her nerves on edge. She had never liked these runestones, and that was before they had been awakened. Yet again she wondered if it had been a mistake to reveal their secrets to her brother.

This will be the end of their war, she thought as she watched Eder stand before the bowl. *Any cost is worth having our family together again.*

Eder withdrew a sharp, slender knife from a small pocket of his robe. He positioned his left arm over the bowl and then pressed the knife's edge to his skin.

"Do you hear us, Father?" he asked, his eyes closed and his head tilted to the sun shining directly down upon him. "We are here."

The knife cut. Blood flowed into the bowl.

"We are *here*."

At first, there was nothing. The blood dripped, and the stones remained silent. Calluna watched, surprised by her deep desire for the ritual to fail. Maybe she had interpreted the mosaic wrong. Maybe Eder had reassembled the runestones incorrectly.

Drip. Drip. And then the blood from Eder's arm coalesced into a solid cord not flowing from the cut but *tearing* out of it. Eder gasped, and he clutched the sides of the pedestal to hold himself aloft.

The light from the runes pulsed brighter, their color shifting from silver to crimson. The humming noise, so faint she sometimes thought she hallucinated it, became a roar.

"Eder!" she cried, but he would not move. More blood ripped free of him and into the bowl. Calluna's eyes, so deeply attuned to radiance, saw its unmistakable shimmer flowing through the blood, and it was immense. Everything that was her brother was pooling into that bowl, and within, it was consumed. It burned. The fires of it flowed through unseen veins hidden beneath the reaching hardstone hands and into the runes surrounding them, empowering them further.

"Eder, stop!"

Perhaps he couldn't. Perhaps he chose not to. She didn't know. His body was rigid, his mouth locked in a silent scream. Panic overwhelmed her. This had to stop. It had to stop!

Calluna slammed into him with her shoulder, and she cried out as the impact snapped her collarbone. Pain flashed through her, her vision swimming yellow and white. Eder staggered away from the bowl, his knife dropping from his hand to clatter upon the stone. The cord of blood snapped, and along with it, the silver vein of radiance.

The light on the runestones paled. Blood smeared across the floor, staining Calluna's dress, but it was nothing compared to the great flow that had once been.

"Calluna," Eder gasped, weak and delirious. "Why?"

"You were going to die," she said, clutching her left arm to her chest. That entire side of her body pulsed with agony from the break.

"It would not be the first."

"But it would be the last!"

Eder slowly pushed himself up to his knees. His eyes focused, the haziness of his speech and gaze replaced with a sudden hardness.

"Explain yourself."

"I saw it," she said. "I felt it. Everything that was you, it was being pulled into that bowl, and…and…*burned* by it." She was crying and didn't know if it was from the pain or from how frightened she'd been in those last moments. "I almost lost you, Eder. I almost lost you forever. This…this awful device, this damned tower itself, it is our deaths. Our true, final deaths. You can't do this. Please, whatever you hope for, it isn't worth the cost."

Eder slid closer to her, still too weak to stand. His gentle hands surrounded her and pulled her into his lap. She cradled against him, enduring the waves of agony from her broken collarbone. Crying, she pressed her face to his chest.

"I know you want this more than anything, Eder, but I'm begging you, don't leave me. Don't make me say goodbye forever."

He kissed the top of her head, his fingers gently stroking her hair.

"I promise," he whispered softly. "And you are right, Calluna. You are right. The cost is too high. Much too high."

She sniffled. "And your war?"

His touch hesitated.

"If I cannot use this tower to reach Father, then the slow-and-steady method must suffice. My church must endure. The cold cells must be spread to all corners of Kaus."

A fresh wave of tears had her closing her eyes and clenching her teeth.

"I'm so sick of it, Eder. I love you, all of you. Must it always come to this?"

He tucked his fingers underneath her chin and forced her to look up at him. He was so handsome, his pale skin warmed by the light of the sun and his star-kissed eyes filled with determination.

"No crowns, no thrones," he said softly. "That was your vow, but it was not mine. I am the only one left who can save this burdened, asphyxiated world. And I will, Calluna. I will. One day, Father will look upon our lives, see our souls cleansed of sins, and he will tell me, 'Good job, faithful servant, now welcome home.'"

"But how do you know?" she asked. "Father? Our sins? These lives? How do you *know*?"

He kissed her forehead, slowly, gently. His answer was a whisper.

"Because in my deepest despair, lost in an endless sea of death and resurrection, *I heard his voice.*"

Part Five

CONQUEST

Chapter 40

FARON

Doremy. Armane. Rudou. Perche. Valois. Forez. Etne. Vivarai. Cevenne. It had taken ten months, but the combined might of western Kaus now numbered twenty-five thousand soldiers in total. All of them, gathered together in the province of Olado to march the road leading through the Sapphire Mountains, smash through the Twin Gates, and emerge upon the grasslands of the Astral Kingdom. And Leliel's chosen would lead them.

"A force anyone should be fearful to engage," Isabelle said as she and Faron looked over the maps and numbers in her command tent. "Though I'd have preferred we received more soldiers over the coin we salvaged from Kanth."

"It will have to do," Faron said, and he tapped Kanth on the map. "Healing the damage the royal family inflicted upon the population will take years. I pray you do not forget them once Racliffe falls and Kaus is united under the banner of the protectorate."

Isabelle sent a mild glare his way.

"Do you not know me by now, Faron? None of this is for personal glory. All of Kaus will benefit from my rule. The corruption of Kanth will not be forgotten, I promise you that. I would see its forests healed and its abandoned villages once more vibrant with life."

Faron smiled to counter her glare. "Forgive me, but I sometimes have trouble trusting those in power."

"Even me?"

He laughed. "Especially you. Those I wish to trust are the ones I should doubt the most."

She waved him away.

"Go and help prepare our soldiers for the march. We can't afford to linger in the mountain pass. Each day we spend there is another day Mitra's forces can ambush us with the terrain to their advantage."

Faron bowed low, to the point of exaggeration, and then exited her tent. The sun shone down on him, still warm despite the approaching winter, and it lifted Faron's spirits. Iris was waiting for him outside the tent, and she stirred, flopped her head side to side as she stretched, and then looked up at him. He scratched behind her ears, then looked out upon the sprawling mess of tents marked with banners from the various kingdoms vassalized into the protectorate.

"Still hard to believe we did it, Sariel," he said. It had taken almost a year, but a conquering force was assembled, its entire might ready to crash down upon the walls of Racliffe and end the Church of Stars. And throughout every conflict, they had guided Isabelle to victory. Not once had she lost.

It was enough to think she might have actually been chosen by a goddess.

"Where are you hiding anyway?" he wondered. Sariel had stuck with Faron and his group of friends for most of the journey eastward, but come this morning, as they prepared to launch the invasion against the Astral Kingdom, he was nowhere to be found. From the moment Faron awoke, Sariel's tent was empty. It was far from abnormal for his brother to be a loner, but this felt strangely sudden.

"I hope you'll forgive me this breach of privacy," he said, and closed his eyes. He let his mind sink into the ground beneath him, flooding the land with his presence. He ignored the teeming mass of humanity, thumping around in armored boots and trampling grass as they folded up tents and kicked out campfires. They were faint little stars in his mind, no brighter than fireflies. What he sought was the blinding sun that was his brother.

Nowhere in the camp. Strange. Faron pushed his presence out wider, expanding the miles while fighting off a worm of worry squirming in his stomach.

There. Two miles out, to the east. Faron breathed a sigh of relief. He didn't even know why he was nervous. Did he think his brother would abandon him now, at the start of their final victory?

"I suppose it's time for a walk," he told Iris, and together they trudged the gentle hills eastward.

•

Faron found his brother standing atop a steeply sloped hill that seemed to roll for hundreds of feet in all directions. A royal whitebud tree grew at its apex, and it seemed as lonely as his brother standing there with Redemption resting upon his shoulder.

"Wait here," he ordered Iris at the bottom of the hill. The coyote reluctantly obeyed. Faron climbed the gentle slope, unsure of what he would say when at the top. It did not help that Sariel did not turn at his arrival. The wind blew across him, teasing his hair. The chill made Faron shiver.

"Took a bit to find you," Faron said by way of greeting.

"Perhaps I did not want to be found."

"Then you should have said so before slinking off and making me worry."

He looked around, trying to understand the importance of this place. They were a few dozen miles shy of the entrance to the mountain path. The nearest towns were miles away. For as long as Faron remembered, no major battles had been fought here, no forgotten cities or major treaties signed beneath the shade of the whitebud tree to lend it importance. So why had...

And then he knew.

"This is where you and Eder dueled," he said.

Sariel stabbed his sword into the earth.

"I used to tell myself here was when everything went wrong," he said. "But that's not true, is it? A wall had grown between us long before I demanded the duel. This was not the start, but the culmination of my every failure."

He shook his head.

"I think on it more than I should, Faron. What I did wrong. How things could have gone differently. What might have happened had I won instead? Would I have been as cruel? As broken and bitter? Or was the reign of the Heartless King fated to rise and fall no matter who won our battle?"

Faron put a hand on his brother's shoulder.

"Do not dwell in the past, lest it drown you," he said. "We all have our faults. We all have our regrets."

"Perhaps," Sariel said, and he looked to the sky. "But they are not equal, are they?"

Faron withdrew his hand.

"No," he said. "Not if one is determined to measure the weight of a sin, I suppose. But that is not my place, nor my desire. You're here with me, looking to fix what Eder has broken. That's enough. The past is set in stone. It is this lifetime alone that you can control."

"And so we march to war," Sariel said, and he ripped his sword free. "At the head of a union of nations, I come to tear down the walls of Racliffe and storm the Tower Majestic in search of my brother." He laughed, so tired, so bitter. "Things do not change on Kaus, do they? On and on it spirals, ever burdened by this bloody cycle."

"That's why we took our vows," Faron said, feeling them itch upon his arm by merely mentioning them. "To stop that cycle."

Sariel rested Redemption upon his shoulder, and he glanced one last time to the tree.

"No thrones. No crowns. If only Eder had shared in the vow. We might have all been spared this second tragedy."

He descended the hill, returning westward to join Isabelle's camp. Faron waited, feeling wrong for having come here. He truly did feel like a spy, crawling in somewhere he was never supposed to be. This tree. This hill. It meant so much to both Sariel and Eder, but to him, it was but a place in a story told to him centuries ago.

Faron glanced at the tree, and he saw the earth near the trunk was freshly dug. Deciding he had already overstepped multiple lines, he let his curiosity get the best of him. The disturbance was small and shallow, the dirt easily parting to his fingers. Buried beneath was a beautiful silver pendant decorated with a lone sapphire. Faron held it in his hand, confused by its significance. Then he flipped the pendant about and saw, carved into the sides, a single name: Agnes.

"You're not who you were," he whispered to the phantom face of his brother. He returned the pendant to the earth. Down at the bottom of the hill, Iris barked, starting to worry. He ignored her as his fingers curled into the soil. The weight of the past threatened him, and the air felt heavy. Of the days of the Four Heroes. Of his time as Barron the Wild Rage. The old war raged in his mind, and the slaughter delivered by his sharpened sword.

"None of us are, and I pray none of us ever become them again."

Chapter 41

AYLAH

Aylah walked the camp, observing the teeming mass of humanity and armor toiling and preparing. The atmosphere was jovial as they crossed the Sapphire Mountains and marched toward Racliffe. Everywhere she went, eyes glanced her way. Far too many contained unhidden lust.

Are the camp followers not enough for you? she thought as she walked. For so long, she had considered herself immune to caring. These humans were little better than animals, so why take offense when they looked upon her beauty and thought the thoughts they were born to think?

Aylah smiled at a nearby soldier, nightmarish images flashing through her mind. No. She was not immune, just numbed.

"Are you well prepared for the next battle?" she asked the man. His banner marked him as from Grenab, one of the last little kingdoms to pledge their banner to Queen Isabelle's protectorate.

"I'd be better prepared if I had a kiss from a pretty lady," he said, and laughed as if he'd told the grandest of jokes. Aylah brushed a hand through her hair, cut short around her neck, and then trailed her fingers lower, barely brushing her breast.

"Just a kiss?" she asked.

The man was not laughing now. He glanced to the other soldiers with him, who were locked in conversation and ignoring him.

"Truly?" he asked. He sounded nervous. Aylah studied him. Handsome enough, with wavy brown hair, and young, maybe just approaching his twentieth year. His smile was ugly, though, his teeth crooked and yellow.

Aylah put her back to him and then glanced over her shoulder. She'd chosen this particular camp for a reason. They were directly beside a nearby copse of trees, a rare possibility for privacy in an army that had swelled in ranks to number over twenty-five thousand.

"Care for a walk in the woods?" she asked, and then proceeded without waiting for an answer.

As expected, he dropped what he was doing and followed.

Aylah carefully stepped through the thickening brush, her boots much too light for such terrain. She wore only a plain pair of trousers, a loose wool blouse, and a thin belt with a dagger buckled into a half sheath. No armor. Every time she imagined donning some, she shuddered at the thought.

Fighting for these humans? No. Not yet. Perhaps not ever.

"So, uh, what's your name?" the man asked as he hurried to catch up. She slid through the forest, silent as a serpent. He tromped like a cow.

"Aylah."

Deeper into the forest. They must not be disturbed.

"Aylah. That's a pretty name." She held her breath. "Not as pretty as you, though."

She hissed it out through her teeth.

"Thank you," she said.

The forest was made of salwood trees, their wide leaves both a vibrant yellow and extremely thin, so that as Aylah walked underneath, it felt like she passed through a land of gold. Dew sparkled from atop the scattered bushes, adding to the illusion. She paused to touch one of the salwood trunks. They were a pale red, and unique to the eastern lands of Kaus. Her fingertips traced the bark.

"Here is far enough," she said.

The soldier stood there, awkward and silent. His neck had turned red-
der than the tree trunks.

"Ground's not exactly soft," he said at last.

She pressed her hand to his chest and pushed him against one of the
salwoods.

"We won't be on the ground."

His breath caught in his throat. His eyes widened. Lust overwhelmed
him, forming a bulge in his trousers, but he was also nervous, perhaps
even afraid. However he expected this to play out, this wasn't it.

Aylah leaned closer, and she let the radiance pool within her eyes. Her
fingers curled around the sides of his face, imprisoning him with her
touch. Of her gifts, this was her weakest, a pittance of the power possessed by Eder or Calluna. This young man, however, was already enraptured, his heart open to her, eager for her acceptance. Silver threads
passed between them, unseen by him, but vibrant spider's silk to her.
They latched on to his mind and burrowed in deep.

"You will not speak," she commanded. "You will not flee. You will not
resist."

A second command pulsed unspoken through her feet into the earth
below. Vines sprouted around the base of the tree. They looped and tangled with each passing second, curving like snakes to bind the soldier
to the bark. First his legs, then his waist, his arms, and last, three coils
tightly encircling his neck.

True to her desires, he did not protest.

Aylah drew her dagger.

"This will hurt," she said as she placed the blade to his face. "But you
will not scream."

She cut him, long, deep, and slow. It started just underneath his eye,
then curved along his jawbone, slicing his cheek in half. Blood poured
down his face and neck, and yet he made not a sound. His eyes, though.
She could see the fear in his eyes. They bulged wide and darted about,
like those of a caught rabbit.

Aylah watched the blood flow, all the forest darkening around her.

"You can't scream," she whispered. "Screaming makes it worse."

She pulled the dagger back and then slashed his chest, cutting open his shirt in the process. A second slash, then a third, each one a little lower. Flaying him, so that his ribs would be exposed.

"You can't fight back, or they'll punish you."

A fourth cut across his abdomen. A bit of his entrails threatened to spill forth. A command, and the vines wrapped over it, keeping him upright. Keeping him alive.

"You can't speak. You can't argue. They don't want your words."

She jabbed the dagger into his shoulder and then carved along the bone, careful not to sever anything major. Even with that care, blood splashed across them both, staining her blouse and trousers. But it wasn't her blood. Not hers.

Her control over him started to weaken, and so she ordered more vines to latch across his mouth, gagging him. Tears trickled down to mix with the blood, and he whimpered softly, pathetically. Aylah watched him, taking in his obvious suffering. She saw the blood, saw the way he clenched his teeth and bit the vines to endure the pain as her dagger punched into his collarbone and wedged it free of the joint, popping it upward within the folds of his skin.

She watched, and waited, to feel anything.

Sympathy.

Pity.

Remorse.

Tears swelled in her eyes. Nothing. She felt nothing. A swift, brutal thrust, and she shoved the dagger between two of the young man's ribs to pierce his heart. Laughter filled her ears. The trees vanished. She saw servants kneeling, cups lifted, howling, someone was howling, was it her? Was it her?

"You can't weep," she said, fighting for her every breath. "Weeping proves part of you yet lives."

And so we lift our glasses in praise of our goddess, Leliel, who delivered unto us this bounty, so that we may taste of everlasting life.

Aylah ripped her dagger free. The man was long dead, but she seethed at him nonetheless.

"Is that all I am to you, goddess?" she asked, and slashed his face. Not the controlled carving as before, but wild and careless.

"A bounty?"

Another slash, and another. She hacked at him, tearing apart the meat, bone, and muscle that made up a human life.

"A gift?"

More savage. With strength to rival Faron's and Sariel's. Snap and break everything that remained.

"A *feast*?"

The vines withered away, and he fell in pieces to the forest floor.

Aylah screamed, choked and strangled so its volume was a whisper, just a phantom enactment of the true rage and horror clawing to be made free within her mind. She sobbed and retched as she stabbed at the corpse, wishing Laurence was there, or Alise, or any of those vile servants who held the cups as she was bled again, and again, and again, night after night, year after year, left to bleed, to *die*, only to wake and be bled once more, cut and bled, cut and bled, sometimes dying, sometimes surviving, but never free, never found, always bleeding, her arm always burning, burning, until, until, until...

She collapsed amid the mess. Her chest heaved with her every breath. She looked to the bones and tissue and didn't even recognize them as human anymore.

A footstep in the woods, crunching a twig. She flinched. There would be no hiding this, no explaining it away. She glanced over her shoulder, her hand tightening around the hilt of her dagger.

"Aylah?" Sariel asked. His face was an emotionless mask.

Aylah had to swallow before she could speak. No excuses here. The truth would have to suffice, even if it was the hardest to give. Three words, and each one deeply hurt.

"I'm. Still. There."

Her brother removed his coat, set it safely aside, and then lowered himself before her. His hands settled around hers, and he gently took away her dagger.

"I know," he whispered.

He used the dagger to cut off her blood-drenched blouse, having to peel it from her wet flesh. When done, he removed his shirt, bunched it up, and began to slowly clean her face and chest. All the while, he spoke in soft, gentle tones.

"What you have suffered goes beyond any cruelty we have ever endured. You were broken, Aylah, and I cannot imagine how deeply. But I also know that you are stronger than any human could ever dream of being. The broken pieces shall be mended. The torn and ripped, sewn together. Time, Aylah. Time heals all things, and it is ever our blessing."

"Time," she whispered. "Time was my curse." She looked to him as he washed the blood from her neck. "I wanted to die, Sariel. To truly, permanently, forever die. And I couldn't."

There wasn't much he could do for her hair, but he tried to clean it all the same, and then brushed it away from her face.

"You aren't the first." He set aside his bloody shirt. "But never forget this, Aylah. I would not walk this world without you. Time is my friend only so long as you, and the rest of my family, are there with me to watch these days and nights spiral forever on."

"Family. Is that what we are?"

He did not answer. Instead he grabbed his coat and wrapped it about her. Its warmth settled over her, but it was not enough. Aylah flung herself against Sariel. His arms wrapped about her, and in that embrace, she finally felt the horrid, raw emptiness within her mind fade.

"I argued with them," she said as the muscles in her back and neck relaxed. She suddenly felt drowsy and weak. "Told them of my past, and all the lives I've lived. I thought if I could convince them I was...that I was real, and alive, they would acknowledge the horror they committed. That they would feel guilt, or regret, for my imprisonment."

She closed her eyes and nuzzled Sariel's chest.

"They only drank. They only cut and drank."

He kissed the top of her head, and she wilted further.

"Are they worth all this, Sariel?" she asked. "These humans? Are they worth everything we have given, everything we have suffered?"

"You ask the wrong brother," Sariel answered. "I care not for them. Only us."

He stood, lifting her to her feet at the same time. His face filled her world, and she ached at realizing how much she'd missed him over those long, miserable decades.

The faintest hint of a smile crossed his lips.

"If you need to release the monsters within your mind, come to me," he said. "You may scream, cry, and strike at me all you like. You may even cut me, if you so desire." He glanced to the mutilated mess. "I'll recover better than the fool who followed you into these woods."

He buttoned the coat to hide her nakedness, then gestured toward the camp.

"Go. I'll clean this up so Faron doesn't find out."

Aylah did as ordered, retracing her path to camp. When almost out of sight, she dared a glance back. Sariel stood in the center of the mess, his head tilted, his eyes closed, and his hands spread wide. Silver threads spread in all directions from his fingertips, piercing the earth to flood it with his call. Carrion creatures swarmed at his feet; ants, beetles, flies, and the like. They feasted upon the remains, stripping them to bone and sopping up the blood.

Disguising her murder. Hiding her sin. Fixing the mess his sibling had made, as he so often did. It was why he had been beloved among them, and why he now led an army upon the Tower Majestic.

It was why his own fall from grace had caused the most ruin.

"I'm sorry, Sariel," she whispered. "But this time, I don't think there's a way to make this right."

Chapter 42

EDER

Eder stood before the sacrificial bowl clutched in the frozen hard-stone altar of hands and lifted a knife to his throat.

"One cut," he whispered. "One cut, and I will kneel in the presence of Father."

He felt the ground tremble so slightly beneath his feet, as if the many runestones quivered with excitement. Once the blood flowed, they would flare with life, crimson and hungry. The Tower Majestic would awaken. His kingdom's purpose, become fulfilled.

The knife pressed harder. Death was familiar to him. He feared nothing. A slice, an opening, and then all else would proceed as intended. If only he could find the courage. If only he could muster the will.

His hand shook. The knife relented, not a single drop of blood spilled.

"Damn it!" Eder screamed, and he slammed the knife to the ground and then slumped with his back pressed to the sacrificial altar. He buried his head in his hands, and he wept as much as he raged.

Eder would never sacrifice one of his beloved siblings. If it must be anyone, it must be him. And yet...and yet...

He looked up to the night sky, wishing he could take comfort from those false stars. Or did he truly know them to be false?

"How great is your faith, truly, if you fear the death that would take you?" he whispered to himself. "How ardent your beliefs if you cannot give everything to see them fulfilled?"

Three words. He had built a kingdom on three simple words, spoken by Father, and heard amid the death and dark. He had told himself his reasoning was sound and his faith absolute. There were no other possible interpretations.

Lies, told to himself beneath the stars. However strong his faith, it wasn't enough. And so he would fail, here and now, at the final step of his journey.

Eder pushed to his feet and made his way to the platform down. He needed rest. His mind felt raw, and the burdens of Luminary heavy on his shoulders. A pull of a lever, and the lift descended. His exhaustion only deepened when he found his Celebrant waiting for him among the rafters.

"Luminary," she said, bowing her head in respect.

"Is something amiss?" he asked as he led her to another lift, one that would take him down to his home upon the Privileged Heights.

"I pray you forgive my forwardness, but we must discuss matters of the Astral Kingdom's defense."

Eder carefully hid his flinch.

"Are we not safe here in Racliffe? The walls of the White City shall protect us."

Madeleine shook her head.

"It is not Racliffe that is the issue. It is our regents. I've been inundated with communiqués from both the north and south. They want to know why we aren't forming an army to meet the protectorate on the field of battle. Some are...insinuating you are content to let Queen Isabelle trample our lands and lay siege to the coastal cities, so long as Racliffe is spared."

"Racliffe will not be spared, because Racliffe is their goal," Eder said as the pair stepped onto the chosen platform. The liftmaster bowed his head to the floor before turning the enormous gear to lower the platform.

"That does not justify complacency," Madeleine said, and when he

glanced her way, she paled. "That...that is their argument, my Luminary. And I fear it goes beyond words. Our preachers are reporting rum-
blings of rebellion, dissidents claiming that if the Astral Kingdom shall
not protect them, they will protect themselves. General Sid's departure
has only made these rumors worsen."

That was a surprise to Eder, and he fully turned his attention to the
diminutive woman.

"Sid left us?" he asked.

"This morning," Madeleine admitted as the platform swayed slightly.
"He has taken a thousand soldiers with him to reinforce the Twin Gates.
All volunteers, I believe. It is how he bypassed our standing orders."

Eder shook his head. General Sid Alafus had been with Eder since the
earliest days of the Astral Kingdom. Eder had expected Sid to helm the
defense of Racliffe, but it seemed that might not be the case.

"Should I muster the rest of our forces to bring him back?" Madeleine
asked as his silence stretched.

"No," Eder said. "Let him do as he wishes. It will not matter. Nothing
will stop Isabelle's army from arriving at our gates."

The platform's descent slowed, the Privileged Heights nearing. Enormous slabs of hardstone both above and below had broken during the
tower's initial collapse ages ago, lending this particular level significant isolation. It was here that members of the Church of Stars resided,
afforded privacy and freedom from the far more crowded environs elsewhere. Homes were built of stone brick instead of wood, another luxury
for those considered chosen by the church. A handful of men and women
awaited the platform's arrival, and seeing Eder, they quickly stepped back
and bowed their heads.

"We will soon begin austerity measures for Racliffe," Eder said, forcing
himself to assume a mantle of leadership. "Our soldiers will be prepared
to meet the coming threat, I assure you. The Bastard Queen's army will
shatter upon our walls like the waves of the ocean do against the Tower
Majestic."

Madeleine hardly looked convinced, but she curled her little mouth
into a smile.

"Of course," she said. "I hold faith in Father to protect his children from the savages. Sleep well, my Luminary. I will come in the morning with reports from our regents, if you are willing to go over them with me?"

Eder paused before a rare sight within the Tower Majestic. It was a garden growing in the heart of the Privileged Heights, positioned so that its wide oval of transported earth received a large amount of sun from the gigantic nearby window that opened up across the wall just above their floor of hardstone.

"Of course I am willing," he said, and made sure his smile was more believable than hers. "Farewell, Celebrant."

Madeleine hesitated, bowed low, and then departed, leaving Eder alone within the garden. He walked its rows, observing the little flowers. Nothing too large or demanding, just tiny elder blooms, yellow caps, and violet irises. Eder knelt before them, his fingers brushing their petals.

"How do I tell her?" he whispered aloud. "She doesn't know. She could never know."

Eder had not mustered a defense because victory and defeat no longer mattered. Oh, he suspected he could crush the protectorate if he gathered the Astral Kingdom's entire might, but to what end? Faron and Sariel would not be stopped. There would always be another rebellion. Another alliance. And if that didn't work, then Sariel would slink through Eder's kingdom, whispering words of sedition. His radiance would seep into even the most loyal, turning their hearts. Civil war would follow. More bloodshed.

It would not stop. It would never stop. And the longer they warred, the more likely that their missing sibling, Eist, would return from their mysterious isolation. Or Aylah would emerge from whatever life she had spent the last decades living, furious at their warring. She had been Crownbreaker once. Might she become that person again?

Eder grabbed one of the irises and ripped it free of the potted earth. The soft petal withered at his touch, blue flame burning away its beauty. If only he could awaken the tower! If only there was a life whose blood he was willing to spill.

"Come, then," he whispered, imagining the faces of his brothers. "Come to my tower, and condemn me for breaking vows I never swore. Tear down the walls of my city. Fill its streets with blood. I will not surrender, not to you. Never to you."

He opened his hand. Ash fluttered away. His tongue felt dry, and his heart much too heavy.

"Come to me, and prove you have the necessary will." He tilted his head so the moonlight spilling through the distant window of the tower could fall upon his tears. "Prove that, when your faith is challenged, you have the strength to shed the blood of our family, for I do not."

He closed his eyes, ashamed of his tears.

"Father," he whispered. "Father. Where are you?"

Silence in the garden, his only answer.

Chapter 43

SARIEL

While there were additional roads to the far north and south, the main passage through the Sapphire Mountains was known as Nature's Path. A river had once flowed through it, in a time so distant Sariel barely remembered when it had been ankle-deep. The unseen shifting of the mountains had slowly dried it up, but the passage remained, taking travelers through the tallest and harshest portions of the blue peaks before the road deviated from the natural flow into the carved paths leading down from the mountains and to the verdant grasslands beyond.

Guarding that passage were the supposedly impregnable Twin Gates.

"These reports are baffling," Isabelle said as her marshal, squadron leaders, and allied kings and queens gathered around her map table. The spires of the Sapphire Mountains rose to either side of them, so that it felt like they walked through the heart of a canyon. "Where are the Astral Kingdom's armies?"

"Perhaps they are skirting north and south, avoiding us to invade our own lands in retaliation?" Oscar suggested.

"And leaving their own homes unprotected?" Isabelle shook her head. "No, I refuse to believe that. They have been much too complacent about the threat of the protectorate. Something is wrong."

"It's not completely unguarded," King Allan said. "By their banners, General Sid has come to helm the defense."

"If Sid is here, then so should the kingdom's army," Isabelle said, still unconvinced. "Instead, they field a mere two thousand within the Twin Gates."

"Two thousand may be more than enough," Sariel interrupted. "Do not underestimate the danger. Our numbers mean nothing if our soldiers cannot bring their swords to bear against their foes."

"Hold faith in me," Isabelle said. "The gates will fall. I only seek to understand the mind of my foe."

Little chance of that, thought Sariel, but he bit his tongue and kept quiet. There would be no explaining Eder's ever-living nature to such a group. They believed his brother a mad priest seeking power and a throne. Eder was many things, but Sariel knew it went beyond a goal so basic. He sought something from the kingdom he built, but what, Sariel did not know.

"The gates are pure iron, layered and reinforced," Prince Druss said. He crossed his arms and frowned at the map of the east. "I hold faith in you, Isabelle, but even our battering rams cannot break them open. How shall you?"

The queen grinned at her vassal.

"When I pray, the goddess provides."

•

Sariel, Faron, and Aylah stood together and watched, along with thousands of others, as Queen Isabelle approached the western half of the Twin Gates. It was an imposing fortress, its gray stone walls stretching from one side of the canyon to the other. The gate itself was monstrously thick, solid metal, and with its outer surface carved into the visage of a viper baring its fangs, the family crest of the original builder, forgotten to time. A matching gate guarded the eastern entrance, and between was an enormous camp purposefully placed where a small stream exited the mountains to ensure a constant supply of fresh water.

"Neither gate has fallen since the shattering," Faron said, scratching his chin.

Sariel winced. "I am aware."

His brother grunted.

"Right. Sorry."

"I remember the siege like it was yesterday," Aylah said, lurking just behind them. Unlike the two brothers, she was not dressed for war. As she had since being rescued, she refused to fight for humanity and was content to remain behind with Rowan in the surgeons' tents. "Three days of assault with our battering rams failed to break it. We ended up using ladders and siege towers to overwhelm the walls instead. Even with our greater numbers, the losses we suffered were horrific."

Sariel leaned against his sword, which he'd thrust into the hard ground, and watched the queen kneel just shy of arrow range.

"We've brought the materials to build both rams and towers in our wagons, but she's not given the order. What trick has she planned?"

Faron shrugged.

"You act as if I can read her mind. I'm here to watch and find out like the rest of you." He frowned. "Though there might be someone who knows."

Priest Reglia walked along the front line of soldiers, looking fine in his white robes. Bells softly chimed with his movements. An endless prayer flowed from his lips as he placed hands on those who knelt and brushed fingers along their foreheads and hearts. When he neared, Faron crossed his arms and gestured for Reglia to come closer. The priest whispered something to the last soldier he prayed over and then accepted the request.

"I suspect you three desire no prayers to Leliel," he said.

"I'd prefer answers over prayers," Sariel said. "Know you what the queen plans?"

Reglia turned to the fortress. Isabelle had settled onto her knees and lifted her arms above her head, a lone figure between the two armies.

"I do, because it was mine," the priest said.

"Then we can blame you when this goes wrong?" Faron asked, only halfway kidding.

Reglia's returned smile lacked any comfort.

"Isabelle is chosen by our goddess and meant to lead us to victory over the wretched Church of Stars. I merely told her if this was true, then it is time she prove to all the world the power of the goddess and the inevitability of our victory."

That sounded more like the priest had devised a test for the queen than any actual plan. Sariel disliked it, as he did the priest's careful, practiced smile.

"You are here to guide and offer Leliel's wisdom and grace to the people," Sariel said. "I pray you are not overstepping your role, priest, nor playing games with those in power."

Reglia gestured to Isabelle, who had lowered herself with her face to the dirt.

"This is no game, Godsight brothers. Either she is who she is, or she is not. And if the goddess is truly with her, then let us not put limits on the power she may bestow."

Sariel could tell the queen was praying, but she was too far away for anyone to hear. Curiosity won him over. He enhanced his senses with a bit of radiance so that her words flowed over him as if he were standing beside her.

Be with me, Leliel, beloved goddess of dawn and dusk. Be with me, Leliel, and look upon me with your loving eyes.

The line of soldiers grew wider, more and more trying to catch sight of the queen. She'd given orders to Marshal Oscar and all her squadron leaders for the army to be ready to assault the Twin Gates at a moment's notice, but few looked prepared for actual war, even if they wore their armor and brandished their swords.

"Hey, hey, Faron!" a familiar voice shouted behind them. Both brothers turned to see Bart pushing through the crowd. Reglia took the opportunity to bow low and depart.

"Be ready for battle," he said as he resumed walking the lines and praying over soldiers. "The goddess expects great things of all of us, but you especially, I think."

"What are you yelling for?" Faron asked Bart once he reached the front line. "Hoping I'll lift you up on my shoulders?"

The young man blushed.

"Just wanted you to make me some space," he said, sliding in beside Faron. "And let you know Iris isn't too happy being ordered to remain behind."

"She's a fine asset in open battlefields," Sariel said, knowing his brother's reasoning. "A close-quartered battle within the fort is another matter."

"Yeah, I tried explaining that to the coyote, and she didn't seem to agree." Bart winked. "Rowan's watching her now. Iris seems to get along with her for some reason, which is lucky for me." He turned his attention to Isabelle, his good humor turning subdued. "Is she praying?"

"To the goddess," Sariel said, trying hard to keep sarcasm or annoyance from his words. "Apparently she will come and open the gates for us."

"She did at Vendom," Bart argued.

"Our army did that," Sariel argued back.

"Does it matter?"

"Silence, both of you," Aylah interrupted. "Can you not sense the gathering?"

Isabelle's power was swelling within her, her innate radiance building into an unseen ball inside her chest. It pulsed gold, and while at first it was visible only to their blessed eyes, the light soon leaked out of her in gentle waves. Murmurs spread through the army, whispers both fearful and hopeful.

Bart, meanwhile, bowed his head and joined in her prayer. He did it quietly, trying not to draw any attention to himself.

"Be with me, Leliel, so in my fear and weakness, I will be strong."

He did not know, but his words were perfectly synchronized to Isabelle's, a fact that unnerved Sariel. He clutched Redemption more tightly and watched a few arrows sail out over the walls of the Twin Gates. They fell harmlessly short.

"Isabelle..." Sariel said as the power flared, the brightness rivaling even that which he and his siblings might produce.

"She's beyond us, isn't she?" Faron whispered, sounding in awe. "I never thought it possible."

Isabelle rose from her prayer, her arms spreading wide. Ethereal wings burst from her back, twelve now, layered and spanning dozens of feet. Her spine arched as if she were in pain, and her voice cried out to the heavens with such power the mountains themselves vibrated in echo.

"Make way for the goddess!"

A pure beam of golden light shot from her chest. The light of its radiance was blinding, but Sariel refused to look away. It struck the massive iron gate. The metal groaned. The stones of the surrounding walls cracked and shifted. The power pressed onward, refusing to give, and to Sariel's shock, the metal itself warped and changed. It wasn't just striking it with a physical force, but a second, overwhelming desire, to be weak, brittle, and thin.

A command of radiance, of creation harnessed and made Isabelle's own. Against that, the gate meant nothing. Its metal shattered, collapsing inward and crushing soldiers pressing against it in a vain attempt to keep it stable.

"Stars have mercy," Aylah whispered, retreating from the front line. In the sudden, shocked silence that followed, Isabelle's voice was a trumpet call.

"Victory for Leliel!"

The army surged forward, and Sariel was all too happy to be swept up in it. He yanked his sword free and charged ahead, determined to be near the front. The protectorate soldiers weaved to either side of Isabelle, parting like a river, and she an immovable stone. Faron caught up with Sariel, and he allowed his larger brother to take the lead. His shield and armor would clear the way. Behind him, Sariel would ever be his deadly shadow.

With the way opened, and Faron leading, the battle was a slaughter. Faron batted soldiers aside like playthings, uncaring of the multitude of little wounds and bruises he suffered. Sariel accompanied him deeper into the ranks, thrusting again and again as if Redemption were a spear, and his brother his protective shield wall. More protectorate soldiers flooded into the expansive opening between the two walls of the Twin Gates.

"Give chase!" Faron bellowed, his voice accompanied by multiple trumpet calls as squadron leaders gave similar orders. The troops within were fleeing out the eastern gate. Sariel saw a flaming phoenix on their banner, marking General Sid among their number. That the leader of the Astral Kingdom's army would retreat so readily worried Sariel, but surely it was born of panic. No one could have predicted the radiant assault Isabelle would unleash upon the supposedly unbreakable iron gates.

When two-thirds of the Astral Kingdom's army were beyond the eastern wall, and the protectorate closing in, the east gate slammed shut with a clang loud enough to be heard over the din of battle. Sariel retreated from the carnage to gain a moment's peace. His eyes enhanced, he scanned the visible chains and gears that opened the monstrously heavy gate and saw them being hacked apart by the soldiers still inside.

"Clever," he muttered. With the gate shut and its gears sabotaged, there would be a lengthy delay in giving chase. Unless Isabelle had another miracle within her, but so far the queen remained back from the battle, a rarity for her. Perhaps the prayer had taken more out of her than he believed.

"Barely worked up a sweat," Faron said, grinning at Sariel as the bulk of the protectorate forces rushed the soldiers trapped against the gates; they threw down their weapons in surrender once their work was done. Faron's smile vanished as he looked past Sariel back toward the camp.

"Smoke?" he asked, confused. Sariel turned, and sure enough, thick plumes rose from the rear of the army.

"An ambush?" Sariel wondered.

"Stop it first, ask questions later," Faron said, and beckoned him to follow. The two dashed through the ranks, weaving between baffled soldiers as they exited the Twin Gates. The smoke grew with each passing moment. Far ahead, Sariel saw what seemed like a dozen smaller skirmishes. Soldiers wearing the symbol of the Tower Majestic battled in a chaotic melee throughout the supply wagons. Many attackers lacked shields in their off hands, and instead wielded torches.

They never meant to stop us, Sariel thought as he tore into the nearest soldier, cutting the man in half at the waist. *Only starve us as we continue east.*

Faron arrived a heartbeat later, roaring into the melee like a furious bear. Sariel split from him, the pair two tornadoes winding through the battle. Where they went, the fighting ended, not that there was much to begin with. The ambushers were horribly outnumbered, and once the full force of the protectorate's army was brought to bear, they quickly crumbled. Hundreds fled west, while hundreds more threw down their arms to be rounded up as prisoners.

Sariel lingered near one of the burning wagons, watching as men and women dove into it, trying to save what they could. All around them, others flung dirt onto the fires, for they had no water they could spare.

Marshal Oscar arrived next, and he started bellowing orders.

"If you're gawking, get lost," he shouted. "We've still a fort to occupy. Now, get moving. I want ranks, not an Araketh market."

Sariel stayed where he was, wanting to hear the final outcome of this ambush. From what he gathered, nearly five hundred soldiers had hidden somewhere farther back along Nature's Path. Where, he did not know, and he suspected they would not find out until interrogating some of the prisoners. Perhaps a path deeper into the mountains, or a cave that went unchecked for fears of angering qiyan within.

"An unexpected ploy, to be certain," Faron said, joining him. Together, they watched soldiers form a tight circle around the several hundred surrendered troops of the Astral Kingdom. "Rather than hold the fort, they went for our supplies."

"Sid weakened his forces within the Twin Gates, but in doing so might have crippled our chance to lay siege," Sariel muttered. "We'd have been forced to assault the walls and suffer tremendously in doing so. Only Isabelle's miracle spared us such a fate."

He quieted. Isabelle approached, flanked on all sides by advisers, nobles, and her marshal. They were arguing about how to respond, their conversation fierce.

"Enough!" Isabelle snapped at them. She stopped before the ring of prisoners. "The future can wait. I want to know how many wagons in total we lost."

"Nine," Aubert answered.

Isabelle shook her head.

"I delivered us victory at the hands of the goddess," she said. "And yet, my reward is this?"

Those with her fell silent, unsure of how to answer. The soldier in charge of the prisoners stepped forward from the circle, and he cleared his throat while saluting.

"Yes?" Isabelle asked.

"We're still hunting down some who fled west," the man said, sounding nervous. "But not counting what few are brought in by nightfall, this here is the sum of all who surrendered once the wagons were burned."

The queen did a poor job of hiding her exasperation.

"And?" she asked.

The soldier stood up straight and crossed his arms behind him.

"I would know your orders, my queen. Shall we bring them with us? Or have them sent west, to be detained at Cevenne?"

Isabelle shook her head. The gold in her eyes seemed to fade.

"They burned what food I might have spared," she said, turning away. Her voice was ice when she gave her order.

"Execute them."

Chapter 44

FARON

The sun was setting when Faron and Sariel arrived at Isabelle's command tent, come at her behest. The brothers stood before her, and she dismissed her handmaidens so they might be alone.

"Thank you for coming, both of you," she said. She sounded tired, and despite the brushing of her handmaiden, her hair was still dirty from the road. Deep circles surrounded her eyes. Faron wondered if she'd slept at all since their battle at Twin Gates.

"We are here to serve, my queen," Sariel said, and he bowed low. Faron detected a hint of sarcasm in the act, and disliked it.

"Indeed," Faron said, and crossed his arms. "Is something the matter?"

Isabelle looked down at her map spread out on her table, illuminated by two lit candles in tin holders. That map had accompanied her steady conquest of both western Kaus and the midlands. Her fingers brushed the frayed edges, and it was a moment before she was comfortable enough to speak.

"I know you two are unlike any others in my army," she said slowly, carefully. "And it is not just in your prowess upon the battlefield. You know things you should not. You carry wisdom of the land like seasoned travelers. You discuss tactics like marshals, despite claiming to be mere mercenaries."

Her gold eyes flicked up from the map, and they shimmered with radiance.

"And when I look upon you, I see a light I do not see in others."

Faron's chest tightened. Would this be it? Would this be when their ever-living nature was revealed to the queen? And why did that thought thrill him as much as it frightened him?

"We are here," Sariel said softly, offering nothing in response to her conjecture. "What do you desire?"

Isabelle drummed her fingers upon the table.

"From our very first battle at Wendway Fort, you two have been instrumental in my conquest. I would have you help me now, when my heart is most troubled."

She gestured to the map, and the figures gathered together to represent the protectorate. So close on the map, so very close, loomed the drawn representation of Racliffe and the triangle in the sea that was the Tower Majestic.

"Those I trust have split their opinions on two paths," she explained. "One is to fall back, secure our positions, and delay our assault upon Racliffe until the winter passes. We'll establish supply lines across the Sapphire Mountains and take several key cities along the edges of the Astral Kingdom. Our enemies' armies will regroup, but so will we, and it is our side that maintains the greater numbers and resources."

"And the other plan?" Faron asked.

"The other is that we make straight for Racliffe, to put an end to this madness once and for all. We still possess the numbers and the siege preparations necessary to breach the walls. With Mitra Gracegiver slain, we cut the head from both the Church of Stars and the Astral Kingdom. I believe the armies that remain, upon learning of this, will sue for peace instead of continuing the war."

Isabelle glared at Racliffe on the map, her fingernails digging deeper into the table.

"Two plans, each with faults and weaknesses. And I don't know which to choose. I would hear your wisdom, you brothers who are still mysteries to me."

The more Faron thought about it, the more obvious the proper response, and so he was shocked when Sariel spoke up in support of a third.

"We should retreat entirely back across the mountains," Sariel said. "The battle at Twin Gates was devastating to our momentum. We are not invincible, and your army is fallible. We need to better prepare our assault on the entire Astral Kingdom, with proper supply lines and even greater numbers. Haste matters not, so long as our victory remains inevitable."

Faron shook his head, unable to believe the suggestion. Even the queen seemed shocked by Sariel's desire.

"You would have us flee?" he asked. "That is ridiculous. Our victory is already inevitable. We need only the strength to see it done." He turned to Isabelle. "March upon Racliffe. I don't give a damn about the other armies or our supplies. Our army is vastly superior. We go, and we claim our victory."

"To retreat after one minor loss," she said to his brother. "You truly think it would be wise?"

"You asked my opinion, and I gave it," Sariel said. "Something about all of this unsettles me. It is as if Eder *wants* us to invade Racliffe, and that alone gives me pause."

"A pause born of fear," Faron insisted, his temper igniting. "You have no faith in this army, do you? Even after all our victories, you are willing to fall back, play matters carefully, and risk nothing, just to ensure your victory."

"Is that not the wise thing to do?" his brother asked, glancing at Isabelle. "I know ourselves, and our numbers, and they are both limited, and both not enough."

"Which means you don't believe in Isabelle," Faron said, stepping closer. "You don't believe in her, or in Leliel."

Sariel's eyes narrowed. "Should I?"

So many conflicting emotions warred within Faron, but as he fought for the right words to say, a sudden clarity overcame him. Of what he believed. Of *whom* he believed in.

"Yes," he said, watching his brother's reaction carefully. "You should.

You and I both know there is no one like her, that there has *never* been anyone like her. No one born with her gifts. No one who has united the people. Not since the breaking of the Anaon Kingdom centuries ago."

Sariel's face darkened at the mention.

"You would reference an evil we created as justification for her being... chosen?"

Faron had never worshiped Leliel. He had lived too long, and seen too much, to hold faith in the goddess. At least, that was what he thought. Now, though, he looked to Isabelle and believed. At least, he *wanted* to believe.

"There has to be something more," Faron whispered. "These powers we possess, the eternal lives we live, there must be a point. I think, for once, I'm willing to believe it is the goddess humanity has worshiped since time immemorial."

Sariel grabbed Faron by the shirt and yanked him close, and his voice decreased to a furious whisper.

"Will you never tire of making the same mistakes?" he asked. "When time claims her, and Isabelle perishes, must I burn you on yet another pyre like I did after Belladonna?"

The name hit Faron like a stone across the forehead. His memory sparked with a thousand casual smiles, whispered nothings, and loving touches. He could not even move, he was so shocked, so overwhelmed. Pain and grief from the memories. Fury at such callous behavior from his own brother.

Sariel, meanwhile, showed not the slightest hint of regret. He shoved Faron away and then turned to address the silent queen.

"You and I both know the truth of your claims," he said. "Trust that the goddess will deliver you Racliffe, but I will play no part in such a farce. If you sacrifice caution, you have only yourself to blame if we stumble and fall at the end of our journey."

Faron crossed the space between them, shoved Sariel's shoulder to turn him, and then slugged him across the mouth. Sariel staggered, blood dripping from his split lip. His eyes flared wide, and he looked like a wild animal suddenly aware of the presence of a hunter.

"If at the culmination of our work, you lack faith in yourself, then hold faith in *me*," Faron said, and he pointed a finger at Sariel. "Not him. If you knew who he was, who he truly was, then you would *never* trust him."

"Careful, brother," Sariel said, wiping his chin.

"No," Faron said, feeling all the more secure in his decision. "Now is not the time for care. Eder is breaking an already dark and straining world upon the back of his sin-obsessed church, and we must be a light to counter that darkness. We will be the hope people need. We will be the faith they lack, and give them the freedom they deserve."

Silence followed, tense like twisted wire ready to snap.

"Eder?" Isabelle asked carefully, her tone measured. Faron winced at the mistake. *Eder*, he'd said, instead of *Mitra*.

"I've said my piece," he insisted, pretending nothing was amiss. "Trust in Sariel if you wish, but do not come to me with the tears that are sure to follow."

Isabelle circled the table, and she reached out for him. "Faron..."

"No," he said, and shook his head. "Just...no. No more arguments. You have never doubted before, Isabelle. Do not let Sariel's poisoned words have you start now."

Faron lowered his voice, once more speaking to his brother of a thousand years.

"I have already marched upon Racliffe to end the reign of a tyrant, and at Isabelle's side, I shall do so again. Make peace with that, Sariel, or begone from us forever."

He exited the tent, marching with feverish energy. He didn't know where to go. He didn't know what he wanted. Fury and betrayal burned, a potent mix in his chest, and when he gazed upon the sprawling camp of soldiers from all nations of Kaus, come together to destroy the Astral Kingdom, he told himself to feel pride and joy at the accomplishment.

...must I burn you on yet another pyre...

Faron collapsed to his knees behind a wagon, turned, and pressed his back to its wheel. He buried his head in his hands.

Her name had been Belladonna. A woman of fierce intellect who had challenged Faron's every learned knowledge, sometimes correctly, sometimes incorrectly, and never caring which. She only sought to learn. Her eyes had sparkled like emeralds, her smile came easy, and her laugh had warmed his heart as he pretended to be a mere farmer, working away his days in a field.

When he met her, Belladonna's hair had been a brilliant blond brighter than the sun. When she passed away in his arms, fifty years later, it had been white as new-fallen snow.

It all flooded back to him, no longer hidden behind a comforting haze. The protection of the pyre faded, as it always did. Tears built, and he was powerless against them. He clenched his fists and pressed them to his face, wishing he could make them stop, wishing he could make the memories go away so the sorrow could not lash him like brittle leather and broken glass shards.

A wet nose pressed to his fists, and when he looked up, Iris was there, licking his face. The simple, caring act was enough to break him completely. Faron sobbed and grabbed the coyote, pulling her so he could bury his face in her fur. She endured it stoically enough, and when he let go, she sat before him, licked his nose once more, and then whimpered.

"I'm all right," Faron whispered, and he wiped away the last of his tears. It hurt, but hurt could be good sometimes. An entire life of marriage was returned to him, and no matter how deeply it cut, at least there were moments of joy and happiness to cling to, memories to give him the strength to keep walking this damned world where age and death would never bless him with their sting.

"I'm all right," he repeated, and gently stroked her fur. "Thank you."

He looked to the stars, and he felt himself falling into a past that no pyre, no matter how fierce, could truly consume.

"But if you would stay a while longer, I would tell you stories of a woman I once knew," he said, and closed his eyes. "A scholar from Reycha by the name of Belladonna..."

Chapter 45

EDER

E der ascended the platform built in the heart of Racliffe. The wood groaned underneath his feet, barely audible over the hum of the crowd. Thousands of people were in attendance, filling the U-shaped curve of the street around the platform. Banners bearing the five stars of the Astral Kingdom fluttered from corner posts. He wore his finest black robe, its belt, tassels, and the jewelry around his wrists and neck all gleaming silver. Celebrant Madeleine, who followed two steps behind him, was dressed in a similar color, though in her fine suit instead.

"General Sid's return from Twin Gates has done little to improve unrest," she said as they both stepped out onto the platform a good twenty feet in the air. "And the austerity measures you are about to announce will harm morale further. Are you so certain Queen Isabelle's army will assault Racliffe? At the least, we could wait until we have confirmation they are on their way. She may choose to claim Edelnoth or Wystra first, or establish supply lines through Nature's Path."

"Is now truly the time to discuss such matters?" Eder asked, and he tilted his head toward the crowd.

Madeleine blushed and crossed her arms behind her. Her gaze shifted to her feet.

"Forgive me, Luminary. I have wished to share this advice but was hesitant. Now is the final time I may do so before you announce these measures to the people."

Eder used the tip of his finger to gently lift her chin.

"I chose you to be my Celebrant for a reason," he said. "Never doubt yourself, for even if you are wrong, the arguments you give may open my eyes to other possibilities I failed to consider."

"Y-yes, Luminary," she said. Her lips trembled as he lifted the finger from her chin to trace a line across her cheek.

"But in this, I hold no doubt," he said, withdrawing his hand. "I know those who are guiding Isabelle's conquest. They come for me, and will do so with confidence in their assured victory. And so we prepare ourselves."

Eder walked to the edge of the platform and looked out upon the city. *His* city, captured heart and soul over the course of two human lifetimes. For so long, he had preached in the streets as Helal, later dubbed Helal Gracegiver by the people. He had worked his miracles and endured the angry words of Leliel's priests and priestesses, and then, later, their violence. He had planted a thousand seeds and then departed to the wilderness.

A decade later, he cut his lengthy hair and returned as his supposed son, Mitra, to assume the mantle taken up by scattered disciples and worshipers clinging to their faith despite Leliel's persecution. The Church of Stars was born in the ashes of a fiery purge of Leliel's temples. The petty king of Racliffe, then a powerful city-state, was all too eager to anoint Eder with control to spare himself a similar fate.

In return, Eder granted radiance to his most ardent followers, and with their power, and the promise of healing, the church spread like wildfire. With it grew Eder's influence. The city-state became a kingdom, and Eder became a conqueror.

"Blessed of Kaus," Eder said, projecting his voice with a flash of radiance. He need not hide his gifts when addressing the public. He was not like his brothers, pretending to be mere humans. He was the Luminary, chosen of Father. Let all hear his words. "I come now to grant you comfort in these final hours before war arrives at our gates."

The crowd fell silent. All would listen. All would remember. His silver tongue would make sure of that. Meanwhile, a line of shepherds surrounded his platform, and they lifted their staffs and their jars of insects, casting a mesmerizing golden glow upon the crowd.

"In spreading the true faith, we have ever faced adversity," Eder continued. "We have endured the barbed words of unbelievers. We have fought invaders of sinful nations. We have sunken the boats of heathen pillagers who worship wealth and flesh over righteousness. Now we face our greatest test. The combined might of the false goddess approaches our fair walls. It is the final gasp of a dying animal. You will hear many rumors. Believe none of them. You will hear fearful lies, and claims from spies who slip through our walls. Dismiss them without hesitation. Hold faith in our Father, and hold faith in his chosen Luminary."

Eder clutched his hands together. They would need a sign. Something to whisper to those not in attendance. Something to cling to when Faron and Sariel's army arrived and food and water grew scarce. Eder let the whispered words of Father echo in his mind, and he answered them with a sudden burst of movement. His hands flung wide, and he screamed to the heavens.

"And when we are victorious, we will shout our glory to the stars, and pierce the heavens with our joy!"

Silver light flared from every inch of his skin. Stars rose from his fingertips, sparkling and wondrous.

"We are here! Joyful! Triumphant! Hold nothing back, my faithful, my children. Let our love be so fierce, and so bright, Father can see it from the very heavens!"

The stars gathered, pulsed, and then exploded in all directions, blanketing the city with light. Eder stood within its center, his head tilted, smiling, as they slowly scattered into sparkling dust. Tears trickled down his face.

"We are here," he prayed. "Right here. One day, you will see."

He took in a deep breath to recover himself, and he looked to the crowd. Their loving expressions gave him the strength to continue. Their...

He froze. Among them, a face he knew so well, watching near the front. Their eyes met despite the distance.

"Madeleine," he said, and gestured her to his side. And then, louder, for the crowd. "My Celebrant will detail the measures we must take in anticipation of the coming war. Listen to her, as well as the orders shared by my shepherds in these troubling days. Fare you well, my people, and may Father forever hold you in his gaze."

Madeleine shot him a confused look, but he ignored it. He had planned to announce the austerity measures himself, but now he had a far more important matter to attend to. He dashed down the steps, then curled around the platform to the line of shepherds organizing the crowd. He pointed as he approached.

"Let her through."

Aylah stepped past, her head held high despite her plain dress and lack of jewelry and other adornments. A few in the crowd muttered their confusion or jealousy, but Eder spared them little thought. Nothing could stop the joy swelling in his heart.

"Aylah," he said, fighting to remain formal before her. She showed little struggle to do the same. Ah, Aylah, ever the proper and noble sister.

"Well met, *Mitra*," she said, amusement sparkling in her silver eyes.

Eder laughed.

"This way," he said, guiding her away from the crowd.

The moment they were out of sight, he spun about and closed the distance between them. She offered her hands to him, and he took them, cradling her fingers as he pressed his forehead to hers.

"I have missed you," he said. "How long has it been? Fifteen years? Twenty?"

"Too long," she said. "And I see you have done much during my imprisonment."

The smile slowly faded from Eder's face. "Your imprisonment?"

She stepped back and pulled her hands free of his touch.

"Thirty years of it, Eder, and at the hands of humans."

Eder swallowed down a sudden burst of rage deep within his chest.

"Come to the Tower Majestic," he said. "And please, tell me everything."

•

Aylah recounted her story as they crossed through Bridgetop. Eder listened with ever-growing horror, horror made worse by the emotionless, factual nature of her telling. As if the chaining, bleeding, and killing had happened to another person, not her. Eder held his tongue all the while, letting her tell the tale in full, until it ended with Sariel and Faron rescuing her from her imprisonment.

Regardless of the watching eyes, Eder turned to her and took her hands in his.

"Please, forgive me, Aylah," he said. "With your vows, I knew you could not grant me your aid. When you did not interfere, I thought it meant you approved of what I built or, at the least, were willing to wait to pass judgment."

He stepped closer, guilt clawing at his mind.

"If I had known you were missing, or worse, imprisoned, I'd have torn apart all the world to find you. Calluna, she told me only that you were hidden, somewhere dark, and I thought... I thought she was lying to me, Aylah. Lying to protect your privacy."

It would be a scandal, Eder knew. An unknown, plain-clothed woman receiving the affection of the Luminary, but he did not care. He wrapped his arms about his sister, needing to hold her, to beg for her mercy.

"Please, Aylah, forgive me. Damn my church, and my kingdom. I should have been there for you."

She pushed him away and smiled as if he were being childish.

"Always with the grand gestures," she said. "But I hold no ill will toward you, Eder. That's not why I am here."

"Then why?" he asked, leading them once more to the tower's entrance. He let the rest of the question go unspoken. *Why here, and not fighting alongside Faron and Sariel?*

"I am here," she said, and then hesitated as they passed through a crowd of folks bartering with a shopkeeper over his suddenly price-hiked bread. Even though Madeleine was just now detailing the austerity measures, rumors had floated about them for days. "I am here because when I was freed, I heard all about this church you had founded, and this kingdom you built."

"Both of which I am certain Sariel cast in a most flattering light," Eder said, unable to hold back his sarcasm. Something about Aylah's presence peeled back his prim and proper veneer. He would never be Mitra Gracegiver, not with her. Just Eder.

"Correct," Aylah said. She gestured to the tower ahead. "But I would hear your truth, Eder, before I cast my judgments. After the shattering, I thought you were done with building empires. What changed?"

He took his dear sister's hand, she who had suffered so terribly.

"I will tell you," he said. "But first, we must visit the cold cells."

•

The entrance to the Tower Majestic was its busiest and most bustling portion. If there had been a door of sorts, it had been gone since ancient times, leaving only a staggeringly large rectangular gap in the hardstone. Into that gap had wedged the jagged protrusion of the broken portion that had fallen and connected the tower to the cliffside where Racliffe was built.

"When was the last time you visited the tower?" Eder asked as he helped her down the gap between the broken portion and the walkway through the grand entrance.

"The shattering," she answered. "I have never been fond of this place, and came only because I must."

Enormous storefronts populated either side, major drop-offs for the exchange of goods ever flowing across Bridgetop. Wooden platforms braced with weights and rope hung over the edges, adding storage and space to an ever-crowded home. Two new additions flanked the entrance itself, statues chiseled from white marble that towered more than twenty feet tall. On the left was disheveled and long-haired Helal Gracegiver, and on the right, the cleanly dressed and finely pampered Mitra Gracegiver. Eder had overseen their construction and used it to add tiny differences, most of them false, between him and his supposed father. Each day, thousands passed by those statues and had their memories of Helal shifted and warped to match Eder's construction.

Aylah paused near the foot of Mitra's and stared up at the marble.

"Your smile," she said. "It's false."

He shrugged. "Are you surprised? It is only with my siblings that I am my true self."

They walked the winding steps downward, circling the tower, passing in and out of giant swaths of daylight shining through the tower's windows. After three steps down, they boarded one of the lifts, with soldiers ordering the other passengers to depart so that Eder and Aylah could ride alone. They traveled ever farther downward, until arriving at the soldiers' camp stationed just above the final step.

Once through, they arrived at Glasga's cabin, where the preacher was deeply involved in his work. Eder guided his sister into the room so she might watch. Witnessing this was important to understanding his goals.

A naked man sat on a pillow before the preacher, his legs crossed and his left arm extended. His other held a small bowl filled with sliced mushrooms. Between them was a small table cluttered with metal instruments. Most were for cutting, but not all. Some were sharp and akin to a pen, and Glasga dipped one into a shallow inkwell, coating it with dye, before pressing it to the naked man's flesh.

"But why did you lie?" Glasga asked as he pricked away at the skin. He shot a glance at Eder and Aylah but did not stop his work. "Think hard."

The man swallowed as if his tongue was too large. His eyelids drooped, his eyes heavily bloodshot.

"I was scared," he said.

Tap-tap-tap.

"Scared of what?"

"Being caught. Being punished. And so I..." He paused. Swallowed. Began to cry. "I told the lawmen it was Jeffry. I said Jeffry did it to me, did it when I didn't want it. That's why I was with child."

Tap-tap-tap. The image was forming now, well detailed and intricately tattooed upon his arm. Glasga could have been an artist, if he so wished. Perhaps he still viewed himself as one. A pregnant woman, crying and pointing. A faceless crowd. In the distance, a noose.

"Your lies killed a man," Glasga said, tapping faster now, his pen flashing back and forth between skin and dye. "Do you understand that, Sven?"

"I do," the naked man said. Despite his tears, his voice was weirdly light, as if he were lost in a dream. "I'm sorry. I'm so sorry."

Glasga set aside the pen, and he reached behind him for the leather handle of a whip with seven individually knotted threads. He glanced at Eder, then pointedly glared at Aylah.

"Go on," Eder said. "She is here to learn."

Glasga shrugged, and as Sven cried, the preacher walked behind him and readied the whip.

"What is your sin?" he asked.

"I am a liar."

A crack, and the whip lashed his naked back, leaving bleeding welts.

"What is your sin?"

"I am a liar."

Another crack. More blood.

"What is the cost of your sin?"

"I murdered a man!"

A third crack. Glasga paused, grabbed a cloth from his pocket, and dabbed away the blood, inspecting each and every wound. When satisfied, he put aside the cloth and readied the whip.

"Again."

Eder guided Aylah out, and then shut the door to muffle the sounds of pained screams.

"I don't understand," Aylah asked. "What did I just witness?"

"Have you encountered blackwall mushrooms before?" he asked. When Aylah shook her head in the negative, he continued. "They grow at the borders of fey lands to serve as warnings. Their intent is to leave a man or woman confused and disordered if they disturb them. Most intriguing is how they do so. They take the soul and confuse it with the memories of its past lives. Problematic, if done unprepared, but with Glasga's help? We can find the sins of not just a person's current life but all their lives, going back dozens of histories."

"And then purify them," Aylah said, finishing for him.

"As best as we can with our methods," Eder admitted.

His sister shivered at a particularly harsh scream.

"But why?" she asked.

He beckoned her to follow. "You will see."

He took her to the very edge of the last step, where the ropes hung over the edge. There were eleven occupied currently, the cold cells swaying above the distant ocean. Eder gestured toward them and waited for Aylah to realize people were inside.

"How?" she asked, suddenly recoiling from the edge. "After what Sariel…"

"Because it is here that I heard Father's voice," he interrupted, peering over the edge to the darkness that hid the ocean. "It is here I felt the thin walls of our world for the very first time."

Aylah was the noblest of the siblings, the one most proud of her resolve and self-control. It was…unsettling to watch her appear so disturbed.

"I thought your speeches of Father were falsehoods," she said. "A way to unite a populace under your rule, with the goddess as a useful foe."

"The goddess must be eradicated if humanity is to be saved," Eder said, shaking his head. "Her doctrine of rebirth and easy forgiveness is a seductive harm. She is false, and her teachings a cancer to be excised from Kaus. The comfort she gives will only lead to our destruction. Father is our true creator, and it is he that we must abide."

Aylah rejoined him at the edge, careful with her balance.

"I have a hard time believing this, Eder, but I have never known you to lie. If you heard the voice of this…Father, what is it he told you? What wisdom did he impart?"

Eder took in a deep breath, letting the memory fill him. He had been in the space between lives, normally black and dreamless, while waiting for his body to recover. But not that time. That one unforgettable moment, the darkness had lifted like a veil.

"No wisdom," he said. "No commands. Just a question, Aylah. One question, and a lifetime of interpretation to follow."

He closed his eyes and spoke with the exact same tone as he had heard all those years ago. The same confusion. The same desperation.

"Where are you?"

The words shocked her silent.

"I have spent many sleepless nights pondering the many implications," he continued. "To be so profoundly lost? At first, it horrified me. I wanted to deny them and cast them aside as delusions or madness. But they never left me, Aylah. They never faded. With each passing year, they grew more true, and so I was forced to reckon with their potential meaning."

He gestured toward Glasga's little cabin and the purification happening within.

"We are lost to our maker. This cycle that humanity endures, it was never meant to be. Life after life, piling on top of one another, until threatening to break under the weight. No salvation, just another lifetime of failure and weakness. Sins are left to fester like rotting meat. It cannot go on."

He stood, and prayed his sincerity, and his wisdom, would be enough to convince his sister.

"We must be found. We must make ourselves known to Father, and in death, go to *his* arms instead of yet one more interminable life. That is my hope. That is my salvation, for which I have built this entire church. These cold cells are but the beginning. When they are stripped of sins and made weightless and pure, I vault their souls into the heavens. They are flares, sharp and piercing, and I send them screaming out to Father. See us! Hear us! But the few I prepare each month are not enough. We need more, ever more, perhaps more than are alive on Kaus, to create a light so blinding Father can see us through the veil that somehow hides our presence from him. But I am not alone in this dream. This hope was shared by the Etemen when they built this tower, and with its aid, I believe I can send forth a light so brilliant it will penetrate any darkness and a call so thunderous it will be heard through any void."

Aylah stared over the edge, watching the cold cells sway. What he would give to know her thoughts.

"Show me," she said, breaking the silence.

•

Upon reaching the Final Ascent, Eder revealed his prized work, the intricately placed runestones, and the key resting in the pedestal of hands.

He walked through their maze of loops and curves while Aylah lingered by the lift.

"We are not the only ones adrift," he said, approaching the key. "The Etemen, I believe, were also separate from Father, but unlike humanity, they were aware of the chasm. They built this tower with the goal of piercing the heavens and crying out their presence."

Aylah knelt by one of the runes, tracing its faint circles and spirals with her fingers.

"Did they ever succeed?"

He shook his head. "Doubtful. Not knowing the great cost that must be paid."

"And what is that?"

Eder pointed to the pedestal.

"For the grand machinery to activate, it requires blood blessed with radiance. *Our* blood, Aylah. Enough to kill us, and grant us a permanent death."

"Permanent..."

Frustration overwhelmed him, and he lifted his fists and bared his teeth like an animal.

"And so here I stand, at the edge of greatness, and I cannot take the final step. I am too weak. Too sentimental. The grandest of causes, and yet..." He lowered his fists and sighed. "And yet I cannot pay that cost. We are so few, this family of ours, and no matter our disagreements, no matter our faults, I will not dare lose a single one of you. You are each too precious to me. And so I do what I can, cleansing souls within the cold cells, purifying all their past lives, and then sending them to the heavens like a flare in the night, screaming for Father to notice us, wherever he may be."

He startled. Aylah was at his side, her hand clutching his arm. Again, he failed to read the look on her face. It was so serious, so... thoughtful.

"Humanity is wretched," she said. "They are broken and adrift. Left as they are, they are beyond redemption. Do you truly believe that?"

He pressed his hand over hers.

"After what you suffered," he asked, "don't you?"

She leaned against him, and he accepted her weight, opening his arms to embrace his beloved sister. She nuzzled his chest as he held her close. She shivered in his grasp, and when she spoke, her voice was a whisper.

"Eder...it need not be us. There is another."

Chapter 46

SARIEL

Sariel stepped into Isabelle's tent. The sun had set, and candles burned in two separate tins on either side of the table. The queen leaned over her map, her weight braced upon the table.

"You summoned me?" he asked.

She looked up, and her expression was impossible for him to read.

"I have made my decision," she said, careful to keep her tone flat.

He approached the table and set his sword down upon it. "And?"

She gestured to the map.

"We may suffer losses on the way, but even doing so, we will arrive with enough forces to take Racliffe. And so we shall march upon the capital."

Sariel crossed his arms. "You go against my wisdom. You favor haste over caution."

Isabelle tapped the table with her fingers, then clenched a fist and struck the wood.

"What I *favor*," she said, "is the trust of my soldiers. They follow me because they believe I am Leliel's chosen. They believe a goddess will grant us victory against all foes. It is a tale I have carefully crafted and, until Twin Gates, never gave my believers any reason to doubt. That faith is shaken, and I cannot risk weakening it further."

"You fear retreating, resupplying, and returning with caution will cast doubt upon your supposed divine backing," Sariel said, having not considered the possibility. "There is some merit to that, though consider the dangers of your current plan. We will march without any possibility of retreat. The minor forces that harry us, fearful to engage directly, will feel no such fear if we are broken upon Racliffe's walls and limp back to your newly founded protectorate."

"Then it is imperative we do not retreat," Isabelle said. "The Tower Majestic will fall. Mitra Gracegiver will face judgment for his crimes against Leliel. That is my order. Do you agree?"

Still she guarded her thoughts. He frowned at her, feeling something else amiss.

"Why am I here, Isabelle?"

The queen pushed away from the table. Her arms crossed over her chest as she paced. Strange. A hint of nervousness? Why?

"Something your brother said has been bothering me," she admitted after a moment. "I would have your explanation."

"And what is that?"

She turned. "He said if I knew who you were, who you truly were, I would not trust you."

There. There it was. Her doubt. Her fear. He said nothing, only let his gaze linger. If she wanted the truth out of him, it must be earned.

She circled the table to stand before him. Her hand reached out, then paused, hovering in the air between them.

"Will you assuage my doubts, Sariel Godsight?" she asked. "Will you explain away the fears Faron's words put into my breast?"

He took her arm by the wrist and held her as if she were his prisoner. Wisps of silver leaked from his eyes as he stared into hers.

"Will the tale change your course of action?" he asked.

"No."

"Then why should I tell you?"

"Because I *want* to trust you," she said. "More than anything. More than myself."

Her touch was fire, her gaze electric. He released her wrist and retreated a step. Different versions of her flashed through his mind. Triumphant and enveloped in golden light during her coronation. Naked and defiant as he held a blade to her neck. Fearless as she demanded he serve despite his hand about her throat. Unstoppable. Unbreakable.

And so very beautiful.

"It is a long tale," he said. "And much of it is unpleasant."

"The night is young, and with how aflame my mind feels, sleep was never in my fate." He noticed her left hand absently rubbing where he had held her wrist. "And I am used to a bit of unpleasantness."

Sariel walked around the table to her bed, his own mind racing. He had rarely told this story, and when he did, it was only to Isca, in the lifetimes where he deigned to trust her fully. Sometimes, he was believed. Sometimes, he was dismissed as a madman. He wondered which would be Isabelle's reaction.

"I will speak only the truth to you," he said as he sat on the edge of her bed. "I will neither lie nor soften the cruelties my family and I committed. Whether or not you believe me, I ask that you let me finish, for there are a great many wonders and truths I must share. You will doubt, at first. I pray, by the end, you do not."

"I am listening," she said, sitting beside him on the bed, so close that their legs touched.

He closed his eyes and let the memories surface, both his and those of his family, whom he had questioned extensively to learn of what had transpired outside his presence. This had been both his greatest accomplishment and his greatest failure. In its wake, he had vowed to never walk in ignorance of who he was, or what he had done.

He opened his eyes and let Isabelle see the starlight within them.

"Then let us begin four centuries ago, at the birth of the Anaon Kingdom, and the prelude to the shattering."

Part Six

KINGDOMS

Chapter 47

SARIEL

I'm not sure it's wise to trust Lord Endal," Sariel's lead marshal, Hugh Fenwick, said. "Rumors say his greed is unmatched, and he has eyes on his king's crown."

Sariel watched the black dragon land just shy of the forest and turn to face the soldiers on horseback giving chase.

"He'll uphold his end of the bargain," Sariel said, and clapped Hugh on the back. "Have a little faith."

"I hold faith in our soldiers and in my king," Hugh said. "All else, I distrust."

No horse for Sariel, for he would not risk his life to an animal's instincts in a battle against a rampaging dragon, no matter how well trained it might be. He drew his shining steel sword and lifted it high so the rows of soldiers behind him could see.

"The beast is tired and frightened," he shouted to them. "Are you ready to carve its corpse?"

His soldiers cheered, but their cheer was half-hearted. Not even the radiance in his voice could chase away the fear of battling a dragon. Sariel did not let it worry him. No stubborn dragon from the south would interrupt his plans, already a decade in motion.

"With me, my brethren!" he cried. "Drown it in steel!"

Sariel led the charge, his sword held high like a banner. Up ahead, knights circled the black dragon, explicitly ordered not to engage, only occupy its attention. Fire blasted through their ranks and carved burning grooves across the field. The dragon's claws lashed out, often missing, but when it did not, it tore rider and horse apart. What had been one hundred was already down to fifty, but they served their purpose. The tired dragon, chased northward by the army of Anaon for two straight days, lashed out angrily and with little thought to its surroundings. It was done fleeing. It wanted blood on its tongue.

Sariel's army crashed into it, and the beast got what it desired. Its jaws crunched soldiers, whose armor meant little to its overwhelming might. Its every movement sent men flying, often with limbs snapped and legs twisted wrong.

"Be not afraid!" Sariel shouted, and this time he poured all his power into those words. They pierced the battlefield, and they lifted spirits that might have been broken and kept firm feet that might have turned to flee.

As for Sariel himself, he weaved closer to the dragon's chest, seeking an opening. Fire roared overhead, a panicked belch that charred two dozen soldiers in its wake. The movement required the dragon to stretch out its head, exposing its neck directly above Sariel. That opening was all he needed. He leaped into the air, far higher than any human could hope to. His sword slipped between two scales to plunge into the soft flesh underneath. It sank so deep Sariel hung there, clutching his sword, as the dragon shook and roared.

When it scratched at its neck, trying to dislodge him, Sariel pulled the sword free and then fell, but not before hacking at a claw for good measure. The steel bounced off after carving the faintest groove.

Sariel landed lightly on his feet, his sword twirling in his hand. Above him, the black dragon loomed, its yellow eyes glaring down, overwhelmed with fury. It hurt Sariel to see the majestic beast so driven by bloodlust, but it seemed every dragon eventually gave in to its baser instincts as its life stretched on for centuries.

It opened its mouth to breathe flame. No escaping it. Sariel crossed his arms, bowed his head, and surrounded his entire body with a shield of radiance. The fire washed across him, but it could not break through. Even the heat was subdued, no greater than the warmth of a nearby campfire. The dragon fire ended, and amid the blackened earth, Sariel stood tall.

His surviving soldiers, briefly lost to despair, were overwhelmed by the sudden miracle. Some cheered. Others wept. Sariel knew stories would travel across Kaus, and he'd twist them to suit his needs in time, but for now, he pointed his sword at the baffled dragon, knowing this, too, would be remembered.

"Your rampage is at its end," he bellowed.

The dragon retreated a step, and within the wildness that had overtaken its mind, Sariel saw a hint of recognition. The black dragon realized it faced one of the ever-living, and it was afraid. That fear only grew when nearby soldiers took up a shout.

"Lord Endal is here!"

Riders of the province of Angloss slammed the dragon's other flank with their lances. Weapons snapped, but for each that broke, another slid underneath the scales to bury into flesh. Black blood flowed across the field, and soldiers of both armies followed, swarming over the dragon like ants. They stabbed and hacked at whatever they could reach. It was a death by a thousand cuts, and each drop of blood the dragon shed was one more closer to its death.

"Embrace your death, dragon," Sariel shouted, still baiting its attention. Furious and driven mad by the pain, it snapped for him, seeking to crush him within its jaws. Sariel rolled aside, his speed pushed to its absolute limit, and then leaped. His hand caught the hollow crevice that marked the dragon's ear. A pull, and his momentum carried him up atop the creature's head. He gripped his sword with both hands, propped its edge underneath a scale, and then rammed it forward with all his strength. It sank in deep, and blood flowed out like a river. The beast shuddered, and it roared out a pained, rattling cry. Too much. It had lost too much blood and expended too much of its energy on the rampage leading into the battle.

It collapsed, its claws scraping enormous grooves in the dirt. Soldiers swarmed over it, slashing and chopping at its body until it was clear the beast was dead. Cheers followed, and the armies of Anaon and Angloss rushed one another to exchange greetings and cheers.

Sariel climbed down from the body, and his soldiers fell to their knees to mark his passing. He curled around the dragon to meet Lord Endal of Angloss, waiting at the front of his army. Sariel stopped and stood, saying nothing, so that it was the other noble who must first make introductions.

"I promised we would come," a beaming Eder said, embracing Sariel. "And I am glad to see you survived the beast's rampage prior to our arrival."

"I never once doubted," Sariel said, grinning at his brother as, all around them, soldiers clapped and hollered in joy.

•

Hours later, the two armies had set up camp, keeping a mandated distance away from the dragon's body. Sariel and Eder stood before it, glad for the privacy.

"I thought Faron was with you, pretending to be one of your knights," Sariel said as they watched the first hint of starlight fall upon the black scales.

"He was," Eder admitted. "But even that took great convincing. He's of the same opinion as Eist and Aylah. They think this grand endeavor is pointless and doomed to fail. In all our lives, Kaus has never been united under a single banner, and they believe it will remain that way."

"That will make it all the sweeter when we prove them wrong," Sariel said. "So what did Faron do? Abandon you when he heard you were to face a dragon?"

Eder laughed.

"Stars above, no. He left my side months ago. Fell in love with some carpenter woman he met at a tavern. He wished to invite you as a marriage witness but feared there was no way to justify inviting the king of Anaon to a lowly knight's wedding."

"Then I'm glad this crown has some advantages, for it spared me from needing an excuse to refuse," Sariel said with a grin. The amusement did not last long. "But let him live his life. Let all our siblings remain distant, and at peace, so long as they do not interfere."

"I have been given no reason to believe they will," Eder said. He circled the dragon's corpse, studying it. "And so long as neither of us becomes a cruel tyrant, it shall stay that way."

The two left the beast's head to stand somewhere much closer to its stomach.

"There is much to do," Sariel said, observing the body, which was beautiful despite its bloodied stillness. "Even with your province's allegiance, I rule but a third of Kaus. Your betrayal of your king will shock many, but that advantage will amount to little if we do not capitalize on it quickly."

Eder placed a hand on the black scales. A smile lit his lovely face.

"My shifting of Angloss's loyalty from King Vran to you and Anaon will be understood by all, for you were brave enough to ride out and face the dragon assaulting our lands, while King Vran cowered in his castle. Hold faith, Sariel. This is but the start of the needed wars. With our forces united, and you as king, no power in all the realm can stand against us. Cowardly King Vran will be the first to learn that painful lesson."

Sariel hoped he was correct. The task they sought to accomplish was daunting, but it soothed his mind knowing he did not seek to achieve it alone. Still, wars for kingdoms and empires were in the future, and right now, they had the matter with the dragon to settle in the present.

"Shall we let its soul return to its egg?" he asked, knowing the same question was on his brother's mind.

Eder shook his head.

"I have spoken with the beast before. Asruma is its name, and this is not the first time it has ravaged humanity for sport. The beast's cruelty goes beyond what I can accept. Over two thousand dead humans, and for what? It was not even provoked. Its black soul sought cruelty, so let it die, and remain dead."

Sariel's brother approached where the dragon's second, secret heart remained slowly beating and slid his sword underneath one of the black scales. He pushed it within, so deeply his arm sank up to the elbow. Black blood poured across him, and the dragon's corpse shuddered in a final, true death.

"A shame," Eder said, pulling his arm free and shaking off what he could of the gore. "But at least something good will come of its passing."

"And what is that?" Sariel asked. "It was a good excuse for our alliance, true, but we could have concocted dozens more if necessary."

"No, not that," Eder said, eyeing the dragon's head. "A gift, if you would grant me the patience to build it."

•

Three days later, Eder invited Sariel to his tent.

"As promised," he said, and offered him a finely polished wooden box of surprising length. Sariel removed the top, and from within the padded cloth interior he retrieved a sword.

It was carved from the slain black dragon's jaw, with the hilt beginning at what had been the hinge. The grip was surprisingly soft, and its weight much lighter than expected. The blade was long and sharpened on only one side. Sariel dared to run a finger along it, and it immediately came back red with blood.

"How?" he asked. "Dragon bones are unbreakable."

Eder hovered his hand over the edge, and after a whisper, silver light shone in the center of his palm. Slowly, carefully, he ran it along the dragon bone.

"I have carved these weapons with radiance," his brother said. "Shaped them by that which all creation must obey."

"Them?" Sariel asked. In answer, Eder reached underneath the table to retrieve a second box, and from within he lifted an identical sword carved from the opposite side of the jaw. He held the weapon above him, admiring his handiwork.

"Twin weapons," he said. "Unbreakable. Unmatched. Nothing shall ruin their edge. They are a promise, dear brother. Of our resolve, and our collaboration."

Sariel clacked his sword against Eder's. Though it was bone against bone, the impact sounded more akin to steel against steel, so sharp were their edges scraping against each other.

"Such rare, exquisite weaponry," he said. "They deserve names."

"Then let us name the other's blade," Eder said. "What better way to signify their bond?"

Sariel agreed, and he thought a moment. What name to give Eder's?

"We should immortalize our purpose, so it may never be forgotten," he said. He tapped Eder's sword once more. "I name yours Atonement, so that it may aid us in redressing humanity's myriad failures."

Eder's smile revealed his approval before he spoke.

"A good name. And if I am to name yours by your purpose, I can think of only one name that is worthy." He stroked the flat edge of the weapon, lovingly caressing the work of his hands and his radiance.

"Redemption."

Chapter 48

SARIEL

As the grand island of Kaus steadily fell under the banner of Anaon, Sariel made a point of visiting each and every little town and village under his sway. His stated reasons to his advisers and army leaders was building unity among the people and showing them he was not oblivious to their fears of offering their loyalty to a new king.

The true reason was his eternal search for the specific color that marked Isca's reborn soul. If he meditated at night, when the stars shone down upon him, he could expand his consciousness for hundreds of miles in all directions, seeking out that color, and whatever new life Isca had made for herself in her current incarnation.

In the little town of Creed's Mill, Sariel found her.

"We are honored by your presence," the town's mayor said, bowing low as several other prominent landowners came to greet the arrival of Sariel's group of soldiers and knights. Creed's Mill was along the northern border of a newly annexed province of Windshew, the transition largely bloodless. Their former king wisely understood the tide he faced and relinquished his hold so that he kept large portions of land under his control as a lord.

"An honor I wish to share with as many of my people as I can," Sariel said, smiling widely. His mood could not be more jovial. At last, he had found her. His search was at its end. "Do you mind if I walk about? I would see the water mill you are known for, as well as the people whose work and sweat keep it running."

"Of course, of course," the mayor said, both flattered and proud of their namesake. "Shall I accompany you to explain its inner workings?"

"No, thank you," Sariel said. "I will be fine on my own. If you might instead work on finding accommodations for my escorts here? We have spent many nights underneath the stars, and we would greatly appreciate some warm beds."

With that, Sariel had his privacy. He pretended to wander, but that vibrant soul color was a beacon to him, and he followed it closer to the mill on the eastern side of the town. He found her just outside, loading bagged flour onto a cart for transport.

Her hair was a reddish brown this time, hanging down past her waist and tied behind her with several thick ribbons. Her nose was small, like a rabbit's. Her eyes were a different hue than the last few incarnations, this time a dark green that reminded him of cave moss. If he were to guess her age, she was just approaching her twentieth year. Unmarried, he hoped, for it complicated matters greatly otherwise.

She eyed him warily as she shouted something to the miller inside, and he wondered if she knew him. Not who he was fully, not the truth of their couplings across dozens of lives, but if she knew him as King Sytha of Anaon.

Perhaps he would remind her, once she was his queen. Perhaps not. It was always a risk, laying his hands upon her and drawing out the memories of her past lives. Sometimes it allowed them to resume their marriage as if the decades between were nothing. Sometimes it broke her mind and ruined whatever love might have bloomed.

"Hello there," he said. "Such hard work seems unbecoming of one so beautiful."

"Being pretty don't put food on the table," she said. "At least not in a place so small as Creed's Mill."

"Then perhaps you were not meant to live in a place so small?"

The woman arched one of her eyebrows, and she seemed momentarily uncertain of his motivations.

"Can I help you with something, my liege?"

"I wish merely to exchange words with a pretty lady," he said.

"Twice now you've called me pretty." She stretched her back, wiping her hands on an apron as she did. "Say it a third time and I might begin to believe you mean it."

Sariel beamed a smile in her direction. She had wit, and enough confidence to talk back to her own king. He couldn't be more pleased. Though her appearance was always different, and the different upbringings resulted in many changes large and small, her personality was always familiar.

"May I have your name first, before I make such a commitment?"

"Agnes," she answered after a moment's hesitation.

"Well then, Agnes," he said, and offered her the crook of his arm. "Might you be my lovely guide this evening through your quaint little corner of Windshew?"

"Beautiful, pretty, and now lovely," she said. "I change my mind, I don't believe it at all. You lay it on thicker than swamp mud. What is it you're after, my liege? Perhaps you might even have it, if you ask honestly. You're handsome enough."

Sariel's smile could not be truer.

"I would spend my day in the company of one whose tongue is sharper than a sword and whose mind is as quick as a fox," he said. "Consider your beauty a lovely diversion for my eyes as we speak."

At last, she returned his smile. She awkwardly joined him, standing at his side, and after a pause, she slid her arm through his. Sariel's insides warmed as he once more felt the touch of his precious Isca.

"All right," she said. "But not for long. I have work to do, and you're keeping me from it."

"Of course," he said as they walked arm in arm beside the river that ran alongside the mill. "Not for long at all, I swear."

•

The wedding was held a month later, a joyous affair in the grand promenade of Cevenne. The people showered the streets with rose petals and told and retold the story of how a mere common maiden had stolen the heart of King Sytha. It was a tale Sariel himself dictated to the bards and ordered them to sing as if it were their own construction.

"A fine enough ceremony," Eder said as the two of them drank during the raucous after-party. Tables filled the city square, loaded with carved turkeys, split potatoes, and bread layered with more honey than sense dictated. No wine, though, a prelude to the coming cleansing laws Sariel would enact when his kingdom was fully established. A troupe of five men and women sang bawdy songs while two more played on five-stringed lutes.

"Agnes deserves the best," Sariel said, watching her dance in the center of the square. Blue ribbons fluttered in her hair, matching the color of her dress. Unlike the currently favored trends, Sariel had styled her dress after the one she wore at their very first wedding centuries ago. Slender shoulders instead of poofy, with much of her back exposed, while the dress furled out near her feet, expanded with layers of additional white and silver silks. A silver pendant hung from her neck, and the sapphire set within it gleamed in the light. Agnes had brought several friends from her home in Creed's Mill, and they surrounded her, laughing and clapping as they sang along with the troupe.

"Even in wartime?" Eder asked, and sipped at his water. He had made the journey to witness the wedding, though his troops remained on the distant front line in their current war against Orlea.

"Especially in wartime."

A lord approached their table, drink in hand and a grand smile on his face, but Sariel waved him away. He wished for privacy with his brother, there in that little corner of Cevenne.

"This is the grandest accomplishment of our long existence," Sariel continued. "With the establishment of my kingdom, we will finally corral humans into better lives, whether they wish for them or not. Of course I shall have Isca with me, to be queen at my side amid a reign that shall span decades and shape the future of all of Kaus."

Eder watched the woman dance, his gaze unreadable.

"I pray for joy, for the both of you," he said. "But will people accept her? You have swept her up from very humble beginnings."

"The people will accept the romanticized stories I tell. It will do, in lieu of the truth."

"The truth," Eder said, shaking his head. "You are a sentimental sort, Sariel, even if you pretend otherwise."

Sariel laughed, and he lifted his glass in a toast.

"Is there a better time to be sentimental than at one's own wedding?" he asked.

Eder returned the toast.

"To the destruction of Orlea," he said.

"And the creation of my perfect kingdom," Sariel said, and drank.

Chapter 49

SARIEL

Sariel watched the city of Erzden burn with a smile on his face. This was it, the culmination of years of work. Archers fired flaming arrows over the walls, while hundreds of soldiers climbed ladders to reach ramparts no longer protected by Orlea's defenders.

"The city is taken," Marshal Hugh said, joining him at his side. The pair stood just beyond the city's main gates, which would soon fall to the battering ram smashing against it. "And reports are coming in from Sivik and Tallas that our troops have successfully breached the defenses there, too."

Sariel's smile grew. It was a coordinated attack, his split forces assaulting each of Orlea's remaining forts and cities in one single, glorious night of conquest. Eder's troops would be doing the same, sweeping along the southern coastal cities. There would be nowhere to flee and no chance for aid. The wars were done. Kaus was tamed, the chaotic, flawed human race yoked to two ever-living siblings.

A glorious night.

"Come with me," Sariel said as the gate collapsed. "I would wait at the docks."

"As you wish, my king."

The streets were overrun with soldiers. Screams echoed from afar. Sariel's order had been clear. The king of Orlea had been given multiple chances to surrender, and its people given ample opportunities to either rebel or flee. His sympathy had limits. Anyone who wore the tabard of Orlea, or was a member of its nobility, was to be dragged out into the street and executed. Even their homes would burn, the smoke and ash a warning to all of Kaus what fate awaited those who resisted the inevitable.

"Is the document ready?" Sariel asked as they walked through the bloodshed.

"Drawn up as requested," Hugh answered. "I believe Marisa has it."

"Fetch her, then, once we reach the docks. Assemble your finest soldiers as well. We will want an audience for the signing."

When they reached the water, Sariel strode across the thick wooden dock planks and gazed out upon the sea. All the ships had fled. Some were part of Orlea's fleet, others merchants seeking far less dangerous trade. Sariel cared not a whit for any of them. All he sought was a single ship bearing the flag of Angloss.

An hour later, when the fires across Erzden were dwindling, Sariel saw it. A slender schooner flying green flags marked with a white crown. His smile spread from ear to ear as he watched it dock, and down the gangplank marched a victorious Eder and his closest soldiers and advisers.

"I see Erzden is yours," Eder said, embracing Sariel. "Does the good news continue in Sivik and Tallas?"

"All of northern Orlea is claimed," Sariel said. "And the coastal cities?"

"Captured or burning," Eder said. His smile matched Sariel's. "Victory is ours, brother. Our long work is at its end."

"Not quite."

He gestured for Eder to follow. Near the docks was a long table dragged out for the occasion, along with two inkwells and multiple quills. With Orlea broken and the wars ended, all that remained was to officially mark the creation of the island-spanning kingdom and Angloss's place within it.

Atop the table waited a large scroll. An older woman, adviser Marisa, stood beside it like a proud parent. Written upon the scroll, prepared weeks in advance of the final conquest, was a listing of rivers and coordinates marking out the individual provinces that Kaus would be divided into, with Sariel ruling over all of them as king. Beneath those details was a listing of laws governing the hierarchy of power, how disputes would be settled between provinces, and the ways in which humanity's worst instincts would be quelled. The cleansing laws, they were called.

Hugh had summoned the crowd Sariel requested, and at a word from Eder, his own advisers and soldiers joined them to form a circle around the table.

Eder paused to read the list, and he nodded in approval by the end. Within the listings of territories and provinces, Angloss was given special consideration, for while Sariel intended to guide the rest of Kaus with a firm hand, he needed no such considerations for his brother.

"Just as we discussed," he said. "I see nothing to change."

"Then let us sign it!" Sariel shouted to a great roar of the crowd. He grabbed a quill, leaned over the first scroll, and then hesitated. "What shall we call it? I feel as if these documents should have a name."

"Considering where we are, let us not complicate matters," Eder said. "This shall be the Erzden Promise, outlining humanity's greater future with you as king."

That was good enough for Sariel. He dipped the quill in ink and signed along the bottom.

I, Sytha Penaga, do swear to honor this Erzden Promise, and treat fairly with all my subjects.

He offered the quill to Eder, who signed below it on a separate row of lines, where all provincial regents would renew their vows upon the end of the wars and the conquering of all of Kaus.

And I, Endal Frae, as regent of Angloss, so swear to honor the Erzden Promise, to serve my king faithfully, and to enact his laws for the betterment of all.

When he finished signing, the gathered crowd burst into applause. Sariel and Eder embraced, and there was no hiding their joy.

"Give us some space," Sariel ordered the bystanders once they separated. "And tell our cooks to prepare a feast. Our soldiers will be hungry, and they deserve to celebrate with the rest of us."

Soldiers and advisers of both nations reluctantly departed, chatting with one another as they imagined what the future might hold. Sariel waited for them to leave, his eyes lingering on the twin scrolls.

"We succeeded," he whispered softly. "At last, our glory is built."

Eder put a hand on his shoulder and squeezed.

"What will you do first?" he asked.

"Fully establish my cleansing laws," Sariel said. "Mankind's faults and sinful urges must be addressed. After a generation or two, few will remember their hedonistic ways, nor will they care, once they have known peace from their earliest childhood days. What of you?"

His brother shook his head.

"I do not trust laws as you do, Sariel. I will enact your ideals in Angloss, but do so by appealing directly to their hearts through their temples. Leliel's teachings are amenable enough to my own beliefs that I believe I can form a new faith to merge them. Such a reformation will be fraught, as you can imagine, but I believe it the only solution that will truly shape the lawless hearts of man."

"I wish you the best of luck, Lord Endal," Sariel said, and offered his hand.

"And to you, King Sytha," Eder said, accepting and shaking it. "To a land of eternal peace."

"And a future of civility and joy," Sariel agreed, as behind them, the port city of Erzden burned.

Chapter 50

SARIEL

Sariel stood before the grand window of the Tower Majestic, the sun's rays flowing across him. The red and gold of his vest sparkled. Such finery. It felt unbecoming. So much easier the armaments of war. So much easier to conquer a foe than sway their hearts. Behind him waited a dozen advisers. They had been called into his home on one of the highest floors of the tower but given no explanation as to why.

"I have read your reports," Sariel said at last. His voice was hard enough to break steel. "And I dislike what I am being told."

Still they remained silent. Sariel turned to face them. They were a mixture of the young and old, each one handpicked to help oversee a province of his kingdom. They exchanged daily letters with regents, bringing to Eder that which was deemed important. And what they brought was a cavalcade of failures.

The cleansing laws were being resisted in every province. Gambling rings in Sovoth. Brothels in Erzden. Sariel flooded their streets with guards, and he increased the severity of punishments, from whippings for the smallest theft to brutal public executions for murderers and rapists. None of it helped. All of it seemed to make matters worse.

"Marisa," he said, and gestured to the stack of papers on the table separating him from the finely dressed crowd of advisers. "You said the regent in Windshew hung fifty men as punishment for the recent riots. Was this your idea?"

A demure woman with graying hair stepped forward.

"It was," she said.

"And did it work?"

Marisa's frown looked like she was trying to swallow her own lips.

"No," she admitted. "It made the riots all the worse the next night."

Sariel could imagine the scene and feel the anger of the people. Damned fools, all of them, clinging to their vices. If only he could cleave the sin from humanity like he did the limbs from his opponents. How much easier a task it would be. But then again, he and Eder had not built their kingdom because they thought it would be easy, but because they sought to create something incredible.

"Two attempts have already been made on Gavin's head in Sovoth," Sariel continued, his ire growing. "And despite our total bans, I read here that the amount of wine and beer flowing into western Kaus is *higher* than it was a year ago."

"It's not my fault," one the younger advisers said. He paled a bit at Sariel's glare but continued. "My regent patrols the borders, but we are confident much of the wine is flowing in from Angloss. We suffer from their leniency."

"Indeed," Marisa agreed. "I've read credible reports that the rioters in Windshew are instigators from Angloss. They are spreading a unique brand of Leliel dogma, and it is the sweetest poison upon our people's tongues. Instead of abstaining from their sins, Leliel would not call them sins at all, and too many are using this as an excuse to attack the cleansing laws directly."

More murmurs of agreement. Sariel wanted to scream. Of course they would blame Eder. Anything to excuse their own failures.

"I will speak with Lord Endal about these matters, but they do not excuse your own culpability," he said. All the stars help him, it'd been only ten years since he'd formed his kingdom, and already he wished he could return to battle.

The problem was, that might even happen.

"With all due respect, my king, it is not an excuse," a third adviser said. He was the oldest of the lot, his beard a bright shade of white and hanging down to his waist. "When a river overflows, it is not the fault of the levy builders that a flood approaches. I understand Lord Endal's aid in the founding of the true Anaon Kingdom was instrumental, but the special privileges he has been given are a rot we are incapable of fighting."

"At least give us permission to hunt marauders across Angloss borders," argued another adviser. "If Endal will not tame his own province, at least allow us to do what must be done to protect ours."

Sariel clenched his jaw. Eder's special privilege had been a sore spot for the various provincial regents since the day the Erzden Promise was signed. If Sariel was honest with himself, it frustrated him as well. Eder consistently and cleverly enacted only the barest minimum of the cleansing laws, and his protestations at the cruelties necessary for its enforcement had grown over time. It'd been a year since Sariel had last seen him, his brother storming off after yet another argument in the dead of night over ways to cow the unruly human populace.

"I will speak with Endal and ensure this matter is settled," he said, and few there bothered to hide their disgust. And why would they? This was a promise Sariel had made countless times before. "But that does not free the lot of you from your own failures at—"

The heavy doors to the meeting room opened, and in stepped a visibly pale Marshal Hugh.

"Forgive my intrusion," he said, and pointedly glared at the advisers. "I must speak with our king. Alone."

Sariel's insides clenched. For his marshal to demand both privacy and urgency did not foretell good news.

"Leave me," he said, dismissing the advisers. "When I next see you, I want each of you to have a plan to turn about the ills of your province."

The fifteen advisers quickly bowed and left, leaving Sariel and Hugh alone in the grand room. Sariel turned to the enormous window of the Tower Majestic, staggering in its size so that this was but the upper half of it. The meeting room was the top floor of an impressive mansion of wood and stone and was built so that a large portion of the wall was open, allowing sight of the ocean. The sunlight felt grating on Sariel's skin, and he winced as he approached a small drink table nearby.

"What brings you with such urgency?" Sariel asked as he poured himself a drink of water mixed with smashed grapes and sliced strawberries to add a bit of sweetness. "Did Franz go and provoke another battle across the border?"

"No, Your Highness," Hugh said. "It's about Agnes."

Sariel froze, the glass held to his lips, but he did not drink. The tightness in his stomach worsened.

"And?" he asked, refusing to face the man. He did not want to see the look in his marshal's eyes. He did not want to assume things that were not there. Instead he stared at the sea, stretching unending to the east.

"My king, she...the queen was found in Olado, not far from the border into Angloss. She and her entire escort, they...they were...Forgive me, Sytha. They were murdered."

The glass shook in Sariel's hand. Water spilled across his lips and chin.

"Murdered," he whispered, and then shattered the glass at his feet. The pitiful break was nothing compared to the breaking in his mind. "How? Who was responsible?"

"Regent Franz says bandits were responsible," Hugh said. "He raided one of their camps and found the...the bodies."

Sariel slowly turned, a cold fire sparking to life within the hollowness of his chest.

"Bandits," he said. "Angloss bandits?"

The marshal slowly nodded. "It seems so."

Sariel slowly approached the table holding the many reports from his advisers. He glared at the rolled pieces of paper as if each one were a venomous snake.

"Olado?" he asked. "Why was Agnes in Olado? She told me she was going to Araketh."

"I do not know," Hugh said softly.

Sariel fell silent. He couldn't move. Couldn't breathe. His marshal and friend shuffled his weight from foot to foot. It was the only sound in the room. A minute passed. Two. Thoughts warred in Sariel's mind, so strong, so brutal and violent, he feared they would rupture his body in half.

"My king?"

"Leave me," Sariel snapped, the paralysis finally ended.

The man quickly obeyed. The moment the door closed, Sariel lifted his fists and smashed the table in half. The wood splintered, and reports fluttered into the air. He grabbed them, crinkling them in his fingers before ripping them to shreds and casting them aside. One after another, tearing, snarling, breaking portions of the table further and flinging them out the window to fall to the sea.

"Why, Agnes?" he asked as he slumped in the middle of the wreckage. He glared at his hands, speckled with blood from splinters and cuts from the papers' edges. "Were the warm markets of Araketh not enough? Why go west?" Tears swelled in his eyes. "Why leave me at all?"

Sariel wept, even as he told himself he could find her again. Her soul would be reborn. He could wait. Age meant nothing. Once the people were properly subdued, perhaps he could even reveal his immortal nature. A perpetual king of a truly sinless nation. And then...then he would find her, anoint her, make her his queen once more, this time gifted a proper land.

He scraped bloody fingerprints across the stone.

Angloss bandits...

Sariel cleaned his face, retrieved a blank scroll from a shelf on the opposite side of the room, and then grabbed the quill and inkwell stored next to it. So often he wrote lengthy proclamations with them, but this time, it would be a single letter, quick and concise. With the table broken, he used the floor. When finished, he would seal it with wax and trust only Marshal Hugh to carry it across Kaus to the seat of his brother's power in Vendom.

Eder, he began. *My wife is dead. We must meet, and I will tell you where...*

Chapter 51

EDER

Just west of the Sapphire Mountains stretched the valleys of Olado, which swooped low before rising into gentle green hills. Atop one such hill grew a lone royal whitebud tree. It flowered twice a year, both times flooding the branches with wide, pale flowers whose petals would flutter away upon the wind.

Hundreds of years ago, Sariel had married Isca underneath that tree, at a wedding attended by all of his siblings. She had been named Elena then. Eder himself had overseen the vows.

Eder waited at the top of that hill, his back pressed to the whitebud. Its branches were barren in preparation for the coming frost. He wore plain dark trousers and a gray shirt. Simple garb to pass unnoticed and unattended at the borderlands between their kingdoms. Atonement lay in the grass beside him, and he touched it for comfort when he saw his brother approach. Sariel was a figure clad in black, wrapped in grief, and carrying his own sword across his shoulders.

"Welcome, brother," Eder said. "I pray you are well?"

"How could I be?" Sariel asked. He reached into his pocket and pulled out a familiar silver pendant and threw it at Eder's feet. Sunlight glinted off the sapphire in its heart. "Agnes is dead, and the blame lies upon your head."

"Does it?" Eder asked, careful to keep his tone neutral. The discomfort in knowing his brother was hurting could not affect him, not at this critical moment. The fate of Anaon would be settled, Eder felt certain of that in his bones.

His brother pointed an accusatory finger.

"Do not play the fool with me. We both know the state of your lands. My people suffer, and all for your foolishness."

"It is not foolish to patiently change the nature of a heart," Eder said. "The faith I am building will take time, and the people's conversion must be honest, not pressed at the edge of the blade. As the rest of your own country's excesses so succinctly prove."

"Enough!" His brother jabbed Redemption into the earth and crossed his arms. "No more words. No more pointless banter. You cannot remain in charge of Angloss. You have failed, Eder."

"Failed, because I must honor a vow sworn to you and your cleansing laws, whose ineffectiveness are proven with every passing rise and fall of the sun."

"You would refuse me?" Sariel asked.

"The truth is irrefutable. All of Anaon suffers from the crown upon your head."

Wind blew across them, cold from the mountains, and it fluttered Sariel's coat and Eder's loose shirt.

"A duel," Sariel said. "I propose a duel."

Eder tilted his head slightly, intrigued.

"A duel?" he asked.

"For everything. You and I, right here, with all of Kaus as the stakes. If you win, I will step down from my throne and elevate you as ruler over all of Anaon."

"Not all will agree to this," Eder said, imagining how his various regents would react. "There will be civil war."

"And that war would be child's play for you to crush," Sariel insisted. "But if I win, you will abdicate your role as regent of Angloss. Afterward, you will join me in the Tower Majestic. For one hundred years, you will serve me, Eder. You will use your brilliance, and your wisdom, to *help* me enact the dream I have envisioned for all of Kaus. And then when Isca is reborn, and I find her anew, you will spend a year of that hundred pleading to her for forgiveness for the crime you committed against her."

Eder imagined such a life, one hundred years bound in servitude to his brother, and was filled with revulsion. That revulsion paled against the alluring idea of sitting upon a throne he had been quite content to let Sariel sit upon...until the disasters of his reign made themselves evident.

"This is the cleanest way," Sariel said when Eder hesitated. "A duel between us, the fate of the kingdom settled by our own blades, and no one else's."

Eder reached for Atonement beside him, then hesitated when his fingers touched the hilt. This...this would be it. There would be no reconciliation between them. Blood would be shed between brothers. In time, perhaps such a duel would be romanticized, but not here. Not now. It was failure, and sorrow, and swords clashed.

He lifted Atonement from the earth and slashed the air before him.

"I accept your terms," he said. "At least our differences shall be settled honorably."

Sariel readied Redemption, holding it before him in a high grip. His legs braced. His eyes narrowed.

"Until death or surrender," he said, dictating the terms.

"Until death or surrender," Eder agreed.

A cold wind blew.

Sariel lunged first, the aggressor, as he was in all things. Eder retreated step after step, his sword held in one hand as he blocked each and every hit. The clack of bone against bone became the only noise. Sariel shifted the angles of his swings, seeking openings, but Eder left him with none. No matter how high or how low he struck, whether a chop at his shoulder or a cut at his side, Eder batted them all away.

Since Eder wielded his weapon one-handed, Sariel shifted tactics. He planted his feet with each swing, trying to overwhelm Eder with sheer strength. He was stronger than him, too, and perhaps it could have worked if the ploy was not so obvious. Eder shifted his own tactics. When an overhead swing threatened to split him in half, he sidestepped while parrying it. Not much, just enough for safety, each deflection using Sariel's own strength against him.

Sariel's frustration grew. He slammed his sword down twice, trying and failing to break Eder, and then pivoted backward, set his right leg, and lunged forward with Redemption thrusting. It would have impaled Eder if his reactions had been any slower. Instead the weapon cut a thin hole in Eder's shirt as it slid harmlessly past. Atonement was out of position, but Eder made the most of it by shifting his arm so his elbow slammed into Sariel's throat.

The pair separated, Sariel coughing and hacking to regain his breath.

Eder set his feet and lifted his sword, taking the hilt in both hands. He eyed Sariel, daring him to make another attack. His brother turned, spat blood, and then bounced on his heels, building momentum, building speed, before a sudden explosion of movement. He leaped sideways, then dashed inward, attempting to surprise Eder with the change in direction and shift in angle.

Child's play. Sariel was too used to fighting humans, where his speed could overwhelm them and his skills dwarfed their own. He had not trained as Eder had. He did not spar against their siblings, whereas Eder and Aylah had spent more than a decade honing their abilities in mutual isolation, pushing each other to greater heights.

Sariel believed himself superior. Eder *made* himself so.

Eder parried the thrust high, twisted his sword, and immediately blocked the looping counter Sariel attempted. Their weapons crossed, but Eder was braced, and Sariel in mid-charge. Eder shoved Redemption aside, twisted so his elbow and shoulder struck his brother in the chest upon their collision, and then pirouetted away. Atonement lashed out amid his twisting, slicing open Sariel's chest. The coat and shirt parted, revealing flesh, blood, and a hint of cracked bone.

Pain and fury mixed together in a wordless shout from Sariel's lips. He slashed twice, an X pattern with strength born of desperation. Eder blocked both, his concentration sharpening, the speed of the entire world slowing as he observed every shift of his opponent's feet and hands. Before Sariel leaped into a thrust, Eder already knew the movement coming, and he charged right back. They passed by each other, weapons flashing, each seeking openings, but only one sword struck true.

Eder slowly eased out a held breath as Sariel collapsed behind him and coughed blood.

"Do you yield?" Eder asked, turning. His strike had ripped the tendons of Sariel's right arm as well as broken more of his ribs. Based on the blood and the raggedness of his breathing, Eder suspected at least one of those ribs was twisted inward and puncturing a lung.

Sariel said nothing, only glared.

Eder approached, and he held Atonement to its full length. Its eternally sharp tip pressed to Sariel's throat.

"Do you yield?"

"I do," Sariel said through labored breaths. He dropped his weapon to the grass. "And so your reign shall spread across Kaus. How many lands will fall to bandits and thieves? How many families will lose their loved ones like I lost Agnes due to your 'patience'?"

Still Sariel blamed him for his wife's death. Eder's resolve weakened, and he knelt before his wounded brother.

"You don't know, do you?" he said. "I thought to spare you the pain, but I see doing so will only lead to hate festering in your heart."

Sariel glared silently, further confirming the need for truth.

"There is a reason Agnes was in Olado," he said. "She was fleeing *you*."

His brother's eyes widened. "You lie."

Eder shook his head.

"I wish there were a gentler way to break this, Sariel, but I can only offer you the truth. Agnes sent me letters, asking if I would grant her asylum. She told me where to meet her, and though I sent soldiers to the rendezvous, she never arrived. I suspect bandits saw her little caravan, and the treasures it carried, and ambushed it without ever realizing your queen was among them."

Sariel's gaze drifted to the pale grass. His fingers dug into earth stained by his own blood.

"Why?" he whispered. Even asking the question sounded like it required tremendous effort.

Eder laid his blade flat across his knees as he crouched.

"She dreaded the world you were building," he said. "Every crime, every failure, must be punished, and she feared that she would one day fail you. Humanity is not perfect, Sariel, and never will be. She understood that, and she understood that your enforcement would continue to escalate until all of Anaon was bathed in blood. And so she wrote me, seeking a new life in Vendom. Forgive me, Sariel, but I obliged. I hoped that, once she was with me, it might finally be the light needed to pierce the darkness that has clouded your vision."

Eder turned away from his broken brother, and though the need for the duel still chafed, he relished his sudden sense of freedom. At last, all of Kaus would be his. He need not fear his brother's influence as he expanded his temples. Already Leliel's Beloved, his newly established religion, had overtaken the west. Soon its temples would sprout in the east, furthering their influence. The salvation of humanity was at hand.

Eder smiled, and he felt a tremendous burden lift from his shoulders. All was as it should be. One day, even Sariel would understand, and forgive the steps taken to achieve it.

And then Redemption pierced his back, the tip punching out through his ribs in a rupture of blood and bone. Eder gasped, his breathing suddenly wet and difficult. The blade twisted, flooding him with pain. Atonement dropped from a hand too weak to hold it. His knees went numb, and he collapsed, held upright only by the weapon impaling him.

"Mine is the only throne," Sariel said, and ripped Redemption free, tearing innards and bone with it. Eder collapsed onto his side, unable to form words. The sword had ruined his lungs. Silently retching, he glared at Sariel, overwhelmed by the sense of betrayal. In all their years, amid all their differences, they had...they had never...

Sariel knelt before him, and despite his naked rage, there were tears in his eyes. He put his hands on Eder's face and softly kissed his forehead. His condemnation was a whisper.

"Forgive me, Eder, but Kaus is mine, as are you, for I shall have my hundred years."

Chapter 52

AYLAH

Aylah stood at the rocky ledge overlooking the distant city of Racliffe. They were near the bottom third of the Sapphire Mountains, which formed a barrier against the west, on a secluded stretch of flat rock marked by a stubborn, scraggly red oak.

"This is it," she said. The last three decades lay heavy upon her shoulders. "There is no turning back now."

Faron joined her, standing at her side, an enormous sword and shield strapped to his back. He wore a horned helmet, and his armor was more fur than metal. Barron the Wild Rage, the people called him, hero of the Crowning uprising.

"There was never a time to turn back," her brother said, and shook his head. "Only Sariel could have stopped this, and not once has he shown a sign of regret. This must be done, the damned fool."

"He is no fool," Eist said. The most enigmatic of their siblings stood near the path that led to the rocky ledge. They wore a brilliant gold robe and wielded a thick staff carved to resemble a curling snake. Eist had led the rebellion along the conquered reaches of Orlea across the south. Known only as the Prophet, they had used their mastery of radiance to overthrow their regent and declare a holy war against Sariel. Eist's head was perfectly shaven, and a myriad of runes that meant nothing were tattooed across their forehead. Most of their followers worshiped the goddess, Leliel, and Eist was careful to never alienate those who clung to those beliefs.

"How else would you describe him?" Aylah asked.

A smirk marred Eist's otherwise beautiful face. "Ignorant."

Aylah did not agree, but she rarely did see things as Eist did. Instead, she saw Sariel as a tyrant and a butcher. When Eder vanished, the brutality of Sariel's cleansing laws had increased tenfold. The Anaon Kingdom. What a miserable creation her brother had birthed.

"I don't care what he is," Calluna said, sitting on the cliff's edge with her legs dangling. Her long hair was tied in a ponytail that hung far past her feet to sway through the air. She wore a flimsy black dress laced with gold, and its center was cut with a sharp V that exposed much of her chest. She had not fomented her own rebellion, but instead allied with Faron during his. Luna the Banshee was her chosen moniker. She gestured to Racliffe, rattling the dozens of silver bracelets on her slender arm.

"I just want to know where Eder is. I want to know that he is safe."

Aylah clenched her teeth to hold back her frustration. Thirty years ago, Eder had vanished, and his province of Angloss had been brutally scoured of any and all remnants of the church he sought to build. Though Calluna could find him when she scried, confirming he was somewhere alive, she saw only pitch-black darkness. Whatever water she peered from was so far away she could not hear him if he ever responded. When asked, Sariel refused to answer a word about his missing brother.

"His guilt is unquestionable," Aylah said. "And at this point, there is nowhere else Eder might be. He is imprisoned somewhere in the Tower Majestic. We will find him, and free him."

"Assuming we break the walls and take the city," Faron said. He grinned to show how certain he was of that prospect.

"With Barron the Wild Rage leading my charge, how could we ever fail?" Aylah asked. "Stay strong, my kin. The work of these long years shall finally come to fruition."

"And what a bitter fruit it is," Eist said.

Aylah placed her helmet atop her head, closed her eyes, and braced herself for what must come next.

The people need your confidence, she told herself. *They need your rage. Give them both, so they hold no room to doubt.*

Aylah paused to dip her head in respect to her sibling Eist, and then continued down the path. It wound along the eastern edge of the ridge before sharply descending toward Nature's Path, which knifed through the mountains. The Twin Gates had long ago crumbled before their combined might. From there, they traversed the road, enduring the occasional ambush, until nearing its end.

Beyond awaited miles of yellow fields, and then Racliffe, the White City. Above it, rising from the sea itself, loomed the Tower Majestic.

Her sword drawn and her golden platemail shining in the midday sun, Aylah stepped out from a side path onto a jut of rock that overlooked the combined might of three rebellions. Seven thousand swordsmen from the kingdoms across the Crowning, along with another two thousand trained in axes. A thousand archers from Vendom. A thousand more from Sovoth. Five thousand spearmen from Orlea. Four thousand skirmishers, and five hundred mounted knights, brought from Windshew and deeply loyal to Aylah. They were a little over twenty thousand in total, come to see the city of Racliffe burn.

And leading them all, the acknowledged champion of what was known as the Rebellion of the Broken, was Aylah herself. She raised her sword as she bellowed out to the armies, her voice carrying over a mile with the blessing of radiance. She was Seraphine the Crownbreaker, and all would remember her words.

"My soldiers, my fighters, my friends," she cried. "The way is clear! The White City awaits, and within it, the swords of the enemy. Within, they cower. Within, they fear our rage, and our justice. Will you give it to them, my brethren? Will you defy the will of the Heartless King?"

Twenty thousand cheers answered her, a thunderous wave that shook the mountains. Soldiers stomped their feet, and others slammed their swords and axes against their shields. Aylah readied her own shield, her armaments raised high. Behind her, the Banshee, the Prophet, and the Wild Rage joined her upon the rocky overhang. They were the Four Heroes, and the sight of them together heightened the people's cries.

For thirty years, Sariel had brutally enforced his cleansing laws, with both blade and tainted radiance in the hands of his most ardent believers. He had broken the Unity of Leliel in Racliffe, burning the temple to the ground. The goddess was declared heretical, her priests banished to the wild, and her followers threatened with death if they did not abandon their beliefs. Butchery followed. The cleansing laws grew ever more gruesome, until the crimes committed were so great that Aylah had gathered her siblings and declared that enough was enough.

Thirty years. At long last, justice had come.

"Then march with me, free people of Kaus," Aylah roared. "For I am the Crownbreaker, and come Racliffe's fall, I will prove the truth of my name!"

Chapter 53

FARON

The walls of Racliffe fell, and with them, the morale of its defenders. Faron led the charge across the narrow streets of Bridgetop, a dozen of his finest soldiers at his sides, all howling and wielding blood-soaked axes. What defenders remained crumpled, lines breaking and panicked men and women fleeing into homes or down wooden stairs to hide in the dark of Underbridge.

"Scour every inch," Faron ordered his soldiers, pointing his sword at one of the entrances. "No cockroaches shall be stabbing us while we sleep."

The men charged with wild abandon, eager to follow his orders. Faron was not concerned with such ambushes, though. He only wished for privacy as he crossed the last remainder of space leading to the entrance of the Tower Majestic. There were no doors or gates to close, but a distant row of some thirty soldiers stood ready with their shields to defend the tower with their lives. Most dangerous among them were the three Wise and their hulking focus carrier.

"I hope you weren't planning on entering without me," Aylah shouted, dashing to catch up with him. Blood painted much of her face and breastplate and stained her hair. Behind her trailed Eist in their pristine gold robes alongside a wide-eyed Calluna, who had painted her face with long blue streaks from her eyes and lips down the sides of her neck.

"Enter the Tower Majestic without the Crownbreaker?" Faron asked, and grinned. "I wouldn't dream of it."

"I have given orders for the soldiers to hold the entrance to Bridgetop," Eist said as they approached, their every step punctuated with a clack of their staff hitting the hardstone. "If we enter the tower, we enter it alone."

"Good," Calluna said. "That's good. No one else needs to confront Sariel but us."

Faron nodded in agreement. So far, despite the collapse of the walls and the fierce initial fighting, there had been no sign of their brother. As the Crownbreaker's forces overran the city, there was nowhere else he could be lurking but somewhere within the ancient tower.

"What about Eder?" he asked, and nodded at the tower. "Is he in there?"

Calluna briefly closed her eyes.

"Yes," she said, her voice suddenly quiet and distant. "Somewhere in there. Somewhere dark."

"Then let's not wait any longer," Faron said, readying his shield. "I'll open the way."

He sprinted, not caring if his siblings kept up with him. His blood was pumping, and he could smell the stink of desperation in the air. That thin, quaking line of defenders would collapse before the rampaging might of the Wild Rage. He bellowed to announce his arrival, and a spray of blood followed as his sword removed limbs and opened throats with each swing. No one could resist his might.

Aylah arrived in his wake, her sword gleaming, her each movement lethal. Together, brother and sister, they stood back-to-back as the soldiers surrounded them, knowing their numbers should grant advantage but failing to find it. Aylah's sword chopped through armor. Faron's sword cleaved off heads. They needed to be quick, for Sariel's appointed Wise had their arms raised and their radiance growing.

The Wise, their brother had named them. Red-robed men and women dedicating their entire lives to the cleansing laws. As reward, Sariel taught them to wield radiance, but they could not channel it on their own. No, they needed a focus, and that came from the enormous muscle-bound man standing in the heart of the trio. His face was covered like a headsman's, and his body wrapped in black. He carried an enormous gibbet on his back, a naked criminal held captive within the iron cage. The three Wise lifted their hands as they chanted, and the captive man thrashed and howled as rivers of golden light tore from his body, leaving black welts and bruises upon his exposed skin. The vile practice sickened Faron's stomach, and he pushed onward, his disgust adding strength to his swings.

"Cleanse the unclean!" one of the Wise shouted as all three pointed. Sickly yellow fire burst from their fingertips, and it lashed the hardstone road. Faron roared as he crossed through it, enduring the burns. It would not twist and warp him like it had hundreds of rebel soldiers outside the walls of Racliffe during the initial siege. It would not leave him as a twisted hulk with remade limbs and skin turned to scales and feathers. He pushed through, side by side with his sister, to slay the last of the soldiers.

And then Calluna and Eist arrived, both eager to share in the fury against the Wise, who released a second burst of flame, to the great torment of the imprisoned criminal. Calluna lifted her hands and bellowed out a wordless denial. A silver shield rolled outward from her breast, encompassing their family, and against it, the sickly fire withered and died.

"Cease this torment," Eist shouted, slamming their staff to the ground. Reverberations traveled unseen across the hardstone and then erupted at the feet of the gibbet carrier. It was a shock wave of pure force, and it turned the bones of the giant man's ankles to jelly. He howled and collapsed as the Wise chanted louder, demanding obedience with the mad furor of those facing death.

Faron was all too happy to give it to them. He broke through Calluna's shield, lopped the head off one Wise, and then buried his sword to the hilt in a second. Aylah claimed the third, her shield breaking his nose and ending his concentration before he might summon another foul attack of radiance. She cut his throat, and as he died, she turned her attention to the whimpering gibbet carrier and the naked prisoner within.

"There is no forgiveness for this," she said, and thrust her blade into the skull of the weeping giant. Then, for mercy, she ended the life of the prisoner. There would be no saving him, not after what he had endured. His skin was almost entirely black from bruises, and his eyes wild with madness as his blood leaked out his cut throat.

"Come on," Faron said, wiping a bit of an opponent's blood from his face. What pleasure he'd taken from fighting a victorious battle drained out of him. "I'm sick of this already. We need it to end."

The greatest collection of buildings within the Tower Majestic was at the very entrance, along with the many platforms rising to various levels circling the sides. Forming a line of muscle and steel where the street was narrowest were the last of Sariel's ardent defenders. Fifty men, armed with spears and swords. Faron approached them with the confident walk of a predator.

"One chance to surrender," he said. The sunlight through the gargantuan windows did not reach them, and so he grinned in the flickering flames of lanterns burning from lampposts. "Otherwise you will witness the Wild Rage."

"Our life for Sytha!" one of the soldiers shouted, lifting a spear.

Faron swooped his sword lazily through the air. "So be it."

This time, it was Calluna who led the charge. The soldiers tensed, confused by the approach of an unarmed little woman dressed in black, but then she opened her mouth to scream. It was wordless, without explicit command, but it was bathed in the power of her radiance. It carried a cacophony of desires; to laugh, to cry, to cower, flee, or fight to the death. All fifty soldiers were locked in place, their minds overwhelmed as the Banshee's wail slammed into them with the subtlety of a battering ram.

Eist followed up with magic of their own. They pointed their staff, and a blazing silver flame leaped from its tip to strike the center of the formation. It splashed like liquid and burned like fire as it melted through their armor to sear flesh. Screams followed, pained and frantic as what few men still possessed of their faculties tried to wipe away the burning silver only to have it coat their hands and fingers.

It was into this stunned, panicked line that Faron and Aylah charged, and they broke the ranks in seconds. When half were dead, Calluna let loose a second scream, its volume seeming to shake the very air.

"FLEE!"

The rest obeyed, sprinting past them toward Bridgetop. Faron let them go. He had no desire to punish those conned into service of his brother. The blame, so far as he was concerned, rested solely on Sariel's shoulders.

"Many ways to go," Eist said, pausing beside Calluna. "Where to now?"

Calluna bowed her head to concentrate. Her eyelids fluttered as she peered into darkness.

"So close, and yet..." She snapped her eyes open. "Down. We go down."

"Down it is," Faron said, and led the way. They passed homes locked tightly shut. Frightened citizens of Racliffe cowered within. He heard the cries of children and the frantic prayers for safety from their parents. Faron did his best to ignore them as he led his own family down the long platforms that formed steps to the ocean at the far, far bottom of the hollow tower.

At last, they reached the final descent. A braced wooden wall with a locked door blocked the way, and Faron smashed it open with a single kick. Beyond loomed the last dozen feet of hardstone, barren but for a large slab of stone near the edge. Beyond that, emptiness, and the distant roar of the ocean. Still no sign of their brother.

"Are you certain Eder is here?" he asked Calluna.

She passed through the door, closed her eyes, and murmured something unintelligible. Immediately after, she shuddered, retreating a step and grabbing Eist's robe so she could cower like a child in need of comfort.

"There," she said, pointing without looking. "He is there."

Faron approached the edge, unsure of what she could mean. As he neared the slab of stone, he noticed a rope tied around it, and his stomach sank.

"No," he whispered, sprinting to the edge and grabbing the rope where it hung off the side. He pulled, disturbed by how little weight resisted him. Aylah joined him as Calluna and Eist hovered by the doorway. Her horrified look said it all as Faron lifted a tightly bound sack of leather onto the ledge. A cut of his sword opened the top, and from within spilled out a naked Eder. His body was so severely emaciated, his bones poked out against his pale, sun-starved skin. His hair, normally long and beautiful, stuck to him like brittle straw. Faron thought him dead, but his eyes loosely focused, and he reached a trembling hand to lovingly brush his fingers against Faron's jaw.

"Brother," he whispered, and then closed his eyes. "Thank you."

Faron lifted Eder into his arms and carried him from the edge. Calluna dared look up from Eist's robes, and seeing Eder, she let out a horrified sob.

"I will take him," Eist said, offering their arms. Faron handed him over, glad to be relieved of the burden. It was too light. No body of theirs should be so light.

"Where is he?" Faron asked. His words came out as a strained whisper, for his self-control was warring with a rage so deep it frightened him.

"Somewhere near the apex," Calluna said, gently stroking Eder's forehead. She kissed his cheek, and her tears wet his face. "Stars above, how could he do this?"

"I don't know," Faron said, storming through the gate. "I don't care."

His footsteps were a blur beneath him. His surroundings were dull and irrelevant. Soldiers who fought to defend the last bastion of the Anaon Kingdom were playthings to be cast aside. Nothing would stop Faron. Nothing. He climbed the steps of the Tower Majestic, butchering anyone who dared try. He smashed through barricades devoid of defenders, for the city was taken, and few remained willing to die for their Heartless King.

Higher. Higher. To one place. One person.

At last he reached the rafters, dozens of strong-armed men cowering in fear at the edges. Faron ignored them, for he saw one last platform, and he climbed its rope instead of demanding that any of the liftmasters raise it. Moments later, he pulled himself up to the Final Ascent, a barren stretch of hardstone whose surface was strangely marked with swirls and symbols unlike any other place in the tower.

Within the center, with his back to Faron as he stared out the distant window to overlook a burning Racliffe, stood Sariel.

"Draw your sword," Faron said, readying his own.

"Why?" Sariel asked, refusing to turn about.

"Draw it, damn you."

Two dragon-bone swords lay at Sariel's feet: his own and Eder's. Seeing the weapons added to Faron's fury. He bared his teeth like a savage animal, and he lifted his sword for a thrust.

"We found him down there," he said. "Hanging. Starved. Did you ever feed him, Sariel? Or did you let the radiance revive him night after night, that he might suffer a few waking moments of consciousness before the hunger clawed him back into death?"

Finally Sariel turned. His face was as passive as a statue. His eyes burned with stars.

"Do it," he said. "Kill me, and let me sleep away the breaking of all I ever built."

Faron crossed the distance, his sword leading. Instead of a lethal cut, he veered its aim so it only sliced his brother's chest. His elbow followed, slamming into Sariel's nose to break it. A knee, then a fist, beating flesh, breaking bone, but leaving him alive. Sariel collapsed, and still Faron let loose his wrath. It never felt like enough.

They had fought before. They had even killed each other before. Such were the consequences of a never-ending cavalcade of lifetimes.

But such cruelty.

Such malice.

"Fight me!" Faron shouted as he dropped his sword, pushed his fists together, and smashed both upon Sariel's back. "Hit me! Strike back!" He kicked his brother in the ribs and felt bones break. "Or are you such a coward?"

Faron grabbed Sariel by the neck and lifted him with one hand. His brother's beaten, bleeding body hung limp from his fingers. Still, he did not resist.

"Even you cannot defend what you have done," Faron said. His anger solidified into something darker, and he hated the way it burned sick in his chest. "Then why keep Eder imprisoned? Why torture him for years unending?"

Sariel's left eye was swollen shut, and his other dared to shed a tear.

"I don't know."

That sickness inside him hardened. It would be so easy to give in. Rope, manacles, and a dark cave somewhere would be enough to subject Sariel to the same torture he had inflicted on Eder. Faron's fingers tightened, threatening to strangle Sariel, and it took all his willpower to loosen them so his brother might draw breath. They had discussed this. They knew what must be done so this could never be repeated, and he let that hope keep him from committing horrors he would one day regret. Sariel had to live. He did not deserve the kindness of death.

"Wrong answer," Faron said, and slammed Sariel's head to the hardstone, sending him into merciful unconsciousness that he did not deserve.

Chapter 54

EDER

Darkness enveloped him, but it could not swallow him. The cold licked across his exposed skin like a cruel tongue, but it did not awaken him. Eder swayed within a cold, cruel cell, sometimes alive, mostly dead. At both times, he dreamed. Dreams of freedom. Dreams of starlit fields. Dreams of his brother, and the last time he saw his face.

The first of your hundred years begins here, Sariel had told him as he sealed the thick burlap. *Consider this your penance. When the pride of the world is broken upon my cleansing laws, perhaps I will lift you up to witness the beauty of my work.*

But that work must not have been so beautiful, for year after year passed, and Eder was not brought out to bear witness. He withered, hunger so constant a companion he no longer recognized it as anything other than pain in his chest and abdomen. Thirst, though, he always knew that one. His tongue was swollen within his dry, cracked mouth. He fantasized about water. He pawed at the thick sack enclosed around him, futilely, pathetically, without strength to even fray its interiors, but struggling nonetheless because he could *hear* the ocean below at the base of the Tower Majestic, sense its waves, imagine its spray, cold and thick with foam. To fall within its embrace? To open his mouth and let its icy kiss rush down his throat? To choke, to drown, even that death would be a relief. Let the creatures of the sea devour him, if only so he might one day reawaken upon the shore, naked and gifted another chance at life.

Nothing. Just the sway of the cell. The groan of the rope. The howl of the wind, and the roar of the ocean.

Night after night, he died. The light of sun and stars was denied him, but he felt the passage nonetheless, an innate sense that grew ever stronger. Night after night. Year after year. Minutes became hours became days, all indistinguishable from one another.

Sariel never visited.

"Please, brother," Eder whispered, his face pressed to the interior of the sack. Sometimes moisture seeped into it from the dank, dark tower, and if he held his tongue against it, he would feel its faint gift. It was the weakest of balms, but he cherished it nonetheless against his parched tongue and his peeling, cracked lips.

"Please, kill me true. Kill me forever. This life? I cannot. I cannot."

Years. Years and years and years.

Eder was dead more often than he was alive. He used to cherish the escape. No longer.

When the delirium took him, his head gone light and his body numb and cold, he felt himself fly. Perhaps it was the last of his sanity. Perhaps it was a dream. Eder did not know, nor did he have the presence of mind to dwell upon it. The very act of thought hurt him now. He only sought to exist, catatonic, within the blanketing darkness while rocking inside his cold cell awaiting the next embrace of dying.

And then it would take him, and he would soar heavenward, past the many floors of the Tower Majestic, through the broken top, to the skies beyond. The stars would burn bright before him, swelling in size. What started as cool and comforting turned to searing fire. They scorched him, and whether it was a delusion, dream, or truth, it did not matter, because it *hurt*. It hurt in a way he did not know he could feel pain. It hurt in a manner that pierced through the fog and the hunger and the swaying silence that stripped away so much of his mind.

As the stars burned him, and the night sky imprisoned him, he hung there, weightless for a moment that might have been seconds and might have been hours, before plunging. The stars would fade, and the pain with it. His body would return. He'd open his eyes, see darkness, feel hunger, taste dry thirst, and then weep. No moisture for the tears, the radiance inherent within him granting his body only enough liquid to wake for a few hours.

More years. More deaths. More trips into the sky. The stars charred his flesh; at least it felt as if they did so, though he could not see his own body. There were only the lights amid the dark field. Eder endured, for what choice did he have? But he steadily felt his mind break. These momentary escapes from his body were so much worse, because at the start of each one, he would feel a wondrous sense of freedom that would always be revoked.

"Stop it!" he screamed as the stars worked their evil upon him. "Stop it, please, give me death, but not this! Not this!"

Eder expected no response, and why would he? Every instance before, he experienced this wretched non-death in solitude.

But this time?

This time, he felt a searching. A yearning. It was not like when his sister Calluna occasionally scried for his presence. That was like a tickle in his mind. This was a crushing weight. It engulfed him. His nonexistent limbs bent and broke. The stars pulsed silver, and within their centers burned an array of colors, many of which bore no name. The world shook. The sky rumbled. For the briefest moment, no longer than a flash of lightning, he felt something pierce through. It touched his mind, and it was so familiar, so precious, it made him want to weep anew. It was a feeling of love, and care, and deep-seated fear. The voice of a loved one. His master. His creator. His Father.

Where are you?

Then the presence was gone, and Eder was alone. Abandonment crippled him, its wound all the more brutal because of the echo of love that still shuddered within his mind as he struggled to awaken from this strange, dreamlike delirium.

"Here!" he screamed as he fell. "Father, I am here!"

Eder awoke gagging in his burlap sack, retching in a futile attempt to vomit something from his empty stomach. Still no tears, but he sobbed nonetheless. His voice was a pathetic warble he did not recognize. It had been so long since he last spoke, but he forced air into his lungs. He had to try.

"Here," he gasped. "I'm here."

Each syllable tore his throat, but he shouted it with his every breath.

"I'm here! I'm here!"

Shouted until the words were drowned out by the faintest of winds and mocked by the crash of the distant waves.

"I'm here!"

Death came. He flew. He screamed.

I'm here!

I'm here!

I'm here!

The burlap shifted. The rope groaned. Light, dim light, poured through a tear in the burlap. More movement. Arms around him. He was free. Through the pain, he squinted up at his rescuer and saw Faron's face.

"Brother," he whispered, and then closed his eyes. Relief settled over him, thicker than any blanket. "Thank you."

Sleep came. Sleep, not death, and it was blessedly empty of dreams and flight alike. However long it lasted, he did not know, for he drifted in and out of it so easily. Voices washed over him, meaningless yet comforting. Movement. Being carried. Warm blankets. A fire.

He awoke with a longing, deep and permanent within the pit of his stomach. To be seen. To be found. To hear those words again, and feel the embrace of that being whose presence filled him with more love than all his years upon Kaus had granted. His senses returned. The crackle of a burning campfire. Quiet conversation. His eyes fluttered open. His family was around him, his whole family, Eist and Calluna, Aylah and Faron, even Sariel, bound in rope before a fire. It should have soothed Eder. It did not.

For the first time in years, the light of the stars was upon him.

The false stars.

The imprisoning veil.

He closed his eyes and wept as sleep carried him away, the darkness pierced again and again by the same three words, pounding at his mind, scraping it raw with an undeniable, unexplainable longing.

Where are you?

Where are you?

Where

are

you?

Chapter 55

SARIEL

Sariel sat beside a burning fire, its warmth his only comfort. Redemption and Atonement lay nearby, salvaged from the capital's collapse. His siblings surrounded him, their harsh faces lit by the fire's orange glow. They gathered a third of the way up the mountain path, off a little diversion that ended with a ledge, a lonely red oak, and a majestic view of Racliffe burning in the distance.

"It is not a question of forgiveness," Aylah said, arguing with the others. She looked radiant in her golden armor, fine plate worthy of the woman who had given herself the moniker Crownbreaker. "It is a matter of assurance. I thought we were already in agreement."

The rest kept silent, each hesitant to meet their sister's iron gaze. Faron stood behind Sariel with his arms crossed, guarding him, as if there were any chance of Sariel fleeing with his wrists and ankles bound in steel. Stars above, he could barely breathe after the beating Faron had administered. Eist paced nearby, their flowing gold robes fluttering in the faint midnight wind. Calluna huddled against the red oak, curled up in a ball with her knees to her chest and her hair hiding her face.

As for Eder, he lay on a pile of blankets on the opposite side of the fire, having said little beyond incoherent mumbles since he and Sariel were both smuggled out of the Tower Majestic amid the chaos.

"And what is it you have agreed upon?" Sariel asked amid their awkward silence. "Is destroying my kingdom and burning my capital not enough?"

"You speak as if we took joy in the devastation," Eist said. They gestured to the burning in the distance. "To imply it was our intention is an insult, dear brother."

"Forgive me. I'm sure you marched upon Racliffe with only kindness in your hearts."

Aylah reached down to grab Sariel by the jaw, her blazing eyes alight with radiance.

"And you insult us with your willful blindness," she said. "All of us united against you, and not once did you consider you might be in the wrong? Stars above, how could you *live* with yourself, knowing the state you left Eder in?"

Sariel tried to meet her gaze, but she wielded the one weapon that could pierce the armor about his mind. What he had forced upon Eder had been cruel, but it was also necessary. That was what he had told himself. No matter his promises, Eder would not have stayed hidden during the purging of the sinful and the enforcement of the cleansing laws across Kaus. Eder would have returned, the vanished regent now a savior. War would have followed, and the Anaon Kingdom would have been fractured for an untold number of years until Sariel succeeded. *If* he succeeded.

"I did what needed to be done," he said, his bluster robbed by his inability to match her gaze.

"As must we," she said, and let him go.

More silence. It was common among them, for they knew one another so well. They could sense one another's emotions and read one another's faces as clearly as one observed words written on a page. Radiance crackled among them, further heightening that communal sharing. The anger and ire among his siblings further worried Sariel. He knew they disagreed with his kingdom, but to feel it so vehemently…

"A blood oath," Calluna said from underneath the tree. She peered at them from above her crossed arms. "We cannot endure a war like this again. Make him swear it in his flesh."

Sariel looked to his family, realizing what they desired. It was something often discussed but never tried. Were they truly so desperate?

"A blood oath," he echoed. "Surely you jest?"

"Would you rather we inflict the same cruelty upon you as you did Eder?" Aylah asked. "Perhaps three decades rotting in a gibbet above a cliff, to be eaten daily by crows? You should consider this a blessing that we seek not to punish but instead ensure a better future."

"And what would you have me swear?" he asked.

"To never again rule a kingdom," Eist said, still staring at the capital. "No crowns. No thrones. We are not meant to rule."

"We are the *only* ones deserving to rule," Sariel snapped, already tired of this argument. "How can any of you not see that?"

"Because we see the death it has caused," Faron said. "And we see the schism it built between us. That cannot repeat itself, either. We are *family*. We must *remain* family."

Of course softhearted Faron would believe thus. He was content to battle in the humans' wars for the pleasure of it, but thrones were ever tedious and unwanted by him.

"One more vow," Eist continued. They finally turned, their beautiful face hardened with resolve. "Radiance must never be given to humanity. It is meant for us, and us alone."

"And so the contradiction remains," Sariel said. "We coddle humanity, claiming them capable of ruling themselves, but we also fear them and deny them knowledge of our radiance. Neither a yoke, nor enlightenment. It is a joke I have no heart to tell."

"Is that why you taught them how to wield radiance?" Aylah asked. "You think them better than they truly are?"

"I taught them how to wield radiance as a reward for their willingness to turn against their own broken souls and accept my better way. It is earned trust, akin to a parent toward their child."

"Such pride you still exhibit," Eist said. They approached, their head tilted slightly as if they found Sariel terribly amusing. "Despite everything, you are not broken. Commendable, if it were not born of foolishness."

They knelt before him, so close Sariel could smell the lavender bathed into their robes. Their voice deepened, and Sariel was suddenly held prisoner to their speech. Eist was the strongest of them all when it came to lacing their words with radiance, granting them a power that shook even the others' resolve.

"Your kingdom was in shambles before any of us took up the sword and staff," they said. "Your people loathed your reign. You fostered no love. You built no loyalty. The sins you thought to deny continued all the same, for fear is no way to change a heart. You are a *failure*, Sariel. All you accomplished amounts to naught but ash and shadows. Humanity has not been elevated, and even if we immortal had abstained from the inevitable rebellion, someone else would have answered the challenge to shatter your shameful edifice. If you are still blind to this truth, then there was never hope for your success. To be so ignorant is to be a painter who sees but one color and decries as false the existence of all others. I have not dragged you from your Tower Majestic out of spite or hatred, Sariel, but out of *pity*."

Sariel's insides withered. He looked to his siblings, each hailing from a different region of Kaus, guiding the various nations of the island into a unified Rebellion of the Broken. For them to have built their army so easily, and his every lord and vassal to turn against him at the first opportunity...

But it was more than that. He was not blind to his failure. He read the reports his advisers delivered. The crimes continued. The sins and deviancies did not slow. His iron grip failed to hold a single heart, and high in his tower, he had struggled for answers that never came.

Sariel closed his eyes, and he let it all crumble to dust. His kingdom was in ruins. His cleansing laws were broken and scattered, as were his dreams. He might hold no faith in humanity, and no regrets for the actions he had taken, but he still held faith in his siblings. If they were this united against him, then he must have erred somewhere, and badly.

"A blood oath," he whispered. "So be it. Unbind me, and bring forth the blade."

Faron was quick to do so, the iron manacles unlocked and discarded.

"You vow nothing we don't all believe in," Faron said, pocketing the key. "This is for the best. None of us should rule, and none of us should give humanity a weapon as frightening and powerful as our radiance."

Sariel accepted the offered dagger, and he turned the soft leather hilt within his fingers. A shadow of his pride returned, and he addressed his siblings before making the cut.

"I will swear these vows, but only under one condition," he said. "All of you shall swear the same."

Faron scoffed. "We're not the ones who built a cruel kingdom."

"And yet you insist you share in this belief," Sariel argued. "You say none of us should rule. No crowns. No thrones. Yet if you believe it so ardently, why am I the only one to suffer this humiliation? Let it not be a curse but a shared promise among equals. Or are your convictions not so commonly shared as you claim?"

"I'll do it," Calluna said before the others could argue. She brushed a bit of hair away from her face. "I'll swear it. I've never desired a throne, and humanity is much too fickle and short-lived to be trusted with our gifts."

"A promise among equals," Eist said. They exchanged an unspoken glance with Aylah and Faron. "My convictions are neither hypocritical nor cowardly. I will share in this vow."

The other two nodded in acceptance. That was good enough for Sariel. He settled onto his knees and rolled up the sleeve of his left arm. Once ready, he held the dagger over the fire, letting it heat the blade. He repeated the words of the vow, ensuring all others heard and agreed.

"No crowns. No thrones." He withdrew the blade from the flame. "Radiance shall never be given to humanity."

Sariel lifted his arm. He didn't know how, but he saw runes glowing upon his flesh already, awaiting the carving. They only needed his blood drawn, and radiance pulsed into them to make them real.

He closed his eyes, memories of his coronation flooding him. The pride he felt at finally uniting all of Kaus under a single banner. The satisfaction in watching his laws spread across the realm to curb the people's worst habits. All of it, every grand accomplishment, paled compared to the guilt he had felt when he lay down for sleep, knowing where Eder also slept.

And yet despite that guilt, despite the collapsing of his kingdom as his siblings stoked rebellion after rebellion, he kept Eder there, hanging in his prison. That was proof enough that he needed this vow. Let the knife cut. Let the radiance bind him, if it meant becoming a better brother than he had been before. The effort was immense, but he swallowed his pride, bowed his head, and forced himself to become small.

"No crowns," he whispered, and pierced his flesh with the knife.

Pain flared throughout his entire arm, far beyond what should have resulted from such a shallow cut. Radiance sparked like lightning across the blade. Sariel carved, perfecting each and every movement despite the blood that soon smeared his arm to obscure his work.

"No thrones."

Agony seized the entire left half of his body. He felt chains lash his mind, cruel, self-inflicted manacles flooding him with unnatural agony.

This is just, he told himself as he lifted the dagger to carve the next rune. *This is necessary.*

"Radiance shall never be given..." He had to stop to collect his breath. His vision swam. Each twist of the knife was an ocean of pain washing over him. "To humanity."

He sliced the final mark and then collapsed to his hands and knees, blood trickling down his left arm to pool upon the rocky ground. The fire crackled before him, and on a whim, he thrust his arm into its heart. Blood hardened, and though his flesh burned, its searing was a far cry from the pain he had experienced.

Sariel withdrew a blackened arm now free of blood. The runes, though, shimmered with silver light. He lifted his arm so all might bear witness.

"My vow is made," he said, his voice raspy and weak. He offered the dagger. "Now keep your word."

The others paused until Calluna pushed off from the tree.

"Cowards," she muttered, and grabbed the knife.

She screamed at the pain halfway through, but nothing stopped the carving. When finished, she held her arm over the flame. The blood cracked and flaked away. When done, she revealed the runes, now black and appearing like inked tattoos.

Faron went next, enduring the cutting with his teeth clenched tightly shut. Aylah followed, then Eist.

"No crowns, no thrones," they said as they held the dagger to their flesh. "As it should have been from the start."

When finished, the five of them joined Eder around the fire, quiet and absorbing one another's presence. It had been nearly a century since they were all in one place. Sariel suspected it would be a century more before they were so again.

"What happens now?" he asked.

"Now the Four Heroes who broke the kingdom shall fade into myth and memory," Aylah said. "And we will watch as the humans squabble among themselves for the remaining pieces. Kaus will collapse into little kingdoms, some adapting your laws, others casting them off entirely. Many will turn to Leliel for comfort, and I suspect her temples shall rise in prominence as the people seek stability amid the change."

"And what life shall await me?"

Eist stood, and they removed their gold-laced robe and tossed it upon the fire. Clothed only in a pale undershirt and breeches, they lifted their left arm so the moonlight fell upon the newly carved tattoos.

"The life you create for yourself," they said. "Same as ever before."

They paused to offer quiet Calluna a kiss upon the forehead and then departed past the red oak tree down the path. Faron was next to follow.

"There's many I care for in the armies who followed me," he explained. "I would guide them safely home before the chaos starts."

Calluna slid closer to Sariel until she sat with her hip pressed against his. She leaned into him, her long hair falling across his bare chest as she pressed her cheek to his rib cage. Her fingers traced his broken ribs and bruised flesh from Faron's beating. Her silver eyes peered up at him, filled with sorrow and hope in equal measure.

"You don't have to be alone," she whispered before departing. "Even if I know that is what you will always choose to be."

And then it was only Aylah, Eder, and himself. His sister sat beside his sleeping brother, her legs crossed and her drawn sword laid out across her lap. She would guard him until he recovered. Sariel wished he could feel insulted, but was not.

"I suppose I will disappear into the west," he said, finally standing.

"For your sake, grow out your hair and keep your face hidden," she said. "I will spread tales of your gruesome execution, and how I cast your remains to the sea. For your sake, give no cause for people to doubt."

"Of course." He lifted Redemption and then gestured to the sleeping Eder. "What of him? He has not sworn our vow."

"You would have him suffer it now?" Aylah asked. "Your brother barely clings to life. Give him time. When he is recovered, I will inform him of our shared vow. He will partake. I am sure of it."

Sariel shrugged. He held no desire to argue the point.

"So be it. I will make no demands of him. Guard him well, Aylah. And when he wakes, tell him..."

He paused. What message was there to convey? What might he say that would absolve him of thirty years spent imprisoning Eder within the cold cells?

"Tell him whatever he must hear, for nothing I offer will ever suffice."

He settled his sword over his shoulder and turned away. To the mountain path. To a life hidden in exile, waiting for the memory of the Heartless King to fade, that memory become story, and then that story become history.

Part Seven

DREAMS

Chapter 56

SARIEL

Sariel fell silent in Isabelle's tent, the hour-long tale told as best he knew it. His tattoo itched upon his arm, and he stood from the bed, needing to stretch his legs.

"You were the Heartless King," Isabelle said. She had kept silent the entire time, speaking up only now that he was finished. "You...that would make you hundreds of years old."

"Older," Sariel said. "Though how old, we do not know. The past fades into a gray fog once enough centuries are past. We remember ourselves, grown as we are now, and we remember humanity, already built into little cities and kingdoms. Nothing beyond."

The queen folded her hands on her lap, and she stared at her open palms.

"I know it mad to believe you, but given what I've seen, the monsters in Kanth, my own gifts..." She hesitated and looked to him. "The beauty in your eyes. How do I deny the possibility?"

Sariel blinked away the radiance within his irises, forgetting he had allowed it to linger during his tale.

"Believe or disbelieve, it is your right," he said. "You asked for who I am, and why my brother would have you distrust me, so I have told my truth."

"I care not for your brother's opinion," she said. "What you were...Do you regret it, Sariel? Do you feel guilt for your time as king?"

In answer, Sariel rolled up his sleeve to reveal the runic vows carved into his arm.

"Guilt?" he asked. "Shame? No. If my siblings and I allowed ourselves to feel regret for the decisions we have made, we would never leave our beds due to the crushing weight. Who I was then is not who I am now. That is all that matters. If it will ease your mind, know that even without these vows, I would never again sit upon a throne, nor seek to change your sinful nature. Let humanity rule humanity. I will live amid their unique brand of chaos. This war we fight, it is only to undo the damage Eder has done, and revoke the knowledge of radiance from those unworthy."

"That vow..." She glanced at his arm. "I assume Eder—*Mitra*—never took it when he recovered?"

"Our brother fled into the wilderness, and none of us were willing to chase him. When he reemerged, he refused, correctly arguing he had never agreed to partake. The matter died, for among all of us, why would we fear Eder? Why would we think the one who suffered the most would seek to build a kingdom? And for our ignorance, it is Kaus that now suffers."

Silence fell. Sariel crossed his arms, and he waited. He didn't want to admit it to himself, but he was achingly curious. How would Isabelle react? Would she reject him now? Cast him aside and trust Faron to be her adviser in the coming battle?

She looked back to her hands, her fingers absently rubbing against each other. She was nervous. Why?

"How do you endure?" she asked softly. "The loneliness? The isolation? Everywhere you go, you are...different."

Sariel sat beside her on the bed. A hundred lifetimes riffled through his mind like brittle paintings.

"Many times, we don't," he said. "Faron, for example? Every life, he falls in love. It's inevitable as the rising sun. He meets a woman, loves her, marries her...and then she ages. He does not. She grows old and weary. He remains young and strong. Sometimes he abandons her before it becomes apparent, but that's rare. Most times he confides his truth, and then they move about, disguising their true relationship with one another, until eventually she passes on."

He shook his head and sighed.

"My brother, the softhearted fool, wishes more than anything to be *human*. To live and love and grow old and die. But he can't. It's a foolish dream, so he does what he can to pretend. When his beloved dies, he burns himself upon a pyre. His return takes decades. During that time, all the people he knew, the friends he made, and the relatives of his deceased wife, they age and move on. He awakens, his memories dulled, and his pain eased into the past." Sariel bitterly laughed. "And then he does it all again."

Isabelle squirmed beside him, her leg bumping against his. "And what of you?"

"What of me?"

She sneaked a glance in his direction. "Is your cold heart ever warmed by a loving embrace?"

Sariel debated answering, and then relented. He had told so much of himself to Isabelle, did it matter if he relinquished this one last truth?

"Yes," he said softly. "Unlike Faron, whose love spreads limitless and latches on to a new woman with every life, I cherish the same unique soul. I cannot remember when I first met her. I just know I have always loved her. Her name, her oldest name, was Isca. When she perishes and her soul is reborn, I find her. I learn her new name. I look upon her features, see the change in the color of her eyes or texture of her hair. Sometimes she learns to love me in return. Sometimes I am rejected. Each life of hers, a new face to remember, and yet I am always a stranger."

He clenched his hands.

"These last few lives, I have not had the heart to try. I am not my brother. I do not need a pyre to endure the pain. But there is pain. Every time."

She reached out, callused fingers settling over his own. "Have you found her in this lifetime?"

He nodded.

"Her name is Tara. A simple farm girl in a town called Barkbent. I've watched over her since her parents died of plague. A protector to her. I can do no more. To watch her age and die, cradle to grave, again and again, sometimes remembering me when the radiance shines brightly in my eyes and I call forth memories of her prior lives...our time together, so fleeting..."

Her grip tightened, and he closed his eyes and focused on the pressure.

"I cannot do it anymore. That is what I tell myself. I cannot. But what does it matter, my protestations? I still love her. I still look upon her soul, collected of a dozen lifetimes of us spent together, and I see moments of happiness, friendship, and love. I yearn to hold her in my arms once more. To protect her from this horrid, miserable world, and all the hardships that would assail her."

He laughed.

"Faron is right, Isabelle. I am equally a fool. I only pretend otherwise."

"You are not a fool." She leaned against him, her head turned and her golden eyes swallowing his gaze. The soft touch of her hair fell across his neck.

"Not a fool," she insisted again, quieter this time. "Just hurt in a way time will never heal, for time is the reason for the wound."

She was so close, he could feel the warmth of her breath against his skin. Her leg pressing against his. Her eyes, enrapturing.

"Is that what I am?" he asked. "Forever wounded?"

She pressed her lips to his. He froze at the shock of her boldness. Undeterred, she gently curled her hand around his neck, her fingertips lightning against his skin. His shock eased, and he returned the kiss, enjoying the softness of her lips. Even so, his mind cried warning.

"We shouldn't," he whispered, breaking the contact.

"I don't care."

Again, pressing against him, one hand about his neck, fearful to let him go, the other tracing lines along his cheek and jaw. Sariel felt a stirring in his groin, felt his heart speeding, his resistance fading.

Isabelle leaned back onto the bed, and he fell with her, maintaining the kiss as his weight settled atop her. He pressed harder, self-control threatening to break, as he briefly slipped his tongue inside her mouth. She shivered beneath him, even as his mind screamed for sanity.

Stop, stop, stop!

Sariel withdrew from the kiss for a gasp of air. He gazed down at Isabelle, looking unreal in her beauty with her hair curling about her face and neck.

"Are you certain?" he asked.

The light in her eyes flared brightly, and she answered not with words. The faintest of golden tendrils spread from her hands. He felt her presence pulse into him, only this was not an overriding command, as they were so often used. This was a sharing. Isabelle's emotions flooded into him, and Sariel gasped at the desire. She wanted him. Needed him. It was an overwhelming flame that burned away what remained of his resistance. Yet amid it, like a coal of ice in the heart of a campfire, he felt fear. Fear of rejection. Fear of loneliness.

"Isabelle," he whispered, and then gave her his own emotions. His awe at her beauty. His admiration of her resolve. And yes, a desire to be accepted, and known, in a way only Isca ever could. Forever living. Forever alone. She gasped, and he braced himself for shock, for pity, even repulsion.

Instead, she wrapped her arms around his neck and pulled him close so she might resume the kiss. Sympathy flooded inside him, so strong it nearly brought him to tears. Her lower back arched, and she moaned beneath him. Her legs curled around his waist, pulling him closer so his crotch ground against hers as her exhalations grew rapid. Her desire reached a fevered peak, for it was meant to drown out her own lingering sorrow. Since the day of her birth, she had been different. Sometimes, she had hated herself for it. Sometimes, she felt guilt, or fear. But with him? In his arms?

"Not alone," she said when the kiss ended, both a promise and a confession. "Not tonight."

He was naked to her long before she grabbed his trousers and pulled them down to his knees. When he thrust into her, he dug his fingernails into the muscles of her back, and he shifted his kiss so it latched on to her neck, then trailed downward toward her breasts. She pushed him upward, removed her blouse, and then lay back down so the path of his kisses might continue. He tasted sweat. His tongue felt softness.

Their connection never broke. He felt wrapped in threads, silver and gold, and with his every movement and her every cry, the pleasure pulsed back and forth between them, shared and then magnified. It added strength to his every thrust. It added desperation to the journeying of his hands. Through it all, a little voice, easily drowned out amid the pleasure, refused to fall silent.

A mistake, for certain, as his lips pinned her to the bed with the force of his kiss.

A mistake he would gladly make.

•

Once Sariel was dressed, he slipped out to the night. In the dark opening of his own tent, he sat upon the grass and stared at the stars. A dozen different memories warred within him. The fear of revealing himself fully to a woman who was not Isca. Of how Faron would react if he found out. Of how Isabelle had arched beneath him.

"Wrong," he muttered, as if speaking it aloud might convince him. "Wrong, dumb, reckless, foolish, naïve..."

So many words. For months now, rumors had persisted that Isabelle was bedding either of the Godsight brothers, with some salacious tales insisting both at the same time. But they were just rumors, and most were unbelieved. The majority saw Isabelle as pure, and her heart as dedicated solely to the goddess, Leliel. With victory so close, it was beyond foolish to risk success on a midnight tryst. The satisfaction of flesh could come later, once victory was secured.

Sariel shivered within his tent. He'd put no thought into what future awaited him once they shattered the Astral Kingdom. Expectations of the past had him assuming he would just drift away afterward, to be forgotten as the remaining human kingdoms squabbled with one another and Isabelle attempted to maintain her protectorate. The idea that he could remain with her, guide her, perhaps even marry and become...

Sariel clenched his teeth to deny his scream. His midsection cramped, and he collapsed onto his back as his left arm rose above him, its every muscle locked tight. Silver fire burned across the unreadable runes, charring through the skin of his forearm. Blood leaked to his elbow and dripped upon the grass. Sariel forced himself to breathe through his nostrils as he endured the waves of pain.

No crowns. No thrones. I will hold no crowns, no thrones. Not with her. Not with anyone.

The pain faded. The silver fire wafted away as smoke, leaving behind only blackened skin that would take a long time to heal, especially for him. Sariel pulled his sleeve back down to hide it as he waited for his heartbeat to settle.

"You knew this was a mistake," he told himself in a shaking voice.

He had to fix this, immediately. He had no future with Isabelle, not with her destined to be queen. Letting her believe so, for even a moment, was wrong.

Once fully recovered, Sariel strode back through the camp, quiet and dark. Dawn was far enough away that even those responsible for preparing the morning meal still slept. He made for Isabelle's tent, his every step careful. Being seen returning could be problematic. When he reached the closed flaps, he hesitated. Telling her this would not be easy...but she knew of his vow. She knew his limitations. She would understand. He had to trust she would understand.

The way it must be, he told himself, and ducked inside.

Her bed was empty.

"Isabelle?" he whispered, looking about. Nothing. Silence.

Sariel slipped back out, telling himself to remain calm. Maybe she needed to relieve herself. He made his way in that direction, stopping halfway toward the latrine trench to address a guard sitting bored at one of the little crossroads through the rows of tents.

"Have you seen Queen Isabelle?" he asked.

"The queen?" the soldier replied. "No. Why?"

"Nothing," he said, continuing. "It's nothing."

He thought to wake Faron, but what would he say? What excuse could he offer for sneaking into Isabelle's tent in the dead of night?

Calm down, he told himself, but he made for the main road nonetheless. The camp was enormous, and surrounded by loyal soldiers. There was no reason to panic. No reason to assume the worst. He pulsed a bit of radiance into his eyes, brightening the night. A speck of a familiar golden aura in the distance filled his stomach with iron.

His hurried pace became a run, and then a sprint. He reached the main road leading toward Racliffe, and the farthest extent of the camp. Nearby were the temporary stables, and from within them burst a speckled horse. Aylah held the reins, sitting tall and stiff in the saddle. Lying bound and unconscious behind her was Queen Isabelle.

"Aylah!" he cried out. His sister tugged on the reins, turning the horse aside so she could face him. Their eyes met.

"I'm sorry, Sariel," she shouted back. "But this must be done."

A kick of her heels, and the horse galloped away, chased only by his futile screams.

Chapter 57

FARON

Faron paced within the tent that had once been Isabelle's. He kicked over the bed that she slept on, and he smashed the table that held the maps she once pored over.

"Why?" he screamed at Sariel. "Why would Aylah betray us? She took the same vows as us. She knows what Eder is doing is wrong, and still she...she..."

He couldn't even say the words, and so he hit the table again, splintering its thick boards. His teeth clenched, grinding together as he fought a losing battle to contain his rage.

"I don't know," Sariel said, calmly watching from the opposite side of the now ruined table. "Her time spent imprisoned within the Grand Castle broke a deep part of her. Perhaps something of Eder's philosophy appeals to her in a way that we cannot."

"Broke?" Faron asked. "But Aylah's always been so strong. I thought she had recovered."

"Yes. I suspect you did."

Faron grabbed one of the table pieces and flung it aside, the chunk ripping through the tent's fabric.

"Damn it, Sariel, now is not the time to gloat! So I'm ignorant, fine, but damn it, if *you* knew, then why did *you* not do something?"

His brother's gaze lowered, and finally Faron saw a bit of contrition.

"I tried," he said. "I thought I had helped her. Perhaps not enough. Or perhaps I did not understand the nature of the wound."

Faron tried to regain control as he fumed. He couldn't lose his temper like this. He had to keep a clear head. Too much was at stake.

"Let's think this through," he said. "Aylah captured Isabelle instead of killing her. That has to mean something, right? Maybe there's a chance to save her."

"Or Eder plans to make an example of her with a public execution," Sariel said, barely above a whisper.

"No," a familiar voice said from outside the tent. "Not...not that. Not exactly."

The brothers turned, and Faron's eyes widened as Calluna slipped inside. Her head hung low, and her hands were crossed behind her.

"What do you know?" he asked his sister. "Was this your doing?"

"No!" she protested, her eyes widening. "At least, not taking Isabelle. But I know *why* Aylah took her. And that...that it's...it's because of me."

Faron exchanged a glance with Sariel, neither certain how to proceed.

"Explain yourself, sister," Sariel said at last. "We will both reserve judgment until you have spoken your truth."

Calluna squirmed before them.

"I don't know what the tower does, but I know it can be awakened. I...I showed Eder how to awaken it. A hidden temple, and a key within. That key, though, that should have been the end of it! For it to work, it takes a sacrifice. Someone whose blood is blessed with radiance. And the one who is sacrificed, they won't just die. Not the death we know."

She looked at them, tears building in her eyes.

"A true death. A final death. No rebirth. No return. The sacrificed would become less than mortal, denied even the cycle of humanity."

Faron clenched his fists, and his voice shook with his fury.

"Why would you give Eder such a monstrous gift?"

"Because I didn't think he'd use it!" Calluna shouted back. "He's been

obsessed with the Tower Majestic since we freed him, and so I thought...
I thought once he learned the cost, a cost he'd never pay, then he'd finally
abandon his dream. Then there wouldn't need to be a war, and we could
be at peace again. We could be a family."

Sariel's voice was colder than mountain frost.

"You are right, Calluna. Our brother would never sacrifice one of his
own." He stepped closer. "But Isabelle is not one of our own, is she?"

Calluna retreated a step.

"I didn't know," she insisted.

"You tried to kill her once before."

"So what if I did?" Her little face suddenly looked so much older than
them all. "Let Eder sacrifice her! Let the tower awaken! I don't care anymore. I hate you, all of you. Murder each other, make a game of it, but
must I always be the one stuck between?"

She fled the tent, and Faron had not the heart to chase her.

A clearing throat turned both of them toward the tent's open flaps.
Marshal Oscar stood at the entrance, his arms crossed behind him. His
eyes were puffy and bloodshot.

"You two are the strongest and bravest of my queen's soldiers," he
said, stepping inside. "I pray neither of you have lost all hope. My fastest
horses are in chase, and we may yet overtake your sister if she is headed
toward Racliffe as we presume."

Faron understood Oscar's reasoning but knew it was hopeless. Yes,
Aylah's horse was burdened with a second rider, but their sister could
also grant her radiance to the beast, strengthening it so it might run for
days if necessary without rest. There would be no catching her.

"While we pray for her safe return," said Sariel, "we should plan as if
she will not."

"Indeed," Oscar said. "Which is why I have come for you. Soldiers
rally to you. They trust you. And I...I will need that support. The vassal
kings, queens, and representatives are coming here to discuss the future
of the invasion. Will you stay with me, Godsight brothers? Will you lend
me the strength you have lent my queen for so long?"

Faron and Sariel exchanged glances. Oscar had been a most loyal servant to Queen Isabelle, but if he were to have their support, there was one thing they must first know.

"That depends," Faron said. "What future do you see for this invasion, now that Isabelle is captured? Will we continue, or will we withdraw?"

"We will *not* withdraw," Oscar said with surprising harshness. He paused a moment to gather himself. "We will not withdraw, for Isabelle made it clear to me she is willing to die a martyr for her cause. The Church of Stars must be destroyed, and the Astral Kingdom sundered. If Mitra threatens Isabelle's life, then we counter with our own threat. If our queen is executed, so, too, will we execute every man, woman, and child who lives within Racliffe, the Hanging City, and the Tower Majestic."

"The purge of tens of thousands, all for the life of one," Sariel said. "Are you willing to go through with such a measure?"

"Aren't you?" Oscar asked, and neither brother could deny it.

"All right," Faron said. "That's good enough for me. You have our support, Oscar. This war must continue, and we will win it, so long as these fickle kings and queens remain loyal to the protectorate."

"A fact we will soon discover," Oscar said, and gestured to the tent entrance and the approaching men and women visible outside it.

Faron recognized most of them, some draped in finery, others in armaments of war. They were all vassals of the protectorate, though a few had been folded directly into Doremy itself. Some were kings and queens, others sent to speak in their rulers' place, such as Prince Druss. By and large, Faron cared little for their presence. They were a distraction, all too eager to bring their own troubles and opinions to Isabelle. There was but once voice Faron wanted Isabelle listening to, and it was his.

"Thank you for coming," Marshal Oscar said to each of them. The friendliest face was that of King Allan, for Armane had joined Doremy on the day of Isabelle's coronation. Least was King Jehan, the dour, dark-haired man dressed in fine black leather armor. Among them was young Prince Druss, speaking for Rudou, King Yarrick of Forez, the elderly Queen Ulma looking pristine in a black-and-teal dress, leading her soldiers of the newly surrendered Grenab. Even Reglia had joined, the priest who spoke for the grand city-state of Cevenne. Several more lords accompanied them, as well as elected spokesmen for the three nations of the Crowning.

They crowded into the tent, as they had so often when Isabelle discussed strategy. A pang of nostalgia hit Faron, and he had to force it away.

"I suspect this is a waste of time," King Jehan said, his green eyes mirthless. "But let us hear your plans, Marshal."

"Rescuing our queen is a waste of time?" Druss asked, sounding legitimately shocked.

"Watch your tone," Yarrick was quick to add, his relationship with Jehan brittle ever since he abandoned the Blue Rivers Alliance. Jehan sneered but said nothing. He didn't need to. The representatives of the Crowning were already talking about the burdens of the invasion and how they were so horribly taxing on lands left to rot and fester at the hands of the slain Silvein family.

Faron heard it all, and it washed over him like hot air. None of this was new. None of this was interesting. Lifetime after lifetime, he had watched royalty wage war against one another, listened to them claim poverty while upon golden thrones, and seen them sacrifice anyone and anything to have their way. They would scheme and argue and try to turn Isabelle's capture to their advantage, however little.

Enough.

"I will have silence!" he shouted, cutting off any potential arguments. He looked upon the nobles, these kings, queens, princes, and lords who had been swept up in the great flood that was Isabelle's protectorate. Some had joined to preserve their power. Some had sought to spare their people the brutality of a losing conquest. Others were opportunists, seeking to grow their influence and become mighty within the empire they expected Isabelle to build.

All of them had spent their days marching beside Isabelle, listening to her words. Hearing her passion. And unknown to them, perhaps even unknown to Isabelle herself, they had been shaped by her radiant voice. Their wills had been steadily bent and made pliable over the course of

months. Centuries ago, Faron had done similar as the Wild Rage. While
he had been unneeded as of late, he stepped up to the role now. He spoke
and let silver radiance imbue his tongue. His words flowed into the gathered people, and it was so easy, like rainwater gathering in already carved
ruts and ditches.

"We will not abandon our queen to the Luminary's mercy," he said,
projecting all his power. "We will not bow before the cowardice of a kingdom that would abduct their foe in the night instead of facing them honorably in battle. This war was never about giving Isabelle a throne. It is
about sundering the evils of the Church of Stars. It is about striking the
hand of a tyrant that is reaching ever more greedily to the west."

He clapped his hands together, and he gave so much of himself that
silver sparks fell from his fingers. The crowd did not react, too deeply
engrossed in the spell he weaved.

"Will you stand now, tall and proud, and rally behind Marshal Oscar
as he leads the assault against Racliffe? Will you cry out, defiant to the
cruelties of the Astral Kingdom? Will you march alongside me, the Ram
of Doremy, as we free our queen?"

Faron's radiance pulsed throughout them, filling them with confidence. Sariel was quick to join in. He was not as skilled with such manipulation, but he aided in his own way when he slammed Redemption to
the dirt and scowled.

"Or will you abandon your queen and flee east, to forever mar the
honor of your family name?"

Sariel's radiance flowed, this time an opposite feeling, one of fear. Fear
of failure. Fear of being seen as a coward. Fear of what might happen if
Isabelle were freed and they had not remained loyal to the protectorate.

It was a heady mix, one they could not resist. Perhaps in a few days
they would wonder, or question their decisions, but by then the momentum of war would have swept them up once more, and crashed them
against the walls of Racliffe.

"I have been loyal to my queen since the earliest days of her reign,"
King Allan said. "I am proud to call my lands part of Doremy, and will
not abandon her now."

"The people of Rudou will not falter, either," Prince Druss said, speaking for his mother.

"I am not one to cower before adversity," King Yarrick said.

Nation after nation answered the call, even King Jehan, whom Faron had feared the most likely to break. Etne might have been spared the destruction Vivarai suffered, but the man had seen firsthand Isabelle's potential cruelty at Lossleaf Castle in her war against the Blue Rivers Alliance.

"Thank you," Marshal Oscar said when it was clear none would resist. "As of now, our plans remain unchanged. We will assault the walls of Racliffe with our catapults, smash its gates with our rams, and claim the city from her cruel masters. Prepare your troops. I shall send runners to check on you shortly. We move out before midday."

The various lords departed, until Marshal Oscar stood alone with Faron and his brother. There was no hiding the man's relief.

"That went better than I could have dreamed," he said, wiping his sweating brow.

"I'd like to think we helped with that," Faron said. "I suppose now we must pray the Luminary will keep Isabelle alive and barter her for his own survival."

Faron suspected little chance of that, given what Calluna had told him, but what else might they do? They still didn't know what the Tower Majestic did, or why Eder was so obsessed with awakening it.

"We can do more than that," Sariel said, once confirming the three were alone in the tent. "There is a small tunnel leading past the walls of Racliffe, through the cliff, all the way to Underbridge. It was to be my escape, if I needed it. I chose not to use it when I realized my entire family had come to challenge me."

Oscar frowned, confused but still clinging to the basic idea.

"A tunnel," he said. "Then we can use it to break their defenses!"

"We will do no such thing," Sariel said. "It is a tight tunnel, and one would have to crawl. The exit is in Underbridge, which means any force we sneak inside would be far from Racliffe's outer walls and would be quickly spotted and surrounded. But if I slipped inside during the initial assault, the path toward the Tower Majestic should be far less guarded."

"No," Faron said. "Not you. Let me go instead."

"You?" Sariel asked, and Oscar was quick to join him.

"You are the heart of our warriors," the marshal argued. "It would do such good to have you on our front lines when we make the assault."

Faron approached Sariel, and he lowered his voice, addressing only his brother.

"Please, Sariel, let me do this," he said. "I will be no good in a fight, not when my mind is on you and your task. Let me instead know I did all I could to rescue Isabelle from Eder's clutches. Take to the battlefield in my stead. Show Eder's forces the true wrath of the ever-living."

Sariel put a hand on Faron's shoulder and sighed.

"I will be a poor replacement," he said. "But I will not deny you. When the time comes, I will trust you to bring her back to us."

Faron smiled, feeling the first inklings of hope since awakening in the dark of night to learn of Aylah's betrayal. His brother left, so that he was now alone with Oscar. The marshal bent down to retrieve the discarded map. He rolled it up gently, and then one by one, began picking up the little wooden pieces to hold in his other hand.

"Thank you," he said, careful to keep his attention on his task. "When I heard, I feared...well. Ignore my uncertainties. You two Godsight brothers are far better men than I could ever hope for."

The marshal dropped to one knee, and he stared at the remaining pieces in the dirt as if they were a burden too great to overcome.

"I made a promise to King Henri on the day we marched south to initiate the attack upon Argylle lands. I swore I would guide Isabelle and protect her as she waged her war. I would stay at her side in her first battle and be her shield against her foes. And each and every step of the way, I have watched her grow. I did not believe her when she spoke of Leliel's blessing, not at first. My promises to her father were enough to ensure my loyalty."

He crumpled the map in his shaking fist.

"But I did begin to believe. Not because of the glory she revealed at her coronation. Not even because of the prowess she displayed on the battlefield. I believed, because within her I saw a resolve unbreakable to the last. And now, on the very cusp of achieving true greatness, I have failed her. My vows are air. I want to hold hope, I want to keep faith that the goddess would not have delivered Isabelle unto her enemies without reason, but I..."

He closed his eyes and looked away.

"My faith has never been in the goddess, only in Isabelle. And I beg that it not be broken."

Faron knelt beside him and gently placed his hand upon Oscar's wrist. Their eyes met.

"No man can overcome all trials. The best one can do is promise to try. Do not fear her fate, Oscar. Do not regret the decisions that led to her capture, nor blame yourself for the failures of the past. The future is all you may mold, and I say mold it, my friend. Take this army into your fist and wield it as a weapon to make Isabelle proud. Rise to the challenge. All else must fall as fate decrees, be it cruel or kind."

Oscar smiled faintly.

"I never thanked you for saving my life from the qiyan," he said. "So thank you, Faron Godsight. For being there when I needed you most, now twice again."

Faron smiled back, and he clapped the man on the shoulder.

"Think nothing of it," he said. "Now, get to work. We have an army to march, and a lot of fears to quell. I'll join you in a moment."

The marshal nodded, and he exited the tent, still carrying the map. Faron watched him go, suddenly anxious and exhausted.

"Fate," he muttered. "Must you always be cruel? Or will you, for once, spare us your poisoned lash?"

He exited and began aimlessly wandering the sprawling web of tents. All these humans, clinging to ideals meant to be so much grander than their own meager lives. Fighting, killing, and dying in hopes of a future kinder than the present. Individually so small, and yet together, powerful enough to topple empires. Their scurrying reminded him of ants, and he could not shake the feeling of them crawling across his skin.

He needed to get out. He needed to get away from prying eyes, fearful expectations, and the looming haze of war. He picked a direction and walked, hating that even now he kept his head held high and his face determined lest he worry Isabelle's soldiers. He once joked to Sariel that the reason his brother disliked humanity was because he feared to be himself around them.

Perhaps Faron was not truthful around them, either, only unlike Sariel, he closed his eyes to the differences.

Tents became empty fields. Stomped dirt became yellow grass. Smoke of campfires scattered to reveal a somber blue sky. Faron gazed upon it, wondering when he had become so tired. Everyone he loved outside of his family died. It was an immutable fact of the world. He knew this. He had experienced this a thousand times. Yet it always hurt. Always.

He was tired of hurting. Tired of fighting. He saw Isabelle's face in the horizon, and he wondered if he must suffer that hurt once more. This time, it felt like another funeral pyre would not suffice to erase the hurt. How many years must pass for him to forgive Eder for such a crime? How many pyres?

Faron sat on the grass, put his palms to his eyes, and screamed silently at himself to not cry. He had to be strong if he was to save Isabelle. He had to be a hero for their army, brash and brave, to keep resolve from breaking. Racliffe must fall. Eder must die. Isabelle, his queen, must live. He gnashed his teeth, dredging up his anger. If hatred was what he needed, then let him hate Eder, if it gave him the strength to carry on.

Behind him, he heard a soft rustle of grass. It seemed solitude would not be his for long. He turned, a reprimand on his lips, but a sudden, soft bark dispelled it.

"Iris?"

The coyote stood a few feet away with her head lowered. She pawed at the ground, as if fearful to approach. The sight added a new ache to his already burdened heart.

"Please," he said, and offered her his hand. "Never fear me."

Instead of accepting the petting, she suddenly bolted to him, slamming her entire body against his chest. He wrapped her in an embrace and pressed his face against her fur as she licked his arms. All his rage and betrayal bled away, if only for a moment. But in that moment, he let his fear and sorrow surface, and he wept tears upon Iris's fur.

"I'm so scared," he whispered. "I don't want to lose her, Iris."

The coyote twisted in his arms so she could face him, and her tongue licked his face, cleaning away his tears. He laughed despite everything, and gently scratched behind her ears.

"You're right," he said. "Now's not the time to despair. She's alive. She has to be. And so long as she is, there's a chance to save her." Iris barked. He smiled. "Thank you, little one, for your kindness when I need it most."

He stood, patted her on the head, and started walking to camp, his spirits lifted.

"Your faithful are strong," he whispered to the blue sky. Never before, in all his life, had he prayed to the goddess, but he spoke to her now. "They are loyal. When we march upon Racliffe's walls, our foes will discover the rage of your beloved; that I promise."

He touched his sword, envisioning the pleasure of holding it aloft as he entered the Tower Majestic.

"And Eder will know it, too, when I take his head from his shoulders and cast it to the sea."

Chapter 58

AYLAH

Thank you for accompanying me," Celebrant Madeleine said as they rode the lift. The woman stared out into the yawning abyss in the heart of the tower, her hand clutching the rope railing. "It would do my mind good to have someone speak with our Luminary, and you are the only one allowed to join him in the Final Ascent."

Aylah glanced sideways at the diminutive woman. No radiance was needed to detect the jealousy that Madeleine tried and failed to hide. What was the Celebrant to her brother? Friend? Confidant? Lover?

None, Aylah suspected, from what she knew of Eder. It made her pity Madeleine, who no doubt wished she were all three.

"I cannot promise much, but I will attempt to persuade him to rest and partake of a good meal," Aylah said.

The Celebrant nodded. Her grip on the rope tightened.

"Eder said I should trust you as I trust him, but he spoke little else of you. How do you know the Luminary? Were you friends before his blessed return to Racliffe?"

Aylah had discussed a story with Eder for them to use, for he had always insisted he was the only child of his "father," and therefore she could not reveal herself as his sister. This was hardly the first time in their lives they'd needed such measures, and the lie was familiar on her tongue.

"We were friends as children," she said. "It seems not so long ago he was pulling my hair, and now here he is, with a nation and church under his thumb."

Madeleine's face twitched. "You demean all he has accomplished with such language."

Aylah grinned at the woman.

"No one is a prophet in their hometown. He may be Luminary now, but he will forever be as a brother to me, softhearted and prone to obsessions…to the point where he forgets to eat and sleep, as you yourself have so clearly noted."

The lift arrived at the rafters, and Aylah suspected that was the only reason the Celebrant did not argue further. Instead she stepped off and gestured for Aylah to follow. They weaved through the mess of rattling gears and pulleys, accepting the respectful nods of the liftmasters.

"This is Aylah, whom Eder has given permission to join him," Madeleine explained to the soldiers guarding the lift to the Final Ascent. They moved aside so Aylah could step into the little platform's center. Madeleine crossed her arms, frustrated and worried.

"Please, for his sake, convince him," she said as the platform rose.

This was the first time Aylah had visited the Final Ascent since Eder explained their purpose, and she was startled by the change. More than half the runestones shimmered with silver light, illuminating the intricate symbols carved into their centers. They glowed because they were bathed in Eder's blood, and the amount required was frightening to observe as she walked through their mazelike pattern.

"Eder?" she asked. Her brother knelt over one of the runestones, a bloody knife held at his side. He was still and did not turn at her voice.

"Eder?" she repeated, touching his shoulder. He startled and spun about, his bleary eyes wide.

"Aylah?" he asked, struggling to focus upon her. His voice was frighteningly weak. "Oh, forgive me. I must have…dozed off."

Aylah frowned at the lie.

"This blood," she said, and gestured about her. "It is too much for you to shed at such a pace."

"But I must," he insisted, and tried to stand. When he wobbled, Aylah grabbed him by the arm and aided him to his feet. He felt thin beneath her touch. This was no ordinary bleeding, of that she was certain. When Eder painted those stones, he was giving a part of himself to them, a faint replication of the true sacrifice required at the altar of hands.

"Your people are afraid," Aylah said. "Queen Isabelle's army marches toward Racliffe. Your marshals seek guidance, and your faithful, encouragement."

"General Sid has returned to lead the defense," Eder insisted. "As for my people, my work here is the culmination of their faith. There is no better use for my time."

"If you must, then why not use Isabelle's blood to paint the runes?"

"No," Eder said, shaking his head. "She is born of radiance, that is true, but it is still thin compared to ours. Tainted with humanity. I fear it may not be enough for what the machinery demands, and I would be foolish to risk matters further by using her blood, and not mine, to power these runestones. I can only pray my radiance overcomes the deficiencies in hers."

"Then at least be patient. You drive yourself to the brink of death."

"Death," her brother said, and laughed. "Death comes for us all, and in the name of the goddess, Leliel. I know our defenses. I have read my scouts' reports. We cannot win, Aylah. The protectorate will destroy us. My only hope is that our walls hold out long enough that I may awaken the Tower Majestic to fulfill its true purpose."

Aylah glanced at the altar and its sacrificial bowl clutched in a crowded array of six-fingered hands. Her stomach clenched at the sight of it.

"And if it is not enough?" she asked.

Eder pushed her away to stand on his own strength. "If it is not enough, then I hope Faron will be kind and not toss my body to rot in the ocean below."

He smiled as if it were a joke. Aylah was not laughing, and when Eder teetered, she closed the distance between them to catch him in her arms.

"Enough," she said. "You are resting, whether you wish to or not, Eder."

"Fair enough," he said, leaning more heavily against her. "I suspect I could not resist you if I tried, and I will spare myself the indignity of being carried."

•

Built against the farthest center edge of the Privileged Heights was Eder's home. An iron fence surrounded it on three sides, with the rear built against the platform's edge to overlook the yawning chasm. Its construction was still fairly humble for the Heights. It lacked the great pillars meant to replicate the older styles found in Racliffe, and though it was two stories tall, that second floor was small and cozy compared to the grand mansions with outer decks overhanging their apportionments.

Twin torches burned at the gate's entrance, which was watched by a lone soldier. He saluted them both and then unlocked the gate so they might pass. Another soldier waited inside, guarding a locked room. Aylah dismissed him, then guided Eder to the interior living room, set him on a padded couch, and then began the process of lighting the many candles throughout the home. Unnecessary, given their blessed eyes, but after decades spent in purest black, Aylah preferred the light of a flame.

"Ever my caretaker," Eder said, smiling at her as she offered him a cup of wine poured from a little cask kept in his pantry.

"Someone must," she said, and sat beside him. "Since you won't."

Eder sipped the wine, his gaze drifting off into nowhere.

"Thank you," he said softly. "It has been...hard, doing this on my own. I am glad that, come the culmination of my grand work, I will not be alone."

Aylah wished she could feel so confident. She sipped from her own cup, unsurprised by its strong, bitter taste. Eder was never one to indulge himself in sweetness. It would take far too much to intoxicate her, but she enjoyed the warmth the wine spread within her belly.

"You hold such faith in the voice you heard in the dark," she said, carefully broaching the subject that had been bothering her since her arrival with Isabelle. "And even more in the machinations of the tower, built by the Etemen long before we walked the lands of Kaus. But say they work. Say you succeed. What does that even mean, Eder? What will happen once you pierce the firmament?"

Eder slowly swished the wine in his cup.

"I do not know," he admitted. "But I cannot deny that we are lost to our creator. I heard it, not only in his words, but in his confusion. His desperation. We are a lost lamb, Aylah, and I will send our bleating cry to the shepherd. If he is truly our creator, our Father, then how could he not react with joy?"

He drank the last of the wine and set his cup down upon the little wooden table before him.

"As for what will happen? We will be free, my sister. Surely you sense it as well as I do. This entire world is *wrong*. Humanity's souls were never meant to live a multitude of lives. Neither were the fey, whose offspring devour their parents, or the dragons, whose souls reenter their own dormant eggs, quickening them. Even our own eternal rebirths are wearing on us, scraping our minds raw and clouding our pasts. Everywhere on Kaus are cycles without end, and after each cycle, we grow more tainted, more broken, and more impure."

He laughed, tired and mirthless.

"We are insects trapped in a jar of stars, Aylah. When the Tower Majestic roars to life, I will shatter the glass and set us free."

It was such a grand goal, one undeniably worth the blood and sacrifice, and yet Aylah could not shake the instinctual terror that flooded her chest at the thought of uniting with her creator. She glanced at the nearby door leading farther into the house, and her heart sank.

"Faron and Sariel will never forgive me for what I have done," she said. "I pray you are right, even as I fear what awaits us when you tear open the skies."

Eder pushed to his feet, and he gently patted her shoulder.

"They will understand, in time," he said. "Good night, Aylah. Sleep calls, and I have denied it for too long."

"Good night, Eder."

His bedroom was up the circular flight of stairs in the corner, and she watched him vanish. The cup of wine shook in her grasp, and she had to clench her teeth to summon the concentration to render it still.

"Will they understand?" she wondered aloud. "Or will your tower reveal only the failure of the Etemen, earning my brothers' condemnation forever?"

Aylah stood, retrieved a candle, and walked to the nearby door that had been guarded by the soldier during their absence. When she grabbed the doorknob, she hesitated. Since returning, she had spent her nights sleeping on that couch, refusing any finer accommodations. After a lifetime spent hanging in chains, those goose-feather cushions were more than adequate.

You don't have to do this, she told herself. She could return to that couch, curl into the blankets, and sleep away her guilt. Easy, cowardly thoughts.

Aylah pushed the door open and stepped inside.

In a room stripped of any shelves, bed, or decorations dwelt the captured queen, Isabelle Dior. Her mouth was gagged, and her hands and feet expertly bound behind her back. She dwelt in total darkness and squinted at the light of the candles that seeped from the open door.

"Hello, Isabelle."

Aylah set her candle down on a small bedside table that had been moved when she was creating the prison and then sat on her knees before it. She observed the bound woman in the candlelight. Isabelle returned that careful study with surprisingly fierce resolve. The days of imprisonment had not cowed her in the slightest. Even now, she tested the bonds.

"You're fierce, aren't you?" Aylah said, remembering when she had captured the woman in her tent. Even with surprise on her side, there had been the briefest moment, when golden light sparked from her eyes and crackled like lightning around her hands as she lurched from her bed, when Aylah had feared her efforts doomed. A solid blow to the temple had knocked Isabelle unconscious, preventing the release of her power. Power that she should not have.

"The mighty warrior queen of Doremy," Aylah continued. "You

probably thought yourself destined for greatness. But this world does not reward greatness. It murders it."

Isabelle's glare was cold enough to freeze the swiftest river. Aylah was briefly tempted to remove her gag. Memories of golden lightning banished the temptation. Her silence would have to be enough.

"I do not suppose you know who I am," Aylah said, shifting closer. "But we are bound to one another, connected by blood."

There was no hiding the connection. Isabelle's face strikingly resembled Aylah's, with the same jaw, the same high cheekbones, and the same broad nose. The only difference was in her hair and eyes. Whereas Aylah's were the stark black of her brethren, Isabelle's were the golden hue of stolen radiance, now tainted by humanity.

"My blood," she continued. "Stolen from me by the cruel masters of Castle Kanth. My siblings...we cannot bear or sire children. We have tried. But you...I suspect you were still in the womb when your parents partook of my blood. You were conceived by those already drunk with radiance, but then stolen away before the balance built within you at birth could be tipped askew. A rare child."

Aylah slid closer on the cold floor as Isabelle's eyes widened.

"*My* child," Aylah whispered. "If viewed in a certain way. You have inherited my beauty, my grace, and my command of the lesser."

There was no stopping the horrid guilt that stabbed her like a cruel assassin in the spine. No longer willing to hide from it, nor pretend it false, Aylah confessed to this captive stranger.

"When you were raised a bastard, I was held in chains," she said. "I could not be there to watch you grow. I could not be mother to you, the first child of my blood, for my imprisonment was the very reason for your blessing. But I wish, so much I wish, that I could have been. I would have told you of the gifts you possessed, of the power of radiance, and all the wonders you are capable of."

She dragged her fingernails across the stone hard enough for one to crack.

"I would have kept you from becoming a tool for my brothers' games," she seethed. "I would have slaughtered the vile royalty of Castle Kanth so you never needed to wage your war. I would have taught you, embraced you, loved you, and ensured a throne awaited you without claims of godhood to act as your crutch. By your own strength and grace, you would have ruled. Not as a puppet of Faron, or Sariel, or the goddess, Leliel. Your own strength. Your own might."

The possibilities of a different life flashed through Aylah's mind, aching and cruel. If only she had not been imprisoned. If only her brothers had found her sooner, before Isabelle had become a woman grown. She put her hands on the sides of Isabelle's face and let Isabelle see her tears.

"I would have given you all these things and more, but in the end, it doesn't matter. You aren't of my flesh. You aren't of my loins. Your radiance, it was not gifted. It was stolen. You are birthed of a crime. In that, you are blameless, but that changes not the truth of your being."

Aylah stood, and she felt her insides tremble and grow cold.

"You are not my daughter," she said. "I am sorry. You are not, no matter how much I wish it to be. Which means the choice is not a choice at all. You will die. Please, know you are not sacrificed out of hatred, nor in vain."

Aylah blew out the candle, blanketing them both in total darkness.

"I hold no faith of my own," she whispered, and wiped away her tears. "But I hold faith in my brother. It will be enough. It must. And against that hope, your death is but a single ripple amid an ocean."

Isabelle screamed something into her gag, but Aylah held no desire to hear it. She exited the room, shut the door, and pressed her back against it. More screams, angry, hurtful, and accusatory. Muffled as they were, they were enough to strike Aylah like wicked little barbs. She endured them as she must, and clung to the promised future for strength.

"A brand-new world," she whispered, and looked to the nearby window, but there were no stars to see, only a great, empty chasm of nothing.

Chapter 59

FARON

The army of Leliel's Protectorate marched upon the white walls of Racliffe, but Faron and Iris were not among them. The pair kept back, at the entrance to what appeared to be little more than a wide gopher hole near the end of the yellow fields. A trio of stones marked the slope, identifying it as Sariel's prepared escape tunnel.

A trumpet sounded, the signal that the assault would begin in roughly half an hour. The time was now, but Faron did not crawl into the hole yet. Instead he knelt beside Iris and set his hands upon her.

"Listen to me, and listen well," he told the coyote. "When you joined me, I promised to show you the world. I meant to travel with you as my companion. You were to visit wondrous falls, fields of flowers, and forests filled with game for you to hunt."

He pressed his forehead against her snout.

"Instead, I dragged you into our war. I brought you to the horrors of Frostlash Forest. Instead of beautiful fields, you trotted alongside a tide of humanity as we marched from battlefield to battlefield. It is a betrayal of my promise, and so I release you from it."

He leaned back and met Iris's eyes.

"Leave me, Iris. Live your life as would best make you happy. Where I go now, it is dangerous, and there is a good chance I will die. I would not have you die with me."

Faron did not know how she would respond, but he was caught off guard by her sudden snarl and baring of her teeth.

"Iris?" he asked, standing. The coyote leaped between him and the hole, her fur raised. Another snarl.

"Don't be foolish," he shouted at her. "This isn't your war! Go on, be free somewhere!"

She hunkered down further, her growl hurt and unending. Shocked by such a furious refusal, he closed his eyes and extended a hand. Little slivers of radiance shot out between them, piercing unseen into her mind. His thoughts mixed with hers for the first time since he designated her as his companion. Again he swam amid a sea of emotions and senses, but her months spent with him, and the blessing he imparted upon her, added words to the thoughts. They were rough and simple, but they struck Faron like arrows to the chest.

Not abandoning.

Not be abandoned.

Iris. Faron.

Together.

Faron opened his eyes, and his expression softened.

"Have it your way," he whispered. "We do this together."

Iris's aggression immediately eased, and her growling halted. He offered her his hand, and she licked it as a sign of peace.

"I do not deserve you," he said, and stroked the tawny fur along her face and neck. "Now, come. We have a queen to save."

Faron extended his arms as if diving into water and then slid into the hole. His sword was buckled securely to his side, but he left his shield behind, knowing it would snag during such a crawl. The fit was tight, and dug for a man slender like Sariel rather than someone as bulky as Faron and his armor. He had to wiggle and drag himself, relying on his strength to push through the dirt. After a dozen feet or so, it thankfully widened, and he need not exert himself quite so much.

"You back there, Iris?" he asked, pausing after a few minutes of crawling. In answer, he felt a gentle nip at his toes.

"Just checking."

Faron continued onward, sometimes more sliding than crawling when the tunnel shot downward for several feet. As he moved through the dark, he wondered how the assault against Racliffe would go. They had the numbers and all the proper siege machinery to both break open the gates and climb the walls. Still, he couldn't shake the feeling that Eder had put little effort into stopping the invasion. From talks with prisoners taken after battle, it seemed even Isabelle's minor loss at Twin Gates had been of General Sid's plotting, not Eder's.

Had they been baited into an attack on Racliffe? Or was Eder's focus solely upon whatever mysteries Calluna had alluded to within the Tower Majestic? He didn't know. All that truly mattered was that he managed to rescue Isabelle from his brother's clutches before he sacrificed her in his mad plan to awaken the tower.

After what felt like a miserably long time of crawling, the tunnel expanded higher and Faron could walk. He assumed this meant the exit neared. Sariel said it would emerge deep in the bowels of Underbridge, where the cliff met the collapsed portion of the tower. Faron had been to Racliffe rarely, and he did his best to remember the layout from his visits. There'd be stairs leading to Bridgetop all throughout Underbridge, slipping around the sides or up through what had once been windows. If he could reach the surface, he could find his way toward the tower with ease.

Whether he could make it through whatever guards were stationed there was another matter.

One last steep pitch downward, and Faron reached the end of the tunnel. Stones were stacked together before another hole, which he assumed was meant to hide the entrance. He began piling them aside until uncovering a gap large enough for him and Iris to slide through, and then they exited into Underbridge.

The hole was a good six feet above the very bottom of the collapsed portion of the tower. The smell hit him immediately. Generally in Underbridge, the farther you were from the surface, the poorer you were considered, and this seemed to be the absolute farthest one could be. From what he could tell, he was within a dilapidated building that might have been a storefront years ago. Broken shelves leaned unevenly throughout the space, and the cupboards on the walls were open and barren. It smelled of piss and shit, and from what mess he saw on the floor, he suspected the destitute used it at night for refuge.

Faron dropped to the ground, then turned for Iris to catch her. Instead the enormous coyote leaped down on her own and then glared at him.

"Right," he said, and laughed. "I forget how strong you've gotten." He turned to the building's exit. "To the surface, and the tower."

A familiar voice halted him halfway across the room.

"I'll take you there myself, Faron, but only if you surrender your sword."

Faron froze. Beside him, Iris growled.

"Happy to see you, Aylah. You left so quickly after your last visit."

His sister stepped around one of the broken shelves. There was no light that deep within Underbridge, and no torches to shine within the building, so it was with the starlight of his blessed sight that he looked upon her brilliant silver armor, molded and carved with an impression of wings across her chest. Her shield bore the five stars of the Astral Kingdom painted in black. Amethysts were encrusted on the hilt of her sword.

"You look nice," he said. "Gifts from Eder for your betrayal?"

"Don't be like this," Aylah said, standing between him and the door. She raised her shield and braced her legs. "You were a fool to come here."

Faron drew his sword and held it in both hands. Worry scratched at his mind, and he pushed it away. His armor might be inferior, and he lacked a shield, but he believed himself capable of holding his own against Aylah.

"And you think whatever madness Eder has planned is worth what you've done?" he asked, tightening his muscles for a thrust. "You need a mirror, Aylah, to see the true fool."

Her attack came first, an overhead chop aimed at his shoulder. Her shield was expertly placed, leaving no opening, and so he blocked the strike. Steel hit steel, lighting up the darkness with a shower of sparks.

Twice more their weapons collided, and then she bodied him with her shield. Faron dug his heels in, refusing to move, and with a defiant cry, he shoved her away.

Iris chose that moment to lunge, her teeth snapping for Aylah's leg. The coyote badly underestimated his sister's speed. Her sword lashed out, cutting across Iris's shoulder and flinging her away.

"Stop!" Faron shouted, as if Aylah would listen. He closed the distance between them, hacking and slashing to force his sister to go on the defensive instead of finishing off the coyote lying stunned and bleeding near her feet. The ringing of their weapons grew in his ears, the sparks an unwelcome burst of light to his blessed eyes. With every hit, his trepidation grew.

This was not the broken woman he had rescued from a lightless cell. This was the Crownbreaker who had united all of Kaus through her sheer might.

Faron used that fear to give him strength. He took the offensive, hammering into Aylah's shield, forcing her back. She stumbled over a broken plank of wood, lost her balance further from a bite from a revived Iris, and then faltered when Faron barreled into her. The pair smashed through one of the broken shelves, scattering wood as they rolled. He flailed to take advantage, but his sword struck her armor and failed to penetrate.

His own reward was a cut across his stomach, shallow but bleeding heavily. He came up to his knees, slashed for her leg, and had it blocked at the last possible moment by the tip of her sword. He retreated, the both of them springing to their feet. Faron grimaced against the pain from his cuts, and he wished more than anything he had a shield so he could better go toe to toe against his sister.

"You don't have to do this," he said as Iris crouched beside him, preparing for another lunge. "Eder suffered at Sariel's hands, but that does not mean we must bow to his madness."

"Madness is us allowing Kaus to fester and rot," Aylah said, standing firm before him. "We've walked these lands for countless lives. All our achievements are ephemeral, all our attempts at improvement doomed to fail. Humanity is vile, Faron. Their souls are rotten to the last, so if Eder has found a way to wash them clean? If the Tower Majestic can drag this spiraling world into becoming something better? Then let him try. That hope is far better than the dreaded complacency we face now."

Faron slowly circled his sister, desperately searching for any opening in her perfect defenses.

"What happened to you was a tragedy, Aylah, but I will not condemn all of humanity for the actions of a few."

Aylah lifted her sword.

"It was not a mere *few* who drank."

She dashed into him with quick, efficient strikes, slowly guiding the movement of his sword as he parried. He added strength to his hits, trying to bash her away or catch her off guard, but her footing was forever firm and her shield ready to block whatever retaliation he attempted.

"Whole families toasted their health to my blood," she shouted. Her sword slipped past his parry and nicked a cut across his forearm. He grimaced against the pain, kicked her away, his heel hitting her shield, and then immediately brought his sword back up to block an overhead chop.

"An entire city was ruined by my stolen radiance."

Her rage gave her strength that Faron struggled to match. Every slash of her sword was like a battering ram. He staggered, pushed back toward the wall. Iris recovered from her blow, and she lunged at Aylah, attempting surprise. Aylah reacted without ever acknowledging the coyote's return, her shield snapping sideways with brutal speed so that Iris slammed against it. Blood shot from her nose, and she whined as she went tumbling away.

"Iris!" Faron shouted, thrusting for Aylah's stomach. Her sword parried it, and then her shield snapped back in with blinding speed, the metal striking him across the chin. His head twisted hard, and he fought to maintain his balance.

"Years!" she screamed at him. "Years upon years, as their food, their pleasure, their goddess, and all they did was cut and drink, and drink, and drink!"

They collided, chest to chest, his sword locked out to the side, hers tucked underneath his armpit and her shield pinning his other arm to the wall. Her forehead pressed against his as he struggled to break free.

"I'm sorry, Faron, but I have seen humanity's true face."

Aylah sliced upward with her sword, cleaving through the bone and muscle of his arm. Faron screamed at the overwhelming pain. The limb dropped, his sword still clutched within its fingers. He shoved her away with his other arm, though he suspected she let him, believing the fight over. He put his heel upon the severed wrist, grabbed the sword with his lone hand, and wrenched it free.

"Still you fight?" she asked, watching him as he staggered unevenly. Blood poured down his side. "Do you even know why?"

Faron kept his weapon at the ready as he fought off dizziness from the loss of blood. Iris was nearby, still bleeding from the cut on her side and the hit to her nose. She was watching him, waiting for the right moment, and Faron swore to give it to her. He leaned back, his rear leg tense as if he was about to attack, and then spun in place. The hilt of his sword slammed the door, bashing it open.

"Run, Iris!" he shouted. "Hurry, be free, before…"

Aylah's fist struck the back of his head. His vision swam, and he staggered several steps before collapsing to his knees. His sword clattered to the hardstone.

"A sentimental fool to the last," Aylah said, boots clomping as she approached. "Never change, Faron."

The last thing he saw was Iris in the distance, sprinting through the cramped streets of Underbridge, before Aylah's boot crashed into his face and sent him into darkness.

Chapter 60

SARIEL

The trumpets blew, the signal for the assault to begin. Sariel could only hope that Faron had reached the Tower Majestic unnoticed. He suspected he would not know Isabelle's fate until his army marched victoriously upon the entrance of the tower.

His army, he'd thought, but that wasn't true. *Isabelle's* army, and officially led by the nervous man beside him.

"Will you stay with me to observe?" Marshal Oscar asked. He wore his military finest, his armor gleaming and his scalp freshly shaved. Ahead of them, two covered and reinforced battering rams rolled toward the closed gates. Far to their sides, massive siege towers rolled on thick wheels toward six different locations of the White City. Meanwhile nine catapults readied their stones to smash holes in the pristine walls.

"My place is where the fighting is at its thickest," Sariel said, shaking his head. "Do not fear for my safety, Marshal. I will not die here at the culmination of all our efforts."

"It's a rare man who chooses when and where he dies," Oscar said.

Sariel grinned at him. "And am I not the rarest sort of man?"

The marshal returned the grin.

"I suppose we shall discover that when the battle is done. Go as you believe best, Sariel Godsight, and I will command the troops in your absence."

Sariel bid him goodbye and then marched through the lines. They were expertly disciplined, even with the soldiers' obvious nerves. Sariel walked among them, letting them find courage in his presence. He stopped near the front, at a familiar little battle squadron.

"Will you be fine without him?" he asked the young man, Bart, who always seemed attached to Faron's hip.

"Don't got a choice, do I?" Bart asked, not needing an explanation of who "him" might be. They all sorely missed Faron, though Sariel could give them no explanation for his absence.

"Don't worry," Derek said, nudging Bart with his elbow. "I'll be strong enough for the both of us. You stick by me, and I'll get you clear and through."

Sariel smiled at them both before continuing to the front lines, which had halted just shy of potential arrow reach. Not that there were many arrows. It disturbed Sariel how perfunctory the defense of the city appeared. Surely his brother had known this invasion was coming for months, so why had he not prepared? Why hadn't armies met them on the pass through the Sapphire Mountains, or gathered eagerly behind the walls of the White City?

Perhaps he expected to lose. Perhaps, having seen the might of the Crownbreaker in ages past, he thought victory impossible. Still, that didn't sit right with Sariel. Eder would always seek a path to success. Which meant the city meant nothing to him. Then what did?

Let Eder sacrifice her! Let the tower awaken!

Sariel wished he could banish every word from his mind, but they would not leave. He glared at the Tower Majestic and wished he possessed the knowledge to break hardstone so they might tear the tower down and cast its broken pieces into the sea so it never plagued them again.

Catapults let loose their stones as the first battering ram reached the gate. Meanwhile, the siege towers struck the walls, their ladders latching on to the sides and the men inside pouring out to fight the defenders.

Sariel watched the blood flow, already knowing the outcome. Their numbers were too great, and Racliffe's too scattered and few. The fate of the city would not be decided here, but by whatever deviousness Eder planned within the Tower Majestic.

"And so dies the Astral Kingdom," Sariel whispered as the battering ram smashed open the entrance and the catapults opened huge chunks in the wall. The gates swayed loosely on their hinges, and through the broken gap between them, he saw defenders readying to hold the line.

This was it. Sariel lifted Redemption high above him as soldiers shifted, eager and nervous for the coming charge.

"This day, we end this war," Sariel shouted, radiance flooding his throat. All would hear him, no matter where they were upon the battle-field. "This day, the goddess shall have her victory."

No going back, he thought, taking that first step, then another. A walk became a run. A run became a sprint. His soldiers rushed with him, roaring a jubilant battle cry. Sariel kept the lead, his speed beyond human. No longer would he hide his true nature.

"This day, we save our queen!"

When this battle ended, he would need to travel west, with a new name and face to disguise his accomplishments. But until then? He would not hide his radiance. Let the people attribute it to Leliel, no differently than Faron had the healing of his wound. As for the form of that radiance?

Silver gleamed across the edge of Sariel's blade, mimicking the power Isabelle summoned in battle. He had never thought to use it in such a manner, but it called to him now as the gates opened and soldiers formed a line ten wide to battle the charge of the protectorate. Sariel focused his power into Redemption, imagining it building, sharpening, and prepar-ing for release.

"For the goddess!" he screamed.

Moments before crashing into the line, he swung. An arc of silver radiance slashed through the air. Armor bent. Shields crunched inward. Limbs fell, severed from those who did not protect themselves. The entire front line staggered, and then Sariel was among them, and the blood flowed.

Dragon bone was unbreakable, and with radiance shimmering across its edge, nothing could withstand its strike. He cut through Racliffe's soldiers, his every swing long and wide like a reaper harvesting a field. The defenders panicked, frightened by radiance and the way their shields broke in half at his cuts, and then the rest of Isabelle's army arrived.

Onward. Deeper. Sariel refused to let anyone else be the spear point. He twisted and turned as he moved, a macabre dancer among gore and corpses, his sword twirling to lop off limbs and open throats. A leap, and he pushed past the next line, finding himself in the middle of dozens of the Astral Kingdom's soldiers. Sword gripped in two hands, he spun in place, extending its length to its limit. Dozens fell, cleaved in half. The gore spilled across the street, accompanied by the screams of the men and women meant to fill the line in their place.

Sariel slashed the air, and a second flash of radiance crossed the space, decapitating one man and cleaving the arm and shoulder of the woman beside him. There would be no reinforcements. There would be no battle lines. Racliffe's defenders broke, retreating deeper into the city as Sariel's troops blew horns and shouted their victory. The walls were similarly overrun, the soldiers there finding stairs and ladders to climb down into the city to rejoin the main force.

Up ahead were the streets of the White City, eerily empty. People were hiding within their homes, praying they would be spared the horrors that befell a conquered city. Sariel gave them not a thought. He had but one goal, and it was within the Tower Majestic looming over Racliffe from above the sea.

Soldiers gathered around him, their eyes wide, and many were silent in their awe. Sariel shook the blood from his sword, and he stood tall over them, wishing he did not feel such pleasure in allowing his true glory to be known to humanity.

"If there is a defense, it will be along the lengths of Bridgetop," Sariel shouted to them. "We stay together, and we march upon it in full force. Our goal is the Tower Majestic, and the Luminary within. Do not spread out. Do not falter. The hour of victory is at hand, and by my blade and my might, I shall lead you to it."

Whispers spread among the soldiers. Names forming, titles given. Another chosen. Leliel's champion. Isabelle's savior. Sariel let them speak it. Tales would warp in time, his name shifted, his purpose forgotten. Only one thing mattered.

I'm coming, Isabelle, he thought as he stared at the tower in the distance. The mass of soldiers flowed through the streets of Racliffe, encountering little resistance. Slowly their number spread out, greedy men seeking to loot or force themselves upon women. They, too, knew the supposed spoils of a conqueror. Sariel pushed those with him onward, hoping haste would prevent any doubts or further splintering. This war was not yet won.

True to his expectations, the remaining soldiers of Racliffe gathered in the narrow passage across Bridgetop. They were stacked five wide and dozens deep. Slapdash barricades blocked the way, made up of anything the soldiers could find; crates, overturned carts, and chunks of wood nailed together to form crude X's.

Marshal Oscar should be the one leading, but Sariel had given up that pretense. This was his army, as it was always meant to be. Eder had crossed too many lines and dragged his family down with him. Sariel lifted Redemption and let its edge shine silver.

"Make way," he said, his voice thundering. It seemed the entire bridge quaked at his words. He slashed, cutting down the front line. The effort was taxing but worth the reward when fear spread in the defenders' eyes.

The ground rumbled before he could order the assault. Shouts from both armies spread as a low humming built in their ears. Sariel's eyes widened, and panic sliced through him as an otherworldly light shone from the top of the Tower Majestic as a tremendous beam racing toward the sky.

"Isabelle," Sariel whispered, as the tower, and all its ancient magics, surged to life.

Chapter 61

EDER

Eder slowly walked the winding circles of the runestones. Blood dripped from an open wound across the top of his arm, running down his fingers to drip into the little pail he held. Within the pail rattled the dagger that had made the cut. His other hand carried a brush, and with it he painted the last of the runes.

"The answer comes," he whispered to give himself strength. The last few days had drained him, but there could be no delay. Racliffe's walls were likely already breached, and soon his siblings' army would march for the tower.

"Eder," Aylah said, stirring him from his thoughts. "He's awake."

Eder stood, set aside the pail, dagger, and brush, and clutched the wound on his arm. A brief pulse of radiance sealed the cut and ended the flow of blood. That done, he turned about to address his sister.

"Good," he said. "I want him to be."

Faron lay on his side not far from the platform that gave access to the Final Ascent. Behind him, Aylah stood guard, her sword at the ready. Faron groaned as he sat up on his knees. The stub of his cut arm was black from where Aylah had burned it to stop the bleeding, and he clutched at it with his left arm. His fingers felt the burns, and after a moment, he lurched forward to vomit.

"Steady yourself," Eder said. "You need a clear head for when you witness this first miracle."

"We've already overthrown one mad king in the Tower Majestic," Faron said, and he spat. "Nothing miraculous about that."

Eder smiled, glad to see his brother's spirit remained intact.

"That is not how this day will end."

He approached the sacrificial bowl and the woman bound before it. Isabelle's wrists were tied behind her back with thick white rope, and her arms bound to her sides. Her ankles were also tied, ensuring she could not flee. She lay on her back, her mouth gagged. Beside her was a long, rectangular wooden box, still closed. Above her head loomed the grasping stone hands clutching the tower's catalyst.

"Even now, a fire burns within you," Eder said, kneeling beside the queen. He lovingly brushed his fingers across her cheek. "But I know the secret of your birth. You are radiance stolen, and it must be reclaimed. Consider this an honor, Isabelle. The failed world shall be broken and made anew, and your blood will be the key."

"Is that what you think will happen?" Faron asked. His stomach seemed under control at last, and on his knees he glared at Eder. "That somehow you will fix the world?"

"*I* will not fix the world," Eder said. "Have you learned nothing from all our failed attempts? My church labors just to cleanse the sins from a mere handful of chosen devouts. Sariel's kingdom used both blade and law to enforce a sinless life, and in return, the people rose up in hatred and resentment. The redemption of an entire world is beyond us, even we who are ever-living. But we need not bear this task alone."

He grabbed Isabelle and hoisted her to her feet, then bent her so she leaned her chest and head over the lip of the sacrificial bowl. Faron cried out, wordless and afraid, but the deed would not be done yet. Eder withdrew his beloved knife from its leather sheath. So many devouts sent to the heavens with this steel. If the stars were kind, this would be the last.

"Whatever this world is, it is wrong," Eder said, leaving Isabelle draped over the stone. He raised his knife and pointed it to the sky as he approached the center of the runestone formation. "A facsimile of celestial bodies. A doomed, spiraling loop of sin and death. We are children, flailing outside the sight of our parents, but Father is searching for us. I heard his words. I felt the desire in his heart. He is desperate to find us, to look upon us and return us to his arms."

Eder imagined the knife puncturing the blue sky above as if it were a canvas he could rip and tear away. What would lie beyond? What joy would he feel when he finally looked upon the face of their Father?

"I know you hate me, Faron," he said softly. "I know it will take time for you to forgive me. But I will endure it. All the slings. All the curses." He smiled at his beloved sister. "Aylah has accepted the need. Calluna, too, is willing to see the answer to this eternal mystery, for why else would she have revealed to me the key?"

He lowered the knife, and his chest felt light. One last kill. He must burden himself with just one last kill.

"Yours is a kind heart," he said, turning back to Faron. "It bleeds with love and aches with loss. But you need not say goodbye forever. Death will become meaningless for everyone, not just us. All souls will be rescued from this cycle of torment. In Father's gaze, we will be found and made free. Your grief is misguided, brother, and its pain ephemeral."

"You don't know this," Faron said. "You don't know *any* of this. You tell me only your dreams and hopes."

Eder closed his eyes and smiled.

"Perhaps," he said. "But is it not a beautiful dream?"

"Listen to him," Aylah said, adding her own voice to the plea. "Those few humans you find and love do not erase the horrors that their kingdoms inflict upon one another. They are a savage people, and their cruelty only grows with each life."

Faron rocked on his heels, his lone hand scraping its fingernails upon the hardstone.

"You of all people would know," he admitted. "But do not ask me to condemn them. Do not ask me to sacrifice those I love."

"You need not hold the knife yourself," Eder said. "Only watch with your eyes open and your mind clear."

His brother laughed faintly, the right side of his lips curling into a bitter smile.

"And what dream survives the opening of one's eyes?"

Faron sprang to his feet, slamming his weight into a surprised Aylah. She toppled, and while she did, he dashed for the pail Eder had left behind, snatching the bloodstained dagger within.

"Faron, stop!" Eder shouted, radiance burning brightly upon his hands as he prepared to defend himself. Except Faron did not attack. He rushed to Isabelle, grabbing her and pulling her away from the sacrificial bowl. She leaned against his chest, helpless within her bindings.

"Stubborn fool," Aylah said, holding her sword in both hands and slowly approaching. "What are you even hoping for?"

Eder gestured for her to keep back.

"Be reasonable, Faron," he said. "You cannot hope to beat the both of us with a meager dagger wielded in an untrained hand. You have no escape. You cannot stop what must be done."

"What must be done?" Faron asked. "Are you that determined to see this madness to its end?"

Eder stood tall. With every ounce of his conviction, he answered, hoping that it might be enough to reach through his brother's stubbornness.

"It is not madness," he said. "It is freedom, and yes, I am. We will pierce the heavens. We will look upon the face of Father and at long last hear his voice ring clear and true. And for that, Isabelle must die, her blessed blood the catalyst for the Tower Majestic's great awakening. That price *must* be paid, no matter how loudly you gnash your teeth and wail."

Faron clutched Isabelle tightly to his chest. His expression softened, and he almost looked ready to weep.

"Forgive me, Isabelle," he said, and looked down to the queen. "One day you will understand."

He flung Isabelle with all his might, sending her crashing into Aylah, who had to frantically toss her sword aside lest the queen be impaled. The pair tumbled, a tangle of limbs. Eder shouted, confused, uncertain, but the look in Faron's eyes, it frightened him. It was too sad. Too broken.

Too final.

"A price paid," Faron whispered, then placed his head above the clasped hands of the sacrificial bowl and sliced his throat open.

Eder's eyes spread wide, and he screamed out his shock and denial.

"*No!*"

This was far from the trickle Eder had used for his first attempt. A massive gush of blood poured into the bowl, splashing along its sides, and at the contact, the entire tower shuddered. The runes flared with brilliant silver light. Eder staggered forward, but there was no stopping this. The blood *ripped* out of Faron, draining him dry in seconds. The light left his eyes. He collapsed a corpse, withered and dry.

"Faron," Eder whispered, his voice choked with a sob. Not a spark of radiance remained within Faron's body. He was a husk. Empty. Barren. Never to resurrect. Never to return. The softhearted fool had taken Isabelle's place.

"Eder, you have to stop this," Aylah begged, shouting to be heard over the strange humming that grew ever louder from the runestones, whose glow had shifted to crimson. She pushed aside the bound Isabelle, who rolled to a halt in the center of the stone formation. "Make it stop!"

But there was no stopping it. The blood burned, the consumed radiance flaring with a light so bright Eder could not look upon it. He squinted and turned away as the humming reached its crescendo.

A beam of purest silver streaked to the heavens from within the bowl. Its speed was immense, its power unparalleled. It pulsed unending, crossing an unfathomable distance to strike the blue sky. As Eder had hoped, had dreamed, it pierced the firmament to reach the lands beyond.

The sky opened.

At first it was but a small black dot amid the blue, forming a black ring amid the silver beam that was so thin near the top it resembled a piece of thread. A heartbeat later, the black spread wide, a gaping, colorless hole thrice the size of the moon. Just looking upon it filled Eder's chest with warmth. His eyes watered, for though there was no color and no light, it made him squint as if he were staring into the sun.

On and on the silver beam flared, powered by the blood of his brother.

"Faron," Eder whispered as he wept. "If only you could see."

Colors emerged. A ring of red along the edges, curling like fire, followed by pulsing waves that stretched outward across the blue sky as a strange mixture of violet and gold. Within the center of the black appeared a white dot, and then it streaked down like a meteor. Eder had no time to react before it struck the center of the runestones, slamming directly into Isabelle's bound form.

The woman's body flailed with seizures, and she shrieked so loudly the gag did nothing to subdue her cry. Radiance swam across her, silver and gold, burning her skin before being absorbed within, somehow leaving her unconscious but alive.

Eder had no time to question it, no thoughts in his mind to spare.

A noise like thunder rolled unending from the radiant chasm burning the sky, and from within it swelled a second orb of light, swirling with all the colors. To Eder's blessed eyes, it was purest radiance, untainted, untouched by mortal hands, not even those of the ever-living. It grew and grew, a perfect orb. A tear, swelling within the dark abyss. A blazing fire, yearning to be unleashed.

And then it fell upon the city of Racliffe, and all was consumed in the glorious flames of creation itself.

Part Eight

MADNESS

Chapter 62

Bart stared mesmerized by the hole in the sky and the growing orb of wondrous light in its center. The shaking ground and screams of frightened soldiers could not tear his eyes away.

"Are you behind there?" he asked Leliel, wondering if perhaps this was the moment the goddess decided *enough with all the world* and brought them all to her heaven.

And then the orb fell, struck the Tower Majestic, and rolled outward in a sudden wave of fire.

"What?" he asked, stumbling backward. "What is that?"

Soldiers panicked all around him, retreating from Bridgetop. The Racliffe soldiers reacted no better, some rushing to die on protectorate blades, some freezing horrified in place, and most scrambling for the passageways down into Underbridge. Everywhere was chaos, and then piercing above it all was Sariel's thunderous voice.

"To me!" he roared, so loud it seemed the earth itself quaked. Bart's mouth dropped at the sight of Faron's brother standing with his arms raised and his sword stabbed into the ground. Silver light lashed about him like lightning, swirling into the palms of his hands.

The wave rolled closer, moving like a storm front, its height twice that of the highest spires within the city. Its surface crackled with silver lightning, and its sides, though rippling like fire, swirled with every manner of color. To even look upon it made Bart's stomach dance and loop.

Sariel clapped his hands together.

"We shall not burn!"

A dome of silvery light rolled outward from Sariel's chest, washing over the vast majority of the army. It shimmered like mist, and it was so beautiful, so wondrous, Bart felt compelled to tears. His mind was empty. His chest was tight with fear.

"What are you?" he wondered aloud as he stared at Sariel. The light continued to pour out of Sariel as his feet rose from the ground. His head arched backward, a scream of defiance on his lips as the rolling, ethereal flame struck the dome. It flowed across it, unable to penetrate. The flames continued, and Bart tilted his neck and watched it travel over and above him. He felt no heat from its passage, but what he did sense was an undeniable *wrongness* that made him shiver.

The wave continued, and the silver dome cracked.

"I can't," Sariel shouted, suddenly dropping to his knees. His back bent as if burdened by a terrible weight. "I can't. I can't. Faron!"

The dome shattered, and the last vestiges of the fire washed over Isabelle's army before continuing throughout Racliffe like an unstoppable tsunami. Bart's jaw dropped as the color touched him, so faint and yet so horrible as it peeled into his skin and set his entire mind alight. His bones ached. His joints locked. His eyes opened wide, and he saw things he could not explain, saw stars and swirling things and open teeth and a thousand moons turning and turning and upon them cities and oceans and life upon drops of water and then he was screaming, he was screaming, and screaming, and screaming.

The fire passed. A strange silence followed, everyone within too shocked and exhausted to make a noise. The first to scream were not the protectorate soldiers, but those upon the bridge.

Everything spun. Bart was barely able to stand, he was so dizzy, but he looked to the soldiers of the enemy and saw...

He saw...

They were no longer people. They were white and gold, feathered, multi-limbed, clawed, and drooling. They squawked and shrieked, and he felt like he was back in Frostlash Forest, lifting the jaw of a wolf to see the dead eyes of a human face staring back at him.

"No," he screamed, then turned and fled. He didn't know where he was going. He didn't care. He couldn't stay. He couldn't stay. The streets of Racliffe were foreign to him, and flooded with soldiers fleeing and people staggering out of their homes. Buildings grew long, walls that might have been painted white now composed of marble and silver. The ground cracked. Moss, vines, and flowers bloomed wild, in vivid colors and shapes Bart had never seen.

Trumpets from the protectorate army called for a retreat, but Bart was far enough away that he barely heard them. He fled past homes where, through windows, he saw people changing, heard the screams of those within who did not. Up ahead, a hand the size of a building rose from the stone, six-fingered and encased in gold, to block the path. Bart turned aside, cutting into a cramped alleyway that stank of feces. He raced to the end, flung his back against a wall, crouched, and then rocked in place.

"Her hand upon my heart when I am in pain," he prayed, his hands clenched and his eyes squeezed shut. "Her eyes upon my face when I am in doubt."

A pained shriek from the road, followed by a breaking sound, and then a meaty tearing. No more shrieks.

"Her words upon my mind when I am in need."

All around him, he heard stone groan and crack. He dared a glance up and immediately regretted it.

The wall opposite him was still a wall, and yet it had opened three eyes to gaze upon him. Their whites were bloodshot, and their irises solid gold. Bart's mind went blank. The remaining words of the prayer left him.

"Leliel, please, goddess, please," he whispered, paralyzed by his fear. What he'd give to be home in Clovelly, safe with his family. To have never joined Isabelle's army. To have never come to this forsaken city.

Hands rose from the ground, the stone moving like flesh. The street itself opened several mouths, exhaling hot air as they spoke in unison.

"Who?"

Bart closed his eyes and crouched into a tight ball as he wept.

"Please, goddess, save me, please save me, I don't want to die. I don't want to die. Please, I don't want to die."

More hands from the wall, grabbing him, holding him. He felt the heat of another exhalation, deep words rumbling across his body from a mouth shockingly close.

"What? Am? I?"

Hands dragged him. He screamed. The mouths opened, and their teeth were blunt, but strong, so strong, as they smashed the bones of his legs and then swallowed, dragging him deeper and deeper into their maws.

•

The call for retreat sounded from the trumpets, as if anyone needed the order. Marshal Oscar led the way, hollering for anyone and everyone to stay together.

"Bart?" Derek shouted, spinning, trying to find the young man. He'd promised Faron that he would keep an eye on him, protect him, but damn it, where had the kid run off to? The whole world felt wrong, too bright and too fast. Nightmare creatures writhed upon the Bridgetop crossing, and he dared not look at them.

"Bart!" he cried again, sprinting in the center of the chaotic mass of humanity fleeing west. "Damn it, where are you?"

His heart leaped. There, fleeing down the street, north instead of west. Derek almost let him go. He didn't have to do this. It was stupid to risk his life for the young man. The sane thing to do in a world suddenly insane was to flee with the rest of the army.

Derek drew his sword and ran after him. His chase was almost immediately halted by an elderly man blasting out of his home with such strength, the door broke off its hinges. Only it wasn't just an elderly man. A second person grew from the torso, bare-chested and young, and he flailed at Derek with wild abandon. Derek swung, cutting across the throat of the elderly portion, but it did nothing to halt the attack.

Arms beat his body, and he staggered under the blows while forcing himself to keep fighting. He thrust, burying his sword in the stomach of the younger half. Both heads screamed, blood gurgling from the cut throat of the older, and then the...thing...dropped to the ground.

Derek ripped his sword free and stared at the corpse.

"This..." he said, his eyes wide and his heart pounding. "This isn't happening."

Wailing to his left. A mother, cradling her daughter as she emerged from her home. Every bit of the mother's skin was a metallic gold. The daughter, a babe not even a year old, was fully encased in silver.

"She's not breathing," the gold woman shouted at him. *"She's not breathing!"*

Derek ran. Simple commands jumbled through his mind. Find Bart. Flee west. Exit Racliffe. And so he ran. More people emerging from homes, twisted beyond rational possibility. He ignored them. A man with bark for skin and vines for hands tried to grab him. Derek shoved his sword into his chest, piercing where he hoped a human heart remained.

"Bart!" he screamed, hoping against hope the young man might hear him. "I'm here!"

Nothing. It was hopeless. Derek bit down a curse, glanced over his shoulder, and saw far too many twisted things between him and the retreating army.

"Damn it all," he muttered, and searched for a different path. Perhaps if he cut across to the next street, he might find a way. That hope died the moment he emerged. A lion blocked the street, only its face was that of a human. Wings sprouted from its back and then folded inward. Instead of fur, it bore pure white scales that seemed to vibrate.

"Fuck off," Derek shouted at the thing and raised his sword. "I've no business with you."

The human face stared back. No emotion. Seemingly no thought at all. It made Derek's skin crawl.

"I said back!" he shouted, and then swung his sword. It cut the lion's side, and to his surprise, deep red blood flowed across the scales. He retreated another step, his stomach churning as he realized the scales were not scales at all. They were alive.

"Lost," the lion spoke. "Faithless."

Hundreds of leeches fell from the lion's sides. They squirmed and flowed in a river toward Derek, their white bodies shimmering like marble. The horror of it made him pause, unable to believe that such a mass flowing at him could be leeches, that they could be real, and then he turned to flee.

He made it only two steps before something struck his back. He stumbled, then felt heavy weights across his legs. Every step became a burden as pain flared throughout his body. He stumbled, and despite knowing nothing good would come of it, he glanced behind him.

The leeches. They could leap, and they did, flying onto him by the dozens. Their teeth sank into his armor and bit at his clothes, not all of them finding flesh, not yet, but their weight piled onto him, heavier and heavier. He rolled across the stone, trying to smash them underneath his armor. Many died, but not enough. Not enough.

They were on his neck. His face. He pulled at them, screaming, but they were on his hands now, sinking into his fingers, draining them of color, of life, until he couldn't move. Couldn't breathe.

Could only lie there as even more piled atop him, biting his face, his lips, and squirming through the creases of his armor to find the flesh underneath.

Above, the now skinny lion watched while licking its lips.

"Lost, and now found," it said, and bared teeth of gold.

•

Rowan trailed a half mile behind the army, in a group of surgeons preparing to set up tents in the heart of the city to treat the wounded. She had been tending to a man who had limped along, ignoring an arrow wound until the blood loss had him collapse, when the otherworldly fire approached. She dove atop the soldier as it passed, offering him what meager protection she could.

It isn't fire, she thought as her skin tingled and her mind went white. *But goddess help me, it burns.*

When it passed, the chilling silence lasted but a moment before the screams began. Rowan sat up, expecting to see burns, but instead men and women writhed, clutching themselves and flushing red as if suddenly afflicted with fevers. It was strange, for Rowan herself felt so cold, and so numb.

"Miss?" the wounded man said beneath her. She looked down and screamed despite herself.

He was not one man now, but three, each sprouting from the same waist. Their faces were different, as were their voices, as they twisted and flailed like newborn babes unable to control their limbs.

"Sara?" one of the faces, bearded and scarred, asked her.

"Merri?" one of the faces, young and handsome with long red hair, asked her.

Nothing, asked the third, the original face, for his eyes were wide, and he was screaming mindlessly.

Rowan fled. Her vows did not matter. Her duty did not matter. To her left was a woman with a scorpion tail sprouting from her back. To her right was a man whose hands had become claws and whose face resembled that of a white-feathered vulture. Deeper in the city, she saw the remainder of Isabelle's army retreating toward her, but she couldn't bring herself to wait.

Run. Run. Chase the fire.

It burned in a wave ahead of her, rolling without stopping. Buildings trembled at its passage. The colors swirled, shifted, never the same and yet always a perfect mix of seemingly every shade to have ever existed. The road vibrated beneath her feet, and suddenly it rose, a hill forming from nowhere, and it sent her tumbling to the bottom. She hit her head against a wall, and the pain was hard enough that she felt an urge to vomit.

Hold it together, she told herself. *On your feet, now!*

Her vision was like a boat on rocky waters, yet she pushed to a stand and moved. She didn't know where; she only saw a street and hurried down it. If she continued west, eventually she would find the outer wall, and then the gate, or perhaps one of the gaps broken by the catapults. *Keep moving. Keep fighting.*

"Please," a woman shouted, her upper half suddenly lunging out an open window. Her hand grabbed Rowan's wrist. Her eyes were wide. When she spoke, her tongue was forked. "Please, help me, I don't know what happened to my husband!"

Rowan saw a shape moving behind the woman, skin like ivory, face like a lion.

"Let me go!" Rowan shouted, and ripped her hand free.

"Wait!" the woman cried. Rowan ran, her hands held to her ears to block the sounds that followed. Screams, first of horror, then of pain. The rattle of a door. Then silence.

The street shifted, stone become pebble, pebble become dirt. Buildings turned to bronze. Somehow, she saw water running through them, and up ahead, an impossible stream. Little blue fish startled and fled as she splashed across. Rowan stumbled near the edge, the cool water flowing across her hands as she caught herself.

"Wait," she heard a guttural voice say, and looked to her left, farther upstream in this body of water that could not possibly flow through the accursed city. A man crawled toward her, naked but for a torn shred of cloth around his waist. His body was muscular, his skin somehow shifted to an unnatural shade akin to obsidian. Water glistened off him, and she realized his skin was not skin at all, but deep black scales.

His face was not a face. It was a gaping, open-mouthed creature of the sea, eyes wide and sightless. Little whiskers wiggled from the sides of his face as he forced out his speech.

"Please. Wait."

Rowan ran and ran, until the ground turned to grass, and the buildings groaned and stretched upward with their sides deep brown bark.

"This...this can't be real," she said, slowing to a walk. Ahead was a small clearing, and in the center, what appeared to have once been a well. A towering tree grew from its center, fifty feet high at least, its sprawling branches spreading out in all directions to cover the clearing with violet leaves. Figures gathered underneath, men, women, and children. At least, they were, once.

Their bodies were vine and bark, root and stem. They stood in place, locked in whatever poses they had been in when the strange fire washed over them. Rowan approached one, a woman, her mind too overwhelmed to feel fear. It was too strange. Too much.

"Are you...there?" she asked the woman. Her lower half was entirely bark, and her feet were sunken into the earth. Her skin was the light brown shade of exposed sapwood. Flowers had replaced her clothing. Green vines wrapped about her head for her hair. Through those vines, eyes like frozen amber stared back at her. They moved, ever so slightly.

Lips parted. Rowan saw teeth like thorns.

"Do you hear it?" the woman asked. Her voice was as soft as petals. "The song?"

Rowan retreated a step, a cloud lifting from her mind. Somehow, this was real. It *was* real, and horrible, and she was trapped.

"Do you hear it?" a man behind her asked. She spun. His hand stretched out, dripping with vines. She tried to flee, but her ankles would not move. Her legs felt numb. She looked down, saw vines wrapping about her shins and knees. Crimson thorns sank into her flesh deep enough to draw blood, and yet she felt them not at all.

"The song is light," two small children said in unison to her right. Vines rolled from their legs to crawl across the ground, joining the growing mass from all directions. They wrapped higher, higher, curling into her waist. Rowan twisted and flailed, but she could not move. All sensations were leaving her. The vines crawled, to her chest now, and then her arms.

The skin on her hands parted. Flowers sprouted from her fingertips. She opened her mouth to cry out, to plead for help, but then the vines slithered down her throat, choking her. Numbness took her lungs. Her eyes refused to close as more vines wrapped along her forehead.

"Do you hear it?" the people of wood and vine asked her.

Blood dribbled down her chin as the thorns tore deeper into her. More twisted up her nostrils and into her ears.

"Do you hear the song?"

The bones in her legs snapped. Her clothes, shredded by vines, fell away, and in her nakedness, she saw thick bark replace her flesh. The numbness began to fade, replaced by pain.

"Do you hear? Do you hear?"

It hurt. It hurt so much.

The vines ripped her jaw from her face. What should have been a rupture of blood was instead a wave of blue poppies falling like a blanket from her neck to cover her chest and waist.

"Isn't it beautiful?"

•

With Mitra remaining inside the Tower Majestic, Madeleine had taken it upon herself to encourage Racliffe's defenders, and so she was in the heart of their formation defending Bridgetop when the otherworldly fire was birthed from the opened sky.

"Do not fear!" she shouted to them as they cowered at its approach. She held her arms to her sides and her head high. This fire...this had to be the cleansing Mitra had always spoken of. This was the hope for all of Kaus, and she would meet it with her heart open and her soul brave. Eyes closed, she offered herself to Father.

Forgive my sins, so your will may be done.

Silence encompassed the world as the fire touched her. She gasped, and her eyes flitted open against her will. All traces of her prayer were banished as pain tore across her entire body. Her mouth opened to scream, but she could not manage even that. Her lungs would not draw breath.

And then it passed. She gasped and dropped to her knees. A bit of drool fell from her lips to the stone of Bridgetop. Her mind reeled. Her skin squirmed. Hot. It was so hot, and it itched. She scratched, but her vest was in the way, and so tight now, much too tight. She ripped at her clothes, tearing buttons, needing to get it off her.

As she cast aside her shirt, she saw the color of her skin was changed. It was white now, pure as new-fallen snow, and covered with the smallest and softest of feathers. Claws stretched from her fingertips, perfectly clear. Her stomach heaved, and then she screamed as the bones in her knees snapped and then reshaped, bent in the opposite direction. Her entire back ached, and she felt a tearing there that traveled all the way up and down her spine, the worst pain focused around her tailbone.

Soldiers screamed all around her, but she had no mind for them.

Her vision swam. She held her hands before her, and somehow she saw herself. She saw her hair, now fine gold thread, and she saw herself... looking at herself. The vertigo overwhelmed her, and she had to fight down an impulse to vomit. With her proper pair of eyes, she looked upon her arms and saw two new eyes opened just below the wrists, and they blinked back up at her.

The vertigo passed. What seemed impossible for her mind to accept became proper, and she lifted her hands higher, taking in the gorgeous smoothness of her skin, the glowing gold of her eyes, and most shocking, the wings sprouted from her back. They were like those of an albino bat, leathery and thin. With a thought, they fluttered, and the wind of them put a smile to her face. But that was not all.

A scorpion tail stretched from her lower back, its sides covered with blue veins, its flesh translucent. A gold stinger marked the top, and now that she was aware of it, she flexed the tail, curling and uncurling it with but a thought. Madeleine looked to herself, and the wonder she had become, and cast aside the last of her clothing. She would not hide Father's beauty from the world.

All around her, she saw the change overtaking Racliffe's defenders. Many fled down into Underbridge, but most were too overwhelmed to do anything other than lie there. Madeleine walked among them, offering her encouragement.

"This is the will of Father," she said, spreading her arms wide. "This is the purification of mankind."

Two lions awaited ahead, their faces those of the men they had once been. Seeing her, they bowed low and folded their wings. Between them, a third soldier fled, his eyes wide and his mind broken. He was seemingly unchanged, and he tried to run past Madeleine toward one of the entrances into Underbridge. Madeleine intercepted him with a flutter of her wings. Her hand closed about his throat, and it was so easy to lift him so that his feet dangled off the ground. His face turned red as he struggled to free himself from her grip.

"Do not despair," she told him. "Not all will be chosen in their lifetimes, but your soul is still promised to be his."

Her tail snapped past her shoulder. He gasped as the stinger sank deep into his chest. Madeleine quivered, feeling a strange pulse of pleasure as poison pumped through the stinger and into him. It was...sexual, in a manner she did not anticipate. The man's scream quickly ceased. His mouth locked open. His skin hardened, and she withdrew her stinger lest it be trapped within.

When she let him go, he dropped, his skin gold, his imperfections made beautiful in death.

"Gather our faithful," Madeleine told the lions as she looked past them to the fleeing protectorate army. Somehow they had endured the flame, but perhaps she should not be surprised an army dedicated to a false goddess would reject Father's gift. "We have a battle to fight."

"We are few," one of the lions said. "And they are many."

Madeleine turned to the Tower Majestic and the blazing hole in the sky. Its light washed over her like that of a second sun, and she lifted her arms in gratitude.

"We are the blessed," she said, closing her eyes and relishing the pleasure she felt. "And I have been anointed among you to lead."

Her tail curled excitedly. She turned back to the lions, spread her wings wide, and beckoned all the survivors to gather and become the army they were destined to be.

"Mitra shall soon come forth to survey the work of his hands," she told them. "And I shall ensure he sees victory. Come, my brethren; the cowards flee, and we, the purified, must give chase!"

•

Everything of the city was so much bigger than anything Iris had ever encountered before. It had taken too long to reach the surface of the strange, twisting place of wood underneath, but up above was little better. So many people. So many smells. Tracking anything or anyone was impossible, she felt so overwhelmed. She had heard the fighting, though, and recognized the sound of steel hitting steel. Thinking Faron's brother might be there, she rushed toward it, doing her best to ignore the angry or frightened shouts of the far, far too many people.

And then the fire came. It washed over her, and she had no warning, no way to hide or flee before she was yelping and dashing through an open door in a frantic bid for safety. Her limbs trembled, and within, she heard a human child screeching. Iris panted, and then she yelped as a horrible pain burst sudden and fierce across her shoulder. Her entire right half suddenly went numb, and she staggered unevenly.

Her vision pitched, and she found it hard to stand. Not far away, the child continued crying, the sound deeply unpleasant. There, in a little crib by a window. The human mother lay on the floor, not attending the child. Unable to attend it. Her body was marble. Her hands were still lifted to the air. No scent came from her. No sound of a heartbeat.

Hunger pierced Iris's stomach, but at last she could stand. She shook her head as if just emerging from a stream, and then bared her teeth. To her right, another coyote. A...second coyote, but it couldn't be. The head sprouted from her own body, sharing, no, *stealing* the right half of her body from her control. Its fur was a stark white compared to her gray, and its eyes a bloody red. Iris also felt taller now, and stronger. As for why she struggled to stand, she realized she bore six legs, not four, a third set sprouting directly underneath her stomach.

Her hunger spiked. The second head drooled, its gaze locked on the crib. The unwanted thing's thoughts intruded on her own.

Feast. Savor. Be full.

Her paws stepped toward the crib, but Iris fought against it. The left half dug her claws into the floor, pushing back. The other coyote snapped at her, teeth nipping across her lip.

Proper. We hunt the weak. We eat.

The child was crying louder, and Iris hated the noise, hated it so much, she wanted to leave. Not eat. Leave, and find Sariel. Faron was hurt. Faron was in trouble. Someone had to help him.

No, she thought. Not the word, but the entire concept of it, a revulsion of everything this unwanted head sought.

No? it questioned, once more nipping at her snout.

Iris pushed with all the strength in her three legs, slamming herself against the side of a table. The wood broke, and she rolled across the pieces. When righted, she bit at the other coyote, surprise and savagery her two best weapons. This thing must be put down. It must be killed. It twisted and snapped at her, but her teeth found purchase first. Her jaw locked tight.

A tear. A pull. Blood on her tongue.

Iris released her grip, and the other head dropped limp, blood pouring from its opened throat. Immediately she felt light-headed, but at least control over her limbs was mostly returned to her. She sniffed at the crib, and she felt a desire to help, but how? What could she do?

Iris turned away. To the door. To Sariel. To anyone who might help. She could not run, and so she limped, the slain head hanging like a broken limb, its black tongue dragging along the ground.

The street frightened her, but Iris traversed it nonetheless. A scent was on the wind, and she followed it as best she could. To the bridge. To the tower. To wherever Sariel lived, and fought, in a city too great, in a place lost to madness.

Chapter 63

SARIEL

After his silver shield broke and the last of the radiant fire washed across the protectorate forces, Sariel fled.

The army he commanded shouted confused orders, and all the world was breaking, and yet Sariel hid.

A multistory home was near the entrance to Bridgetop, and within its second floor, inside a cramped little closet, Sariel cowered, Redemption cradled against his chest.

"Isabelle," he whispered as his skin burned. His body was weak and his muscles sluggish, but it was nothing compared to the sensations striking through him. That fire...it was radiance. Pure, untainted radiance, of a scale he had never experienced in all his lifetimes. If he and his siblings were stars, then he had bathed within the heart of the sun.

In the dark, he looked to his shaking hand. His exposed skin bubbled and broke. Underneath, he saw shades of gold, then feathers, and then stone. Creation magic sought to remake him, change him, without focus, without reason. He felt memories of the past try to tear free and become tangible. Other times, he felt a desire to become something new, beautiful and monstrous. Each time, he forced the crackling waves of radiance away, reminding himself of who he was.

I am Sariel, ever-living child of Kaus. I am no creature, no beast, no monster.

It was a confession he might have once denied, or made begrudgingly, but now he clung to it with all his heart.

I am HUMAN.

At last the sensations passed, and he felt himself again. He slumped against the wall and worked to control his breathing. All the while, his mind raced, seeking answers for things he could not begin to comprehend.

"What did you do, Eder?" he whispered, and then felt a pang in his chest.

For it to work, it takes a sacrifice. Someone whose blood is blessed with radiance.

"You killed her. How could you? And for what? For this?"

He could hear the screams outside, and he did not wish to imagine the changes being wrought upon the populace of Racliffe. If creation's fire had threatened to unmake him, what hope had others unaccustomed to its gift?

At last, he could hide no longer. He stood and opened the closet door.

A man and woman lay dead on the floor, slain by his hand. They'd been writhing together when he entered, their mouths open and locked in pain. The change had overtaken their corpses even after death. They were both composed of bark, their legs merged like tangled roots, their upper halves pale wood and coated with vines and flowers. Sap leaked from where he'd cut their throats.

"I can't," he muttered, turning away. "I can't."

The floor was soft beneath him, the wood turning to black earth. Grass was sprouting from the walls. At a window rimmed with vines, he looked out upon Bridgetop. An army of nameless swarming things marched out from it, led by a woman with beautiful gold hair and a curling scorpion tail. Sariel watched them go, and he hoped that whoever commanded the remnants of the protectorate army was quick enough to get the soldiers out of Racliffe while there was still a chance at survival.

When the monstrous army had passed, Sariel climbed out the window, dropped to the street, and crossed the narrow path through Bridgetop.

It was remarkably empty, with most everyone having fled beneath. The noises coming from below were enough to chill Sariel's spine. But it was not all empty. Two pained voices cried out from an open window to steal his attention.

Within writhed both one man and three, for protruding from his waist were two additional bodies. They flailed about like newborns, crying out wordlessly and wrestling for control of the shared flesh of their legs. Sariel stared at them in horror, realizing what he looked upon.

The past lives. The two additional bodies were the man's past lives, split from his soul and remade in the flesh.

A scaled lioness burst from the next house, its face that of a human woman. She turned, saw Sariel, and lunged at him, her eyes wild and unthinking. Pure, frightened instinct. Sariel sidestepped the attack and slashed with his sword, opening the beastly body from chest to crotch. The lioness collapsed, but the threat was not yet past.

The scales crawled from the corpse. No, not scales, but white leeches, fat, living marble with teeth. Sariel clenched a fist and summoned his fire.

"Begone from me," he said, and lashed the street with blue flame. It roared with power, and the leeches curled and writhed in their deaths. Sariel watched, unable to deny what he felt. His mastery of radiance was growing, and why wouldn't it? Radiance permeated the very air.

Sariel pushed onward. Nothing would stop him from reaching the Tower Majestic. Halfway across the bridge, the buildings turned silver, and from within crawled a six-legged man, his face that of a spider, his arms gold, and his many legs shining bronze. Sariel buried his sword in the thing's head.

A pair of six-winged women assaulted him next, beautiful and naked, their heads become horses, one white, one black. Soft white hair covered their bodies, and their legs were now bent backward like the legs of beasts. Their voices, though, were still distinctly human as they plunged from the air, and they shrieked mindless, frightened cries as they kicked and clawed and sought to tear him apart.

Sariel cut one in half the moment she was near. From the other he endured a brutal kick to his side, the bruise an acceptable trade-off to drive his sword straight through her chest and out her back. A pull, and he slammed her to the ground to lie forever still. Sariel rubbed the injury, hoping against hope no bones were broken.

More creatures assaulted him as he crossed. More creatures died. Bark and scales and fur parted to Redemption's dragon-bone blade. His mind grew numb to the changes. The horrors were beyond comprehension. All that mattered was reaching the Tower Majestic, and at last, he stood before its gaping maw.

Waiting alone before the entrance stood Aylah, resplendent in her silver platemail.

"I pray this is everything you wanted," Sariel shouted as he approached. "All this slaughter, this madness, because you couldn't forgive."

Aylah drew her sword and held it limply at her side. Something about her stance worried him. She wouldn't meet his gaze. Where was her defiance?

"Sariel..."

"No," he said, readying his sword. "You don't get to feel guilty now, dear sister. You don't get to plead for forgiveness. Isabelle is dead because of you, and now we live through the horrors of your decision."

"Isabelle isn't dead!"

Sariel froze. "But Calluna said..."

At last, Aylah met his gaze. Her eyes were red, and wet with tears.

"It wasn't Isabelle," she said. "Faron...Faron gave himself in her place. He's dead, Sariel. Our brother is forever dead."

It felt like Sariel's feet were melded to the hardstone. The world darkened, and his every breath was a struggle. Words tumbled around in his mind, leaving him unable to give voice to his broken thoughts.

"No," he said, the only thing he could say.

"It is true," she insisted. "So just...leave, Sariel. Leave us, and let this end as it must. To stop it now would render his sacrifice in vain. I won't do it, and I won't let you do it, either. Eder's dream is now our only hope of ever seeing our brother again."

At last, Sariel felt himself freed. He imagined the raging fire of radiance sweeping across all of Kaus, of civilizations twisted by creation, and the world ripped asunder and left incomprehensible. It was a fate he would wish upon no one, not even the worst of humanity.

"No," he repeated, and lifted Redemption. "I'm ending this, Aylah. Make way."

"Must you fight?" she asked, readying her shield. "Have you not committed enough sins upon Eder?"

"This is no sin."

He crossed the space between them, his thrust aimed directly for her forehead. She sidestepped as he expected, and he angled his sword during the descent, seeking to cut her at the knees. Her sword batted it aside, the skilled woman also predicting the deviation.

The moment their weapons touched, it seemed something broke between them, and the battle began in earnest. He took the offensive, lashing back and forth with his dragon-bone blade, relying on its sheer length to attack without fear of retaliation. Redemption carved grooves across her shield, and with every hit on her blade, a bit of metal nicked from the fine edge. His desperation increased, for he knew his sister's prowess in battle. Overwhelming strength and rage were his only advantages, for if he relied purely on skill, victory would be hers.

Yet for all his efforts, he could not break her defenses. Sweat poured down his neck as he thrust for her abdomen. His blade struck the center of her shield, scraped across, and then she was upon him, finally closing the distance. He twisted to avoid her counterthrust, then cried out as her shield smashed his elbow. He swept his sword sideways, attempting to force her back, or cut through her waist if she refused to block, but she did neither. Aylah smacked the blade with her forearm, relying on the fine metal of her platemail to absorb the impact.

Redemption cut through it, but the injury was shallow, a bit of blood along her forearm. It was nothing compared to the gash she opened across his side with her sword. Only his sheer speed kept him from being impaled.

Fully on the defensive, he retreated, trying to regain the separation required to fully utilize Redemption's reach. Aylah refused to give it to him. Her every step was coupled with a quick slash or jab, sometimes even a strike with her shield, so that the frantic waving of his sword was but an inconvenience to her. Once again he was reminded of the decade she had practiced with Eder. His skill surpassed any pinnacle humanity might achieve, but against his siblings, Sariel felt slow and incompetent.

Another cut, this across his abdomen. Sariel punched her in the face with his free hand, then kicked her to knock her away. Finally given a moment to breathe, he lifted his sword, its tip aimed for her throat.

"It's not too late," he said, as if he were the one winning the fight. "Come with me. Help me stop the tower and save us from Eder's folly."

Aylah spat a bit of blood from where his punch had split her lip.

"You were always the greatest fool among us, weren't you, Sariel? Look around you. There is no going back from this. The sky is torn. The world is judged. You only risk damning yourself."

Sariel's grip tightened. Radiance swelled across Redemption's edge.

"Then let me be damned. I am not leaving without Isabelle."

He lashed out, a silver blade arcing through the air. Aylah lifted her shield to block, and she cried out in pain as it crumpled inward from the hit. The impact staggered her, and he followed up with a second slash aimed at her neck. Another blade of silver.

"*No!*"

Brilliant light exploded from Aylah, encasing her armor and shining across her skin. His attack dissolved into nothing. His sister charged him, her movements bewildering with their speed. Her shield struck his forehead. The hilt of her sword punched his chest, then his stomach. Nothing lethal. She did not want him dead, though she could have.

"Do you not feel it?" she asked as he staggered, barely able to hold his weapon as two more punches stole the breath from his lungs. "It fills the air. It sweeps the land. Whatever we are, whatever we are meant to be, originates from beyond that pierced sky. How can this not be right? How can this not be our truth?"

Her fist struck his mouth, denying him an answer. He dropped to one knee, and before he could move, her sword tucked underneath his chin. She pulled his gaze upward, forcing him to look upon her as she held his life within her grasp.

"Eder's wisdom must prevail," she said. "Will you live to see it, or must you die, and discover the world we have made when you reawaken?"

Sariel stared at his sister. Her eyes were blazing silver lights barely touched by the darkness around the irises. Radiance swirled about her skin, sparkling like cold lightning. She was wondrous. She was beautiful. And she was wrong.

"There is no wisdom here," he whispered. "Only suffering."

The tip of her sword pierced the tender flesh of his throat, just enough to draw a drop of blood.

"Damn it, Sariel," she whispered back. "I never wanted this."

Her arms tensed. Her eyes narrowed. Sariel held his breath, waiting for the killing sting.

A gray-and-white monster slammed into Aylah, six-legged and twin-headed. Aylah cried out, stumbling off balance as the creature, a coyote, clenched her teeth about Aylah's face and held on with a feral grip. She dropped her shield so she might grab the coyote by the throat. With a wordless cry, Aylah flung the creature aside, blood flowing across them both.

Sariel stabbed Redemption through her biceps, severing the muscles. As she screamed, he ripped his sword free, looped it about, and then sliced through the armpit of her shield arm, separating tendons and muscles there, too. She staggered away, her beautiful face marred and her arms hanging limp at her sides, unable to hold her weapons. She had no words for him, just anger and frustration.

"Leave us," Sariel said, readying Redemption for one last cut. "Or you die here in the shadow of the tower."

Aylah retreated a step toward Bridgetop.

"Nothing good awaits you within," she said.

"I enter nonetheless."

His sister shook her head and then fled across the broken piece of hardstone.

Once he was sure Aylah was gone, Sariel turned to his unlikely savior. The coyote wobbled unevenly. The fur standing on her neck and back flattened, and she dropped to the ground. Sariel knelt before her, and he gently stroked the top of her true head.

"Thank you, Iris," he said. "I owe you this life."

Her tail wagged. Her yellow eyes watered. She whimpered softly, her every breath appearing labored. He gently petted her, his bruised and bloodied hands stroking the gray portions of her fur, giving her the affection she deserved. It gave him time to pause. It allowed him to delay confirming his greatest fears.

At last, Sariel turned his attention to the head hanging limp from her neck. Blood soaked its throat, and its tongue lolled about from its open mouth. Sariel's stomach sank at the sight, and it took him a moment before he could speak.

"You're so strong, I know you're strong," he told the coyote. "But it's killing you."

Iris struggled to stand on her six legs, but they shook beneath her, and she abandoned the attempt halfway. Instead she rested her healthy head on his lap and stared up at him. Sariel's throat hitched.

"Does it hurt?" he asked her.

She whined.

He closed his eyes, gathered himself.

"I can end it, if you wish."

When he opened them, she was still on his lap, but her own eyes had closed, and her muscles relaxed. She whimpered with each breath, but the sound was quiet, suppressed.

Sariel lifted Redemption, having to hold it by the flat edge, for it was too long, and she, too close. The tip pressed to the base of her neck, just between two vertebrae. He held it there, not even deep enough to draw a drop of blood.

But how to sink that blade farther? He stared down at Iris, hating himself, hating Kaus, hating every single second of this horrid nightmare world. Faron was gone. Before him was the last true remnant of his brother, a creature gifted by his radiance. To kill Iris was to kill what remained of Faron. To say goodbye to both. To have that blood stain his sword.

Her whining increased, and she shuddered in his lap.

Sariel pushed the sword.

The vertebrae separated; her body jolted and then lay still.

Her head, in his lap.

Sariel's hand slipped from the blade. The light left Iris's eyes, as did the radiance, passing away unseen. Sariel's teeth clenched, and he buried his face in her fur, wetting it with his tears. His lips trembled. His jaw ached from the strain. It wasn't enough. He could not contain it. Nothing could.

He arched back and screamed to the sky, a wordless, broken, primal cry that tore from him unending, until all breath was gone from his lungs, and still he screamed and screamed.

Chapter 64

SARIEL

At last there was nothing left within Sariel to scream, and he gently lifted Iris's body off him. That he had no time to give her a proper burial infuriated him further. He pulled Redemption free and shook the blood from the dragon-bone tip. The weapon gave comfort, where none else could be found.

Sariel turned, all the world flat and gray in his mind. Only the Tower Majestic burned within it, aflame with radiance and ruled by a mad king at its highest peak. The cavernous entrance loomed, an open mouth from which shrieked and squawked the twisted populace born of a staggering curse of radiance. He lifted his sword. He hardened his heart. There was no room for weakness. No forgiving the unforgivable. A brother, forever lost. The debt must be repaid. High above, the thin silver beam continued to pierce the heavens. The hole in the sky writhed with fire.

"Eder," Sariel said, the name a curse upon his tongue.

No soldiers remained to guard the tower. Sariel did not wish to imagine what the radiance had done to those within, but that initial floor was blessedly empty. Up above he heard a chaotic mix of pain and fear, but let the people squabble and devour each other, for they did not matter to him.

There were many lifts at the edges of the hardstone, and Sariel knew them all. He approached one in particular, wrapped his arm around the rope on one side, and then swung his sword to cut the other free. The balance ruined, the rope shot him upward, carrying through the great empty expanse in the heart of the Tower Majestic. As he rose, he looked upon homes that had once been simple wooden structures and saw them made of jade, bronze, silver, stone, and sapphire. Denizens within them slaughtered one another, tearing apart flesh with clawed hands or biting with teeth now jagged and strong.

And then it was all below him. He passed through the gap into the rafters and then swung his legs while letting go to land on the enormous platform. To no surprise, the liftmasters had abandoned the level, if they had even been allowed to remain while Eder performed his monstrous ritual above. Sariel crossed the space to the only lift that continued higher, and he did not attempt to raise it on his own. Instead he grabbed the side rope, climbed high enough to reach the floor, and then hoisted himself up to the Final Ascent.

Eder stood on the far end, beside the bowl blazing with radiance stolen from his slain brother. Nearby lay the corpse of—

No, don't look at it, don't think on it, not now.

Dozens of runestones shimmered around them, glowing with crimson light. The sight of them put a thorn in Sariel's aching mind. Within their center, lying perfectly still, was the body of Isabelle Dior.

"Isabelle!" he shouted, and rushed to her side. His hands cupped her head, and to his relief, he saw her eyes flutter. Not awake, but alive.

"I'm glad you're here," Eder said. His gaze was locked on the hole in the sky. His arms stretched out, his palms tilted upward. "No one should witness this alone."

"Halt this foul magic," Sariel said. He glared at the sacrificial bowl, which even now burned away all that had once been Faron. "Stop it, while there's still a world to save."

Eder slowly turned. His skin was paler than usual, and dark circles ringed his eyes.

"Stop it?" he asked. "Why? Do you not feel it? How beautiful it is to be seen?"

Sariel gently lowered Isabelle back to the floor and stood, Redemption at the ready.

"Faron is dead because of you."

Eder shook his head.

"You see only what is before you," he said, approaching a long wooden box lying beside the altar. "But Faron is not lost forever. He has merely gone to the death we all should be given when our lives end. Once Kaus is made pure, we shall join him and be together in Father's paradise."

"Pure?" Sariel snarled. "Paradise? Do you not see the monsters all around us?"

Eder removed the lid to the box. Within was filled with purple velvet, and he dipped his fingers into the cloth.

"Monsters?" he asked as he withdrew Atonement, the velvet smoothly sliding off its immaculately sharp edge. "No, brother. I see no monsters. I see change, and the burning light of creation."

Sariel stared at the sword and felt himself falling hundreds of years into the past. Not since their fated duel had they crossed blades. He'd not even looked upon Atonement since the shattering. Seeing it threatened to drown him in guilt, and he denied that guilt with his fury. Redemption rose, and he braced his legs for the attack to come.

"Destroy it," he said, and nodded toward the bowl. "Or I will."

Eder placed himself in the way, Atonement held in both hands.

"There is no stopping this," he said. "Let it end, Sariel. Let it all end, so we may become something new."

Sariel dashed toward him, his sword swinging. Eder blocked, barely needing to move his arms. As the dragon-bone weapons connected, it felt like a fire ignited within them, calm words and stances exploding into a frenetic back-and-forth clash. The long reach of their weapons allowed them to dance as they circled each other, testing each other's defenses. A slash here, aiming for a leg. Another for the throat. Sariel kept light on his feet, and he struck at Eder as if trying to batter down a wall. Every swing, blocked to perfection. Every thrust, easily parried.

Anger pushed Sariel harder. He leaped closer, sword up in an overhead slam. Eder blocked, his legs braced and arms up. Sariel struck again, and again, forcing his brother to deepen his stance. On the third, he feinted a hit and then leaped to the side, Redemption angling around for a slice at his brother's waist. Eder twisted, reading it perfectly, the edge of his blade shifting positions and then deflecting Sariel's swing harmlessly above his head.

And now Sariel was out of position. Eder closed the space between them with blinding speed, Atonement's hilt cracking into Sariel's ribs. He cried out, swung a punch with his off hand, and missed. Eder twisted, his shoulder slamming Sariel to gain separation, and then came the killing slash, with power and sharpness to cleave Sariel in half. With strength born of desperation, Sariel managed to pull his sword in the way just in time, but it was weak, and his weapon was easily shoved backward. It robbed the attack of momentum, though, so when it hit Sariel's side it only cut through his coat and opened a thin slash across his skin.

Sariel batted it aside again, this time harder, and then retreated a step. His sword rose, its tip hovering in the air mere inches from Eder, whose stance mirrored his own. Sariel's heart hammered in his chest. Sweat dripped from his brow. He felt so exhausted by the day, and his wounds from his fight against Aylah ached with fresh pain. His only hope was that Eder appeared to have fared little better. Their bodies were both pushed to their limits, but then again, there was more to them than their bodies.

Radiance permeated the air to a sickening degree, but it need not solely be a curse.

"Stop debasing yourself," Eder said as he calmly parried a series of thrusts. "This time, I will not turn my back to your blade. Cowardice and dishonor were your only path to victory, and they shall not work here."

Sariel heightened his aggression, needing his brother's attention preoccupied. Their swords slammed through the air, colliding with such loud cracks they were like boulders crashing together on their way down a mountain.

"Do you think I have not improved?" he asked, drawing closer with every swing. "Do you think I have wasted my exile?"

The air was so thick, it felt difficult to breathe, but Sariel pushed onward. He was tiring, and Eder knew that, too. His brother kept defensive, waiting for Sariel to make a mistake. It'd work, too, if Sariel's tactics remained unchanged. His next thrust was too shallow, and Eder risked a counter. Sariel twisted away from it, his long hair flailing behind him. Eder's edge sliced a significant portion of it, and it fell to the hardstone.

Sariel came out of the turn swinging, the low edges of their swords colliding, and he pressed closer, strength against strength, weapons rattling, their faces so near. Stars burned within their eyes, and shadow swept away the whites. They clenched their teeth, the effort taking their all as their weapons locked together.

A thousand steps had led them across this journey to this moment, but in Sariel's mind, the rise of the Astral Kingdom and the Church of Stars began in a small cave in the far west. It began with fire, and it would end in fire. Blue flame flicked across his knuckles as he pushed, testing his brother, demanding he use all his strength to keep that dragon-bone blade from cutting him in twain.

"Don't do this," Eder said, pretending to wield greater strength than he possessed. "Stay with me, so we may witness rebirth together."

A shift of Sariel's feet. Closer now, their faces nearly touching, Redemption and Atonement vibrating between them. Sariel stared into those eyes, and for the first time in all their long, long lives together, he saw madness. His brother was gone.

Sariel relented in his effort, his entire body sliding sideways to avoid being split down the middle by Eder's blade, and then he reached out. He drew radiance, not only from himself, but from the air, the tower, and, yes, even the damned hole in the sky. So many forms, but he demanded fire. Blue flame burst from his palm, an eruption of power far beyond anything he had ever formed in his life. It blasted across Eder, charring his clothing and blackening his skin. His brother cried out, but not in pain. In fury.

The air rippled as an explosion of silver light rolled outward from Eder's chest, banishing the fire. Another shock wave, tossing Sariel aside as if he were a child's doll. Eder rose into the air, hovering several feet above the hardstone, as his burned skin glowed. He was majestic in his beauty, his hair fluttering on a mystery wind as he drew radiance into his body.

"You would turn our gift against me?" he seethed. "You would defile the divinity we wield? Then let it purify you in turn."

Eder lifted his hands above his head, and fire swelled within his grasp. It shimmered a dark violet, gathering in power, and to Sariel's blessed eyes, it was blinding in its brightness. He dropped to one knee, his sword held close. He felt lightheaded, and the effort of the fire left him drained. One chance, he saw only one chance, for Sariel would not be the only one blinded by that overwhelming light.

The fire flew, an orb of intense heat and power, with enough radiance within it to send buildings crumbling. It crackled and burned, a newly formed sun. Sariel slashed his sword, all his remaining strength pooled into a silvery echo that struck the orb at its midpoint between them. The fire detonated, awesome in its power, a swirl of colors that consumed the air and knocked Sariel to the floor.

The slash continued onward, unseen amid the burning glory. It struck Eder across the chest, cleanly slicing through his robe. It lacked the power to cut through him completely, but it severed flesh and shattered his ribs. Eder gasped, blood spurting from his mouth to stain his lips. The glow about him faded, and he dropped awkwardly upon the hardstone.

Sariel staggered to his feet, swaying unevenly on legs that did not wish to move. He approached his brother, who lay on broken limbs. Underneath him was a slowly growing pool of blood.

"This...this won't stop it," Eder said, having to pause to cough. "The sky is torn, and nothing will close the wound."

"We'll see."

Sariel grabbed Eder by the hair and lifted his head. In his other hand, he raised Redemption.

"I still love you, brother," Eder said. Blood dribbled down his chin. "Even now, I await you in Father's arms."

Sariel swung, severing the head. He watched the stars leave his brother's eyes, replaced with bloodshot whites and pale gray irises.

"Damn you, Eder," he said, and dropped the head. He fought off the temptation to toss it to the ocean far below. Such cruelty was beyond him, even if Eder's demented vision had led to the death of Faron.

Faron…

Sariel slowly approached the body, his legs turning weak and his throat tight. It was strange. So strange. He had witnessed his brother burn to death upon a pyre multiple times, but this was different. No light remained within the corpse. No glimmer. No soul. He collapsed to his knees and wrapped his arms about his brother's enormous frame. He buried his face in his unmoving chest.

"Faron," he whispered. "Damn it, Faron, why?"

No answer. There would *never* be an answer, and the truth of it struck him like a spear. He wept and gnashed his teeth, but it would not change. There was no coming back. For once, there was no coming back.

That sorrow turned to rage as he looked up to the altar of hands and the bowl they held. This miserable, wretched relic of a dead people. Sariel gripped his sword, hatred flooding through him. Who would build such a thing? Who would desire this madness, and why must it destroy the only thing sacred in a world so broken as Kaus?

Sariel struck the bowl with Redemption, dislodging it from the hands. It landed with a loud clatter. The runes sputtered. The great silver beam faded from the sky. Nothing else changed. As Eder had promised, the damage was done. Sariel could only hope the sky healed with time, and that gaping wound sealed over and was forever banished.

He glanced once more to Faron's body. It felt wrong to leave him there, but there was no soil to bury him within, and he would not suffer his brother the indignity of the ocean.

"One last pyre, then," he said, and wreathed his hand with fire. It fell upon the body. It burned his clothes. It charred away the skin. Sariel watched it consume, his insides twisting hollow and draining of life.

"Not now," he said, forcing the pain away. Time was not on his side. There was at least one life he might save amid this nightmare day. He rested Redemption over his shoulder and turned to Isabelle. She remained where she'd been, eyelids open but eyes not seeing. He gently put his free hand underneath her and lifted. Her feet moved, attempting to walk.

"That's right," he said. "Just hold on to me, and I shall see you safe."

Together they approached the broken lift, and once they were on it, he kicked the nearby lever to lower it. Sariel scanned the lifts on the rafters until he found his desired choice, a platform that would drop all the way to the entrance. He lifted the catatonic Isabelle into the crook of his left arm, careful to position her so she was not cut by his sword, and then wrapped his right arm and leg around the rope. His jacket and trousers were his protection from the friction as he slid down into the chasm of the Tower Majestic.

Once his feet were on solid ground, he shifted Isabelle's weight so she was carried in both his arms and Redemption lay atop her. His heart heavy, he exited the Tower Majestic to the narrow crossing of Bridgetop.

Hundreds of former residents of Racliffe formed a wretched gathering at the entrance. They stared, snarled, and squawked, depending on what deformation had overtaken them. Unlike earlier, when they seemed lost to madness from the change, their eyes shone with frightening clarity. Sariel was too exhausted and broken to imagine fighting them all. What hope might he have against an entire city, and with him burdened as he was? Accepting his fate, he merely walked, Isabelle clutched tightly in his arms.

Four lions formed the vanguard of the monstrosities, and at his approach, they separated, turned sideways, and then pressed their faces to the hardstone. Others were quick to follow their example. A gap spread through the ranks to the very end of Bridgetop. The sight chilled Sariel, but he dared not question it, only forced himself to place one foot in front of the other.

Sariel slowly crossed through the otherworldly army, Isabelle muttering incoherently in his arms, as one by one, the creatures and people dropped to their knees, lowered their claws, stingers, and wings, and bowed as if in the presence of their king.

Chapter 65

CALLUNA

Calluna walked the streets of Racliffe, and despite the *things* that walked around her, she had never felt so alone. They peered at her with squirming gold eyes, and though they bowed and showed reverence, she dared not say a word. It wasn't just them she feared, either. The city itself felt alive. Too often, she saw its eyes and felt the exhalation of its mouths.

There you are, she thought, stopping before the broken door of a home.

Aylah rested within, her eyes closed, her wounded body safely curled into the embrace of an enormous lion. Its human face bared its teeth but quickly ceased upon seeing Calluna and sensing her aura. These creatures, these monsters, they obeyed the radiance within her. What that meant, she dared not think on.

"Hello, sister," Calluna said. She tried to project her greeting as excited and loving, but instead the words came out like a whimper.

Aylah looked up, blinking as if returning from slumber. The swollen leeches were padded pillows to her body. Along both her arms, several more leeches crawled, nibbling and biting and leaving clean, healing skin in their wake.

"Calluna," Aylah said. Her voice was as cold as the ocean. "What are you doing here?"

"I...I was hiding in the city when it happened," she said, trying to think of an answer that wasn't so pathetic. "It struck me, and it was awful, it was terrible, I cried so much, Aylah. I cried, and I wished I was somewhere with you, with any of you, and not alone. I don't want to be alone. Not now. Not ever."

Her sister sat up, causing the lion to stir. A soft growl escaped its throat.

"You hid," Aylah said. "As Faron sacrificed himself, and Sariel destroyed everything, you hid?"

Calluna stood tall and struggled not to cry against the strange and sudden hate flowing off her sister in waves.

"Faron?" she asked. "What happened to Faron?"

Aylah shook her head, refusing to answer.

"You," she said. "You showed Eder where the key was. That's what he said. You showed him what he needed to activate the Tower Majestic. This is all your doing."

"Me?" Calluna took a step back, her eyes widening. "But you...you're the one who captured Isabelle."

"And I wouldn't have if I had known," Aylah said, standing. "I knew only what Eder told me, but he was wrong, wasn't he?" She stepped closer. "Did you know, Calluna? Did you know the purpose of the tower? You scoured its secrets. You learned more about it than any of us. Did you know?"

"Please, Aylah..."

"*Did you know?*"

Calluna struggled to keep her words firm despite the tears swelling in her eyes.

"I knew the Etemen had activated the tower once," she said. "Only once. I thought it saved them. I thought it took them to a better place."

Aylah drew her sword and pointed its sharp edge toward the door.

"Get out," she said.

"Aylah, no, I can't, don't do this."

"I said get out! Go to the Tower Majestic. Look on all you've done with your meddling."

Calluna fled, sobbing and screaming and furious. She ran through wild, untamed streets, hating the way the monstrous beings bowed their heads as if she were a princess. As if they couldn't see how broken she was.

"I didn't know!" she screamed, not caring who heard. "I didn't know, how could I have known? And Eder, he should have refused. He should have stopped. I didn't start this war. I didn't start any of this!"

Her flight took her east, toward Bridgetop. More of the creatures congregated there, and they quickly formed a path to allow her to pass. Calluna sniffled and wiped her tears, better composing herself now that she had put some distance between her and her sister. She observed the things as she walked, appreciating them as a distraction from her own misery.

There was an order to them, a guidance among the chaos that had enveloped the people when the crackling radiance had washed over them from the hole in the sky. Calluna sorted them into various races in her mind, for though they seemed random, that randomness was repeated throughout the city. The harpies with their equestrian heads. The leaf and thorn people. Animals with two heads and six limbs. Those lions with their human faces and their bodies pulsing with fat, recently fed leeches the color of marble. Among them, most pitiable, were the mere humans split asunder by their past lives. Rarely did they live long, if at all.

At last, she stood before the Tower Majestic. Calluna craned her neck to peer up at it, Aylah's chilling words striking her heart.

...Faron sacrificed himself...

Stair by enormous stair, Calluna climbed the tower. It took so long, and she was sweating by the end, but the exertion did her good. It helped her collect her thoughts. It helped brace her for what she feared she would find.

...Sariel destroyed everything...

At last, she arrived at the rafters, and the little lift up to the Final Ascent. There was no one to operate it, and so she hopped, grabbing ropes and climbing until she curled up around the edge and onto the rune-strewn floor.

The first thing she saw was Eder's body. The second was his head, lying beside it.

"You sweet fool," Calluna said, approaching both. She dropped to her knees beside the body and cradled Eder's head in her lap, her slender fingers gently stroking his lovely face. It was frozen in death, but it would not be for long. Once she buried his body, head in its proper place, he would soon return, in a few years. But what world would he awaken within, with the sky ruptured and waves of radiance steadily spreading throughout Kaus?

She turned to the key, the damned sacrificial bowl she herself had given Eder, and felt her insides freeze.

"Faron?" she asked. Slowly, she stood, Eder's head cradled to her chest. Her every footstep was smaller than her last as she approached, until she was tiptoeing toward the charred corpse. Her lips trembled. Her grip on Eder's head tightened.

"No," she said. "No. No, you didn't, Faron, you didn't, you didn't…"

The final sacrifice. The true death. It was him. Not Isabelle. Not anyone else. Her wonderful, softhearted oaf of a muscle-bound brother had given everything. There was nothing left. No life. No soul. No returning. Cold flesh tightening into rigor mortis.

Calluna collapsed beside the burned ruins of his body. She tried to lift what remained, to cradle him against her, but he was too heavy, and she too small. She bent over, weeping as her hair fell across what had once been his face.

"Why?" she asked. "Who could be worth this? Or were you sick of it all? Was this your one last pyre?"

She lifted his head and slid her legs underneath him so that it settled onto her lap. There she cradled it, Faron's head in one arm, Eder's in the other. She wept. She screamed. She fought against the voice of guilt that seethed within her mind, so heartless, so cruel, to disregard the actions of others and insist that, yes, this was all her fault, her fault and no one else's.

She wept until she heard the sound of ringing. Calluna looked up, enduring the dizziness she always felt when staring into that swirling, burning black hole in the sky. There, in its very center, she saw the thinnest beam of white light. It was like a crack in the darkness, splintering, growing. The tower shook underneath her, as if all the world groaned from the effort.

Calluna stared, eyes wide, tears burning away, as the white light grew. Her mouth dropped. Her hair whipped about in a sudden wild wind. Hope and fear pulsed in her heart.

"Faron?"

Chapter 66

SARIEL

Sariel trudged away from the wreckage that felt wrong to call a city. Isabelle was limp against him, awake just enough to aid in walking as they crossed the yellow expanse of grass to the mountains beyond.

Behind him, Racliffe squirmed and sighed like a beast well fed.

Don't look back, Sariel thought as they traveled. *And don't you dare look at the sky.*

Sariel need not search hard to find the hidden path upward. He more carried than guided Isabelle along the rocks, needing only twice to leap over little gaps and crevices. Perhaps it was nostalgia that brought him here, perhaps a twisted sense of irony, but after half an hour of hard climbing, he arrived at the flattened clearing halfway up the Sapphire Mountains and laid Isabelle down in the shade of the lonely red oak, remembering how Eder had been propped in similar fashion the night the Rebellion of the Broken had ended the Anaon Kingdom.

Back then, the night had been deep and the stars bright, when Sariel knelt humbled before his siblings and swore his vows. None were with him now. Eder lay beheaded atop the Tower Majestic. Aylah was wounded and had fled somewhere unknown amid the mad city. He could only guess where Calluna lurked during all this, and no one had spoken with Eist in decades. And of course...

"Faron," he whispered, and slumped to the dirt. "Why, brother? Did you always wish to leave us? Was this everything you wanted?"

He was too tired for tears, but the sorrow still ached in his breast. The sight haunted him. Faron's empty eyes. The color drained from his body. The way he resembled not himself, not the ever-living bodies that would recover from any injury, but a hollow shell. A dead thing. Real death. True death. Sariel's throat tightened. He would never speak with Faron again, never laugh with him, never chide him for his kindness or his attachment to his mortal lovers.

He struck the ground. This loss. This suffering, it was never meant for them. They were never meant to say goodbye and weep over pyres lamenting the lost. That... that misery was for humanity, and humanity alone.

"Not us," he whispered, and it seemed he was wrong. There were still tears left in him to fall. "Never us. Faron. Please. Faron. Why?"

At last, he looked to the east.

To his relief, not all of the protectorate's army had perished in the aftermath of the sky's opening. It seemed a third had managed to retreat beyond Racliffe's walls, through such heroics as he could not begin to imagine. They fled west, toward Nature's Path, and Sariel wondered if he should rejoin them. They would want their queen, after all...

Sariel glanced at Isabelle, still groggy and empty-minded as she slumped against the trunk of the red oak. She was not fit to lead this crisis. Bringing her in such a state might only worsen their morale. Not that much morale remained, he suspected. Not after today's cursed events.

At last, he willed himself to look upon Racliffe. A cloud of smoke hovered over the White City, adding to the strange discolored haze that emanated from the radiant fire. Said fire still burned fierce, and even as he watched, it continued its steady progress outward, swallowing the edges of the city as well as portions of the grass beyond.

The more Sariel watched, the more he saw. Strange beings crawling across the rooftops. Six-winged creatures hovered in circles above the spires. Much of the city was no longer white. Some portions were covered in vines, some turned brown like stripped bark, and others sparkled silver and gold, blinding to look upon in the midday sun. The ache of its light was nothing compared to the sickly, shimmering gold that swallowed everything if he dared allow his eyes to bear witness with blessed vision. The entire city blazed with the hue of uncontrolled radiance.

And all that paled compared to the gaping hole in the sky. Just looking upon it made Sariel's stomach twist and threaten to vomit. Even its dark center, seemingly black, felt like an illusion, as if it were composed of so many colors his eyes could not see any of them. The outer rings burned red, gold, and violet, rolling outward in waves that faded like smoke. Though it made not a sound, Sariel swore he could hear it burning.

Once Kaus is made pure, we shall join him and be together in Father's paradise.

Sariel shook his head.

"If this is the paradise you sought, I want no part of it, Eder."

A sharp intake of air stole Sariel's attention. Isabelle sat up, her arms curling about her legs and her head leaning forward. Her eyes were as wide as saucers, the whites deeply bloodshot. And then she screamed.

Sariel held her as she thrashed. He endured her scratches, and he whispered as if all were well.

"Shush, Isabelle. You are safe now. Listen to me. Listen. You are safe with me. Isabelle...Isabelle..."

The woman suddenly froze, her entire body stiff. It seemed to take her enormous effort to force out the next three words.

"I'm...not...Isabelle."

Sariel released her, and she scurried away from him like a frightened animal. Her movements were unsteady, and she stumbled onto her side, sliding across the hard ground and scratching herself on the loose rock. As she bled, she glared at him with her golden eyes.

"Leliel," she said. "My name...is Leliel."

Sariel slowly stood, his every movement carefully controlled lest he startle her like an alerted deer.

"No, it is not."

The body of Isabelle frantically looked over her shoulder to the east. Her gaze fell upon Racliffe, and the instant she saw the gaping hole in the sky, she let out a horrified shriek and recoiled from it, crawling on her hands and knees to the nearby tree.

"No," she moaned, and pressed her spine against the bark and held her arms over her head like a frightened child. Her entire body quivered. Her fingernails dug so hard into her skin, she drew blood.

"No, no, no, no no no no no no."

She rocked back and forth, beginning a new horrified mantra. Her words slid like poison into Sariel's mind as Racliffe burned and the sky wept radiance like tears from a lidless eye.

"We are seen. We are seen. *We are seen.*"

The story continues in…

Book TWO of the Astral Kingdoms

Author's Note

Welcome to my little space at the end of the book, where I get to pull the curtain back and talk about characters, the writing process, and just whatever comes to mind now that I've had a moment to breathe. So if you'll indulge me, let's ramble a little.

Novels of mine often start in my head with the characters, but *The Radiant King* was unique in that it started entirely with the world-building... and that world-building took *forever*, at least for me. The amount of incarnations it had is kind of ridiculous. The first idea I had was that the entire world had the regenerative powers of the six ever-living siblings, and it was far, far faster. No matter who you were, if you died, you came back to life at midnight.

Now, you can imagine how this might make it a bit difficult to build stakes. And I had ideas—I did! I had plans for sadistic prison sentences, and warfare was going to be a brutal affair focusing on capturing those you defeated so they couldn't fight you again. But the idea was just a little too out there, and it didn't help that my plan was to have traditional "death" arrive in the world in a big event... but then I'm taking a weird interesting world and literally having the whole story arc be about making it less interesting and magical. Which... That's not fun. Worse was the issue of who would be the main characters. Why would they be interesting? What would be the major story arc worth following?

So the idea kept bouncing around in my head while I was writing the final two books of Vagrant Gods. There was a germ of an idea intriguing me, but I couldn't get it to work. I thought about shifting it from full immortality to reincarnation. Shades of this still linger in *The Radiant King*, just not to the massive extent I had planned. People are aware of their past lives and are able to delve back into them. I had ideas of wealthy people paying companies to find their reincarnated selves to then deliver all their assets. Kingdoms would have assigned days to remain celibate, because those would be the days they executed criminals, with the hope that their souls would therefore not be reincarnated.

Again, I ran into the same issue. Whom do we follow? Why would we care for them? I had unique world-building, but it was just barren scaffolding, and I had nothing to fill the rest with. So around and around in my head it bounced. I kept tweaking things, the scenario, the reasons for people living forever, until I finally had a (seemingly) simple idea: What if it wasn't everyone who kept returning, but a few specific people?

That got things moving again. Because suddenly a lot of interesting questions popped up. Why those people? What makes them special? What would they be like, if they lived for so long?

But finally, finally, I felt like I had something tangible. Before I had figured anything else out, before I'd created the rest of the family, I wrote the scene where Faron is burned alive, except at the time, he was completely alone. Just him, consuming himself upon a pyre, and then waking up years later to insects crawling through his body. If I was going to have a cast that could withstand even death and return, then I was going to make that abundantly clear from the very beginning, and I'll admit, I had an absolute blast writing such a macabre scene.

From there, I zoomed out, figuring out the rest of the family, the world they were in, the reasons for their eternal life, and the conflicts that would arise. But it all started with Faron.

Which is why it's hilarious that the Faron you have read is not the Faron I first started with.

This might be revealing a bit too much behind the curtain, and it might seem impossible given how the later portions of the novel unfold, but when I first started writing *The Radiant King, Faron and Sariel were the same character*. Basically, Sariel didn't exist. Instead, Faron was meant to have a darker side. He was to be kind and loving to nature and to humanity in general, but frightening to those who committed crimes or dared transgress against his family. And it just...did...not...work. I hated trying to reconcile the kindhearted Faron who was so patient and loving with Iris with the cold and ruthless man who was supposed to hold a sword to Isabelle's throat and threaten to kill her for possessing radiance.

The solution came on a walk, as they often do with me. It's stupid and obvious in hindsight, but at the time, I had five siblings in this ever-living family. All of them are pretty similar to their final incarnations, too. But as I was trying to figure out what to do with Faron, I had a very simple thought: There could be six siblings, not five.

And that's how Sariel came to be. What if I took the cold, callous, and dangerous parts Faron was meant to be repressing and just...made a sixth brother. So to test this idea, I wrote the chapter where Sariel is drinking in the tavern and gets roped into helping a fledgling rebellion. A few thousand words later, I knew I had a character I adored. Originally, Faron was the one who killed the preacher at the start of the novel with the jar of bugs, a startling murder for one portrayed as so calm and kind, but now Sariel was the one to do the deed. Sariel would be willing to murder Isabelle. Sariel could be the heartless king that Faron could not.

From this point on, everything fell into place. I had my trio of brothers, Eder, Faron, and Sariel, all working together to make an absolute mess of a world. And I hope you found that world interesting, because it's clearly about to get a whole lot weirder.

All right, time for the obligatory thanks. Thank you, Bree, for looking over the initial pitch for *The Radiant King* and helping me craft it into something solid. Thank you, Megan and Essa, for being there for my every rant and moment of despair about the publishing industry. Thank you to my fisher friends in FFXIV, whose absurdities have helped keep me sane over the past two years. Thank you to my editor, Brit, for showing excitement for this story exactly when I needed it. Thank you, Michael, for sticking with me as my agent over all these years. Thank you, Stephanie, for swooping in seamlessly during Brit's maternity leave.

Last, but certainly not least, thank you, dear reader. For the past twelve years, I've been able to support my family by telling stories. If I am able to do this for another twelve years, or even another two, it will be because of readers like you. Despite all the brutality and betrayal, I hope you found enjoyment in this story, and a tale worth the effort to read it. Thank you for that time and for your trust that I might actually know what I am doing. I will always and forever do my best to repay both.

David Dalglish
December 5, 2023

extras

orbit

meet the author

North Myrtle Beach Photography

DAVID DALGLISH graduated from Missouri Southern State University in 2006 with a degree in mathematics. He has self-published more than twelve novels, as well as had seventeen books traditionally published through Orbit Books and 47North.

He also has a lovely wife and three beautiful daughters, with all four being far better than he deserves.

Find out more about David Dalglish and other Orbit authors by registering for the free monthly newsletter at orbitbooks.net.

if you enjoyed
THE RADIANT KING

look out for

The Gods Below
The Hollow Covenant: Book 1

by

Andrea Stewart

*In this sweeping epic fantasy comes a story of magic, betrayal,
love, and loyalty, where two sisters will clash on opposite sides
of a war against the gods.*

*A divine war shattered the world, leaving humanity in ruins.
Desperate for hope, they struck a deal with the devious god Kluehnn:
He would restore the world to its former glory, but at a price so steep
it would keep the mortals indebted to him for eternity. And as each
land was transformed, so too were its people changed into strange new
forms—if they survived at all.*

*Hakara is not willing to pay such a price. Desperate to protect
herself and her sister, Rasha, she flees her homeland for the safety
of a neighboring kingdom. But when tragedy separates them,
Hakara is forced to abandon her beloved sister to an
unknown fate.*

Alone and desperate for answers on the wrong side of the world, Hakara discovers she can channel magic from the mysterious gems they are forced to mine for Kluehnn. With that discovery comes another: Her sister is alive, and the rebels plotting to destroy the god pact can help rescue her.

But only if Hakara goes to war against a god.

1

Hakara

561 years after the Shattering

Kashan – the Bay of Batabyan

The mortals broke the world. They took the living wood of the Numinars, feeding it to their machines to capture and use their magic. Once, the great branches reached into the sky, each tree an ecosystem for countless lives. By the time the Numinars were almost gone, the world was changed. The mortals tried, but they could not repair the damage they'd caused. As the skies filled with ash and the air grew hot, the mortal Tolemne made his way down into the depths of the world to ask a boon of the gods.

And the gods, ensconced in their hollow, in the inner sanctum of the earth, told Tolemne that the scorched land above was not their problem. The gods ignored his pleas.

All except one.

Maman lied when she told me there were ghosts in the ocean. Cold water pressed at my ears, the breath in my lungs warm and taut as a paper lantern. Shapes appeared in the murk below, towers rising out of the darkness. Strands of kelp swayed back and forth between broken stone and rotting wood with the ceaseless rhythm of breathing. There were no ghosts down here – just the pitted, pockmarked bones of a long-dead world. I forced myself to calm, to make my breath last longer.

A shark swam above, between me and the surface, its shadow passing over my face. I hovered next to a tower wall, not even letting a bubble free from my lips, my elbow hooked over the stone lip of a window. An abalone lay in my left hand, the snail curling into itself, the rocky shell of it rough against my palm. My blunt knife lay in my right. A shimmering school of small fish circled next to me, light catching their silver scales like so many scattered coins. I willed them to swim away. There was nothing interesting here. Nothing to see. Nothing to eat.

Somewhere beyond the shore, Rasha curled in our tent, silent and waiting.

The first time I went to the sea, my sister had begged me not to go. I'd held her face between my palms, wiped her tears away with my thumbs and then pressed her cheeks together until her mouth opened like a fish's. "Glug glug," I'd said. I'd laughed and then she'd laughed, and then I'd whisked myself to the tent flap before she could protest any further. "That's all that's down there. Things that are good to eat and to sell. I'll come back. I promise."

Always told her I'd come back, just in case she forgot.

I imagined Rasha in our tent, getting the fire going, sorting through our stash of dried and salted goods to throw together some semblance of a meal. The fishing hadn't been good lately and now I had a snail in hand, as big as my face. I could begin to make things right if I could make it home.

If I died here, Rasha would die too. She'd have no one to defend her, to care for her. I counted the passing seconds, my heartbeat thudding in my ears, hoping the shark would swim away. My throat tightened, my chest aching. I was running out of time. I could hold my breath longer than most, but I had limits.

There was a stone ledge far beneath me – the remnants of a crumbled balcony. I had two things in hand – my abalone knife and the abalone. I *needed* that abalone and they were so hard to find these days. Each one would buy several days' worth of meals. But it wasn't worth my life. Nothing else for it. I dropped the snail and moved, slowly as I could manage, around the tower.

Its shell cracked against the ledge and the shark darted toward the sound.

I swam upward, the tautness of my chest threatening to shatter, to let the water come rushing in. The bright shimmer of the world above seemed at once close and too far. I kicked, hoping the shark was occupied with the abalone. My breath came out in short bursts when I broke the surface.

I swam for the closest rock, doing my best not to splash. Any moment, I imagined, the beast from below would shear off a leg with its bite. The water that had welcomed me only moments before now felt like a vast, unknowable thing. And then my hands were on the rock and I was hauling myself out of the water, my fingers scrabbling against slick algae and barnacles, doing my best not to shake. A close call, but not the first I'd ever had. Another diver was setting up on shore. "Shark in the ruins!" I called to him. "Best wait until it's cleared off."

He waved me away. "Sure. Children always think they see sharks when they're scared."

Did he think just because I was young that my eyes didn't work right? Went the other way around, didn't it? "Go on, then." I waved at the water. "Be a big brave adult and get yourself eaten."

He made a rude gesture at me before fastening his bag to his belt and dropping from the rocks into the water. Not the wisest decision, but he was probably just as desperate as the rest of us. I could smell the shoreline from my rock – sea life rotting under the heat of the sun, crisped seaweed, thick white bird droppings.

I wrapped my arms around my knees and watched him submerge

as I breathed into my belly, calming my too-fast heartbeat. Waves lapped against the shore behind me. Early-morning light shone piss-yellow through the haze, the air smelling faintly like a campfire. Not the most auspicious start to the day, but most mornings in Kashan weren't. My smallclothes clung to me, trickles of water tickling my skin. I'd head out again once I thought the shark had moved on. Or once it had taken a bite out of the other diver and had a nice meal. Either way, I'd slide into the water again, no matter the dangers.

I think Maman told me about ghosts in a misguided attempt to scare me. Like I was supposed to look at her, round-eyed, and avoid the ocean ever after instead of eagerly asking her if underwater ghosts ate sharks or people's souls. Had to admit I was a bit disappointed not to find spirits lurking around the ruined city when I'd finally hauled my hungry carcass to the shore and plunged my face beneath the water. Would have had a lot of questions to ask my ancestors.

Maman wasn't here to warn me away, and our Mimi had rid herself of that responsibility when she'd sighed out her last breath a year ago. We had no parents left. Besides, who was Maman to warn me against danger when she'd walked into the barrier between Kashan and Cressima? At least our Mimi had died through no fault of her own.

Sometimes I could hear Maman's voice in the back of my head as I swam down, down, so far that I started free-falling into the depths.

Don't go too far. Don't push yourself too hard. Stay safe.

And each time that voice in my head spoke up, I stayed down a little longer, until my chest burned, until I felt I would die if I didn't gasp in a breath. I couldn't listen to Maman's voice. Not with Rasha counting on me. Mimi had told me to take care of my sister. She'd not needed to say it, but I felt the weight of her last words like the press of a palm against my back.

This time of year, when the afternoon sun bore down on the water like a fire on a tea kettle, the abalone I fished for retreated deeper. They clung to the sides of the ruins, smaller ones hiding in crevices, their shells blending in with the surrounding rocks. Hints of metal and machinery lay deeper down, artifacts of the time before. All broken into unrecognizable pieces, or I'd have gone after them instead. There was always some sucker with money fascinated by our pre-Shattering civilization.

Rasha and I could eat fish, but abalone we could sell – the shells and their meat both – and children always needed things. It seemed I could get by on less and less the older I got, my fifteen-year-old frame gaunt and dry as a withered tree trunk. But Rasha was nine and I knew she needed toys, warm clothes, books, vegetables and fruits – all those little comforts she used to have when both Maman and Mimi had been alive. Every year got a little harder. More heat, more floods, more fires. Kluehnn's devoted followers prayed for restoration to take Kashan, to remake its people and its landscape, the way it had realm after realm. It was our turn, they said.

Couldn't say I relished the thought of being remade. I'd run if it ever came to that. I'd make for the border with Rasha and I wouldn't look back. Kluehnn's followers said that was a coward's choice. I was perfectly fine with being a coward if it meant I kept my bodily self unchanged and all in one piece.

I frowned as I glanced back at the shore, rocks fading into yellowed grasses and wilting trees. There should have been more divers out by now. I might have always been first, but others usually followed quickly, jostling for the best fishing spots.

It was deserted enough that I managed to find three more abalone once I got back into the water; only one other diver made her way into the ruins. My mind picked over all the possible reasons. A fire come too close? Rasha knew what to do in case of fire. A sickness passing through camp? It had happened before. I cut my diving short and walked back to our tent barefoot, the well-worn path soft beneath my feet, the scattered remains of dried seagrass forming a cushiony surface.

Ours was not the only tent pitched near Batabyan Bay. Together with the others we formed a loose settlement. This morning, though, three flattened areas of grass lay where tents had once been pitched. They'd been there when I'd left for the ocean.

Rasha had started a fire in the pit, the musty scent of burning dung drifting toward me. A covered cast-iron pot hung over it, the lid cracked to let out steam. She ran toward me, nearly bowling me over with a hug.

I squeezed her back until she wheezed. Maybe got a bit carried away, but she didn't complain. Her long black hair had some indefinable scent I only knew as home. Something of Maman and Mimi clung to the thick walls of our tent, permeating our clothes and our skin. I waved away the pungent smoke as I let her go, gesturing toward the empty campsites. "What happened over there?"

She shrugged. "They left just as I woke up. All three. Packed up their belongings and just hauled them out."

I smoothed the hair from her forehead. It was quick as instinct, the way I moved to soothe away her worries. Worrying was for me, not her. "Did they leave anything behind?"

She gave me a tentative smile before holding up a comb and a horsehair doll. I held my hand out for the comb. That one had been left by mistake. Tortoiseshell, carved with the face of Lithuas, one of the dead elder gods. Her hair flowed out to the tines of the comb, which had been left smooth. I should have been excited by the find; instead, uneasiness rose like a high tide. Most people would have scoured their campsite. Most people would have taken the time to find what they'd lost. The people here weren't rich, and the comb was a luxury, one that had passed hands from one generation to the next. No one carved the elder gods into combs anymore.

I lifted the abalone in my mesh sack. "I got something too."

Rasha's eyes sparkled, and her expression was a bulwark against anxiety. "Is it enough?"

I gave her a mock-startled look. "For what? What do you mean?"

She laughed before grabbing a pole to take the pot off the fire. "You know what."

"Pretty sure you called me stupid the other day, and stupid people have terrible memories."

"I was *joking*."

"Yes, being called stupid is a very funny joke."

"I said 'don't *be* stupid. You can't go to the mines.'"

I mussed her hair. "Please. Same difference. Besides, if the ocean stops giving us what we need, I might be able to find work at the sinkholes. I have to consider it."

She spooned out the porridge with the air of someone who'd come to the realization that this shitty gruel was her last meal. "No, you don't."

Ah, I'd ruined the mood in one fell swoop, hadn't I? Count on me to crush delicate hopes with the clumsiness of a toddler wandering into a seabird's nest. "We have enough, and I can dive deeper than most. Let's not think about it. Not when we have this, eh?" I brandished the comb. "I'll sell it at market with the abalone. And then yes, I'll see about the garden you want."

Wished she would answer me with a sly "So you *do* remember", but she'd never been as able as I was to recover a good mood. It was a big ask. We both knew it. I could buy the seeds and we had water, but the weather was unpredictable. Crops had to grow quickly to be harvested before heat or flooding ruined them. Only thing that would make them grow more quickly was god gems, and I wasn't going to risk the black market.

Magic wasn't for the likes of us.

Follow us:

[facebook] **/orbitbooksUS**

[X] **/orbitbooks**

[youtube] **/orbitbooks**

Join our mailing list
to receive alerts on our
latest releases and deals.

orbitbooks.net

Enter our monthly
giveaway for the chance
to win some epic prizes.

orbitloot.com